Ali McNamara attributes her overactive imagination to one thing – being an only child. Time spent dreaming up adventures when she was young has left her with a head bursting with stories waiting to be told. When stories she wrote for fun on Ronan Keating's website became so popular they were sold as a fundraising project for his cancer awareness charity, Ali realised that writing was not only something she enjoyed doing, but something others enjoyed reading too. Ali lives in Cambridgeshire with her family and beloved Labrador dogs.

To find out more about Ali visit her website at:
www.alimcnamara.co.uk

Follow her on Twitter and Instagram: @AliMcNamara
Or like her Facebook page: Ali McNamara

Also by this author

From Notting Hill with Love . . . Actually

Breakfast at Darcy's

From Notting Hill to New York . . . Actually

Step Back in Time

From Notting Hill with Four Weddings . . . Actually

The Little Flower Shop by the Sea

Letters from Lighthouse Cottage

The Summer of Serendipity

Daisy's Vintage Cornish Camper Van

Secrets and Seashells at Rainbow Bay

Kate and Clara's Curious Cornish Craft Shop

Hope and Happiness in Bluebell Wood

Ali McNamara

sphere

SPHERE

First published in Great Britain in 2021 by Sphere

1 3 5 7 9 10 8 6 4 2

A CIP catalogue record for this book is available from the British Library.

ISBN 978-0-7515-8099-0

Typeset in Caslon by M Rules
Printed and bound in Great Britain by
Clays Ltd, Elcograf S.p.A.

Papers used by Sphere are from well-managed forests and other responsible sources.

FSC
www.fsc.org
MIX
Paper from responsible sources
FSC® C104740

Sphere
An imprint of
Little, Brown Book Group
Carmelite House
50 Victoria Embankment
London EC4Y 0DZ

An Hachette UK Company
www.hachette.co.uk

www.littlebrown.co.uk

'Do not be overcome by evil, but overcome evil with good'

~ Romans 12.21 ~

Prologue

'Where is the exit?' I cry for what seems like the hundredth time. 'I can't find it!'

All around me are people. People crying. People shouting. People panicking.

None of us can find the exit. None of us is going to get out of here.

But then the deafening noise of the voices that have engulfed me for so long stops, and I can hear nothing. Not a sound.

The silence is a welcome relief, but at the same time weighs heavy upon my already weary shoulders. As the voices stop, so do the people, they stop moving and stand still – too still. Everyone is motionless, frozen like statues in some ghoulish museum. All these people. People with lives. People with families.

This is where it will end for them.

'I have to get out of here,' I cry in anguish, this time into the eerie silence. Otherwise, that's it – the end for me, too.

I sit up in bed – covered, as always, head to toe in sweat.

I reach for my bedside lamp and switch it on. The soft light immediately cuts the cord that joins the trauma of my mind to my physical reality, and allows me to begin my recovery.

I take a sip from the glass of water by my bedside, and try to control my shallow fast breathing, until it returns to something more manageable.

Then I climb slowly from my bed and retrieve the fresh pyjamas I always leave on my chair in case this happens, and I exchange them for my cold damp ones.

After I've splashed some cool water on my face, I return to my bed and, with the light still on, I pick up my phone with the intention of scrolling through monotonous social media posts until I feel calm enough to try to sleep again.

This was nothing new to me. The nightmares, night sweats and subsequent attempts to get back off to a patchy night's sleep have been a constant in my life for over a year now. I'm well practised at this routine, but it never gets any easier.

I look at the screen on my phone – I have a new email notification from the letting company. I open the email and read:

Dear Ava Martin,

You recently registered interest in renting properties in the Cambridgeshire area. I am pleased to tell you that a property fitting your requirements has just become available on a short-term lease in the beautiful village of Bluebell Wood.

Please find enclosed details of the property 'Bluebird Cottage' below.

Please don't hesitate to get in touch with us should it be something you love as much as we do.

Kind regards,

Jenny Magpie

Aviary Lettings

Bluebell Wood... I think, as I click on the link and look over the property they've suggested – a pretty cottage in a quiet and attractive village.

You could be just what I need...

One

'Are you sure you're going to be all right here on your own?'

I turn away from watching my scruffy grey-haired dog tear around on the unmown grass and look at my daughter.

'I'll be perfectly fine,' I try to reassure her. 'This is what I want right now, Han. No, correction: this is what I *need*.'

Hannah sighs. 'But this cottage, it's so ... remote,' she says, looking at me with concern. 'And so quiet. Listen ... '

I listen with her for a moment. 'I can't hear anything,' I say after a few seconds. 'Only a few birds singing in the trees.'

'Exactly. There's nothing around here for miles once you leave these tiny villages.'

'I know, isn't it lovely?'

Hannah sighs again. 'But what if you need something important, Mum? You know your ... *health* hasn't been too good lately.'

'My mental health, you mean,' I correct her. 'Don't be scared about saying it.'

'I'm not. But we worry about you, we both do.'

Matthew, my son, emerges through the French windows of

the cottage to join us in the garden. 'I think that's the last of your stuff in now,' he says. 'I can't actually believe we got all that packed into my car.'

'Thank you, Matt,' I say, smiling at him. 'It was good of you to drive me.'

'Don't be daft, Mum. We wanted to make sure you got here okay.'

'Wanted to nose around my new home, you mean!'

'Well, there is that!' Matt says, grinning. 'This village is so old-fashioned, isn't it? I can't quite believe places like this still exist. There are no modern homes here at all, as far as I can see. It's like something from a cosy Sunday-night TV drama.'

'Cosy is exactly it. Cosy and remote. It's just what I need right now.'

'And that's all that matters,' Hannah says, putting her arm around my shoulders and giving me a squeeze. 'Just as long as you're happy in this cottage, then we are too. Aren't we, Matt?'

Matt nods. 'Yeah, we only want you to be happy again, Mum.'

Again. My children just want me to be happy *again*. Because I hadn't been truly happy for well over a year now.

'You two might not think much of this little cottage, and how remote it is,' I continue, deciding now is not the time to dwell. 'You're both used to living in places with lots of people. But I really like Bluebell Wood. I think I'll be very happy here.'

My new cottage isn't exactly in the middle of a wood, just on the outskirts, to be precise. And contrary to what my children think, the village of Bluebell Wood is really not that small, but it is quiet. Still, it has everything you could need: a tiny village shop with a post office counter, a small old-fashioned primary school, and a very pretty little church. There's even a pub – quaintly named The Daft Duck.

'Plus, don't forget I have my new friend over there to keep me company,' I say, and we all look over to the scruffy little dog keenly investigating his new home. 'I think Merlin will sprinkle some magic over this place, just like his namesake.'

'You're going to keep calling him that, then?' Hannah asks. 'We wondered if you might change his name.'

'No, I like it, it suits him.'

At my children's insistence, before I'd moved from the city to the country, I'd adopted Merlin from a local dog shelter to keep me company in the new, more solitary life I was about to embark on. I'd been hesitant at first; some days I felt I could barely look after myself, let alone a dog. But Hannah and Matt had been adamant that I couldn't live here all alone. So as much to appease them as to help me, I'd relented, and Merlin had accompanied us to my new home in Bluebell Wood.

I watch my new companion carefully sniffing around the base of some overgrown bushes, then equally as carefully lifting his leg to avoid the spiky thorns. 'Merlin!' I call. 'Merlin, come here!' I pat my thighs in encouragement.

Merlin pricks up his ears and looks at me quizzically. 'That's it,' I call again. 'Come here, boy!'

Merlin bounds over to me in great excitement, sits down and looks up expectantly.

'I think he's expecting a treat,' Matt says knowingly. 'Maybe that's what his previous owner gave him if he came when called?'

Merlin's previous owners had been killed in a car accident, which he had miraculously emerged from unscathed. He was a resilient little thing, though, with a happy nature, and I hoped some of his confidence and zest for life would rub off on me as we got to know each other better.

'I'm sorry,' I tell Merlin, crouching down next to him and tickling him under the chin. 'I don't have a treat on me, will a fuss do instead?'

Merlin's dark eyes look directly into mine, then he nuzzles into my hand, turning his head to one side so I'm now rubbing his ear instead.

'That seems to be acceptable,' Hannah says, smiling. 'I think you two are going to get on just fine.' She looks across at Matt.

Matt nods. 'We're going to have to get going soon, Mum. Or the traffic on the A1 will be horrendous.'

'That's fine,' I say, standing up again. 'I really appreciate the two of you helping me move. I know you both have busy lives.'

'Don't be silly, Mum,' Matt says, hugging me this time. 'We wouldn't have let you come here alone.'

'I know. But I'm still very grateful.'

'And you're sure you don't want any help unpacking?' Hannah asks, looking back at the cottage, where boxes and suitcases full of my belongings await. 'We don't mind.'

I shake my head. 'No, it will give us something to do, won't it, Merlin?'

Merlin barks.

'See? He agrees with me.'

Hannah sighs. 'And you're still sure?' she asks again. 'About being here all alone, I mean. I don't think I'd like it.'

'You'd hate it, Han,' I agree. 'And so would you, Matt. So would I a couple of years ago, but things change. What I need right now is peace and solitude, and you two to promise me that you'll be careful.'

I beckon them over and I put my arms around them – marvelling once again at how tall they both are now. When had they stopped being my babies and grown into such wonderful, kind, caring adults? 'Promise me,' I say again. 'Promise me you'll both take extra care at all times – you never know what's around the corner, what people might be thinking . . . '

'Yes, Mum.'

'Of course, Mum,' they both say at the same time. They'd heard me say something similar a few too many times before.

'I mean it. I totally understand you both wanting to live in busy cities – you're young, why wouldn't you? You think you're invincible. I certainly did at your age. But none of us is – not these days.'

'Mum, we'll be fine,' Hannah insists. 'Don't worry.'

'Keep in touch, won't you?' I insist. 'And you too, Matt.'

'Of course,' Matt says. 'I'll text you and speak to you on Facetime as often as I can – although we'll have to get used to the time difference . . . '

'What time difference?' I ask. 'What do you mean?'

Matt looks uneasily at his older sister.

She glares back at him.

'What's going on?' I ask, looking between them both.

'You've *got* to tell her now,' Hannah says, looking and sounding annoyed.

'Tell me what?'

'I'm going to New York for six months,' Matt blurts out, his cheeks flushed. 'As part of my university course. We talked about this ages ago, didn't we, before the . . . thing.' He glances at Hannah, but she simply shakes her head dismissively. 'Only I didn't know where I was going to go then. But now I've been offered a work placement with a firm in Manhattan, and I've accepted it.'

I continue to stare at Matt. I'm trying desperately not to show it, but inside I'm horrified. My little boy in New York.

Yes, I'm pleased for him, of course I am. But why did it have to be there?

'I'm sorry it had to be New York, Mum. I know you'll worry about me in a big city – even more than you usually do. But it really is an amazing opportunity.'

'Yes, yes, of course it is,' I say, recovering enough, on the outside at least, to speak. 'I … I'm pleased for you, Matt; honestly I am.'

I reach forward to hug him, and suddenly his twenty-year-old, six-foot-two frame feels like it's shrunk, and in my arms I'm holding a wiry, short-for-his-age eleven-year-old boy, who needs his mum because he's scared of his first day at secondary school.

'I'll be fine, Mum,' he says, trying to reassure me just as I'd been the one reassuring him back then. 'I'll be as safe there as Hannah is when she visits London for her job.'

I hear Hannah sigh heavily behind us at her brother. She clearly thinks he's said the wrong thing … again.

'Look,' I tell them both, taking their hands in mine, 'you're adults now. I know I can't tell you what to do, where to go and where to live. But I'm your mother, I'll always worry about you *wherever* you go, you have to understand that. All that I ask is—'

'*We be careful!*' they cry in unison.

'Please stop worrying, Mum,' Hannah pleads. 'What's important right now is that *you* feel secure and happy again; and if this little cottage in the middle of nowhere is going to help you to heal, then if you promise not to worry too much about us, we'll promise in return not to spend all our time worrying about you. Deal?'

'Deal,' I say, trying my best to sound as confident as they

both did. But worrying, anxiety and general fear was what I experienced on a daily basis these days. My state of mind was one of the things I hoped this move to the country might help me with. But hearing the news that my son was going to live somewhere I considered dangerous like New York was not getting me off to the best start.

So as Merlin and I wave off my two children, I know in my heart of hearts that promising not to worry about them was a promise I'll never be able to keep.

Two

'Right,' I say to Merlin when I've tackled some of the many boxes and cases that Matt had unloaded from the back of his car. 'I don't know about you, but I've had enough of this already.'

As I'd unpacked each box from my old life, I'd tried hard to find appropriate places to put my things. The clothes had been easy enough; I'd hung them in a huge wooden wardrobe, and folded them into possibly the largest chest of drawers I'd ever seen in the only bedroom of the cottage. I'd only brought casual things with me: I'd put all my work clothes into storage. I hadn't worn them in ages, plus they reminded me too much of my old life, and that was what I was here to forget.

Any kitchen equipment (of which I have very little) went in the corresponding room. I was intrigued to find that the previous occupant of the cottage is clearly a much keener cook than me, and the old-fashioned kitchen is very well stocked for creating all sorts of interesting meals and bakes. Copper pots and pans hang from the ceiling on a wooden airer; blue-striped storage pots filled with spoons, whisks and spatulas sit on pristine scrubbed worktops, alongside large chunky chopping boards and a solid wooden knife block.

My sleek, hi-tech kettle, toaster and coffee maker, all so perfectly matched to my previous minimalist apartment, don't look quite so at home here in this practical yet cosy kitchen.

I'd been very glad to hear that the quaintly named Bluebird Cottage came 'fully furnished'. The rental company had informed me that the previous occupant had gone abroad indefinitely to take care of their ill daughter in Australia, and desperately wanted someone to look after their beloved home until they returned.

The pretty whitewashed cottage had seemed almost too perfect when I'd looked through the details – rural, peaceful, immediate occupation needed – so I'd contacted the company straightaway to express my interest. It came as an enormous, but very welcome surprise that, in fact, I was the only person to show any interest in the property. It seemed idyllic, and my hopes that I'd found the perfect place to get away from everything for a while were confirmed when I paid Bluebird Cottage a brief visit, and put down a deposit and my first month's rent there and then.

It's a charming little place; the one pretty bedroom has in addition to the antique wooden furniture where my clothes now reside, an ornate, comfortable double bed with carved wooden head- and footboards depicting birds and other wildlife. The bathroom next door has a large old-fashioned free-standing bath, with a basic shower at one end, and a solid white sink with pretty vintage taps. Downstairs, the narrow kitchen that runs along one side of the small cottage has a window that looks out to the back garden, and there's a tiny laundry room next door, with just enough space for a washing machine and tumble dryer. Next to that is the largest room of the house – a sunny sitting room, where there's a mismatched set of comfortable armchairs with colourful embroidered cushions scattered over them, a flowery well-upholstered sofa, and, next to a small dining table and chairs, a set of overflowing bookshelves. The sitting room also has, through a pair of French windows, a delightful view of the large well-kept garden, which the previous occupant has obviously take a lot of pride in, but which I might very well allow to go to ruin – my gardening skills, a bit like my culinary skills, leave a lot to be desired.

I'm lucky that currently, I don't have to worry about work. I've recently been awarded a generous redundancy package from the firm that I'd worked for in London, and I've decided to use some of that money to allow me to try living in the country for a while, in the hope it might help me to heal and move on with my life.

A couple of years ago I would never have considered leaving my job, the city, and my very active social life and moving to relative isolation like this. But things change – I'd changed – and I knew I'd never be quite the same again.

I desperately hoped this move would do me good. Perhaps it might even bring back some of the old me. I missed that confident Ava, and I often wondered if I'd ever see or feel like her again.

'Shall we go for a walk?' I ask Merlin. I glance at my watch; it was a dull day in mid-March, and it was already starting to get dark, even though it was only just after five. 'I'm pretty sure we'll be safe,' I tell my new dog friend, who watches me with interest as I pull on my trainers and gather my jacket from the coat rack in the narrow hall. 'I'm sure there won't be too many people around now. Soon it will be summer and the nights will be as bright as the day, though. Maybe then we'll have to go out super early in the mornings if we want to keep ourselves to ourselves.'

Merlin cocks his head to one side so his right ear is pricked up, but his left remains lowered.

I smile at him. 'You don't care, do you?' I say, lifting his new leather lead down from where I'd also hung it on the coat rack. 'As long as you get a walk, I'm sure it doesn't bother you how many people we see.'

Merlin, realising what I've got in my hand, jumps up, bounds over and sits neatly at my feet, both ears now raised as he looks eagerly up at me.

'You *have* been brought up well,' I tell him, clipping his lead to his matching red leather collar. 'Good boy!

'Right, so you've got your lead on,' I say, going through my mental checklist before we leave, 'and I've got my coat on.' I pause, zipping it up. 'I think that's everything, isn't it?'

I'm still very new to being a dog owner, and there's so much you have to think about. I'd got so used to living on my own since the children left home and only having myself to think about, that having Merlin to care for reminds me of when Hannah and Matt were babies. Back then I had to remember so much before I went out anywhere with them. 'At least you don't need nappies, eh?' I say, smiling at Merlin. 'But you do need these.' I tap my pocket to check there's an ample supply of poo bags there and I'm glad to find there is.

'I think I'm getting better at this already,' I say to the patiently waiting Merlin. 'Right then.' I look back into the cottage one more time just to check I've remembered to switch everything off and lock everything up. Then I open the front door, but as usual I hesitate before I step outside.

'It's going to be fine, isn't it?' I ask Merlin nervously.

Merlin barks reassuringly, and again I smile; it was as though he knew what I was saying.

'Thank you,' I tell him gratefully.

We step outside together and I lock the cottage behind us, and with Merlin leading the way we set off through the gate. A small gang of sparrows stops chattering to each other and watches us with interest from a nearby tree as we leave the cottage.

'Hello,' I say to them as we pass. 'I'm Ava and this is Merlin. We're new here.'

The sparrows immediately take flight.

'I don't blame you,' I say, watching them fly up into the sky. 'I don't like strangers much either.

'Which way, Merlin?' I ask the little grey dog as we reach the top of the narrow path that leads up from the cottage, and step out on to the pavement that runs alongside the main road. 'Perhaps this way?' I continue, veering to the left because I know the other way leads towards the centre of the village. 'I'm sure we'll have less chance of bumping into anyone if we go in this direction.'

Merlin doesn't seem to have a preference; he's simply happy to be out for a walk.

We follow the road that runs through the centre of Bluebell Wood towards the outskirts of the village, and to my intense relief the few people we see are in passing cars, so there's no need for interaction with anyone. Merlin, still wary after his accident, cowers a little way into the verge when each car drives past us, so I bend down and try to reassure him it's quite safe. It's clear both of us still have much healing to do.

I'm all too aware in a village as small as this one that it's only a matter of time before a 'newcomer' is noticed, but as far as I'm concerned, the longer I remain anonymous the better. Merlin has his issues with moving vehicles, and I have mine with many things, including people. I'm happy to try to avoid his triggers, and I'm pretty sure he'd have no problem if we avoided mine. We are going to get on just fine.

The pavement suddenly comes to an abrupt halt, as the main road continues out of the village and down a hill. I'm about to turn back, when I spy a hand-carved wooden sign pointing to the left of us. TO THE WOOD, it says in burnt lettering.

I look in the direction of the sign and see a narrow dirt track with a few trees either side of it.

We'll be fine in a wood, won't we? I think, peering as far down the track as I can. It's clearly a well-used entrance: I can still see foot and paw prints from previous walkers on the damp ground. But the light is fading and it's getting colder ... not that either of those things bother me, but what if we bump into another dog and its owner taking their evening walk through the wood?

'Perhaps if we just go a little way?' I tell Merlin. 'So we can scout it out for another time.'

But Merlin is already pulling towards the wood, sniffing the ground in front of him, so I bravely let him guide me down the path towards the trees.

We only have to walk a little way before the narrow path we're on opens up into a clearing. There's a rustic wooden bench on one side, with an information sign next to it; the entire edge of the clearing is lined with tall trees, with many more lined up behind them like rows of soldiers. 'This must be the actual wood the village is named after; I had no idea it was so close to our cottage.' I look down at Merlin, but he seems more interested in being let off his lead.

'I hope you're as well trained as they said you were at the shelter,' I tell him, bending down to unfasten the lead from his collar. We'd been on a few walks together now, but this was the first time I'd attempted to let him off his lead. 'I'm trusting you, Merlin, and you don't know how hard that is for me to say these days – even to you. Please don't run off and let me down, will you?'

Merlin looks up at me with a knowing expression, and I'm more certain than ever that he understands exactly what I'm saying to him. 'You're a smart little thing,' I tell him. 'Just like your namesake.'

I unfasten his lead and Merlin trots off to investigate a nearby tree stump. I watch him for a few moments, still wary. But he doesn't look like he's going to shoot off into the trees beyond; he seems perfectly happy investigating and marking this new territory.

I stand for moment, and with my eyes closed I take a deep breath. I'd done a lot of that lately, usually in response to something triggering my anxiety. But today I do it because I want to. I want to breathe in some of the clean air the trees provide, perhaps I might even absorb some of the strength they exude as they soar up into the sky above me.

I do this a few times, and with each new breath I definitely feel a little calmer, and to my surprise, I also feel a sense of strength begin to pulse through my body.

'Gosh,' I say, opening my eyes again. 'I didn't expect I'd *actually* feel anything.'

I look around me again. There is definitely something special about this place. I can't put my finger on what; all I know is for once I don't feel scared, it's almost as if I'm being comforted by the age and wisdom of the ancient trees, as if their great branches are enveloping me in an enormous protective blanket.

'I had a feeling I'd like it here in Bluebell Wood,' I say, smiling up at them. 'I'm glad you're so close to my cottage. I think Merlin and I might spend quite a lot of time here with you all.'

Merlin is still happily pootling around the clearing, so I wander over to the information sign to see what it says:

WELCOME TO BLUEBELL WOOD.

This beautiful ancient woodland consists mainly of oak, ash and hazel trees. The flora here is diverse, especially in spring when there are good numbers of wood anemones, wild garlic, and a spectacular display of bluebells – hence its name!

Please don't be tempted to pick any flowers to take home with you. Bluebells are protected in the UK under the Wildlife and Countryside Act, 1981, and it is an offence to remove them from the ground.

Enjoy your time here, but please leave our wood as you found it.

Underneath there's a little map showing a few different footpaths that can be taken around the wood. I'm not too sure where Bluebird Cottage is in relation to the paths, but I guess it must be just on the edge of the trees – as the crow flies, not that far from where we are now. There are a lot of tall trees edging one side of the cottage garden; I'd naively assumed they must have been planted there by a previous owner, but now I realise they are most probably a part of the ancient woodland. I wonder if there might even be a secret entrance from the garden directly through to the wood because it's so close, and I make a mental note to check it out tomorrow when it's light again.

I turn away from the sign and look for Merlin, but he's still happily exploring the clearing.

'Shall we wander a little further?' I ask, already feeling so at home here in the wood that I don't want to leave just yet.

He lifts his head to look at me.

'How about this way?' I suggest, pointing to one of the footpaths.

Merlin obediently follows me, and we walk deeper into the wood together. Even though our way is clearly marked by narrow paths, the further we venture, the darker it becomes under the canopy of the trees, and as the trees begin to look even older, the denser the undergrowth becomes around our feet. Some of the trees have gnarled, twisty bark that gives the impression of them being even more ancient, and I wonder as we pass by, how many people they might have seen walk underneath them over the many years they've stood here. I'd hoped to spot some of the infamous bluebells the sign had talked about, but there are only occasional bunches of little white flowers.

'Maybe it's too early for bluebells,' I say to Merlin. 'I'll have to look it up when we get back. As you know, wildlife isn't really my strong point.'

'Mid-April onwards,' a voice calls, making me physically jump and drop Merlin's folded lead. I swivel around to see a man jogging along the path behind me. I'd been so wrapped up in my thoughts and feeling about the trees, I hadn't even heard him. I berate myself for letting my guard drop.

'Sorry,' the man says, breathing heavily. He bends to pick up the lead, then he passes it to me. 'Did I make you jump?'

I nod as I take the lead. Automatically I back away from him a little, my gaze lowered. Then when I feel I'm at a safe distance I look warily up at him.

The man is wearing a grey hoodie, blue tracksuit bottoms and green running shoes. Even though he's wearing his sweatshirt hood pulled up over his head, I have to admit he doesn't look very threatening. He has kind blue eyes, dark hair that pokes out just a little way under the front of his hood, and black stubble peppered with grey covering his chin. He looks with concern at me while he awaits my answer.

'You and Merlin there will have to come back when the wood is in full bloom,' he says eventually, when I don't speak. His breathing is still laboured as he tries to catch his breath, and he stands with his hands on his hips. 'It's glorious here then.'

I nod again.

'Right, well, I'd better get back to my run,' he says, rightly sensing I'm in no mood for conversation. 'No rest for the wicked, as the great man says! Enjoy the rest of your walk.' He glances past me down the path. 'It's entirely up to you, of course, but I should warn you it gets dark quite quickly here. I wouldn't want you to get lost in the wood. I'm taking a loop; I'll be on my way out soon.'

When I don't respond he glances over at Merlin, who's examining the bark of one of the trees. But when I still don't speak, the man just nods at me. 'See ya then,' he says, picking up his speed again and jogging away along the path into the trees.

As he departs, I realise he's not the only one breathing heavily. I put my hand against a nearby tree trunk to steady myself, and then I attempt to control my breathing and calm my racing heart in the way I'd practised so many times in my therapist's office.

The feeling of the tree bark under my hand while I try to steady my erratic breath stirs a distant memory, which I immediately push back down where it belongs.

'No, not now,' I mutter, shaking my head. 'I won't have the serenity of this wood sullied by you.

'Time to go,' I tell Merlin after a minute or two, when I feel a tad calmer and ready to move on. 'The wood isn't quite as empty as I hoped it might be.'

I feel annoyed with myself as I walk quickly back to the cottage with Merlin. The wood had felt like it might be a refuge for me while I was staying here – somewhere to come where I could be calm and in control – but then that jogger had come along, quite innocently tried to engage me in conversation, and as usual I'd freaked out.

It wasn't him – he seemed perfectly nice. I just couldn't cope with being surprised like that. These days I liked to be in control of situations that might put me on edge and where I might have to think and react fast.

'But you coped, Ava,' I tell myself as we reach the edge of the clearing again and take the path back to the cottage. 'Yes, you didn't speak, and that wasn't great, but you survived; you should be proud.'

I look back at the trees as we step on to the pavement again.

Maybe they did help me, after all. Perhaps we might be able to go back again another day . . .

To my enormous relief we arrive back at the cottage without having to see or speak with anyone else, and the moment I shut the door on the outside world, I immediately feel happier. I've only been here a few hours and this cottage has already become a sanctuary to me – but I was determined it wouldn't become my prison.

One of the reasons I'd agreed to taking on Merlin was because I knew it would force me into going out when he needed walking. When I stopped working and was living on my own in London, it had become far too easy to stay inside for days, sometimes weeks, at a time. The only occasion I'd had no choice but to leave my flat was when I had an appointment for therapy, but I'd always rushed back home afterwards. I had no interest in being among people – especially those I didn't know.

It's very dark in the cottage now, so I turn on a few lights, and make up a fire in the hearth in the sitting room to make it seem cosier. Then I feed Merlin, and wait for my own dinner to cook – nothing special, just a ready meal from the little bit of shopping I'd managed to fit in Matt's car alongside all my other stuff. But the familiarity of preparing food for us both helps to soothe me, and I begin to feel calmer.

'We'll have to get ourselves organised tomorrow with some proper food,' I tell Merlin as he happily curls up next to me on the sofa while I eat my dinner in front of the fire. 'I'm sure we must be able to get a supermarket delivery out here.'

I'd become so used to buying everything online in London and having it delivered, I had no intention of changing that habit now we were in the country. There was the local shop in Bluebell Wood, where I was sure I could get a few supplies, but if I ventured out it would mean having to talk to people, and them asking questions, and that was the last thing I wanted.

As far as I was concerned, Merlin and I, tucked away in our little cottage in the wood, was all I needed. And I felt happy for it to remain that way for as long as possible.

Three

The next morning I'm sitting in front of the French windows in the lounge in one of the comfy armchairs, letting the spring sunshine warm me through the glass.

This would have been lovely and relaxing, if I wasn't at the same time preparing myself for a simple but possibly traumatic trip to the local shop.

Last night I'd sat at my laptop and ordered a delivery of food for me and a supply of dog food for Merlin from the nearest large supermarket.

This on its own hadn't been too much of a problem, they'd had everything I wanted, and I'd ordered enough to last me about a fortnight. The problem had come when I'd tried to book a delivery: the earliest slot I could get was Wednesday afternoon – almost two days away.

I probably could have managed if it had just been me, but I certainly didn't have enough dog food for Merlin to last until then – and I didn't think he'd appreciate toast and butter as anything more than a snack, certainly not a substitute for his proper food. It was no use; I was going to have to brave a trip to the village shop to see if they had some food that would keep us going until Wednesday.

Yawning, I decide I'll put it off for a little longer. It's warm and comforting in the sunshine, and I'm going to need all the comfort I can get before I have to venture out.

Why do I have to be so silly about something as simple as visiting the local shop? I think as I sit and look out at the little garden. *Fretting about that was probably one of the reasons you didn't sleep very well last night.*

I never slept that well any more. I spent far too many nights tossing and turning, worrying about the children, myself, and a hundred other things that really didn't warrant me or anyone else worrying about them.

And then there were the nightmares. The awful, unremitting nightmares . . .

Disturbed sleep, or the lack of it, was apparently one of the symptoms – another one to add to my ever-growing list.

To most people, popping down to the local shop seemed such a simple thing, but to me it was like planning a full-on military mission. I'm currently using one of the coping techniques I've been taught – planning ahead. Basically, I have to run through in my mind all the various scenarios that might take place while I'm both at the shop and travelling to and from it. The theory being that then I will feel more in control should any of those scenarios actually happen. Not only do I have to think of anything that might take place, but also how I might feel if it does, so I can prepare.

Still gazing outside, I notice that some of the shrubs that surround the overgrown lawn are starting to look a little unkempt. *I should probably try to keep the garden tidy while I'm here,* I think. *The previous resident clearly cared a lot about it.*

A few snowdrops that have seen better days sway to and fro in the breeze next to some cheery crocuses – currently in full bloom. Daffodils still in bud fight the wind by trying to sit poker straight above them both, waiting for the right time to bloom.

In the middle of the lawn stands an ornate wooden bird table. It's about five feet high, has a little house on top with a roof, and various hooks underneath where some bird feeders, rather sadly, swing empty.

While I'm watching the table, a little robin flies up from one of the bushes and lands there. It rests for a moment, looking around, then it hops about on the table as if searching for food. Disappointed, it quickly flies away.

Goodness, am I going to have to feed you as well? I think as I spot the robin hiding in one of the bushes spying on me. *This cottage is already starting to need a lot more upkeep than I'm used to – a dog, a garden, and now a bird feeder too.*

After I've sat for a few more minutes, watching to see if the robin tries the table again, I can't put off leaving the cottage any longer. I glance at the old wooden mantel clock gently ticking away above the empty fireplace. It's 10 a.m.; hopefully the shop shouldn't be too busy if we go now.

Merlin and I head towards the front door to get ready. I pause as I had the day before to pull on my jacket and attach Merlin's lead to his collar, hoping the familiarity of this routine will make stepping outside in a moment slightly easier. After all, I'd survived our outing yesterday, even when we'd run into a stranger.

I think about the jogger for a moment. How odd it must have seemed to him – me not speaking like that. He must have thought me very rude, or very strange.

But what's new? Most people seemed to think I was a bit weird these days. Not my children, they had stuck with me throughout, but most of my colleagues and many of my old friends had simply faded away when I hadn't returned to my old self, and I couldn't blame them really.

I sigh as I lift a wicker basket from one of the hooks next to where my coat had hung. *You mustn't blame yourself, Ava*, I tell myself in practised fashion. *That was your past; this is your future now. You simply have to make a go of today; don't worry about anything else.* I grip the basket extra tightly, then I nod purposefully at Merlin before I turn the handle of the front door and pull it open.

But yet again I hesitate on the step. 'Come on, Ava!' I tell myself sternly. 'You can do this – what's the worst that can happen?'

My therapist had advised me not to use that phrase. Almost experiencing *the worst that could happen* was what had made me like this in the first place. But I liked the saying; it somehow helped put things in perspective.

The robin appears again. This time it lands on the gate and watches us with a pair of beady but knowing eyes.

'Don't look at me like that,' I tell him as I dither on the step. 'I'm trying. If I do get out, I might buy food for you as well, if you're lucky.'

The robin gives us one last look and then flies up into the sky. *If only I could feel as free as you*, I think, watching it go.

I take a deep calming breath. 'Right,' I say, suddenly feeling brave enough to lock the door behind us. 'Let's do this.'

Merlin, who has been patiently waiting beside me on the step, trots happily down the path in front of me, seemingly without a care in the world. And I follow, feeling more like we're about to scale Mount Everest together.

*

Bird & Son, the sign above the shop window says in bright red lettering, *established 1936.* Merlin and I are currently standing on the opposite side of the road to the shop, just staring at it. Well, I'm staring; Merlin has found some scent or other to amuse him while I try to drum up enough courage to cross the road.

He'd been really good to start with and had sat neatly on the side of the pavement waiting for us to cross. But when several cars had slowly passed and we still hadn't moved, Merlin had become bored with waiting and I'd allowed him the length of his lead to go off and investigate for a bit.

Craning my neck, I try to see through the shop window to determine if there're many people inside. It doesn't look like there are, but the shop is bigger than I'd initially thought when I'd driven past in a taxi on my first trip to the village. It looks like it's a sort of L shape; on the short side there's a shop counter, with a till and a display of newspapers, magazines and sweets, and at the end behind a glass screen, a little Post Office. On the longer side, the shop goes back quite far, with two aisles packed full of food and groceries.

An old man wearing a flat tweed cap comes out of the shop carrying a newspaper and a pint of milk. He looks with interest at me still standing in the same place as when he'd gone in a few minutes ago. He nods and I attempt a sort of half-smile back.

'She doesn't mind you bringing the dog in,' he calls across the road, looking at Merlin. 'As long as he's well behaved.'

'Thanks,' I manage to reply. 'I was just waiting until it's a bit quieter in there.'

'No one in there now,' he says. 'Go on, duck. Jenny will look after ya both.'

The man is still watching us, so I have no choice but to encourage Merlin to cross the road with me.

'Thank you,' I say to the man, who doesn't seem in any hurry to go anywhere.

'My pleasure, duck,' he says, doffing his cap at me. 'You just passing through, are ya?'

I hesitate. I really don't want anyone to know where I'm staying or for how long. But I've never been good at lying, however harmless it might seem, especially when under pressure.

'I'm just visiting . . . for a while,' I reply cautiously. 'I'm renting one of the cottages.'

'Which one?' the man asks with interest.

Inwardly I chastise myself. I'd left myself right open for that follow-up question.

'Bluebird Cottage?' I say, hoping he doesn't know it.

'Oh, Evelyn's cottage,' he says knowingly. 'Lovely little place that is. Such a shame she had to leave so suddenly. But her daughter was very ill, I understand.'

'Yes, apparently.'

'Good to know it's in safe hands. The birds will be pleased, too.'

'The birds?' I can't help but ask.

'Yes, Evelyn loved her wild birds. Fed them every day, doted on them, she did, and they showed her their appreciation in return.'

'*Right* . . . '

'You'll have to make sure you get some food in for them if Evelyn didn't leave you any.'

'I'm not really sure . . . '

'Scraps'll do them for now, though – you know: bacon rinds, that kind of thing.'

'Okay . . . '

'Anyway, duck, I must be getting back,' he says, replacing his cap on his head. 'I got a plumber coming round this morning – me bath isn't draining right. Took me ages to get him to come out – like gold dust they are around here.'

I just nod this time.

'Enjoy your stay,' he says, touching the brim of his cap before shuffling away along the pavement. 'I'm Bran, by the way,' he calls back. 'I'm sure we'll bump into each other again.'

I watch him go, then I turn back to the shop, and I feel my hand grip the handle of the basket extra tightly again.

Right, let's get this over with before anyone else comes along.

'Good morning!' a cheery-looking woman, who I guess must be Jenny, calls from behind the counter as I make my way tentatively through the door.

'Are you Jenny?' I ask.

'Yes, that's me, dear. What can I do for you?'

'The man outside . . . er, Bran I think he said his name was? He said it would be okay to bring my dog in,' I gesture to Merlin. 'He's very well behaved.'

'Ah, of course it is. Hello, lovey, and what's your name?' she asks, smiling down at Merlin.

Merlin wags his tail on cue.

'It's Merlin,' I say. I feel like I should say my name too, but I resist.

'What a good boy!' Jenny says, coming around the counter towards us. I feel myself stiffen as she approaches, but I try not to let it show. 'May I fuss him?'

'Sure,' I say, standing back a little.

'Would you like me to mind him while you get your shopping?' Jenny asks, bending down towards Merlin. 'Is there anything in particular we can help you with?'

'I just need a few bits and pieces,' I say vaguely. 'I don't want to put you out.' I still clutch Merlin's lead tightly in my hand.

'Oh, it's no bother. As you can see, we're very quiet at the moment.'

I glance around the shop. Apart from us it's completely empty. If I let her look after Merlin, I can probably scoot round much faster, and therefore make my exit before anyone else comes in.

'If you really don't mind?' I say tentatively, holding out Merlin's lead. 'I'll only be a couple of minutes.'

'He'll be perfectly safe with me,' she says, attempting to take the lead from me. I notice she has to tug it a little when I don't fully let go. 'Baskets are just over there, dear,' Jenny says, looking at me a little oddly. 'Or you can fill your own if you feel happier?'

'Is that okay?' I ask, glancing down at my basket.

'Of course! We're very trusting here,' Jenny says, already tickling Merlin on his tummy, while Merlin laps it up by rolling over on his back. 'You go for it.'

I hurry off towards the aisles of groceries, where I quickly grab some basic provisions for me. I find some dog food in the small section of pet supplies and grab a couple of tins for Merlin and some dry biscuits. Then I head back to Jenny.

'Find everything you need?' Jenny asks, reluctantly passing Merlin's lead back to me. She takes my basket and looks in it with interest as she carries it back to the counter.

'Yes, thank you,' I say, surprised at how much calmer I feel now I have Merlin back by my side. 'Oh,' I say, suddenly remembering what Bran had said outside, 'I don't suppose you have any bird food, do you?'

'No, I'm afraid we don't stock bird food – too specialised. Do you have birds as well as your little dog?'

'Gosh, no; I meant food for garden birds.'

'Ah, I see! You need to go down to Peacocks for that.' Jenny puts my basket down on the counter and begins scanning the contents through her till.

'Peacocks?'

'Yes, the farm shop on the outskirts of the village. They have everything there we don't – they keep a lot more fresh veg, and a much bigger supply of pet food. You'll get all the wild bird food you need there.'

'Great, thanks. Is it that way?' I ask, pointing in the opposite direction to where we'd walked to the wood yesterday.

'Yes, just follow the road along until you're almost out of the village. Gavin will deliver anything you can't carry. Are you local?' she asks, trying to sound like she's not prying, when clearly she's desperate to know.

I'd been in the heart of the village less than half an hour and already two people were going to know I was staying here. I didn't mind them knowing, they seemed friendly enough, but I really just wanted to keep myself to myself for a while.

I found it so difficult to trust strangers these days – allowing Jenny to hold Merlin had been hard enough. But she had been so helpful, I didn't want to appear rude.

'Yes, I'm staying at Bluebird Cottage,' I hear myself reluctantly reply.

'I wondered if you were.' Jenny nods knowingly. 'Evelyn said she hoped she'd get a tenant to look after the place while she was away. Dreadful business about her daughter.'

'Yes,' I reply, feeling that I should know all about it. Everyone else seemed to.

'Are you staying long?'

'I'm not sure,' I reply cagily.

'I expect Evelyn will be gone a fair while.'

'Yes.'

'Right then, that's £26.74, please. Shall I put it back in your basket for you?'

'Yes, thank you.'

While Jenny loads my shopping into the basket, I find my purse and swipe my card over her payment machine.

'There you go, lovey,' Jenny says, passing me the basket. 'I'm sure we'll see you again if you're staying here a while.'

'Yes,' I tell her, choosing not to mention my online supermarket order due tomorrow, which I'm certain Jenny wouldn't appreciate. 'I'm sure you will.'

Merlin and I are finally allowed to leave the shop. I think twice about whether to go to this farm shop – I'd already had more than enough interaction with people for one day, but then I see a little robin land on the hedge in front of us – I'm sure it can't be the same one from before, but it reminds me that I *will* have to get some bird food sometime soon. Clearly Evelyn had cared about the birds that came to her garden as much as the garden itself, and it was becoming quite obvious she'd only left Bluebell Wood because she'd had to go and care for her daughter. I didn't want things to be spoilt for her upon her return.

So Merlin and I walk towards the farm shop together, with me taking as many deep calming breaths of the fresh country air as I can, and Merlin also sniffing, but instead at as much of the fresh country soil as he can.

Bluebell Wood is a very pretty place, the majority of which is set along the main road that runs the length of the village. There are small roads adjacent to 'Hill Rise', as the main road is called, but many of them are closes, and cul-de-sacs that don't go anywhere except to the owners' houses. At the bottom of the aptly named Church Street I spy a small, pretty-looking church and I wonder how many residents of Bluebell Wood are a part of its congregation.

Eventually, when we're almost at the end of the village, we reach Peacocks Farm Shop. I pause a moment with my hand on the gate. 'Come on, Ava,' I tell myself. 'You coped with Jenny. This will be fine too.'

Two friendly-looking black Labradors come bounding up to us as we enter, and immediately begin sniffing around Merlin. Merlin, knowing his place, stands very still, waiting for them to finish. When they've decided he's friend not foe, they sit playfully back on their haunches with their heads bowed, waiting for him to respond.

'It's okay, they're quite friendly,' a bulky grey-haired man wearing a checked shirt and brown corduroy trousers calls as he comes out of the main shop building. 'You can let him off his lead if he's all right with other dogs?'

I look down at Merlin, who looks eager to be freed. So I unhook his lead and he immediately races off with the Labradors as they begin chasing each other around the yard. Merlin obviously has a lot fewer issues with socialising than I do.

'What can I help you with?' the man asks, smiling at me.

'Jenny at the shop told me you might sell wild bird food here?' I try to inject a confident tone to my voice, even though my insides feel far from this.

'And she'd be right. What type are you looking for?'

'Er . . . is there more than one brand, then?' I ask, surprised. *What if the birds that came to Evelyn's garden have a favourite and I get it wrong?*

'Not brand – type. For instance, do you have pigeons and doves you want to feed, or blue tits and sparrows?'

'Oh, I see. There was a robin this morning; I think he was looking for food.'

'Right, well, that's small birds to start with. Robins like a bit of seed, but they love their mealworms.'

'Worms?' I ask, trying not to grimace. 'Live ones?' I have visions of me attempting, unsuccessfully, to dig the cottage garden in search of worms wriggling through the soil.

'No!' the man laughs. 'We sell dried worms. Although your robin would love you if you gave him live worms – save him digging for them!'

I force a smile.

'Why don't you come in and have a look at what we have – that might help you decide.'

'All right then.' I look around at Merlin still playing with the other dogs.

'He'll be fine with my two,' the man reassures me. 'They won't let anyone in here without telling me about it, and they won't run off.'

I still hesitate – partly because of leaving Merlin, and partly because I'll have to go into the shop without him. He's become my security blanket over the last couple of days – albeit a particularly hairy one.

'He'll be perfectly safe, love. Honest,' the man says again. 'I'd trust those two with my life.'

I glance one more time at Merlin – he looks far too happy to prise him away from his new friends, so I follow the man into a huge barn filled with fresh fruits, vegetables and more pet food than I've ever seen gathered in one place.

'Wow, you have a lot of stuff in here,' I tell him, my guard dropping for a second as I look around me.

'Thank you; we aim to please here at Peacocks. I try not to

step on Jenny's toes by selling anything she does. But I like to give my customers lots of choice. I'm Gavin, by the way,' the man says, turning back to me. 'Gavin Peacock, we're a family business.'

'I'm Ava,' I say, feeling I have no choice but to introduce myself this time. 'And my furry friend out there is Merlin.'

'Great name,' Gavin says approvingly. 'Now here's our wild bird food. Like I said, there's quite a selection.'

I stare at the shelves in front of me. There are packets of seeds, bags of nuts and weird-looking ball things in tubs. Then there are bird feeders of every shape and size, some nest boxes, and at the end of the aisle bird tables – from the simple to the very ornate.

'New to this, are you?' Gavin says kindly, sensing my confusion. 'Feeding wild birds?'

'I am, yes. But I think the lady who lived in my house before me fed them – she had a bird table in the garden.'

'Which house would that be? You must be local – you walked here, didn't you? I have a lot of customers come by car to buy in bulk, see.'

What was it about these people? As hard as I tried to keep my guard up, they just kept breaking it down with their constant friendliness.

'Yes, I'm local,' I tell Gavin. 'I'm staying at Bluebird Cottage.'

'Oh, why didn't you say you were in Evelyn's place? Evelyn used to have a regular order of bird food off me – I think she had all sorts of birds visiting that garden of hers. I'm surprised she didn't leave you some.'

Maybe she had and I hadn't even looked for it – damn.

'But just in case, why don't I give you a few bits now from her regular order, and then you can phone me if you want anything else and I'll pop it round in the van for you? We deliver locally.'

‘Okay. I mean, yes, thank you very much, that would be great.’

Gavin loads me up with a few small bags of bird food, peanuts and dried worms – which I try not to look too horrified about as he pops them in my basket. Then he enquires about Merlin, and makes a few suggestions about food for him to try.

When we eventually leave the shop, I’m completely loaded down. Along with my original basket of groceries from Jenny, I’m carrying a variety of wild bird food, some samples of dog food for Merlin – with the promise from Gavin that he’ll happily deliver any bulk bags of food that Merlin takes a fancy to – and some extra dog biscuits and treats that he’d thrown in for free.

‘I’ve got used to only having me to feed since the kids moved out,’ I half grumble as I stagger back to the cottage, my arms aching. ‘I didn’t know by moving here I’d signed up to feeding half the local wildlife as well as a rescue dog!’

But Merlin, unperturbed, just trots along happily next to me, occasionally sniffing at my basket in anticipation. He seems to have made his mind up he’s going to love living in Bluebell Wood already.

While I’m not quite so sure just yet.

Four

What am I doing wrong? I wonder as I stare at the bird table. *Why aren't any birds coming to feed from this buffet of food I've laid out for them?*

Yesterday, when we'd got back from our excursion to the shops, I'd put our shopping away and popped a little of the mixed wild bird food that Gavin had given me on the bird table, along with a handful of black sunflower seeds and some of the dried mealworms. Then I'd gone in search for more food in the old shed that stands at the bottom of the garden. As Gavin had correctly predicted, there were some bags of food already in there, some of which were useable, and some with holes in the bottom and seed spilling out that looked like a mouse might have got to them.

I'd sorted the good sacks from the bad, and then I'd put the ruined ones out in the dustbin. Gavin was right again: Evelyn had such an amazing variety of bird food that I wondered just how many birds she'd had visiting her garden in the past.

I'd then filled the feeders, added some nuts to them and re-hung them underneath the bird table.

Afterwards I'd sat in a chair by the French windows and watched, expecting to see lots of birds immediately flocking to the table now I'd offered them some food – but to my great disappointment none came – not even the robin that had looked at me with so much expectation had returned.

Merlin and I hadn't done much for the rest of the day. I'd pottered about in the garden, attempting some weeding with some of the tools I'd also found in the shed. I'd nodded off in the armchair in the afternoon in the warmth of the spring sunshine that poured through the windows, and then later I'd taken Merlin back to the woods for his evening walk, pleased and relieved that this time we didn't meet anyone at all. I'd checked when I'd been in the garden earlier to see if there was any way of getting from the back of the cottage directly into the wood as I'd hoped. But all I found was a solid wooden fence that ran all the way around the perimeter of the garden, so Merlin and I would just have to settle for using the same entrance as everyone else for the time being.

It had been a quiet but semi-productive day, and was just the sort of way I'd envisaged spending my time when I'd begun to dream about moving from the noise of the city to the quiet and peace of the country.

But today, as I await my food delivery with Merlin next to me on the sofa, I wonder again why the birds don't seem interested in the food I'm offering them, and why it's bothering me so much that they aren't feeding.

The problem is, you're used to getting fast results, I tell myself. *Back in London everything happened super speedily. You're going to have to learn how to live life at a slower and gentler pace now you're living in the country.*

But I *really* want the birds to come now I've made the effort with them, and I can't help feeling let down that my efforts aren't deemed good enough.

My supermarket delivery arrives just after lunch, and the driver quickly unloads my baskets from the truck. I can't help feeling a little embarrassed at this huge lorry parked outside my little cottage – it seems so at odds with the rest of the village.

'Do you deliver to Bluebell Wood a lot?' I ask the driver as I'm signing his delivery sheet. 'I'm new here,' I explain.

He looks at me as though I've just confirmed what he'd already guessed. 'More than you might think,' he says. 'A lot of the villages around here only have one small shop – if that. Folks these days want variety and choice in their groceries – these village shops are just too small to offer more than the basics.' He passes me my delivery note. 'Don't worry about it,' he says, seeing my concerned expression. 'I'm pretty sure no one will mind!'

I thank him, and then Merlin and I – well, mainly me, Merlin's contribution is sniffing all the food before it goes in the fridge, the freezer and the cupboards – put our shopping away.

'Right, what now?' I ask him when we're done. I look around the kitchen. When I'd done the order, inspired by all the equipment in here, I'd added some ingredients for baking, but now just the thought of it scares me. *I can't bake – who am I kidding? Maybe Evelyn has some cookery books on that huge bookshelf in the sitting room? Perhaps I can find inspiration there?*

I hadn't spent very long looking through the books yet. I'd figured reading was something I could do on a rainy day to keep myself amused. I used to read a lot – always had a book on the go – but recently I'd found it incredibly difficult to concentrate on anything for very long, so reading was something that had fallen by the wayside, like so many other things in my life.

Could now be the time to try to take it up again? I wonder. *I'm already starting to get a little bored, and I've only been here a couple of days.*

I shake my head. 'Stop it. This was what you wanted – remember?' I tell myself sternly, speaking the words as I glance at the mirror in the hall on my way through to the sitting room. 'A quiet, solitary life. You longed for it before.'

The large bookshelf that runs the length and height of the sitting-room wall does, I'm pleased to find, contain quite a few cookery books. Unlike the bookshelves I'd been used to seeing in some of my friends' swanky London flats, which contained only glossy cookery books by celebrity chefs, Evelyn has proper cookery books with battered covers and worn pages covered in splashes of past recipes she'd created. Some of the pages even have detailed notes in the margins suggesting what could be done better next time.

I flick through a few books, and make a mental note of what I might have a go at baking sometime. Then I look over some of the other shelves: as well as the cookery books, there are books on gardening, sewing, DIY and wildlife, including some bird books.

Maybe these will tell me why the birds aren't coming to the table? I think, pulling a few aside to read later. *Can't do any harm to have a look. Oh, what's this one?*

From the shelf where the bird books end, I pull out a leather-bound notebook. I open up the front cover and find a page of handwritten notes detailing all the feathered visitors Evelyn has had to her garden: when they came, how long they stayed, and even what they ate.

'Ah, maybe now I can discover where I'm going wrong.'

I don't know why it was bothering me that much. After all,

why did it matter if a few birds came and fed from a bird table? But I knew it was more than that. I'd been used to problem-solving in my old job; in fact, I'd thrived on it. 'I will get you to feed on my table,' I hear myself saying. 'I don't give up that easily.'

Hold on, I think, catching myself. *That's the old Ava talking. The one I'm trying to get away from.*

But was it the old me I was trying to escape from by coming here? There hadn't been anything wrong with the person I was before. It had been the situation that had changed me, not something I'd done.

'You couldn't control that situation, Ava,' my therapist had told me over and over again. 'You couldn't control what happened that day.'

I knew she was right. But I still felt guilty. I just couldn't help it.

And there was the problem. That day had been out of my control. I couldn't do anything back then to change the events of that awful afternoon, but now I could control something. I could entice the birds to feed on the table again. It was clear from this notebook that Evelyn had done it. And if she could make a success of it, then so could I.

'I might not have been able to do anything back then,' I say purposefully, going over to the sofa and sitting down with the books. 'But I can do something about this now.'

After I've been sitting reading the bird notebook for a while – making my own notes on a pad about what types of bird food I should be putting out and when – Merlin suddenly gets up from where he's been asleep on the floor and puts his head on my knee.

'Hello,' I say, stroking him. 'What's up?'

He lifts his head and drops it on my knee again.

'Do you want something to eat?' I ask him.

He wags his tail.

I glance at the clock. 'It's not quite your dinner time yet,' I say, standing up, 'but let's see what we've got.'

I walk through to the kitchen and look in one of the bags that Gavin had filled for me. Then I produce a couple of dog biscuits, which Merlin sits neatly for. Then he walks over to where his bowls are on the floor, and nudges his water bowl with his nose.

'Oh my gosh, I'm so sorry, Merlin!' I cry when I notice the bowl is dry. 'I'll fill it for you immediately.'

I lift his bowl, rinse it out, fill it with clean water from the tap, then I put it down again and he laps thirstily from it.

I feel awful as I watch him. I had to get used to looking after someone else again. In the past, when the children had been growing up, I'd been used to caring for others. There had been three people as well as me to look after back then, until my separation and subsequent divorce from my ex-husband. Then it had just been Hannah, Matt and me, and then when Hannah went to university Matt had become my only housemate, and then when he eventually flew the nest, it had just been me alone.

It was then I'd moved to the small apartment in central London; it was expensive but I had a good job, was working long hours and I had a busy social life; I didn't need a home, I needed a place to stay. But after *that day* my flat became more than just a place to lay my head at night and keep my things. It became my fortress. I barely left, and when I did, I would usually return a sweaty anxiety-ridden mess.

I look at Merlin; he has water dripping off his chin as he gazes up at me.

'It's not your fault you got taken on by a mess of a human, is it?' I tell him. 'I'm sorry; I'll try to do better.' I kneel down in front of him and look into his big brown eyes as he gazes up into mine. 'I promise I'll learn to take care of you properly, Merlin. After all, I need you just as much as you need me right now.'

It was true, I'd become quite attached to this little dog in the short while we'd been together. Whether he knew it or not, he was providing me with so much more than just companionship: he was giving me the strength to go places and do things that I knew alone I'd have hidden away from.

'Shall we go for a walk?' I ask him as recompense for my shortcomings as a dog owner. 'Would you like that?'

Merlin, like many dogs, clearly recognises the word 'walk' and immediately starts wagging his tail.

'I'll take it that's a yes! I'll just wash my hands then and we'll go,' I say, turning back to the sink. To my surprise I see the water that I'd rinsed Merlin's bowl out with hasn't drained away and is still sitting at the bottom. 'That's odd?' I say. I try to flush some more water down there by turning the tap on again, but that just makes things worse.

'Oh Lord, Merlin, I think it's blocked.'

How the devil do I unblock a sink? The benefit of living in a building of expensive apartments was there had always been a caretaker around to help with these sorts of issues, and before that my husband and subsequently Matt or Hannah had dealt with anything like this. I suddenly feel completely helpless and alone.

Stop it, Ava! I tell myself promptly, before I begin to wallow. *You're a grown woman, you can deal with a blocked sink – you've dealt with much worse. Now, you probably need one of those plunger things that people always use on TV . . .*

I take a look under the sink and in a few cupboards, sure that Evelyn would have such a thing. But my search appears in vain. Then I remember a cork noticeboard that hangs on the wall in the small laundry room. There are a lot of business cards and handy numbers pinned up there; in fact, the correspondence from the rental company had said, in the event of an emergency or any maintenance that I might need doing, to contact the cottage's caretaker, whose details would be listed on the board.

'One moment!' I say to Merlin, who is looking very put out that my preparations for his walk are taking so long, and I hurry through to look at the board.

After I've waded through take-away menus, refuse collection dates and numbers for the local shops, I spy what I need.

In the event of an emergency or
any routine maintenance
please contact the vicarage
on 0456799827

Ah, that's right, the rental company had said that the local church was looking after the cottage, and they should be my first call if I had any problems.

But I really don't want to bother them – and I especially don't want to speak to the local vicar. Knowing my luck, he'll probably only preach at me for being so inadequate at life . . .

I take my phone from my pocket, not to phone the number on the card, but to Google blocked sinks. However, after a couple of minutes I realise that most of the solutions involve either a plunger or some other tool Evelyn didn't seem to have anywhere. I really had no choice but to call the number on the card.

So with a feeling of impending doom, I do just that, hoping that perhaps the vicar's wife or somebody else will answer the phone and I can talk to them.

'Good morning, vicarage!' a cheery voice replies at the other end of the line after a few rings. 'Oh, I do beg your pardon, it's already afternoon. Where has today gone? Good afternoon then, Deacon Finch speaking, how may I help you?'

I'm a bit taken aback. *A deacon? Wasn't that someone quite high up in the Church, like an archbishop or something? Why would they be answering the local vicarage's telephone?*

'Hello?' the voice says again. 'Is anyone there?'

'Yes . . . ' I reply hurriedly. 'I'm here. Sorry, my name is Ava and I'm staying at Bluebird Cottage. It said on the notice-board I should ring the vicarage if I have any problems while I'm here.'

'That's absolutely correct. Hello, Ava, and welcome to Bluebell Wood. What can I help you with today?'

I feel a bit silly again. 'Er . . . well, it's my kitchen sink. It appears to be blocked.'

'Gosh, I see; well, I am sorry to hear that, Ava. Should I get someone to pop round and try to unblock it for you?'

'If it's not too much trouble that would be wonderful, thank you.' I'm relieved: this guy was friendly and being more than helpful.

'I'll try to get someone to come and look at it today.'

'Great.' I look down at Merlin, waiting patiently for his walk. 'Sorry to be awkward, but I was about to walk my dog. Do you know what sort of time the person might come? It's unlikely to be in the next hour, is it?'

'Oh no. I'm sure it will be either later today or more likely tomorrow. Will that suit you?'

'Yes, that will be absolutely fine. But please don't put anyone out, it's not an emergency.'

'Evelyn is an important and respected member of our church. It's our pleasure to look after you while you stay in her home. Please don't worry.'

'Okay. Well, thanks again.'

'My pleasure. Good day to you, Ava.'

'Good day,' I find myself repeating as I end the call.

'Well, that was easier that I thought it might be,' I say to Merlin, who's still waiting by my feet. 'Right, now we can go for that walk at last.'

We walk along the road to the wood again.

I don't feel the need to try to find other routes for us to take just yet. Merlin likes the wood because he can have a good run off his lead, and I like it because it's quiet and we rarely see anyone. The wood is calm and tranquil, and just like the first time we visited, I feel an enormous sense of peace when I'm nestled within its comforting embrace, something I haven't felt for a very long time.

I feel stronger, too. I'm not sure if the trees are passing their wisdom and strength down to me as I walk, or whether I'm subconsciously drawing it from their solid trunks, deeply buried roots and far-reaching branches. All I know is I never feel better than when I'm walking under their protective canopy.

We spend longer in the wood than I'd anticipated. The fresh cool woodland air, the sounds of some early spring leaves blowing gently in the breeze and the birds singing happily above us do more for my state of mind than any of the expensive sessions I've had with my therapist.

When we return to the cottage about an hour later, I've just unclipped Merlin from his lead when his ears prick up, and the hackles on his neck begin to rise.

'What's up?' I ask, looking at him in dismay. 'What's wrong, Merlin?'

Then I hear a sound coming from the kitchen. I stiffen, just like the dog at my feet. Someone is in there.

I stand there for a moment, paralysed with fear. *There's an intruder*, I hear a voice say in my head. *An intruder in your cottage.* It's like I'm under water and the voice in my head is above the surface. It's muffled and slow and difficult to understand. *Someone has broken into your bolt-hole. Your safe place. Your home. Danger. Danger. Danger!*

Merlin growling at the door that leads into the kitchen jolts me from my inner trauma.

Whereas his natural instinct is clearly to approach the danger head-on, mine is the opposite.

'Shush,' I whisper, trying to back out of the hall towards the front door. 'Merlin!' I urge in a low voice. 'Come here!'

But Merlin, usually so obedient, is clearly not happy that a stranger has invaded our home, and stays rooted to the spot.

I'm torn: torn between my fear of what is on the other side of the kitchen door and my loyalty to the little dog that has become my friend.

'Merlin!' I try one more time. 'Come here . . . *please*!'

Merlin ignores me and begins scratching at the door. I hurry over to him with the intention of scooping him up and carrying away from the danger, but his scratching has nudged the door ajar – just a crack, but a crack big enough for a little dog to squeeze through.

'Merlin!' I cry as he scampers into the kitchen at full speed. I don't think this time, I immediately chase after him.

I don't know what I expect to find as we both dash into the kitchen, but it's certainly not a pair of legs protruding from underneath the sink. The legs are wearing khaki combat trousers, and the feet at the end of the legs are clad in tan Timberland boots.

Merlin stands by the side of the legs, barking and growling.

'Merlin!' I call. 'Stop it.'

'Won't be a mo!' a male voice calls from under the sink. 'Does he bite? It sounds like he might, and I'm feeling pretty exposed here.'

'Er . . . no. I don't think so,' I say, somewhat confused by the man's jovial tone. I'd been expecting a knife-wielding attacker, or at the very least some sort of burglar looking for valuables. Instead, I find a man apparently fixing my sink.

I notice my heart, which had been racing so fast I could barely feel it before Merlin had burst into the kitchen, has calmed slightly, and is now only beating at a rate comparable with a hundred-metre sprint.

'I met a little dog called Merlin the other day,' the voice says, as a body wearing a tight white T-shirt slides out from under the sink. 'It can't be the same . . . Oh, it is the same one. Hello, fella,' he says. Merlin visibly calms but still retains an aggressive stancc.

'Good guard dog,' he says to me, as a set of perfect teeth form a smile. 'And hello; we meet again.'

'H-hi,' I say, as I suddenly recognise the jogger we'd met in the wood on our first night here. Now he's without a hood, I can see that his short black hair is peppered with the occasional grey like his stubble had been. He has a few more laughter lines around his blue eyes, and furrows in his brow that I hadn't noticed in the dim light of the wood, and unlike the other day when I'd thought he must be younger, now I decide he's probably in his early forties. 'Are . . . are you fixing my sink?'

'I'm trying to,' he says, grinning, and he grabs a spanner from the toolkit beside him on the floor.

'But how did you get in?'

'There's a spare key at the vicarage,' he says. 'I hope that's okay?'

I just nod. My mind is all over the place. In the space of minutes, but what felt like seconds, I'd gone from expecting an intruder to be in my kitchen to discovering it wasn't an intruder but a plumber under the sink, to then finding out that they were both the jogger I'd met in the woods.

'Almost done,' the man says, as his taut, muscular body slides back under the sink. 'Right, that's your U-bend reattached,' he says after a moment or two, and he slides himself back out again. 'You had a blockage,' he explains. 'Sorry, did I surprise you again? You look quite shocked to see me here.'

'No, it's not that . . . I . . . I didn't recognise you without your hood,' I reply stupidly.

The man grins. 'That's a new one, usually it's something else.'

I wonder what he means.

'I didn't know you were coming yet,' I say, trying to say something normal.

'Didn't Jonah tell you?'

'Jonah?'

'You spoke to him earlier when you rang the vicarage.'

'The person I spoke to said his name was Deacon Finch?'

'Yes, that's right; Jonah is the deacon of the parish here.'

'Oh, I see. Well, he said you'd probably come tomorrow.'

'No time like the present; I had some free time this

afternoon so I thought I'd better come as soon as possible.' He begins to put his tools away into the bag.

'You've managed to fix it, then?' I ask. 'My sink?'

'Let's try it, shall we?' He stands up and turns on the tap. Water flows into the bowl, and quickly drains away down the plug hole. 'Like magic!' he says, gesturing flamboyantly at the sink.

'Wonderful,' I tell him, a fixed smile on my face. Although this man is very pleasant to look at, I never want to be in the company of strangers long these days, so I'm keen for him to leave now. 'Thank you so much for coming out so quickly . . .'

'Sorry, we haven't been introduced properly, have we?' He holds out his hand. 'I'm Callum.'

I hesitate.

'Don't worry, it's clean!' Callum jokes, looking at his hand.

Reluctantly I shake his hand, and as I do, I notice how soft it is. Quite the opposite to how a handyman's hand usually feels – slightly rough and worn.

'Again, I'm sorry if I scared you the other day in the wood,' he says, clearly noticing my apprehension. 'I fear I may have startled you, suddenly appearing like that.'

'You didn't scare me,' I say, desperately trying to appear calm and unruffled.

'Good, I'm pleased. It's just you were very quiet and you looked a little pale.'

'Perhaps I'm just not that talkative,' I reply shortly.

I'm so uncomfortable right now. Small talk with strangers was something I could perform in my sleep before, now I find it excruciatingly painful. I wish he would just go.

But luckily for me, Callum doesn't ask more questions, he just nods. 'Totally. I understand. Not everyone has as much to say as I do.' He smiles again, and I feel my insides, trying so hard to be tough right now, melt just a little. 'It's very nice to meet you, Ava.'

'How do you know my name?' I ask, suddenly forgetting my anxieties.

'Jonah – you told him when you rang.'

'Oh, yes, so I did.' I feel awful. Callum is just trying to be polite and friendly, and as so often happens, my anxiety is beginning to border on rudeness.

'I was just about to welcome you to Bluebell Wood, Ava; I know you're new to the village.'

'Thanks,' I reply, trying to sound a little more grateful. 'That's kind of you. How much do I owe you for fixing the sink? I assume I pay you, or does someone else – sorry, I don't quite know what the situation is here.'

'You owe me nothing. Call it my good deed for the day!'

'Are you sure?'

Callum nods. 'Love thy neighbour as thyself.'

'You live here as well?' I exclaim. I'd now met four locals in two days. In all the time I lived in my old apartment, I don't think I ever spoke to more than one or two of my neighbours and that was only when we passed in the corridor or met in the lift.

He looks at me strangely. 'Yes, just up the road.'

'That's good. Well, if you ever need a favour in return . . .' I blurt out without thinking. It seemed like the right thing to say to one of your neighbours in a small village.

Callum's cheeks flush a little, and I realise what I might have implied with my offer. 'Oh, I didn't mean . . . I meant—'

'It's fine,' he says, waving his hand dismissively at me. 'I know what you mean . . . honestly.' I'm surprised to see him look flustered as he hurriedly picks up his tool bag and a small hammer tumbles to the floor in his haste. 'I appreciate the offer,' he says, scooping up the hammer and throwing it in his bag. 'Now, I'd better be going. I'm sure I'll see you again around the village.'

I accompany him through the hall to the door. 'Yes, probably.'

'Let me know if you have anything else you need sorting – with your cottage, that is,' he says hurriedly, his cheeks pinking again as he fumbles for the door handle.

Callum's bashfulness is quite becoming, and suddenly I don't feel so uncomfortable in his presence.

'Bit of a handy man, are you?' I ask – my smile a tad warmer this time. 'Jack of all trades?'

'We usually are,' he says, smiling as he opens the door. 'We usually are.'

He steps out of the cottage on to the path and turns around to face me. 'Goodbye, Ava, it was nice to meet you, and again, welcome to Bluebell Wood. I do hope your stay here will be a pleasant one.'

'I hope so too,' I say, watching him depart down the path a little before I close the door. His triceps are taut as he carries his heavy tool bag, and his back muscles flex under his white T-shirt as he walks away. *Bluebell Wood suddenly looks a lot brighter than it did a while ago*, I think as I linger a little longer than I should on the doorstep. *Much brighter indeed* . . .

Five

'Ow!' I cry as I turn my burnt offerings out of the baking tray on to a plate. 'That's hot!'

Merlin looks up hopefully at me. My previous effort at baking muffins had turned out so badly that I'd binned all of them immediately, much to Merlin's chagrin.

'You can't have them,' I'd told him, looking at the soggy mess in the bin. 'They're inedible for humans, let alone dogs!'

Now I run my finger under the cold tap, while I survey my latest chargrilled effort. 'I knew I couldn't bake,' I mutter. 'I don't know why I thought otherwise.'

I'd been sure Evelyn's recipes would be foolproof – even to an amateur baker like me. But apparently not. I'd tried quite a few of them over the last few days, and I'm ready to admit defeat – for today, anyway.

When I've cooled my finger sufficiently, and cleared up the remaining mess, I make myself a coffee and sit on the sofa in the calm of the sitting room with Merlin next to me, gazing out at the garden.

'This is more like it,' I say as I stroke Merlin's soft ears. 'At least I tried something new – even if it didn't work out – and that's a step forward.'

I'd lost interest in most things over the last year; I'd found myself staring at the television for hours on end in my apartment in London, not really absorbing anything that was on the screen. It had simply been a comfort to hear voices talking, voices that didn't need me to form any sort of coherent reply.

So my baking didn't work out – no big deal – but I'm determined my challenge of feeding the birds isn't going to fail too. I've already put in too much effort to give up on that one. We've been in Bluebird Cottage for nearly a week now and I still haven't seen any birds on the table since the robin.

'What am I doing wrong?' I ask a sleeping Merlin. 'According to this,' I tap Evelyn's notebook on the side table next to me, 'Evelyn had all sorts of birds visiting her every day.'

I'd tried putting the food in different feeders, and I'd used plates and the flat part of the table to sprinkle seed on in case that made a difference, I'd even chopped up peanuts in Evelyn's food processor so they'd be a bit smaller and maybe tempt some of the smaller birds into feeding, but to no avail.

It's been four days since Callum came to fix my sink. Even though Merlin and I had been for many walks since, each time exploring fresh trails in the wood and discovering pretty flowers and new varieties of trees, we haven't seen or spoken to anyone since Callum.

This was nothing new for me; over the last year I'd become more and more reclusive, not wanting to go out or speak to anyone other than my children. But in London there was always noise, always something going on outside your home, even if you didn't want to be a part of it. Here it was silent.

I could hear the occasional car up on the main road and the

birds singing in the trees of the wood, but other than that, it was only Merlin and me.

I tried to pretend this didn't bother me; after all, I'd longed to be left alone for so many months now. I'd yearned for peace, quiet and solitude. So to be given what I wished for only to now not like it seemed churlish and ungrateful.

My one bright point is that Merlin seems extremely content with his new life, and that does please me. He'd been through such trauma in losing his own family; I was delighted to find I could give him a new life that made him so happy.

'Right, enough wallowing!' I say, finishing my coffee. 'That won't get us anywhere. So what if I can't bake and the birds don't like my food? The one thing I can do well is walk you. What do you say, Merlin?'

Merlin awakes, pricks up his ears and we set about our usual routine to prepare for our outing.

As we leave the cottage I hear a new sound to add to the constant birdsong: the church bells pealing.

'Must be the Sunday service,' I say to Merlin as we walk up the path from the cottage. 'I don't know how religious this village is, but hopefully they will all be in church right now instead of out for a walk in the woods, so fingers crossed we'll have the place to ourselves.'

We take one of our newly discovered routes through the woods, and as I'd hoped we barely see anyone other than a couple of other dog walkers who simply nod at me as we pass. As we leave the trees behind, we're about to head back to the cottage, when I remember I need to buy some plasters and general first-aid bits. I'd cut my finger the other day, and realised too late that I hadn't restocked my depleted first-aid kit before I moved. I'd searched Evelyn's cupboards, but couldn't find what I needed, so I'd sat with kitchen towel around my finger until the bleeding had stopped.

If I keep cooking in the way I have been, I'm definitely going to need those supplies, I think, looking hesitantly down the street towards the shop. There aren't too many people about, the church service must still be going on, so I take a chance and hurry along to Bird & Son.

Jenny isn't behind the counter this morning; instead, there's a young boy reading a magazine. He barely looks up as we wander in, which is exactly how I prefer it.

I quickly locate the first-aid supplies and gather a few things from the shelf. Then equally speedily I take them to the counter to pay.

The boy nods at me. 'Find everything you were looking for?' he asks in a practised fashion.

'Yes, thank you.'

He nods again and begins to add up my few things.

'Need a bag?'

'Oh yes, I do, I forgot my basket,' I say apologetically.

He shrugs. 'That's an extra 5p.'

'No problem,' I reply, keen to get away from here as quickly as I can. I can hear the church bells beginning to ring again, which presumably means the end of the service.

The boy adds the carrier bag charge to my total, then he loads my few items into the bag.

'That's £8.57 please,' he says, looking at me.

'Sure,' I say, reaching for the pocket of my jacket where I usually keep my purse. 'Oh,' I say as my hand finds an empty pocket and I hurriedly tap a couple more. 'Gosh, I'm terribly sorry, I don't seem to have my purse on me.'

The boy just stares blankly at me.

I look behind me down the narrow road opposite the shop; I can just see people beginning to spill forth from the church.

'I'm local,' I tell him desperately. 'I live in the village ... at Bluebird Cottage,' I add, hoping this will help. Everyone else I've spoken to seems to know the cottage and its previous occupant all too well.

'So?' the boy says, shrugging. 'If you haven't got any money you can't have the goods.' He quickly grabs the bag from the counter in case I should try to make a run for it.

'I meant if you can hold on to the bag, I'll pop back later and pay.' I glance again at the people beginning to stream from the church down the road towards us.

'S'pose it will be all right,' he says, looking at me oddly as I keep glancing from the window to him and back again.

'Hello again, lovey!' a friendly voice says, and I turn to see Jenny, in her Sunday best, standing in the shop doorway. 'Lovely to see you back again.' She gives Merlin a quick stroke and heads over to the counter. 'Is everything all right, Arnold?' she asks the boy. 'You look a bit flustered, dear.'

Arnold gives her a withering look that suggests he's never been flustered in his life. 'It's Arnie,' he tells her, 'I've told you before, Mrs Bird.'

'Oh yes, sorry, dear, of course.' She gives me a knowing wink. 'Now then, is everything okay with your shopping, lovey?'

'She ain't got no money,' Arnie says.

'I've forgotten my purse,' I tell Jenny. 'We went from a walk in the woods. I totally forgot I wasn't carrying it.'

'Oh well, don't you worry now. You can pop back in with the money another time.' She gives me a dismissive wave. 'It's not like I don't know where you're staying, is it?'

'Are you sure?' I ask with relief. A few people have followed

Jenny into the shop, and I'm eager to escape before it becomes too crowded. 'I'll pop back later today.'

'Whenever is convenient, lovey.' Jenny seems a little distracted now. She looks past me at someone entering the shop, her eyes lighting up. 'Ah, good morning to you again, Vicar,' she says, her smile wide. 'Lovely service this morning.'

'Thank you, Jenny,' I hear a voice that sounds very familiar say behind me, but I'm too busy trying to retrieve my bag from Arnie to think too hard about it. 'I'm glad you enjoyed it. We had a good turnout – must be the beautiful weather.'

I finally manage to wrestle my carrier bag away from Arnie, and I turn swiftly so we can exit the shop. But a man, wearing the long black robes of a vicar, is now bending down behind me fussing Merlin.

'Hello again, fella,' he says, ruffling Merlin's head. 'Had a good walk?' The vicar tilts his head up and smiles at me. 'We must stop meeting like this! How's your sink – still running freely?'

I stare down into a pair of pale blue eyes that look benevolently back up at me.

'You?' I say at last. 'You're the vicar?'

'Guilty as charged,' he says, standing up now.

'Best vicar we've had in a long time,' Jenny says, keen to still be involved. 'The congregation has almost doubled since Father Crawford took over.'

'Jenny, please, it's Callum. I've asked you enough times now.'

'Sorry, Father Crawford . . . I mean Father Callum.'

'Just Callum is fine.'

'But I thought you were a plumber . . . or at least the local handyman,' I say, still bewildered.

'Just because I wear this,' he says, pulling at his dog collar, 'doesn't mean I can't fix things.'

'No, of course not ... ' I'm still in shock. Especially when I remember some of the things that had run through my mind about Callum when he'd left my cottage the other day. My cheeks flush now. But he'd looked so different in his tight T-shirt, snug combat pants and chin covered with stubble to how he looked now: clean shaven, in his black robes and dog collar. 'Well ... it's nice to meet you again.' And for some reason I give a little bow and my face flushes all the more. 'Come on, Merlin,' I call, my head down, trying to hide my embarrassment. 'We'd better go. Thanks again, Jenny. I'll pop back and pay you for my shopping later.'

I pull Merlin's lead and we race from the shop.

Callum is the vicar here? How had I not known this?

'Hey, wait up!' I hear behind me and I turn to see Callum jogging up the path behind us.

I stop walking and smile politely.

'Sorry if I shocked you back there,' he says, catching up. 'I seem to spend my whole life doing that recently, don't I? I thought Jonah might have said who I was when you rang.'

'Nope, he just said he'd get someone to come out – I assumed it would be a plumber or someone like that.'

Callum shakes his head. 'Typical Jonah. He's so busy trying to say and do the right thing he sometimes forgets the basics. If you'd had something majorly wrong then it would have been a plumber, but I'm quite handy with most things, so I thought I'd take a look first.'

I nod, but I'm still confused. 'Could you explain who Jonah is again? You said he was a deacon or something when I spoke to you before, isn't that quite high up in the Church?'

'You're thinking of an archdeacon. A deacon helps me with my work at the church and in the parish – you might know him better as a curate.'

‘Oh, like a trainee vicar?’

‘There’s a little more to it than that – but yes.’

‘That makes more sense, then. I had visions of someone in full ceremonial robes and a pointy hat answering your phone.’

Callum laughs and I feel my heart beat a little faster in my chest.

‘Well, it was good to see you again … Ava, isn’t it?’ he asks.

I nod.

‘I’d better get back to Jenny – I just popped in for some milk. If I go back to the vicarage without any and Jonah is left with black coffee, I’ll never hear the end of it.’ He rolls his eyes. ‘I sometimes think being married would be easier than living with him!’

I grin now.

‘Hope to see you around again,’ he says, smiling at me. ‘Bluebell Wood is a very friendly village, I’m sure you’ll enjoy being here.’

He turns and strides confidently back down the path towards the shop.

But this time as I watch him go, my thoughts about his departing figure aren’t quite so clear cut …

Six

The next morning Merlin and I are in our new favourite spot. It's a warm day for March, helped by the sun that's shining through the window into the sitting room, so I've opened one of the glass doors just a little to let in some fresh air.

It's lovely feeling a little warmth in the air again. Spring is definitely on the way, and then summer. And in the same way as the weather is warming a little, a day at a time, so are my feelings towards this little cottage and the village I'm living in.

For the first time in ages I feel protected and safe. Both when I'm in the cottage and particularly when Merlin and I are in the wood.

There's something about Bluebell Wood that I can't quite put my finger on – but it's a something I'm growing to love a little more with every passing day.

I gaze out at the garden, enjoying the sun and simply letting my mind wander for a bit (something my therapist had recommended to me, but I'd yet to put into practice very often), when movement in the garden catches my eye – something darting behind a bush.

I'm just wondering what it was, when there's more movement from the bush, and a tiny bird flies across the garden and lands on the bird table.

It's the robin! I think excitedly, as the little bird looks carefully around several times before it goes to investigate the food on the table. As quick as a flash it chooses something and flies off again, back down to the same bush it had emerged from.

Finally! I think, and I find myself smiling. *And it's the little robin again.* But then there's more movement as the robin appears again and repeats his previous routine, before selecting a worm this time and darting off.

'At last,' I comment to Merlin. 'I thought they'd never come.'

It was only one robin, but the sight of a bird brave enough to come to the table and try something new makes me so much happier than I'd anticipated.

Over the next few days the robin returns several times to feed on the table, and then it brings a friend.

A pair! I think, watching them from my now regular spot by the window. *How fabulous.*

When I'd lived in London I'd seen wild birds all the time – sparrows on the window sill of my office, the pigeons around Trafalgar Square when I'd walked from the tube to my work, even the annoying birds that would sit in the trees outside my flat some mornings and wake me up with their incessant coo-coo-cooing. I'd never given them a second thought. But now, seeing the pair of robins that had decided to trust me enough to feed on my bird table brought me more joy than I ever could have imagined.

I didn't always see them from the French windows; sometimes I'd be out in the garden when they'd visit – hanging out my washing or pulling the odd weed out of the flower beds. They didn't seem in the least bit scared of me; if anything, I felt like I was intruding on their patch instead of the other way around.

It said in one of Evelyn's bird books that robins are very territorial, and once they've chosen a garden to feed from they will often try to scare off other birds that attempt to invade their territory. I hadn't seen any sign of that yet with my robins, I was simply honoured that they'd chosen my garden to feed from.

Our days in Bluebird Cottage had developed a routine of sorts. I'd get up in the morning and make Merlin's breakfast and myself a coffee. I'd then go out and top up the bird table if it needed it. I was beginning to think there were more birds feeding there than just my two regulars, as the seed was disappearing far too quickly to only be them. But so far I hadn't seen any other birds, so I guessed they must be coming before I got up in the morning. And that was another thing: I was sleeping better now – I put it down to all the fresh air and exercise I was getting. Often the first thing that would wake me in the morning would be birdsong. I'd awake feeling refreshed, rather than groggy from a mix of sleeping tablets and another fretful night of tossing and turning.

Once we'd looked after ourselves and the birds, Merlin and I would sit by the French windows and look out at the garden for a while, waiting for the first robin to make an appearance.

We'd go for one walk in the morning and another in the evening, and in between that I'd fill my time with reading from the many books on Evelyn's shelves, watching the odd bit of television, and occasionally attempting some more baking, although unlike my success in feeding the birds, my baking still left a lot to be desired.

Our walks would usually take place in the woods, but sometimes we'd venture into the village if I thought it was likely to be quiet. Like yesterday, when it had been bucketing down with rain. So Merlin didn't get muddy, I'd been a little braver, and we'd walked through the village and down by the church, exploring just a little more of Bluebell Wood than we'd already discovered.

I'd paused outside the church for a moment or two in the rain. It was a fairly small building, but that made it all the more attractive. It had a tall bell tower at one end, and a little porch on one side decorated with plants and birds carved in stone. I tried to imagine Callum taking services in there, but for some reason I struggled to.

Callum had crossed my mind more times than I cared to admit since we'd bumped into him last Sunday, but I was still having trouble seeing him as anything but the hunky handyman who had come to the cottage to fix my sink. Even though I'd seen him in his dog collar, I still couldn't imagine him as a vicar, or maybe I didn't want to . . .

Today as we take our usual route towards the wood, I hope that yesterday's rain hasn't made it too wet to walk the paths. I had dog shampoo at the cottage now, but I didn't fancy trying to bath Merlin when we got back.

Luckily for us some of the trees must have acted as a canopy, so although the greenery around us looks refreshed and invigorated by yesterday's downpour, the narrow paths and trails are still easy to negotiate. As always, I breathe in the fresh woodland air as I walk, and as a result any worries I have seem to melt away.

Birds sing in the trees as we pass.

'Why don't you come and try my bird table sometime?' I call cheerily to them. 'It's very nice and there's lots of choice.'

But they happily ignore my invitation and continue singing to each other.

We take a new path today, one we haven't tried before. It looks much like many of the other narrow paths in the wood, except after we've walked along it for a while this one begins to widen out into a clearing. The sun, making the most of the gap between the trees, shines down into the opening and I lean my face up towards it.

'Wonderful,' I say, my eyes closed for a moment. I can hear nothing but the trees swishing next to me, and the now distant sound of birdsong. I open my eyes again, and see Merlin investigating some old stones in the centre of the clearing. He lifts his leg against one.

'Do you ever stop marking your territory?' I ask, laughing at him. 'I'm sure hundreds of dogs have been here before you and hundreds will be here after you.'

But Merlin doesn't care, he continues to sniff around the old stones, which I realise as I get nearer are not, as I'd first thought, natural in their making, but more like stones used for building.

'These are pretty old,' I say, examining those around us. 'Maybe there was once a house or something similar here in the woods.'

But any building here would have been quite remote – we'd walked a fair way into the wood now, and I realise as I hear the sound of running water and discover a small stream running downhill next to us, we've been steadily climbing for a while too.

Merlin stops to take a drink from the cool clear water, and as I watch him I become transfixed by the steady sound of the water trickling over the rocks in front of me.

How peaceful it is, I think to myself. Actually, tranquil might be a better word. Peaceful, tranquil and serene. I can actually feel my heart rate begin to slow as I gaze at the moving water beside me.

'Mind if I join you?' I hear, as a voice bursts my bubble of calm.

Startled, I turn and see Callum jogging towards us on the opposite side of the stream. He's wearing a similar outfit to the first time we'd met him out running – sweatpants, a hoodie and running shoes – and I notice that the stubble that had been missing from his face on Sunday has made a return.

'Your Merlin has got the right idea,' he says, stopping and kneeling down at the side of the stream. He scoops up some of the water in his hands and takes a drink, then he does the same again. 'Can't beat it,' he says, smiling at me as he stands up again, shaking his hands dry. 'It's some of the freshest, cleanest water you'll ever taste.'

'I'll take your word for it,' I say, as he expertly steps over a few stones in the water so he doesn't get his feet wet.

'You surely can,' he says, standing next to me now. 'It's the best, and considering I deal in Holy Water, that's saying something!'

I smile at him, feeling awkward in his presence as usual.

'Is this one of your usual running routes?' I ask, not knowing what else to say.

'Yeah, I quite often come up here. That's the good thing about the woods: there are so many different paths you can take – a bit like life itself!'

I smile politely again.

'Sorry, too many jokes?' he asks. 'I do that sometimes.'

Was Callum nervous too? I wonder. No, why would he be?

'So, how are you settling in?' he continues pleasantly. He

reaches down to fuss Merlin, who has joined us. 'Is the cottage behaving itself now?'

'Yes, it's lovely, thank you. Nice and peaceful.'

'Good. If there's something that Bluebell Wood will definitely give you it's peace. Not too much happens here.'

'Yes, I've noticed that. But peace and quiet is just what I need right now so I'm not complaining.' I bite my lip; I'd said more than I needed to.

Callum looks at me with interest, but doesn't enquire any further.

'I'm glad we're providing you with what you need,' he says tactfully. 'If you ever get tired of peace and quiet, though, just let me know.'

Is he asking me out now? No, surely not.

'There's quite a few social clubs in the village,' he continues. 'You know, WI, that kind of thing. They usually meet up in the village hall. Or if that's not your scene, there's always The Daft Duck. There's usually a friendly crowd in there.'

Of course he isn't! What am I thinking?

'Thanks,' I say, and annoyingly I feel my face flush. 'But I'm fine. I'm not that keen on crowds.' I sigh, I'd done it again.

'Fair enough.' He shrugs. 'Tell you the truth, neither am I.'

I look disbelievingly at him. 'But you're a vicar. You deal with people all the time – huge congregations, weddings, christenings, garden fetes . . . '

He grins. 'I wish I had a huge congregation. I'm lucky if I manage forty, and that's on a good Sunday.'

'Forty isn't bad for one village, is it?'

'It wouldn't be if it *were* just one village. But my church is now the place of worship for all the local parishes. All the other churches in the area have either closed down or fallen into disrepair. I'm lucky mine is still standing, to be honest. It's the only one left.'

'That's a shame.'

'It's the time we're living in,' Callum says pragmatically. 'No one wants to waste time going to church on a Sunday. Too many other things to do. I can't say I blame them. If I wasn't a vicar, I probably wouldn't go either.'

I'm surprised to hear him say this.

'Have I shocked you?' he asks, grinning.

'A bit.'

'Let's just say I'm not your usual parish priest.'

I'm beginning to realise this.

'Where's Merlin?' I suddenly ask, looking around us.

Callum turns too. 'He can't have gone very far,' he says calmly.

'Merlin!' I call. 'Merrrlinn!'

There's a piercing whistle next to me. And I turn to see Callum with his finger and thumb between his lips. He drops them for a moment to listen.

We hear a rustle of leaves, and Merlin appears from a clump of trees, looking completely unaware that anything is amiss.

'Works every time,' Callum says, grinning again.

'Merlin, you mustn't run off,' I say, hurrying over to him. I pull his lead from my pocket.

'You don't need that,' Callum says, following me. 'He's usually glued to your side. He just saw an opportunity and took it. Nothing wrong in that, fella, is there?'

Merlin looks keenly up at Callum, who ruffles his head in return.

'All right then,' I say, putting the lead back in my pocket.

'I'll let you off, but just this one time. I need to be able to trust you, Merlin.'

Callum again looks with interest between us but doesn't comment further. 'Are you heading back yet?' he asks.

I glance at my watch. 'Er, yes, I think we will. We've been out a fair while now.'

'Mind if I tag along?'

'Aren't you supposed to be running, though?'

'I think I've done enough of that for today. A walk back will be my cool-down.'

'Sure, if you want to,' I say, sounding indifferent.

Callum puts his hands on his hips and grins. 'You sure know how to make a boy feel wanted.'

'You're hardly a boy,' I counter, smiling to myself as I head off with Merlin.

'The charm of her!' he calls, jogging to catch up with us. 'So, miss, how old do you think I am, then?'

I turn and look at him. His dark, almost black hair is flecked with grey at the temples, like the stubble on his chin. Close up I can see that below his now twinkling pale blue eyes, along with the laughter lines I'd spotted the other day, are heavier lines. Up on his forehead are the type of furrows that only deepen that far when one has reached a certain stage of life.

'I'm going to be polite,' I say, trying to guess in my head before I share with him, 'and say on a good day forty, and on a bad . . .'

He pulls a silly face.

'Forty-five, maybe -six?'

'It must be a bad day, then,' Callum says. 'I'm forty-six.'

'Like I said, hardly a boy!'

'Sadly no, not any more. I try hard, though.'

'I bet you do.'

We walk on a bit further. It should feel odd having someone walking alongside me, but strangely it doesn't. Callum, a bit like the wood, is a very calming presence.

'What brings you to Bluebell Wood?' Callum asks. 'We're a bit off the beaten track. Not many folk choose to come and live here at your age unless they have a reason.'

'Are you saying I'm old?' I ask, feigning shock.

'No, quite the contrary, actually. I'm saying you look too young to retire here.'

'Is that a prompt so you can guess my age now?' I say, raising my eyebrows at him.

'You *must* be younger than me,' Callum says diplomatically. 'No way you're older.'

I shake my head. 'Flattery will get you absolutely nowhere with me.'

'Somehow I didn't think it would,' Callum says knowingly, looking far too directly into my eyes for my liking.

'If you must know,' I say hurriedly, looking away, 'I'm the same age as you.'

'Really?'

'Yes.'

'You look good on it.'

'Thanks,' I say, blushing, not for the first time. I pretend to look around for Merlin, but he's right beside us.

'You obviously haven't been blessed with children, then?' Callum asks. 'In my experience that usually ages people.'

Does Callum have children? I puzzle this in my mind for a moment.

'Actually, I have – two. Hannah and Matt – well, Matthew.' At the sound of his name my mind immediately begins to fret about his fast approaching move, as it had done far too many times since he'd told me about it. But it's stopped in its tracks by Callum.

'Good Biblical names there,' he says approvingly.

'Oh yes, I suppose they are,' I say vaguely, as my mind is forced back to the present. 'I hadn't really thought about it.'

'Are they with their father? I'm assuming they must still be quite young?'

'No, they're both in their twenties. Hannah works in Lincoln and Matt is at uni in York. He's going on a year abroad soon – to New York,' I force myself to say. I had to deal with it sometime.

'Wow – that will be fun. I wish I'd had a year in New York.'

'Yes,' I say, sounding less enthusiastic.

'Worried about him going?' Callum asks perceptively.

I shrug.

'Nothing wrong with that. We all worry about our loved ones. It's only natural if you care for someone to be concerned for their welfare.'

'Yes, I suppose it is.' I stare at him. Somehow hearing Callum say it made it sound okay.

'Are you all right?' he asks.

'Yes, I'm absolutely fine,' I say, smiling at him, my mind suddenly feeling clearer than it had in a long time. Of course it was all right to worry about your children. I'd be an odd mother not to, wouldn't I? Trying to stop myself from doing so had made me worry all the more.

'So you must have been quite a young mum, then?' Callum says, attempting to fill the gap in our conversation.

I feel sorry for him. It must seem like I'm acting very strangely.

'Fairly young,' I say, suddenly realising how much I'm telling

Callum about myself. When I'd moved here to get away from everything, I'd sworn I'd keep myself to myself, and now here I was sharing everything with the local parish priest; but it didn't feel scary, it felt good. 'You're very good at getting people to talk, you know?' I tell him as we emerge into a more familiar part of the wood. 'Does it come with the job?'

'Partly, I suppose. But sometimes people just interest me and I want to know more about them.'

'I can assure you I'm not interesting in the least,' I say, tapping my leg to get Merlin to come closer, also so it gives me an excuse to look away from Callum again. He has an incredible ability to pull you into his gaze so you don't want to look away, and I really need to pull away right now. For a casual conversation this is already feeling far too intense.

'Well, I disagree,' Callum says, his voice sounding different. He's lost his usual light cheery tone; his voice now sounds more thoughtful as he speaks. 'I think you're an incredibly intriguing person, Ava, and one I would very much like to get to know better.'

Seven

April arrives, and so does a blast of colder weather.

This prevents me from opening the French windows too often, but doesn't prevent the robins from visiting my bird table; in fact, to their great annoyance they're regularly joined by a few other feathered friends – a pair of blackbirds, some collared doves, an odd wood pigeon – and, to my enormous excitement, a blue and a great tit. Evelyn's bird books have been a huge source of information and, surprisingly, enjoyment for me, but I find I need to study them less and less as I begin to recognise any new visitors to the table myself.

I take great delight in watching the robins suddenly appear when one of the other birds decides to visit the table. It doesn't matter what size the bird is, one of the robins will always pop up, bravely trying to defend its territory – just like the book had said they would.

I'm getting so many birds on my table now that I'm fast running out of food for them. I think about ordering some to be delivered online, but then I decide that's just silly when there's a perfectly good shop down the road.

If my birds can be brave enough to try something new, and then keep returning even if others are about, then so can I, I decide. So one morning Merlin and I set off through the village to Peacocks Farm Shop.

Along the way, I find myself hoping that we might bump into Callum again. I hadn't seen him since we'd walked together in the woods, and even though I tried really hard *not* to want to see him again, the truth was I really did.

But other than a few odd villagers out and about around the shop and the school as we pass, we don't see anyone we know. As always, people smile and nod at us, acknowledging our presence, but no one stops to talk, and although that pleases me, for the first time in a *very* long time, there's a tiny part of me that's a little sad.

It's not surprising, I think to myself as we walk, *the majority of your life has been spent constantly surrounded by people, both at work and at home, so to find yourself living alone with only Merlin for company is going to feel a little odd from time to time. You'll get used to it.*

We arrive at the farm shop, and I pause before I push on the gate, taking a deep, calming breath.

'You can do this, Ava,' I murmur. 'You've been here before; you can do it again.'

We walk across the gravel, and Gavin's two Labradors bound up to greet us. 'Hello, you two,' I say to them. 'Do you want to go and play, Merlin?' I ask, perfectly happy for him to stick with me if he wants to; there's no reason he has to go and socialise with other dogs if he doesn't want. But of course, unlike me, Merlin loves company, and his tail wags super hard as he waits for me to unclip his lead; then, keen as mustard, he races off to play with the other dogs.

There are a few people wandering around the shop as I enter and a couple already by the till, so I pick up a basket and head straight to the section Gavin showed me on my first visit.

I find the particular brand of mixed bird food my birds seem to prefer and I pick up a couple of bags, then I get some more mealworms, and some peanuts – I've continued to chop them up in Evelyn's food processor because the birds seem much keener to take them this way. I also get some sunflower seeds and a packet of food specially designed to attract blue and great tits. Then I head across to the dog section and pick up a few dog biscuits and a treat for Merlin. I knew I was spoiling both the birds and my dog, but I was on my own now, who else did I have to spoil?

I think about Hannah and Matt and how every time we'd go shopping when they were small, they'd persuade me to buy them a small toy or some sweets.

They'd both called me frequently since I'd been here, checking to see if I was okay and wasn't getting too lonely all on my own, and I'd assured them both that I was absolutely fine, and I was enjoying all this time to myself. Which was partly true: I was. But I was starting to feel a little lonely, which I was having a hard time understanding after yearning for solitude for so long.

I take my basket to the till, and wait patiently in the short line that has formed in front of me. But there seems to be a bit of a delay at the counter while some gossiping takes place.

'. . . so I said to him, "If you don't do something about that tree overhanging my garden boundary then I'll chop it down myself!" You wouldn't stand for that nonsense, would you, Father Finch?' a small, rounded woman demands.

'Er … well, it's not for me to say really.' I recognise the softly spoken voice from my telephone call to the vicarage, and I realise that the tall young man with brown curly hair standing in front of me must be the deacon that Callum had spoken about.

'I know, but it's blocking out all my sunlight, damn monstrosity. Oh, pardon my language, Father.'

'Please, Mrs Bunting, it's Jonah.'

But Mrs Bunting doesn't seem happy with such familiarity.

'You and Father Crawford keep the vicarage garden looking lovely, you do. No overhanging trees there. It's as neat as a new pin.'

'Well, thank you; it's kind of you to say.' Jonah glances behind him to see who they might be delaying with this chatter. He smiles at me apologetically.

'As lovely as it is to chat to you, Mrs Bunting, I think we might be holding up people who want to pay.'

Mrs Bunting looks to see who he means.

'Oops, so we are! Sorry, my love!' she calls to me. 'It's Father Finch here, he just won't stop talking!'

Jonah gives me a rueful smile.

'Why don't you go on in front of us?' Mrs Bunting suggests. 'I'm in no hurry; are you, Father?'

Jonah looks like he might be, but is too polite to say.

'Oh no, it's fine,' I protest, not wanting to make a fuss. 'I don't mind waiting, honestly.'

'Hello again!' Gavin waves from the shop counter. 'You decided to come back, then – used all your bird food up yet?'

'Yes, almost,' I say, my cheeks flushing as everyone looks at me now. Jonah and Mrs Bunting stand aside, so I have no choice but to move forward into the space they've left for me.

'This lady has moved into Evelyn's cottage,' Gavin says, taking my basket from me.

'Oh really?' Mrs Bunting says with great interest. 'I heard someone new had moved in. We haven't seen you around the village much, have we?'

'Er . . . no. Not really,' I say, feeling very uncomfortable now everyone's eyes are upon me. 'When I go out it's mainly to take my dog for walks in the wood,' I say, hoping this will be sufficient explanation.

Gavin glances out of the window behind him. 'And there he is, having a fine time in the yard with my two again.'

'Is it just you in the cottage?' Mrs Bunting enquires. 'No family?'

'Mrs Bunting,' Jonah protests, 'I really don't think that's any of our business, now, is it?'

'It's fine,' I tell Jonah. 'Yes, it's just me,' I answer Mrs Bunting. 'My two children are all grown up now.'

'Flown the nest, have they?' Mrs Bunting says pragmatically. 'I remember when my two left home, I was bereft for weeks I was; Mr Bunting said he'd never heard me so quiet.'

'Golly, you must have been bad!' Jonah says, turning quickly to wink at me.

I grin back at him, but Mrs Bunting isn't perturbed.

'There's lots of activities here in Bluebell Wood if you're feeling lonely, dear,' she continues. 'We've a lovely WI that meets on the first Wednesday of the month. There's a little Friendship group that meets at the village hall on a Friday morning – you might be a bit young for that, though . . . ' she says, looking me up and down. 'We've a local history group, and exercise classes too. Also—'

'I'm fine, really,' I try, but stopping Mrs Bunting when she's in full flow is like trying to hold back a tsunami.

'Our village hall is where it all happens,' she continues. 'Although,' she looks accusingly at Jonah, 'it's seen better days.'

'I don't know why you're looking at me, Mrs Bunting,' Jonah protests. 'We're trying our best.'

'The village hall is part of the church,' she explains. 'They're responsible for its upkeep.'

'Like I said, Callum and I are doing our best to raise funds to refurbish it.' He turns to me again. 'It's not easy; we also have a problem with the church roof, which is in need of repair, so it's difficult to know where to begin when it comes to distributing the little funds we might raise.'

I try to nod sympathetically.

'Talking of fundraising, can you bake, dear?' Mrs Bunting suddenly asks. 'We've got a fundraising bake sale at the church this Saturday. You'd meet lots of the villagers if you came. We always get a lovely turnout to our bake sales.'

'No,' I say, vigorously shaking my head. 'No, really – I'm a terrible baker.'

'Ah . . .' For the first time, Mrs Bunting looks a little deflated. 'That's a real shame. Evelyn was a wonderful baker. She always made us lots of lovely cakes for our sales.'

'I'm sure she was,' I agree. 'I've seen all the equipment in her kitchen, but it's not for me.'

'Hmm, well, let me think . . .' Mrs Bunting is clearly not a quitter. 'There must be something . . .'

'*Sorry*,' Jonah mouths silently.

'*It's fine*,' I mouth back. 'Perhaps I could just pay?' I ask Gavin hopefully.

I might just be able to escape without being coerced into one of the village's many societies then.

'Of course,' Gavin says knowingly. While Mrs Bunting has

been desperately trying to set me up with a village social life, Gavin has been quietly totalling up my basket. 'That'll be £24.62, please.'

I reach for my purse, but nearly drop it as Mrs Bunting suddenly cries, 'Ooh!'

I turn back to her with trepidation.

'Are you any good at quizzes, dear?' she asks keenly.

'Quizzes?' I repeat.

'Yes, we have a church quiz team here – don't we, Father? Evelyn was one of our founder members, so we're one member short now she's gone, and correct me if I'm wrong, but doesn't the new season start soon?' She looks at Jonah.

'Yes, it does. But we're actually two short. Eileen has gone to live with her daughter in Devon now, hasn't she?'

'So she has, to help look after the triplets – I totally forgot. Her daughter had triplets,' she tells me. 'Can't cope on her own, the father is away in the army.' She nods knowingly.

'But even so, I really don't think that Ava should be pressurised into joining, Mrs Bunting,' Jonah says, to my immense relief. 'It's a pub quiz league we're in,' he says as an aside to me. 'It just so happens that a lot of our team are also a part of our church.'

My ears prick up immediately. 'I see. Who is in your team?' I ask casually.

I really shouldn't care if Callum is in the team.

But I do.

'Well, there's myself, Gavin here,' Jonah gestures to behind the counter and Gavin nods, 'then there's Jenny from the village shop – who I'm sure you've met – and a few other folk from the village who you might not have, including the landlady from The Daft Duck, and the head teacher at the village school. Oh and Callum, of course – that's Father Crawford.'

I nod in what I hope is an indifferent fashion.

'We all try to have a good broad general knowledge, and then we have our own specialist subjects. Mine is music,' he adds proudly. 'I don't suppose you know anything about natural history?' he asks hopefully. 'That was Evelyn's speciality.'

'Not really,' I reply. 'As Gavin here will tell you, I didn't even know what to feed wild birds until I came to Bluebell Wood. City girl me.'

Phew, that was close. Even though I would have liked to see Callum again, the last thing I wanted was to join a quiz team in a pub full of people – that was asking for trouble.

'Ah, that's a shame,' Jonah says. 'We really need some new team members right now.'

'Sorry.' I shrug. Then for some silly reason I keep talking. 'If you'd needed someone who knew about twentieth-century history then I'd have been just the person for you. That's my specialist subject; I've always been interested in it.'

Gavin and Jonah stare at me.

'What?' I ask, looking back at them with concern.

'Each quiz night has a theme,' Jonah says, smiling at me, 'and you'll never guess what the first theme of the new season is . . . '

'History?' I ask weakly, already knowing the answer.

'Exactly! Oh, you'd be perfect, Ava,' Jonah says, beaming. 'Please say you'll do it. You'd be doing me a huge favour. I'm the team captain and I've been having an awful time trying to get someone worthy to take Eileen and Evelyn's places.'

Don't do it, Ava, my mind is very clearly advising me. *Don't do it. You know you'll hate it . . .*

But for some reason my heart is pressing the override button today. I feel sorry for Jonah; he's obviously one of those people that's always trying to do his best by everyone. So I hear myself say: 'Sure, I'll do it. Just let me know when you need me.'

Eight

What was I thinking of? I ask myself for what feels like the hundredth time since I agreed to be a part of the Bluebell Wood quiz team.

It had been almost a week since I'd been pressganged in the farm shop, and I'd worried about it two, three, maybe four times or more every day since.

It wasn't the questions I was worried about, I was actually quite confident in my range of general knowledge, and knowing the quiz had a history theme did make it all the more appealing. No, it was the fact I was going to have to be around so many people at once that was giving me the most concern.

The social side of my life had always been a huge part of who I was before. My ex-husband and I had had lots of friends in the early part of our marriage, and if we'd ever joined clubs, the social life that came with them had usually been what attracted us the most. When the children were young, I joined the school's PTFA, and I was always volunteering to help at fetes and the like; then when they grew too old for school and my divorce came through, I socialised with my own close friends and a few work colleagues; people were always a huge part of my life.

Breathe, Ava. Breathe, I tell myself as I feel my heartbeat begin to quicken. I get up and stand at the part open French windows, drawing in the fresh morning air. *Deep calming breaths. In for a count of three, out for a count of four. In for a count of four, out for a count of five . . .*

It helps a bit. My breathing becomes less shallow, and I feel a little calmer – for now.

I look out at the bird table – that always calmed me down and brought me joy. My regulars were growing in number day by day, and I felt if I didn't go out every morning to top up their food, the birds would be disappointed in me, and might go elsewhere.

So I do as I do every morning and head to the little garden shed to scoop up today's mix of seeds, nuts and dried worms. Then I carry them outside to the table and top up the feeders and the pie dish I keep on the flat part of the table under the little roof.

I'm about to pour my scoop of seed out when I spy something unusually bright among the discarded and unwanted seed.

What's that? I wonder as I reach inside the table to pull something yellow and plastic from the corner. *It looks a bit like one of those plastic wedges from a game of Trivial Pursuit.* 'Wait, it *is* one of those wedges!' I exclaim as I brush some bird seed off it. 'What on earth are you doing on my bird table?' I ask, looking down at the triangle of yellow plastic in the palm of my hand. 'Did one of the birds drop you?'

I look around as if the culprit might still be hiding in the bushes watching me.

Maybe I'd had a magpie visit the table, and he'd dropped

it. Didn't they like brightly coloured things? Or was that shiny things? That must be it, how else would it have got here?

I put the yellow wedge in the pocket of the long baggy cardigan that I'd taken to wearing all the time since I came to the cottage, and continue to refill the table.

Then, as we do every morning, Merlin and I take a walk in the woods.

While we walk I try hard not to think about tonight, and simply enjoy being out in nature once more. I'd grown to love my little cottage and its pretty little garden, but I never felt happier than when I was here in the wood.

But even the trees couldn't absorb all my anxiety today, and my thoughts soon returned to the quiz. Jonah had popped round to the cottage yesterday to check I was still okay to take part. He'd told me the team were 'at home' tonight, so all I needed to do was turn up at the pub and they would all look after me.

All I needed to do.

Five words. Easy to say. Not so easy to do. Not for me, anyway.

'Stop thinking about it!' I say out loud in frustration. 'Stop worrying; it's not going to help, is it?'

But telling myself not to worry was, as usual, easier said than done.

Determined my anxiety wasn't going to win this time, I thrust my hands into my pockets and begin to stomp along the soft spongy ground below my feet. But my hand catches on something in the pocket of my cardigan and I pull the plastic triangle from it.

'Maybe you can be my lucky charm,' I say, looking down at the Trivial Pursuit wedge. 'After all, you do represent the history category in the game, don't you?'

As Merlin and I continue our walk, I find myself smiling. It was only something small and insignificant, but as I grasp the wedge tightly in my hand, I do feel a little calmer, and anything that helped me to feel like that was worth more to me than carrying a precious diamond would have been.

At seven o'clock that night Merlin and I stand in the hall of the cottage. I have my coat on, and Merlin has his lead attached to his collar, so we're ready to leave. The only problem is I haven't yet stepped forward and put my hand on the door handle.

Merlin looks up at me.

'I know,' I tell him. 'I know we've been standing here too long. But I'm not sure I can do it.'

Merlin sits down next to my leg, patiently waiting, and not for the first time since we'd arrived in the little hallway, I sigh.

'Come on, Ava, you can do this,' I tell myself. 'A little quiz in the village pub is safe. Nothing is going to happen to you there.'

I'd even rung the pub at lunchtime today to check it was okay to bring Merlin tonight. I hadn't left the cottage without him since I'd arrived in Bluebell Wood, and I was a little scared to now – actually, I was *very* scared to.

But the pub landlord had been lovely, and said they very much welcomed dogs. He and his wife had two Border terriers themselves, and were huge dog lovers.

I'd ended the call with mixed feelings – yes it was great I could take Merlin to the quiz tonight; any bit of extra support was going to be very helpful in getting me through the door. But I knew a part of me had secretly hoped they'd say no I couldn't bring him, then I'd have used it as an excuse not to be able to go, saying I couldn't leave him alone at the cottage.

'Come on, Ava,' I say again. 'If you don't leave soon you'll be late.'

Merlin is now lying down by my side. He looks like he might be about to nod off.

'I'm sorry,' I tell him. 'I'm being very silly, I know.'

Suddenly, I hear a commotion coming from outside the front door. I glance out of the narrow lattice window at the side and see a cat swiping its paw at some ornamental rocks in the little front garden.

'What on earth is he doing?' I say to Merlin.

Then I see the cat trying to get his paw between the rocks – he must have something trapped in there!

Without thinking, I open up the front door a little and try to shoo the cat away. But the cat just turns its head and looks at me for a moment, before quickly turning back to continue its quest to get its furry paw in between the rocks.

'Merlin,' I call, looking behind the door to a now wide-awake Merlin. 'It's your time to shine!'

I open the door wide so Merlin sees the cat at the same time as the cat sees him.

Merlin shoots forward, his ears pricked up and his tail poker straight behind him. The startled cat stares at him for a couple of seconds before concluding that it might be in his best interests to leave now. He leaps up on to the gate, gives Merlin one last look, then disappears over the other side and into a nearby bush.

'Well done you,' I tell Merlin, patting him and ruffling his fur. 'We make a good team – yes?'

But now Merlin has become interested in what is behind the rocks; he pulls tightly towards them on his lead.

'You just wait there,' I tell him, tethering his lead to the gatepost.

I walk back towards the rocks, and gently move one away from the pile. Trapped in the middle of the stones is a slightly dishevelled-looking blackbird. It stares fearfully up at me.

'It's okay,' I tell it gently, hoping the cat hadn't managed to get its claws anywhere near it. 'I'm not going to hurt you.'

I remove enough of the rocks so that it can escape, then I stand well back.

The traumatised blackbird hesitates for a moment, perhaps wondering if it can trust me. Then it hops forward a little and peeks through the gap I've created while I watch quietly from a distance.

The bird suddenly takes its chance and hops a little further forward, then it flaps its wings and takes off into the air, flying to the safety of a nearby tree.

'Good, I'm pleased the cat didn't get you,' I tell it, its beady eyes still watching me warily. 'If you don't already, why don't you come feed on my bird table sometime? There's lots for everyone, and Merlin will see off any cats – won't you, Merlin?'

Merlin wags his tail, so I go over to the gate to untie his lead.

I'm about to head back into the cottage when Merlin turns and begins barking again.

'What now?' I ask him, but then I hear a male voice.

'Hello!' it calls as I turn to see a face I don't recognise heading down the path towards the cottage.

'Are you Ava, by any chance?' a tall slim man with raven-black hair asks, smiling at me as he arrives at the gate.

'Yes,' I reply hesitantly, looking more closely at him. The man is dressed smartly in a pale blue shirt and navy chinos, a navy-blue wax jacket tossed casually over his arm.

'Ah, good, I'm Lonan. Jonah said I'd find you here. I'm heading to the quiz tonight too.'

'Oh, I see,' I reply hesitantly, wondering what he wants with me.

'I'm new to the village and I thought it would be a good way to meet a few folk. Jonah said that you were new too, so I thought you might like someone to walk down there with. Nothing worse than walking into an unfamiliar situation where no one knows you, is there?'

'Er, no.'

'Looks like I've just caught you,' he says, glancing at the door ajar behind me. 'Just locking up?'

'Yes, but—'

'Great! Is this your dog?' he asks, looking at Merlin, who wags his tail.

'Yes, I'm taking him along tonight. Apparently, they welcome dogs in the pub.'

'Sounds like just my sort of pub, then. Shall we go?'

I nod and turn back towards the door. After I've shut it, I pretend to be fiddling with the key in the lock to buy myself a little time. *How am I supposed to get out of this now? What can I possibly say to Lonan that's a good enough excuse not to go with him?*

I glance back: Lonan has bent down to fuss Merlin.

Maybe he's right? Perhaps it would be easier to arrive at the pub with someone else? There's less chance I'll turn and run back to the cottage if someone else is by my side as well as Merlin. I catch sight of the blackbird still sitting in the tree watching me.

This is your fault! I think, turning the key in the lock. *I would still be in the cottage if it wasn't for you, then Lonan wouldn't have seen me. I should have left you for the cat!*

But I don't mean it; if it hadn't been for the blackbird, I

knew I wouldn't have had the courage to leave the cottage at all. Perhaps I should be thanking it?

'All good?' Lonan says behind me.

I turn back to him. 'Yes,' I say with as much confidence as I can muster. 'As good as it's going to get, anyway.'

Nine

'How long have you been in Bluebell Wood?' my companion asks as we walk together towards the pub.

'Not long,' I answer, knowing I must sound a little brusque.

'Me either,' Lonan continues companionably. 'I moved here a week ago. I'm a writer; I decided I needed some peace and quiet to finish a book I'm working on. So I rented a little cottage and here I am.'

I nod. 'What is your book about?' I ask. I'm trying super hard to be as calm and relaxed as Lonan seems and make polite conversation. It's not this perfectly nice man that's causing the ever-growing knot in my stomach, but the thought of the pub and all those people . . .

'I write historical fiction,' he says, obviously keen to talk about his work. 'My current novel is set in the twelfth century, during the reign of Richard the Lionheart. I've heard this area is full of interesting history, so I thought it would be the perfect place to get my creative juices flowing. I also hope to think up an idea for my next book while I'm here.'

'How interesting . . . '

Lonan laughs. 'Don't pretend to be interested if you're not.'

'I am, actually. I used to work with a few museums in London. I've always enjoyed history – well, factual history.'

'Mine is factual. Just because I write fiction, I still have to research all the facts first.'

'Sorry.'

'Don't apologise, it's fine, I get that a lot. Were you a curator at the museums?'

'No, nothing so exciting, I'm afraid. I used to work in publicity and events; we had contracts with them for promotions, advertising, that kind of thing.'

'Really?' Lonan looks surprised.

'What's that supposed to mean?'

'Nothing, you just don't look the type.'

'And what *type* is that?'

'Sorry, I don't mean anything dreadful by it. It's just in my experience people who work in that type of industry in London are usually a sort. You know, they dress and behave a certain way. And you don't seem like that.'

I'm not sure if this is a dig or a compliment.

'It was a while ago,' I say. 'I'm a different person now than I was back then.'

'Sounds intriguing. Why are you different?'

'I'd rather not talk about it if you don't mind.'

'Sure,' Lonan says, shrugging amiably. 'Your prerogative, of course. I'm terrible for probing questions. It's part of the job.'

We walk on for a few seconds in silence.

'Lonan is an unusual name,' I say, feeling bad that I'd cut him off in the way I had.

'Yes, apparently it means blackbird. My parents are Irish, you see. I was born just outside of Dublin.'

I stare at him for a moment as I think of the bird outside the cottage. 'What a coincidence,' I hear myself saying.

'What is?' Lonan asks.

'Oh, nothing,' I reply quickly. 'I spent some time in Dublin with work. I thought I could hear a Celtic lilt to your voice.'

'And you'd be right! We moved to the UK when I was ten, so my accent has got somewhat consumed by a rather plain South London twang over time, I'm afraid.'

Lonan seems a lot more comfortable sharing facts about his life than I am.

'Did you live in the city when you worked in London?' he asks now. 'Or did you commute?'

'I lived on the outskirts. My commute wasn't too bad.'

'The only time I go into London now is when I have to meet with my publisher,' Lonan says. 'I may have spent most of my teenage years there, but I'm in no hurry to return now.'

'You don't like London, then?' I ask, sensing we might at last have something in common.

Lonan shakes his head. 'No, dirty noisy place. Some of the parks are rather magnificent, but I can't stand all the pollution; and it's become a much more dangerous place to be in the last few years.'

He looks at me to see if I understand what he means.

I do, of course. I'm about to agree when I realise we've reached the pub.

'Ah, here we are,' Lonan says, looking up at the pub sign. 'I like it, The Daft Duck, so much more interesting than The White Horse or The Red Lion.'

'Yes, it's quirky, and seems to suits the village.'

'Shall we?' Lonan asks, holding the door open for me.

I hesitate on the doorstep.

'Something wrong?' he asks.

'No, I'm fine.'

'Are we going in?'

'Of course,' I say, taking a deep breath.

Lonan watches me as I still dither in the doorway.

'Shall I go first?' he asks kindly. 'It's not easy walking into somewhere new, is it?'

I nod and he steps forward in front of me into the pub. 'Come on, Merlin,' he calls and Merlin happily trots after him. Leaving me no choice but to follow them both.

'Ava, Lonan, over here!' I hear Jonah call across the pub as soon as we walk through the door.

I stare across the small bar area we're now standing in and through a sort of haze see Jonah waving madly at us. The pub quiz seems to have pulled in a small but lively crowd, but to me it feels like there are people everywhere, all shouting and chatting and swallowing me up in their euphoria.

Lonan puts his hand up in greeting. 'We'll be over in a minute.' He turns back to me, standing stock-still behind him. 'Can I get you a drink, Ava?' he asks. 'You look like you could do with something alcoholic.'

I hear Lonan's voice as though I'm under water, and realising I need to respond, I attempt to surface from the depths of the cold deep sea I feel like I'm currently drowning in.

I'm about to say a Diet Coke will be perfectly fine, when I realise something alcoholic might actually be quite helpful right now. 'A gin and tonic would be lovely, thanks,' I manage to say, and I pull Merlin a little closer to me for comfort while I look around the pub.

The Daft Duck is a typically quaint English country pub. Its decor is old-fashioned, with dark wooden tables and chairs, and upholstered seats that run around the inside of the uneven whitewashed walls. There are paintings adorning the walls, a mix of landscape and still-life, and photographs of events the pub has previously been a part of – black-and-white or colour, depending on what decade the photograph was taken in. The whole effect is warm and welcoming, and I feel myself begin to relax a little.

I crouch down to fuss Merlin. 'It's going to be all right, Merlin,' I tell him, as though he is the one with the problem, not me. 'We can do this, can't we?'

'Ava?' I hear above me. I look up to see Callum's kind eyes looking down at us. 'Are you all right down there?'

Hurriedly I stand up again, wobbling slightly. 'Yes, I'm fine, thank you. I thought Merlin might have a thorn in his coat. But everything seems to be fine now.'

'Ah, good. I hear you're joining our quiz team tonight?'

'That's right.'

Callum is wearing a green T-shirt and black jeans. I notice he doesn't have on his dog collar tonight.

'Great, I was very pleased to hear that when Jonah told me.'

I smile shyly at him. I don't feel like I'm drowning any more. I feel like I'm floating high on a soft fluffy cloud instead.

'Sorry, I haven't seen you around much lately,' Callum continues when I don't say anything. 'I've been away . . . on a course.'

'I didn't know they sent vicars on courses?'

'Yes, occasionally.'

'Did you learn much?'

Callum grins. 'Nothing I didn't already know.'

'Ah well, I guess it was a change of scenery for you.'

'I'd much rather have been here, actually.' Callum holds my gaze for a moment.

'One gin and tonic,' Lonan says, interrupting us. 'Hi,' he says to Callum as he passes me my drink. 'I don't think we've been introduced, Lonan Adler.' He holds out his hand and Callum shakes it.

'Callum Crawford, pleased to meet you.' He glances at my drink. 'You two obviously know each other?'

'We met about five minutes ago,' Lonan says before I have chance to speak. 'We're the newbies on the pub quiz team.'

'So I've heard,' Callum says, smiling at me again. 'I'm a team member too. Welcome.'

'I hear it's run by the local church,' Lonan says, leaning in towards us conspiratorially. 'Still, I'm sure we can liven it up a little.' He lifts his glass at us. 'Can't have the Bible-bashers ruining all our fun, can we?'

My heart sinks. But Callum to his credit simply lifts his own pint of beer and chinks it to Lonan's. 'Nope, we certainly can't.'

Jonah pops up behind us. 'Ah, there you are,' he says to Callum. 'I should have known I'd find you propping up the bar!'

Callum rolls his eyes at us. 'You've met my wife,' he jokes.

Lonan and I both smile, but Jonah pulls a disapproving expression.

'Can you all make your way over to the team table as quickly as you can, please?' he asks urgently. 'We have a few things to go through before tonight's competition begins. That means you too, Callum.'

Callum pulls a face, which Jonah ignores before he makes his way back over to the team table.

'He may seem a little over-zealous,' Callum explains kindly, once Jonah is out of earshot, 'but he means well. Jonah is very passionate about the quiz team. He's passionate about everything he becomes involved with, actually. But the quiz team is his baby, and he does organise it very well.'

We follow Jonah to the back of the pub, where we're warmly welcomed by the rest of the team, who are sitting around two adjoining tables.

'Welcome!' Jonah says as we take our seats. 'Before we begin tonight, I think we should have some introductions so our newcomers can get to know everyone.'

Jonah, like Callum, is wearing casual attire tonight. But whereas Callum's clothing is super casual, Jonah's is smart – a bottle-green jumper and dark grey trousers – and he still wears his dog collar under his V-neck.

'I'll begin, shall I? I'm Jonah,' Jonah says, placing his hand on his chest. 'I'm the deacon at the church and, for my sins,' he pauses for a moment, delighted with his joke, 'I'm the captain of the quiz team.'

He holds out his hand to the person next to him – who happens to be Jenny from the shop.

'I'm Jenny and I own the village shop, and I'm pleased to say I've met both our lovely newcomers already,' she says nodding with encouragement at Lonan and me. She nudges the man next to her.

'I'm Gavin, and I own Peacocks Farm Shop,' Gavin says next, looking a tad embarrassed. 'I've met Ava here, but not you, sir.'

Lonan grins with delight at him. 'A farm shop – how fabulous! I'll be sure to pop in and see you, Gavin.'

Gavin nods, and looks to a pretty young woman with long blonde hair to his right.

'Hi, I'm Jemima, and I'm the acting head teacher at the primary school,' she says a little shyly.

'Known to most as Miss Swan,' Jenny pipes up.

Jemima smiles at her, and turns to a sophisticated and very striking woman with a mane of bright red hair.

''Ello, I am Alouette Daw,' a sultry French accent announces. 'And I own this pub with my 'usband Jack.'

I can't help smiling at her husband's name; it seems very appropriate for a Jack Daw to be running a pub called The Daft Duck. I glance over to the bar and see a tall, thick-set man in a checked shirt pouring a pint.

'Good evening, I'm Lonan Adler,' Lonan pipes up next to me. 'I've just moved to Bluebell Wood so I don't really know any of you that well. Except Ava here, who I met tonight, and who was kind enough to accompany me on my walk here to meet with you all. Oh and I'm a writer,' he says, just as I'm about to introduce myself. 'Mostly novels – of the historical kind.'

There's a murmur of interest in Lonan's profession.

I wait to see if he's going to add anything else, but he simply nods with encouragement at me as if I'm a small child.

I attempt to swallow my annoyance – not at Lonan so much as at myself. I've obviously given him the impression that I'm shy in crowds and nervous around people. That wasn't true. It wasn't shyness that was my problem at all.

'I'm Ava,' I say in a quiet voice, conscious that everyone is probably wanting Lonan to tell them more about himself. 'And I've not long moved here either. I've met some of you already. But it's good to meet you, Jemima, and you, Alouette.'

The women both smile warmly at me.

'And last, and very definitely least,' Callum says, smiling, 'I'm Callum. And to my delight, I can say I've met *all* of you before.'

'Father Crawford is the best priest we've had here in a long time,' Jenny emphasises for anyone that doesn't already know this fact. 'His sermons draw quite the crowd.'

'Thank you, Jenny,' Callum says, looking embarrassed. 'That's kind of you to say. But as you know the services at St Francis's are a joint effort between myself and Jonah.'

Jonah looks surprised to hear this praise, but nods gratefully at him.

Callum and I both turn to Lonan to see his reaction to this news.

But instead of looking mortified at his earlier faux pas, he simply grins and lifts his pint glass at us. 'Touché!' he calls across the table. 'Greetings, Father Crawford.'

As we await the beginning of the quiz, more and more teams seem to be piling into the pub. I hadn't realised that Jonah had got us all here early so we could get to know each other, and the quiz didn't actually start until eight thirty.

'Are you all right, Ava?' Callum asks me, as once again I cast my eyes nervously over the ever-growing swarm of people packing out the bar.

'Yes,' I turn quickly to him, 'I'm absolutely fine.' But my voice sounds stilted. 'Thank you.'

The others around the table are discussing their specialist subjects, and Lonan seems to have manoeuvred Jemima into having a discussion about his books.

'It's just you look a little pale.'

I take a quick sip of my drink, and realise it's nearly empty.

'I'm not great in crowds,' I tell him honestly, cradling my glass to me. 'And the pub *is* quite busy, isn't it?'

Callum looks across the bar. 'I've seen it worse. But I guess if you're anxious in crowded places then this might seem a bit much. Can I get you another drink?'

'Er, yes. Please,' I reply, looking down into my glass. 'Just a sparkling water will be fine this time, though.'

'Are you sure?' Callum looks with concern at me. 'I might be a vicar, but as you can see,' he holds up his pint glass, 'I still like a drink.'

'It's not you. I just think I'll keep a clearer head if I only have the one.'

'If you're certain?'

I nod.

Callum stands up and heads over to the bar. I remain at the table, all the time feeling hotter and more uncomfortable.

I pull my shirt away from my chest to try to get some cooler air down there.

'Hot flush, dear?' Jenny whispers as she squeezes past behind my chair. 'I know that feeling well.'

'No, I'm just a bit warm tonight, that's all.'

'Ah, lucky you not to have started that yet. I'm a martyr to mine. Always going red in the face I am, and surprisingly it's not just Mr Bird annoying me that's the cause!'

I smile up at her.

'Call of nature,' she whispers, her head gesturing towards the Ladies. 'I'll be right back – that's another downfall at my time of life!'

I watch Jenny go, and then my glance falls over the bar again. Now it's even more packed. There also seems to be some sort of delay at the bar. Alouette has gone to help out, and her husband Jack is pulling persistently on a pump to try to get some beer to flow.

Breathe, *Ava*, I tell myself. *Breathe!*

But it's no good; I can't stand it any more. My head is beginning to swim, and I feel sick and dizzy. I have to get out of here.

Merlin, who willingly seems to have become the team mascot tonight, is currently being fussed by Jonah, and looks perfectly happy.

I stand up suddenly. 'Be right back,' I say to no one in particular, and I make a dash for the door.

But weaving my way through the busy bar area isn't easy, and as I find myself being jostled and bumped a little, I can feel the wave of nausea beginning to rise. Attempting to reach the elusive exit feels like I'm trying to swim up from the murky depths of the sea, searching for the moment I can finally gulp down some fresh air, instead of drowning in this sea of danger.

Eventually, my fingers wrap themselves around the door handle and I'm able to yank it open. I'm aware someone might be calling my name behind me, but I can't stop now, I must get outside, it's the only way to survive.

Finally, I'm able to escape from the pub and stand underneath the edge of the thatched roof. My back is firmly pressed against the cool, whitewashed wall, and this is the only thing keeping me upright. I begin to draw great gulps of fresh air to make up for the oxygen I'd been lacking when I was drowning.

After what feels like hours, but is likely only a few minutes, I start to feel a little better. My breathing returns to normal, and I'm able to focus on my surroundings once more.

It's now dark outside, and a clear night sky has allowed a few stars to appear above me; mixed with the light coming from the pub, they give a soft calming glow to my surroundings, which only aids my recovery.

'Feeling better?' a gentle voice from the dark asks.

I jump and turn towards the voice. Callum steps out of the shadows and is bathed in yellow light from one of the pub's lattice windows.

I stare at him. *No one is ever supposed to see me this way. No one. Not even Hannah and Matt have ever witnessed me like this.*

'Why are you out here?' I demand. 'Are you following me?'

'I wanted to check you were okay.'

'I'm fine.'

'You didn't seem it when you were careering through the pub just now.'

'Was I that bad?' I ask, my voice calming a little.

Callum nods. 'Here.' He passes me a glass. 'It's your water.'

Callum offering to get me a drink seems like ages ago now, but again in reality it's probably only been a few minutes.

'Thank you,' I say, taking it from him. 'I'm sorry I snapped just now.'

'It's fine. You were in some state back there – claustrophobia, is it?'

'Something like that,' I lie.

'That can be very scary.'

'How would you know?'

'I once had a parishioner who wouldn't leave their house. Brought on a panic attack every time they even thought about it. It was very debilitating for them.'

'That's agoraphobia,' I tell him knowingly. 'Claustrophobia is a fear of enclosed and crowded spaces and, loosely, agoraphobia is a fear of leaving the safety of your own home. They can often overlap and are sometimes difficult to diagnose separately.'

'You seem to know a lot about it,' Callum says calmly, taking a sip of his drink.

I shrug.

'You feel better now, though?' he asks in the same quiet, composed way.

'A little.' I glance back towards the pub. The sound of too many voices and too much noisy chatter seems to ooze through the solid white walls – like they're reaching out their many hands to try to suffocate me.

I jump forward.

'You don't have to go back in there yet if you don't want to,' Callum suggests. 'In fact, you don't have to go back in at all.'

I nod and take another sip of my water. 'Won't people be wondering where we are?'

Callum shrugs now. 'Let them.'

I watch him calmly sipping on his pint.

'You're not much like a normal vicar, are you?' I suddenly ask.

'How do you mean?'

'I mean, you don't dress like one when you're out of your . . . ' I struggle for the right word. 'You know, your fancy robes, your dog collar thing,' I say, waving my hand across my neck.

Callum smiles. 'I try not to be too normal. I like to challenge people's view of the clergy.'

'Why?'

'Why not?'

'Fair enough.' I understood not wanting to share every detail of your life with a stranger. I couldn't blame Callum for that.

'I haven't actually been a vicar all that long,' Callum continues, 'not for my age, anyway. I came to it quite late.'

'Don't you mean you didn't get the *calling* until quite late?'

'Some people describe it like that.'

'How do you describe it, then?'

'Look, I don't think the outside of the pub is the right place to discuss something so personal.'

'Oh, right . . . sure.'

'I mean, I'd like to talk to you about it – if you're really interested, that is?' Callum watches me, as if he's checking my sincerity level.

His earnest gaze overpowers me for a moment. 'Yes, I'm interested,' I reply, almost in a whisper.

'Good, good.' He looks secretly delighted. 'Perhaps we could arrange a time to meet up properly?'

Does he really mean a date this time?

I'm about to open my mouth when the pub door swings open.

'Oh, this is where the two of you have got to,' Jonah says, looking mildly irritated. 'I was beginning to panic. We're about to start.'

'Ava wasn't feeling too well,' Callum explains. 'I brought her some water.'

'I'm sorry to hear that, Ava.' Jonah looks at me with concern. 'Are you feeling any better now?'

I glance at Callum. He returns my look with one that suggests it's totally my decision.

'Yes, I'm feeling much better, thank you,' I tell Jonah.

'Good stuff. Will you be okay to come back soon? Because we really need *both* of you when the quiz gets going.' He looks meaningfully at Callum.

'What do you say, Ava?' Callum asks. 'Shall we go back in now?'

I put my hand in the pocket of my jeans and immediately feel the hard plastic of the Trivial Pursuit piece I'd placed there before I left the cottage tonight.

'Yes,' I say, wrapping my hand tightly around it. 'Yes, let's give this a try.'

Ten

The next day I awake, and for once I smile.

I did it. I actually did it.

I hadn't done anything major in a normal person's life. But to me spending the night in a busy pub among a lot of noisy people was just as much of an achievement as running the London Marathon would be to someone else.

Callum had been great all night. He'd kept checking on me, and asking if I was all right – not in an obvious way, but in a quiet considered way, that most of the time no one else would have even noticed.

He'd insisted that I took a couple of breaks outside – at the halfway point of the quiz when everyone paused to buy more drinks, and at the end just before the scoring had taken place.

I'm sure the others must have wondered what we were doing popping outside together. Maybe they thought we were secret smokers? But to their credit no one said anything when we returned. Callum appeared to be a sort of superhero here in Bluebell Wood; no one wanted to criticise him or question anything he was doing – they simply accepted it. They did to his face, anyway; I don't imagine for one second that Jenny won't already be gossiping about this in her shop this morning!

But I don't care. I'm proud of myself, and I felt like I'd made a new friend in Callum.

He'd been so kind and calm that any stress I might have felt at being in a crowded room full of people was quickly dissipated every time we stepped outside into the cool night air.

Nothing had been mentioned again about the proposed 'date', we'd simply concentrated on keeping me calm and getting me through the quiz – which had been a great success for the team. We hadn't won, but we'd come joint second, which Callum assured me was a much higher placing than they usually managed, so much was made of the two new team members continuing on in future competitions.

I wake Merlin, who is snoozing at the bottom of my bed, and we head downstairs. I open up the back door and Merlin wanders out to empty his bladder in his favourite places across the garden.

While the kettle is boiling, I look out of the small kitchen window at the bird table. As usual, overnight the birds had demolished any remaining food, so the table and the feeders look bare. *I must get a lot of 'early birds'*, I think to myself, smiling at my own joke.

'I'd better feed you now,' I say through the window, as I spy one of my blackbird regulars landing on the table. As he pecks around, trying to find something to eat, I'm reminded of Lonan from last night. He hadn't been so bad in the end. He was a bit full of himself, but he'd been entertaining enough, and luckily for the team his broad and varied knowledge of ancient history had helped us through a number of tricky questions, and had balanced well with my knowledge of twentieth-century events.

I'd always enjoyed modern history. Anything from the 1900s onwards was my thing, and I'd been lucky enough to spend a fair amount of time in a few of London's excellent museums, both when I'd been doing work for them and also in my spare time.

That seemed such a long time ago. How different my life was now – my daily commute involved walking to the bottom of the garden to feed wild birds, instead of travelling by tube across the city to my office.

I load up the various paper cups that I'd found in one of Evelyn's cupboards, which I now use to ferry bird seed, nuts, worms and all the regular things I left out for my bird friends every morning, then I head from the shed out into the garden.

I fill up the hanging feeders first. I'm about to empty seed on to the flat feeding platform when I spy something shiny tucked away in the corner.

Reaching my hand under the little roof, I fish out what looks like a broken piece of green glass. No, it's not glass, I realise, as I turn it over in my hand: it's a piece of ceramic with one shiny green side. Then under some husks of seed I notice there's a second piece – this time it's a bluey green colour.

How very strange?

I'm about to turn away with the pieces in my hand, when I notice down on the floor two more shards. These two are both shades of deeper blue and look like they're from the same pattern.

What on earth?

I pick the third and fourth piece up and examine them in the palm of my hand.

'Where did you come from?' I ask, looking around at the trees, as if one of the birds is going to lift its wing and admit to being the culprit. 'I'm starting quite the odd little collection.'

I tip the remaining bird seed on to the table and head back inside the cottage. After washing the pieces of pottery I lay them on the mantelpiece next to the Trivial Pursuit piece from yesterday.

Where have these things come from? It's like the birds are actually leaving them for me on the table.

I laugh. *Don't be daft, Ava. Why would they do that? It must be a magpie. It's the only answer. Maybe he was the early-morning visitor that was taking the rest of the food?*

Later that morning Merlin and I head out for our walk. But as we leave the little path that leads from the cottage, I feel different.

At the top of the path from the cottage, I pause on the pavement.

'Shall we go this way today?' I ask Merlin, beginning to walk in the opposite direction to the woods. Merlin looks quizzically at me for a moment – we nearly always go to the woods – but trusting I know what I'm doing, he happily follows my lead, trotting along beside me like he always does.

This was more than a simple need to walk somewhere new; I felt a newfound confidence, and I had one person to thank for it . . . Okay, maybe two: Lonan for getting me to the pub in the first place, but mostly Callum for keeping me there, when really I'd just wanted to run away to the safety of Bluebird Cottage, make myself a hot chocolate and snuggle under a blanket with Merlin.

I think about Callum now as I walk – his soft voice, his calm demeanour, and the way he looked at me in that caring, considerate way of his. I sigh. *Why does he have to be a vicar?*

It shouldn't matter what he did for a living. But of all the jobs he could have done, why did it have to be this? If he'd been the plumber or the odd-job man I'd first thought he was, it would have made things a lot simpler.

'Bonjour, Ava!' a cheery voice calls, and I see Alouette walking along the road towards me carrying two large bags.

'Hello,' I reply as she draws closer. 'How are you today?'

'I am very good, thank you, and you?' Alouette puts her bags on the ground for a moment and fusses Merlin, who laps up any attention.

'Yes, well thanks. Those bags look mighty heavy.'

'Ah, they are not so bad. I am taking them to the school for Jemima – Miss Swan,' she corrects herself. 'The school is having a – how you say? – a *bumble* sale?'

'Jumble sale,' I correct her, smiling.

'Yes, that is it! These are a few of our unwanted things – mostly Jack's unwanted things.' She grins, and I like how she pronounces her husband's name in the French way – *Jacques*. 'I have had a good clear-up of his wardrobe. Whether anyone will wish to purchase his old clothes, though, I am not so sure.' She looks with disdain at the bags. Alouette, like last night, is perfectly turned out this morning, in a pair of navy cropped trousers, a crisp white shirt and a jaunty scarf around her neck. She makes me feel extremely drab in my denim dungarees, trainers and sweatshirt.

'Do you want a hand carrying them to the school?' I ask with my newfound confidence – although I guessed there wouldn't be too many people at the school right now in the middle of the day.

'Oh, that is very kind of you, Ava; yes please, if I'm not interfering with your doggie walk.'

'No, we can carry on from the school. I think there's a little footpath not far from there that we haven't tried yet.'

'Ah, very good, then.' Ava lifts one bag, then she offers me the handle of the other. 'We shall carry this one together. It is the heaviest.'

I take the handle in one hand, and hold Merlin's lead in the other, and we walk together like a strange three-legged race towards the school.

'Ah, there is Miss Swan,' Alouette says as we arrive outside the school gates and spot Jemima standing in the empty playground looking at a wall. 'Miss Swan!' she calls. And Jemima turns around.

'Ah, good morning, ladies,' she says cheerfully, coming over to us at the gate. 'Hello, Ava. Good to see you again.'

'You too.'

'I have the things I promised you for the ... *jumble* sale,' Alouette says carefully.

'We're holding a fundraiser for the school – half car boot sale, half jumble,' Jemima explains to me. 'We always have one just before the Easter holidays. Well, this is amazing, Alouette,' she says, peeking into the bag. 'Does Jack know you're giving away quite so many of his shirts?'

'It is not a bother,' Alouette says proudly. 'Ma 'usband does not have a good sense of the dress. 'e needs to learn.'

Jemima and I both laugh.

'When is the fundraiser?' I ask.

'Tomorrow, here in the school grounds. You're most welcome to come. I can't guarantee you'll find anything to buy, but we need all the funds we can get right now, so the more the merrier.'

'Actually, I was wondering if I had anything I could give you to sell, but yes, I quite like a bargain. I'll definitely come along,' I say, trying to sound keen. But I knew if there was going to be a lot of people I'd be keeping well away.

'Great, so did you enjoy the quiz last night?' Jemima asks. 'You and Lonan were a real asset to the team.'

'Thank you. Yes, I did. It was fun.'

'I bet it was much fun,' Alouette pipes up, and she winks at Jemima. 'Secret little tête-à-têtes with our 'andsome vicar all night.'

Jemima smiles but doesn't say anything.

I feel my face flush. 'It . . . it wasn't like that—' I begin, but Jemima rescues me.

'Don't pay any attention, Ava. Alouette is just teasing you, aren't you, Alouette?'

'Teasing?' Alouette asks.

'Joking. Having a laugh?' Jemima explains.

'Ah, yes, a laugh. Do not listen to me, Ava, I am – how you say? – jealous. I adore my Jack, but we have been married together for a long time now. Things can be a little . . . dull. You are not married, Ava?'

I shake my head. 'Not any more. But I do have two children – they're all grown up now.'

'You see,' Alouette says, her hands gesticulating in a Gallic way at Jemima, 'she is free and single. I thought so. You can have all the fun you want with Father Callum, yes?'

Again I blush.

'Lovely as this is to stand and chat,' Jemima says, very clearly changing the subject, 'I have to be getting back to my class in a minute. Year Six: they're usually quite well behaved, but if I leave them too long the temptation to misbehave will become too much for them to resist. You're lucky to catch me; I was only out here because we've had a spot of vandalism.'

I'm surprised to hear this. The last thing I expected to find in Bluebell Wood is vandals.

'The Year Threes have been doing a project this term on the Romans, and we built this Roman mosaic here on the school wall.' She gestures back to a wall behind us. 'Only this morning we came in to find bits missing. At first I thought they'd fallen off – not enough glue, perhaps. But the pieces can't be found anywhere. It's a real shame; the children worked so hard on it.'

We all look at the mosaic behind her. It's a large seascape, but it's a bit too far away to see any gaps. 'Which areas are missing pieces?' I ask casually.

'Parts of the sea, mainly. You see where the bluey-green waves are supposed to be?'

I nod.

'Just there. It's very odd. I can't think who would want to deliberately remove pieces from the children's work.'

'Yes, that is very strange,' I say, thinking about the shards of pottery on my mantelpiece. 'I hope you can repair it. It seems such a shame to have it ruined.'

'Yes, indeed.' Jemima turns back towards us. 'Well, thanks again for helping Alouette with her bags. Hopefully I'll see you around a bit more now we've met properly.'

'That would be nice. Right, I'd better get back to our walk or Merlin won't be happy. Are you heading back to the pub, Alouette?'

'I am. We have a delivery due at any moment.'

'Okay, I'll see you both soon. Bye for now.'

They both wave as Merlin and I head off to find the footpath. With Merlin wondering what new scents he was going to discover today, and me, how pieces of a children's school project had been left on my bird table this morning.

*

As we walk along the pretty footpath, I enjoy spotting and naming, thanks to Evelyn's books, wild yellow daffodils, white cow parsley just beginning to bloom, and a few wood anemones with their pretty white petals and yellow centres. We pass fields scattered with new-born lambs, and pass through long canopies of tall trees, which I guess must have been part of the wood at some point in its distant past, before the road split it in two. We walk in a long loop around the outskirts of the village until we're almost back at the cottage and the part of the wood we usually walk through. While we're waiting at the side of the road for some traffic to pass so we can cross safely, I notice that the field we've just walked around the outside of is up for sale, according to an estate agent's board that's nailed to one of the gateposts.

Merlin and I are about to step across the now empty road, when suddenly from nowhere an open-top white sports car speeds past us, taking both of us by surprise.

Merlin cowers back from the road, and I have to catch my breath.

'Hey, it's all right,' I say to Merlin as I crouch down next to him. 'That idiot was driving ridiculously fast. He scared me too!'

We're about to step out again, when to my surprise the car reappears, reversing back down the road.

'Did I scare you?' the driver says as he pulls level with us, one arm around the passenger seat and one on the steering wheel. 'I may have been going a tad too fast there.'

'You were going far too fast,' I tell him angrily. 'This is a village, not Silverstone race track! You frightened the life out of my dog.'

'Apologies!' the man says cheerfully, not seeming in the least sorry. 'I'll be more careful next time.'

He glances at the board behind us, and smiles, and I wonder why.

'Bye then!' he calls, with a casual wave of his hand. 'See you again!' And he speeds off up the road as if nothing ever happened.

I shake my head, and look a little more carefully this time before we step out to cross the road. Bluebell Wood may be a small village, but because it's situated on a long straight road that joins several other small villages and towns, it seems to attract more than its fair share of through traffic.

But luckily, I rarely hear any of it when I'm at the cottage – it's tucked far enough away off the road for it not to bother me.

Our way back to the cottage is through the quieter end of the village. The shop, the church, the school and farm shop are all at the other end, so I feel quite sure we won't bump into anyone we know before we get back home. But as we walk along the long straight pavement, happily minding our own business, I hear a voice:

'Ava!'

I stop and look around but I can't see anyone.

'Over here!' the voice says again, and I realise it's coming from one of the gardens we're passing. I look over the hedge and see Lonan and Jonah standing on one of the paths leading up to a whitewashed cottage.

'Hi,' I say, surprised to see them both, and I walk back a little way to the gate. I'm becoming much more comfortable now in my interactions with the villagers I know in Bluebell Wood – especially those in the quiz team.

'Sorry if we startled you,' Jonah says, walking up the path towards the gate with Lonan.

'Oh no, you didn't startle me,' I say, smiling at them both.

'It was some mad man tearing through the village just now in a sports car. He almost took us out as we were about to cross the road.'

'Oh dear,' Jonah says, while Lonan pulls off his gardening gloves and opens up the gate so he can bend down to fuss Merlin. 'We heard someone driving too fast just now but we didn't see the vehicle. We don't get too many problems with speeding here, but it happens occasionally. Where was this?'

'Just up the road a little way. We were next to that field that's for sale, on the way out of the village.'

'Yes, I know it,' Jonah says, sighing. 'Everyone in the village knows that field.'

'Sounds intriguing,' Lonan says, his ears pricking up. 'What's the story?'

'Ah, it's a long one, I'm afraid, and it doesn't have a good ending. That field was sold a while back to some developers. They want to put quite a lot of new houses on it. The village objected, of course – quite vehemently. But the permission still went through, much to our disappointment.'

'That's a shame,' Lonan says. 'But I suppose it's the modern way, and I'm sure a few new houses won't affect the village too much.'

'If it were only a few,' Jonah says sadly. 'But that field is just the start: they intend to build on many of the other fields that adjoin it too. It's a whole new estate, completely at odds with the rest of the village.'

'How awful,' I say, trying to imagine a brand-new housing estate in Bluebell Wood, with its quaint old buildings and picture-perfect cottages. 'And there's nothing you can do?'

Jonah shakes his head. 'Nope. Like I said, we tried. There were petitions and protests, but to no avail. It's still going ahead. Just between us, I think the developers had someone on the inside and that's how they got their permission. I'm surprised the "for sale" sign hasn't been changed yet to "sold". Maybe they're too scared to come back. Some of the villagers got pretty fierce in the meetings that were held. Anyhow,' Jonah says, obviously keen to change the subject, 'I mustn't stand here gossiping. I'm glad I've seen you, Ava, because it's saved me calling on you again. I knocked at your cottage a little while ago but you weren't in. Now I see why,' he says, looking at Merlin. 'I've just been talking to Lonan about how successful the quiz was last night with you two joining our team, and I just want to make sure you're definitely up for coming again?'

'And as I've just been telling Jonah, I can't wait,' Lonan says eagerly, standing up again. 'I had a whale of a time. As I'm sure you did too, Ava?'

'Yes, of course,' I reply, with slightly less enthusiasm than Lonan.

'That's wonderful,' Jonah says. 'I'm glad you both enjoyed it.'

'I must say this village is turning out to be much more fun than I thought it might be,' Lonan says. 'I never dreamt I'd be sitting drinking in a pub with the local priests.'

Jonah looks a tad uncomfortable. 'Yes, well, a public house isn't usually my favourite haunt. But needs must with the quiz team. It seems to be a popular venue; my choice of the village hall didn't go down too favourably when I suggested it.'

I glance at Lonan, who smiles.

'Your boss, the other vicar chappie, is a great hoot,' he says. 'I've never met a priest that can down a pint as fast as me!'

'Yes ...' Jonah says, again looking uncomfortable. 'The

ability to hold their beer is not a trait parishioners usually look for in their local parish priest. But Callum is very popular, despite his shortcomings.'

I can't help but smile now too. Jonah's obvious disapproval of Callum is amusing.

'He seems particularly popular with the ladies,' Lonan continues, with a glint in his eye. 'Isn't that right, Ava?'

But I don't take his bait, I simply shrug amiably. 'I wouldn't really know, Lonan. I'm new here like you.'

Lonan grins and nods his approval.

'*Yes* . . . ' Jonah says again, obviously uncomfortable with this line of conversation. 'But for all his failings, Callum is a good vicar. He's very popular with *all* his parishioners. Now, if you'll both excuse me, I really must go. I have several other visits to complete before lunch. Again, it's lovely to see you both, and I'm very pleased to be able to welcome you as regular members of the Bluebell Wood quiz team.'

I stand back to let Jonah through the gate.

We bid him goodbye and watch as he heads off down the road back towards the village.

'He's a good chap,' Lonan says, smiling as we watch him go, 'but he's rather uptight. Callum is a lot more relaxed.'

'It's just his way,' I say kindly. 'He'll find his feet. Just as there're all types of people in this world, I guess there are all types of priests, too.'

'You are quite correct, my dear Ava. I stand corrected.'

'I guess I'd better be getting on,' I say, about to move away with Merlin.

'So had I. As you can see, I was just doing a bit of weeding when Jonah caught me.'

Lonan is wearing what I would consider quite a smart outfit

for gardening: he's in brown brogues, long beige trousers, and a white shirt with a burgundy cravat around his neck.

'I didn't have you down as having green fingers,' I say, noticing a large bucket full of weeds behind him. 'You don't look the *type*.'

Lonan's expression is one of surprise, then seeing me smile he realises I'm turning the tables on him from last night. 'Ha ha, touché, my friend! Actually, I don't mind a bit of gardening; it gives me time to think.'

'Writer's block?' I ask.

'No, I'm just trying to work out a tricky plot point in my head. I'll get there. Where have you and young Merlin been for a walk this morning? I could do with some pointers; I've only discovered the woods so far.'

'We usually walk through the woods, but I noticed a little footpath not far from the school, so we've taken that today.' I look at my watch. 'Gosh, we've been out almost two hours, I had no idea. We'd better be getting back.' I tighten Merlin's lead to motion to him we're about to leave.

'Yes, and I must get back to my weeding. We should go for a drink at the pub again sometime. I very much enjoyed our outing yesterday.'

'Er . . . yes, why not?' I reply politely, pretty sure this is just a vague sort of invitation I won't actually have to follow up.

'Great, I'll be in touch.'

'Lovely,' I try to say with a degree of keenness. 'See you soon, then.'

This time I really do guide Merlin away with much greater urgency. We quickly leave Lonan behind and soon arrive at the top of the narrow path that leads down to the cottage and my sanctuary.

I sigh deeply as we step inside and I close the door, leaning against it for support. It wasn't the walk that had exhausted me, it was the social interaction that always seemed to accompany it here.

Although I'm still a long way from becoming fully comfortable with casual chit-chat, I'm secretly pleased to find I am slowly becoming more at ease with it, and that I might actually be starting to enjoy it . . . just a little.

Eleven

Saturday morning, the day of the school sale, dawns clear and bright.

'Someone is looking down kindly on you and your school, Jemima,' I say as I gaze out of the window while I make my breakfast. 'It looks like it's going to be a beautiful day.'

Talking aloud was something I'd found myself doing a lot since I came to the cottage. I didn't feel like I was talking to myself really, more to Merlin or even to my bird visitors outside. I definitely had regulars to my bird table now, and I was learning to recognise them by an odd marking on their feathers or a slightly unusual shape to their head or sometimes even their beak.

Before I'd come to Bluebell Wood all sparrows had looked the same to me, as did all blue tits or robins. But they all had their own distinctive markings if you looked closely enough, and often their own unique characteristics, too.

'Right, Merlin,' I say to a comfortable-looking dog who has just had his breakfast and is happily settling down to bathe in the warm sunlight flooding through the window on to one of the armchairs. 'We need to get out early this morning; we don't want to bump into anyone asking us about the school sale.'

I felt bad now that I'd told Jemima I was going to attend the sale, because of course I wasn't. There would just be too many people, and I didn't want to create a scene like I had at the quiz. Outdoor events with lots of people were a little easier to cope with than indoor ones, but I didn't want to take any chances.

Today when we arrive at the wood, there is the most wonderful surprise waiting for us. 'The bluebells have bloomed!' I tell an unbothered Merlin, wriggling to get off the lead. 'Aren't they beautiful?'

But Merlin isn't at all impressed by the carpet of blue heads bobbing gently in the breeze, so I reach down and unclip his lead from his collar, and at once he bounds off along one of the paths that keep us perfectly apart from the delicate flowers.

I follow him at a slower pace than I might normally, stopping to breathe in the heady scent of the bluebells, peppered with the odd patch of wild garlic whose tiny white clusters of flowers had already begun blooming last week.

'Hold up, Merlin,' I call as we reach a particularly pretty patch where the path takes a sharp bend to the left so you can see bluebells in front and behind it. 'I want to take a photo.'

I pull my phone from my pocket, and take a few photos of the landscape in front of me. It's absolutely glorious, a seemingly endless blue carpet of bell-like blooms. I crouch down so I can get a closer shot of the delicate flowers. Being this close to them is quite overwhelming, their scent is sweet and powerful, and for a moment I feel overcome by their natural grace and beauty. They're so very fragile, and the way their heads bow in deference to the great trees above them is both humbling and amazing to behold.

'You're so small and insignificant, and yet you hold your own year after year against all these other much bigger plants that surround you,' I whisper. 'If only I had half your strength and determination.'

'I'm glad to see you're not trampling all over them to get that photo!' I hear Callum's voice before I see him, and his footsteps jogging along the path behind me.

'Of course not,' I say, standing up again. 'I'm not that silly.'

'You'd be surprised what people do in the name of getting a good photo to post on social media. You trample a bluebell this year and it can take years for it to fully recover from the damage to its leaves. They can't photosynthesise properly, apparently.'

'I know,' I tell him. 'I also know it's illegal to pick them.'

'Well done!' Callum says without sounding patronising at all. 'You know more than most, then.'

I don't tell him I didn't know any of this until I read it on the sign as you come into the wood and also in one of Evelyn's many books.

'I wonder how long these bluebells have been blooming here,' I say, looking around. 'This is ancient woodland, isn't it?'

'Yes, I believe so. I think it's supposed to date back to the sixteen hundreds.'

'Yes, that's what I read, too.'

'But a few folk around here think that there was a settlement here at Bluebell Wood much earlier.'

'Really?'

'Parts of the church definitely date to back to the twelfth century, possibly even earlier.'

'Gosh, how interesting.'

'Yes, I think so too. Jonah knows more than me, though. He's always banging on at me to read more about the church and the history of the area. There just never seems to be time, though – always something to do or somewhere to be.'

I wish I could agree with him. My life used to be exactly like that, but just recently I've had all the time in the world to learn new things.

'Are you going to the sale at the school today?' Callum asks. 'Jemima's hoping for a good turnout. She's worked very hard on organising it all. I'm sure she'd appreciate your support.'

'I was thinking about it,' I reply as non-committally as I can. 'Are you?'

'I sure am. Part of the job, isn't it, supporting local endeavours within my parish.'

I'd almost forgotten for a moment. Callum looks so attractive right now, with a slight flush to his perspiring face, and a damp T-shirt clinging to his well-shaped torso. His appearance didn't say vicar to me at all. It said something very different. Something I was desperately trying not to think about.

'Yes,' I hurriedly say, 'of course it is.'

'There's usually a good turnout to these kinds of things at Bluebell Wood. All the local villages are very supportive of each other.'

'I'll try to pop along then,' I say, wanting to sound supportive. But the more Callum talked the more I knew I was less and less likely to go. I'd assumed it would just be a few local villagers turning up to help out the school, but Callum was making it sound like it might be mobbed with people.

'Get there super early or extremely late, then,' Callum suggests, mirroring my thoughts. 'It tends to be quietest then.' He gives me a meaningful look.

'Thanks,' I say, realising he's trying to help me.

Callum hesitates. 'We still need to arrange to meet up for that . . . you know, we said we'd get together sometime?'

'Yes,' I assure him. 'I remember.'

'I didn't want you to think I'd forgotten; it's just my diary is quite hectic with planning Easter at the church – it's a busy time for us.'

'I can imagine.'

'Perhaps after Easter, when things have calmed down a little?'

'I'd like that.'

Callum nods, looking pleased. 'Right, well, I'll leave you to your photography. Bye, Merlin!' he calls to Merlin, who's sniffing around the base of a tree. 'See you later at the sale, then,' he says to me, and his shy smile makes all the awkwardness and unease I feel melt away.

'I hope so,' I manage to utter, before he jogs away along the path, with me trying very hard not to ogle his disappearing figure too much.

'Oh, Ava,' I say to myself and any wildlife in the forest that might be listening. 'Of all the men for you to fall for . . . why does he have to be a vicar?'

Twelve

After a lot of thought I decide I'll try to go to the school sale this afternoon. I don't want to let either Jemima or Callum down, but I know I'll struggle if it's busy. So I decide to go early, and if it's too hectic I'll just slip away quietly and hope no one notices. I'm about to leave the cottage when I see that one of the bird feeders has been knocked off its hook and is lying on the ground outside. 'I won't be a minute!' I call to Merlin, who is waiting patiently by the front door for us to leave.

I slip through the back door and head over to the bird table. I pick up the feeder, which still has peanuts in it, and hang it back on the base of the table. But as I'm about to leave, something shiny catches my eye.

It's poking out from underneath some discarded bird seed, so I brush the seed away and retrieve it from the table. It's a polished and quite new-looking fifty-pence piece.

'You're leaving me money now?' I ask the trees in the garden, knowing the birds like to hide out there before they come to feed. 'That's very lovely of you, and much appreciated, but fifty pence won't go very far, I'm afraid. Your bird food costs a lot more than that!'

I haven't got the time to think about the coin at the moment, so I shove it in the pocket of my jeans, then I head back through the cottage to collect Merlin.

Even though we arrive at the school gates thirty minutes before the sale is due to start, there's already a number of people queuing outside. Realising I don't know any of them, I just smile politely and stand back a little with Merlin.

Over on the playing field at the back of the school I can see people milling around a number of trestle tables that look to be piled high with things for sale. There are strands of colourful bunting hanging between the tables, and the whole effect looks pretty and very welcoming.

I glance over into the playground in front of us and I can't help but notice the mosaic on the wall. I'm absolutely convinced that the pieces of broken pottery I have sitting on my mantelpiece are a match for it, but I've yet to figure out just how or why they'd ended up on my bird table. The Trivial Pursuit piece and the coin . . . well, it's possible that a bird had dropped them – probably a magpie. But the pieces of mosaic are very odd. I had thought about trying to return them, but what if I'd been caught trespassing on the school grounds, attempting to stick pieces of pottery back on to the school wall? How would I have explained myself then?

'Ava!' I hear my name called, and I realise that it's Jemima that's calling it. 'Ava, over here!'

I walk past the queue of people that's getting longer by the minute towards Jemima. She opens up the gate and beckons me inside the school grounds. I'm sure I can feel the glares of the people queuing behind me as I slip through the gate with Merlin.

'Ava, I've been let down by one of the parents. She was supposed to be manning the toy and book stall this afternoon. I don't suppose you could help me out, could you?'

I stare at Jemima. Visiting the sale was one thing, I could escape if things got too much, but if I was manning a stall and I had a panic attack I couldn't just abandon it and run away.

'Ava?' Jemima says when I don't answer. 'Can you help?'

I'm about to mutter something about Merlin being with me, when someone else says my name and I feel like the cavalry has just ridden in to save me.

'Hello, ladies,' a gentle voice says. 'Did I hear you need someone to look after your toy stall?'

Callum.

'I was just asking Ava the same thing,' Jemima says, looking unbelievably pleased to see him.

'The devil makes work for idle hands,' Callum says, waving his hands in front of him, and I notice today he's wearing his dog collar underneath a pale grey pullover. 'How about Ava and I run the stall together – I expect it will be a busy one?'

'That's very kind of you, Callum, but I was going to ask you to help me out with the refreshments.' Jemima looks quite adamant about this.

'Jonah is much more au fait with cakes than I am. He never misses an episode of *Bake Off*. I'm sure he will make an excellent assistant. Ah, here he comes now.'

'Good afternoon, ladies,' Jonah says, rubbing his hands together as he arrives next to us. 'Where would you like me?'

'Refreshments, Jonah!' Callum says before Jemima can say anything. 'You'll enjoy serving up cups of tea and slices of cake, won't you?'

'I make an excellent brew, even if I say so myself,' Jonah says proudly. 'Lead the way, Miss Swan!'

'Don't worry, Jemima, we'll find the toys and books,' Callum says, smiling at her. 'Won't we, Ava?'

I nod.

'Well ... I guess ... ' Jemima says reluctantly, and she leads Jonah across the playground in the direction of the refreshment stall.

'Will you be all right with all these folk?' Callum asks me as he gestures back at the ever-growing queue behind us.

'I'll try my best,' I say honestly.

'Well done,' Callum says. 'Now I must ask you to promise me one thing?'

'What's that?'

'Don't let me buy all the toys off the stall, will you? I'm a big kid at heart and I must leave some for the children!'

Callum and I make a good job of running the toy and book stall, particularly after the initial rush of people has subsided. The bonus to looking after a stall where most of the customers are children is I never once feel too crowded by the amount of people in front of us, because the majority of them are smaller than me.

Callum keeps a close eye on me throughout, and if he thinks I'm becoming overwhelmed at all he moves in and takes over, giving me the chance to stand back for a few minutes and take a few deep breaths. Merlin is happy just napping at the back of the stall, especially after I buy him a soft toy dog, which he is currently curled up with sound asleep.

I can't help but notice that Callum is quite the popular stallholder, with many of the locals coming to the stall especially to talk to him. Now the stall is a little quieter, he's in conversation with Mrs Bunting about flowers for the Easter services.

'Are you okay there?' I ask a young boy who's been browsing the stall for a good few minutes now.

An apprehensive face looks up at me and nods.

'Is there something you'd like to buy?' I ask gently.

He nods again.

I look at the area of the table he's been browsing. 'Is it the tank you like the look of?' I ask.

He shakes his head.

'The cars?'

Again it's a firm shake of the head.

'The bear?' I ask, seeing an abandoned, but quite pretty teddy bear wearing a flowery dress at the end of the trestle table.

He looks around him and nods hurriedly. 'It's for my mum. She collects teddy bears.'

'That's a lovely idea,' I tell him encouragingly. I lift the bear up and glance at the price. 'It says one pound.'

'I know,' he replies sadly, 'but I only have fifty pence left. I spent the rest of my money on the lucky dip.'

'That's okay. You can have it for fifty pence if you like? I'm sure no one will mind.'

The boy shakes his head adamantly. 'No, it says one pound so I must pay one pound for it!' His voice is suddenly angry, and he looks like he might cry.

A few people look around to see what the noise is, so I hurriedly go to the front of the table and crouch down so I'm the same height as the boy.

'I understand,' I tell him gently. 'You want to pay what the ticket says.'

He nods furiously.

'If I tell you a secret, will you promise not to tell anyone?'

The boy looks suspiciously at me. 'Not supposed to keep secrets,' he says.

I nod. 'Yes, I know, but this is something quite magical.'

He looks at me with interest now.

'You see this fifty-pence piece,' I say, pulling it from my pocket and holding it up in front of him.

'Yes.'

'It was left on my bird table this morning.'

'By a bird?'

'I think so. And do you know what else?'

The boy shakes his head.

'I think they knew I'd meet you today, so they left this for me to give to you.'

The boy stares at the coin. 'Really?'

I nod. 'That's the secret – I think the birds on my table are magical birds.'

'Magical birds?' the boy repeats.

I nod. 'Why don't I give you this coin from the birds and then you can pay the proper price for the bear for your mum. No one other than us and the birds will ever know.'

The boy nods eagerly, so I pass him the coin, then I get up and head back around the table, where I make a great fuss of announcing that the bear is one pound and the boy has got the exact amount of money to pay for it.

The boy leaves the table with a huge smile on his face, and I watch him as he rushes over to his mum, who he proudly presents with the bear. His mum looks delighted, and then the boy points back at me while he's talking to her. Then they both look back at me, and the mother smiles, and mouths the words, *Thank you.*

I feel myself tearing up, as I realise the boy reminds me of my Matt when he was that age. I turn away, pretending to check on Merlin.

'That was a lovely thing you did there,' Callum says, standing next to me. 'You made them both very happy.'

I turn away from Merlin and shrug, blinking back my tears. 'It was nothing.'

'Actually, it wasn't nothing,' Jemima says, walking over to us. She comes behind the stall. 'Robin is on the autistic spectrum,' she says in a low voice. 'He's a lovely boy, but he sometimes struggles with communication. He likes things to be black and white, there are no grey areas with him.'

'So when I offered to give him the bear at the wrong price, he didn't like it?'

'Exactly. You dealt with the situation very well.'

'I didn't really think about it, to be honest. It just seemed the right thing to do.'

'Sorry to interrupt.' Robin's mother has made her way over to us with Robin hiding shyly behind her. 'But I just wanted to thank you for this.' She holds up the bear. 'Robin can get a little bit stressed sometimes when things aren't how he thinks they should be.'

'You don't need to thank me,' I say, smiling kindly at her. 'It was a pleasure to help you do such a nice thing for your mum, Robin.'

Robin peeks his head around his mum's legs. 'Is that your dog?' he asks, looking at Merlin, who has just woken up.

'Yes, would you like to come round here and see him?'

Robin nods.

'Is that okay?' I ask his mother.

She nods enthusiastically.

Robin walks around to the back of the stall, and we kneel down together.

'You can stroke him if you like?' I say as Merlin sits up in front of us. 'He really likes it if you rub his tummy.'

Robin reaches out his hand tentatively towards Merlin.

'That's it,' I say as he begins to stroke Merlin's furry chest. 'See, he likes it.'

'I like him,' Robin says.

'He likes you too.'

'How do you know?'

I'm about to try to explain, when Merlin does it for me. He bends his head down and very quickly licks Robin's hand.

Robin looks shocked, then immediately throws back his head and laughs.

'Mummy, he licked me!' he calls to his mother.

'I know. I saw him,' she calls back encouragingly.

Robin fusses Merlin again, and Merlin laps it up.

'He's very good with him,' Callum says, watching us.

'Is he like that with all children?' Jemima asks.

'I don't know really; I would think so. He's a very calm character. Nothing bothers him too much.'

A few other children have noticed us all watching Robin fuss Merlin.

'Would it be all right if we let some of the other children stroke him?' I ask Robin.

Robin looks a bit put out, and I think for a moment he might kick up a fuss and refuse. But instead he looks at the other children gathered around the stall. 'Yes, I think he would like it.'

'Let's take him out front then,' I say, hooking Merlin's lead on to his collar. 'Would you like to hold him?' I ask.

Robin looks delighted. 'Yes please!' he says, and he proudly takes hold of Merlin's lead and guides him out to the front of the stall, where several other children move forward to pat him.

'No,' Robin says, holding up his hand to them. I notice all the adults freeze when he says this. 'You must come one at a time or you might scare him.'

'Robin is quite right,' I say to the children. 'One at a time.'

While the children take it in turns to stroke Merlin, Robin holds on to his lead tightly. They ask me questions about Merlin that I happily answer – like how old he is, and what his favourite food is – and some questions that aren't so easy – like what he likes to watch on television and what he wants for Christmas!

Eventually, Jemima intervenes and tells the children that Merlin is getting tired now, and might need a nap, and gradually one by one after a final pat they disperse back to their parents.

Robin is the last one to go.

'Will Merlin miss me?' he asks as his mother takes one of his hands and encourages him to pass me back the lead.

'I think he will,' I tell him. 'But perhaps you can see him again if it's all right with your mum?'

'Can I?' Robin asks eagerly, still holding on to the lead.

'We don't want to impose on you,' Robin's mother says.

'It's fine,' I say, standing up from where I've been sat cross-legged on the ground with the children. 'We'd like to see Robin again, wouldn't we, Merlin?'

Merlin looks up happily at me.

'If you're sure?' Robin's mother asks.

I nod.

'That would be wonderful. I haven't seen him so engaged in anything for a long time. I'm Linnet by the way.'

'Ava,' I say, shaking her hand. 'I'm at Bluebird Cottage, just off the main road on the way out of the village.'

'Ah yes, I know. Evelyn's cottage.'

'That's the one. Give me a call and we can arrange something.'

We exchange mobile numbers, and then reluctantly Robin passes me back Merlin's lead.

'Bye, Merlin,' he calls as Linnet guides him away. 'See you soon.'

Merlin wags his tail.

I turn back to the stall. With everything else going on, I'd kind of forgotten that Callum and Jemima are still here too.

Callum smiles at me, and Jemima looks like she's thinking hard about something.

'That was lovely,' she says, coming back to the front of the stall. 'The children behaved so well around Merlin – has he ever been a therapy dog?'

'Not that I know of. I've only had him a short while. I adopted him from a rescue centre.'

Jemima reaches down to stroke Merlin now. 'Might you consider bringing him into the school on a regular basis?' she asks, looking up at me. 'I think he could be an amazing asset for us. Just look at how Robin reacted to him. Merlin had such a wonderful effect on the children.'

'I'm not sure. Won't he need special training to do that?'

'I'll look into it. But actually,' she says, standing up again, 'it's not just Merlin I'm interested in . . . '

Thirteen

Later that day, Merlin and I are waiting outside The Daft Duck.

It's a pleasant spring evening, warm for April, and instead of subjecting ourselves to the hustle and bustle on the inside of the pub, I've chosen to sit outside on one of the wooden picnic tables, which in the height of summer will have a colourful umbrella in the centre shading drinkers from the sun. This evening they are bare, but in the warmth of the setting sun they are perfectly comfortable to sit at.

Luckily for me Alouette had spotted me waiting on the bench with Merlin and offered to bring me a drink out, which I'd gratefully accepted.

While I sip on my Diet Coke, I think about what had happened at the sale earlier.

Merlin had undoubtedly been a hit with the children, particularly Robin, and I could see how he would make a perfect therapy dog. But that would mean I would have to commit to going into the school on a regular basis with him, and although

I didn't have the same issues with groups of children that I often had with crowds of adults, I still wasn't sure I felt ready to make that sort of promise.

'Evening!' Callum says as he arrives outside the pub. As usual he sports casual clothes – a long-sleeved T-shirt, navy gilet and jeans – now he's away from Church duties. 'Glad you decided to come.'

Jemima hadn't been able to stop and talk after her surprise announcement; parents, teachers and children were all clamouring for her attention. So we'd agreed to meet at the pub tonight. She'd very quickly thrown open her invitation to Callum as well, and Callum being Callum had accepted.

'Of course, I said I would, didn't I?' I reply, smiling.

'I know, but I could see how shocked you were when Jemima asked you to become a part of the school.'

'I was surprised; I can't deny it. But I thought it would be polite to at least hear what she has to say.'

Callum nods approvingly.

'I'm not really sure why she asked *me* to come, though,' he says, looking perplexed. 'It's nothing to do with me, is it?'

'Moral support?' I suggest.

'For you or for her?' Callum asks, raising his eyebrows.

'For both of us,' I reply diplomatically. Although I was beginning to get the feeling that I wasn't the only female in Bluebell Wood to find Callum attractive.

'I am pretty good at moral support,' Callum says, winking. 'All part of the job! Now, can I get you another drink?'

I look at my glass. 'Why not? Another Diet Coke will be great, thanks.'

'Nothing stronger?'

I shake my head. 'Nope, that will be absolutely fine.'

I had to keep my wits about me, otherwise goodness knows what I might agree to and later regret.

Callum heads into the pub, while Merlin and I wait outside for Jemima.

'Hello!' she soon calls as she arrives through the pub gate. 'I'm so glad you've chosen to sit out here, it's a lovely evening.' She glances at her watch. 'Not late, am I?'

'No, I just got here a little early. Merlin and I took our evening walk before we came.'

Jemima crouches down to pat a sleeping Merlin. 'Here's the star of the show. Is Callum here yet?' she asks, looking up at me.

'Yes, he's just gone in to get some drinks.'

'Great!' she says, springing to her feet. 'I'll go and find him. Back in a mo.'

I watch Jemima as she heads into the pub. She seems very keen to be with our local vicar . . .

Is Jemima keen on Callum? I suddenly wonder. The last thing I want is to get in her way if she is. Things are just beginning to run smoothly for me here, I don't want to rock the boat.

But is the feeling mutual? I haven't noticed Callum showing the slightest bit of interest in Jemima. He was simply polite and friendly around her when I saw them together. Maybe I'm reading this all wrong? Callum is quite a bit older than Jemima, too – not that it should matter of course, but—

'Here you go!' Callum says, jolting me from my thoughts. He puts two glasses down on the table in front of me and swings his leg over one side of the seat so he's now on the same side as me, straddling the wooden slats.

'You looked completely lost in your thoughts then,' he says. 'Everything all right?'

'Yes ... everything is fine. Did you see Jemima?' I ask, testing the water. 'She went in a little after you did.'

'Yes, I'd already paid for our drinks, though, and I was heading back to you when I got stopped by one of our bell ringers – Bran. Jemima passed me on her way to the bar and I said I'd see her outside in a minute.'

'Ah, okay,' I say, taking a sip from my new drink. That doesn't tell me much.

'What are you going to say to Jemima when she comes out?' Callum asks, lifting his own pint.

'What do mean?' I ask, shocked he'd apparently read my mind.

'About taking Merlin into school?' Callum says, looking puzzled. 'What did you think I meant?'

'Oh, right, yes,' I reply, relieved. 'Er, I haven't decided yet. Like I said before, I need to hear what she's proposing first.'

'You coped very well with the children when they were crowded round you this afternoon. That situation didn't make you feel trapped at all?'

I shake my head. 'No, it didn't.'

'Was that because you were outside, do you think? Is it usually when you're indoors you have problems with crowds?'

I like the way Callum doesn't steer away from my problems like a lot of people I used to know would do, under some false pretence that if they don't mention it, it's not really happening. He just seemed happy to talk with me about it, as if it was perfectly normal.

'Not always, but indoors tends to make it worse. The fact they were children makes it easier.'

'Because they're smaller?'

'More likely because they don't pose any danger,' I say without thinking. I immediately regret my words.

Callum looks at me with a puzzled expression. But I look away, making a great fuss of placing a clean beermat down under my drink.

'Gosh, it's busy in there!' Jemima calls, emerging from the pub with her drink. She heads over to us and sits down directly opposite Callum.

'Sorry I couldn't get you that,' Callum says, looking at her glass, 'but old Bran cornered me about the bells on Easter Sunday.'

'Don't worry about it,' Jemima says with a vibrant smile. 'There's always another time.'

Callum just nods. 'What's this plan you have for Ava, then?' he asks. 'I'm sure she's eager to hear it.'

Jemima turns to me. 'So, Ava, like I said earlier, after seeing you with both Robin and the other children, I suddenly had this amazing idea. I've worked in other schools before that have had what are often called therapy dogs.'

I nod. 'Yes, I've heard of them.'

'And I think that your Merlin could make a wonderful addition to our school. I'm sure he would help not only the children with learning disabilities like Robin, but *all* the children. Dogs have this incredible effect on humans. The dogs I've seen coming into schools before seem to calm the over-active children and bring the quieter ones out of their shells.'

'But wouldn't he have to have special training?'

'Possibly some in the long term, but I've done a quick check, and bringing animals into the school seems to be at the discretion of the head teacher. Since I'm acting head teacher right now, then as long as we get the governors' approval, I think it would be a wonderful idea.'

I'm still not sure.

'I'm one of the school governors,' Callum says, 'and I concur. I believe both Merlin and you, Ava, could do so much good here.' He smiles at me in that gently encouraging way he has as he holds my gaze.

'We'd need to run it by the parents as well,' Jemima says keenly. 'But if you were all for it, Callum, then I'm sure they wouldn't say no to us having Merlin in the school on a regular basis.'

'It's up to you, Ava, of course,' Callum says quietly. 'Merlin is your dog.'

'It's not just Merlin who I think would be an asset,' Jemima continues at a pace, in stark contrast to Callum's calmer approach. 'It's you too, Ava. You were so good with Robin and the other children. Wasn't she, Callum?'

Callum nods. 'But if Ava is wary then perhaps she should see how she gets on bringing Merlin to the school once, rather than commit to a regular slot, and then if that goes well we can go from there? That might be easier and less pressure on everyone. What do you think, Ava?'

They both look at me, eagerly awaiting my answer.

'Well, if everyone agrees,' I reply eventually, 'then I guess we could give it a try and see how it goes. Merlin might not like it, so it would have to be a very small group of children first, just in case.'

I glance at Callum; he looks back at me knowingly. He knew it wasn't only Merlin that had to see if he liked it.

'Of course!' Jemima says excitedly. 'Oh, I'm so pleased

you've agreed to this, Ava.' She lifts her glass in the air. 'Let's have a toast, shall we?'

Callum and I both lift our glasses.

'To Ava and Merlin, and the joy they will bring to Bluebell Wood Primary School!'

'To Ava and Merlin,' Callum repeats. 'And the joy they've brought to *all of us* in Bluebell Wood already . . .'

Fourteen

I stagger sleepily downstairs on Sunday morning with the intention of making some coffee, feeding Merlin and heading outside to feed the birds. We'd slept later than we usually do because it had been quite a late one last night. We'd stayed on at the pub with Jemima and Callum, and later Lonan, who had unexpectedly joined us halfway through the evening, entertaining us with stories of his research trips abroad and his publishing career. When it got too cold to sit outside, Jemima suggested we all move inside to continue our evening, but it was a Saturday night and the pub was heaving with people, so to my regret I'd had to decline.

As we'd all stood up from the table, and I said I was going to head home, Callum had hesitated in following the others. Jemima had wasted no time in sliding her arm companionably through his to encourage him to continue the night with them. But Callum clearly had other ideas, and said he had an early start in the morning with the Sunday service and he would walk me home first before heading back to the vicarage.

My heart had leapt as high as Jemima's had likely fallen when he'd wriggled from her hold and walked over towards me, and we'd left the pub together, leaving Jemima and Lonan to carry on the rest of their evening together.

'Thanks for offering to walk me home,' I'd said before we left the pub. 'But you don't have to; Merlin and I will be fine.'

'Don't be silly, it's my pleasure. Between you and me, you gave me just the excuse I needed to leave. I enjoy our local pub, but I really don't feel like it tonight. A nice walk and some fresh air seem much more appealing right now.'

We'd then enjoyed a lovely moonlit amble back to the cottage, not talking about anything in particular, simply enjoying being in each other's company.

When we'd got to the top of the path that leads down to the cottage, Callum had insisted on walking me right to the gate. Then we'd paused and said our goodnights.

'I'm glad you and Merlin are going to give the school a chance,' Callum said, reflecting back on what had taken place earlier. 'I think it will be a good move for everyone involved.'

'Perhaps,' I'd replied with a little less confidence.

'You have so much to give, Ava. It's a shame you don't realise it.'

'Have I?' I'd asked doubtfully.

Callum had nodded. 'I suspect you could do great things if you put your mind to it.'

'And I think you might have had one beer too many!' I'd joked in an attempt to lighten the conversation.

But Callum had remained solemn. Then to my surprise he'd reached out his hand and gently allowed his soft fingers to caress my cheek.

'I . . . I must go,' he'd said hastily, with the slightly startled expression of someone who's just been woken from a really intense dream. 'I'll see you soon – yes?'

I'd simply nodded, feeling just as astonished by his touch as he'd looked dazed. Then I'd watched as he'd walked briskly up the path away from me and away from Bluebird Cottage.

This morning as I gaze out of the kitchen window, still sleepy, I reach out my hand and gently touch my cheek where Callum's fingers had been last night.

Then I feel Merlin nudge my leg impatiently.

'Sorry, fella,' I say apologetically, 'I'm getting it now.'

I make Merlin's breakfast, and then we both head out to the garden to top up the bird feeders.

'Good morning!' I say to a cheery little robin and a beady-eyed blackbird who are brave enough to sit watching me as I cross the grass towards them. 'How are you both today?'

But as I get closer to the bird table, my heart drops. I can see something bright red lying against the base. I pause for a moment, there's movement: it looks like tiny feathers moving in the breeze.

Oh no, I think, staring at it. *Has a cat had one of my birds? Is it lying there covered in blood?*

With much trepidation I move closer to the table, but my concern turns to relief as I see what is actually lying there. It is indeed a feather I can see moving, but instead of being lots of little feathers covered in blood, this is just one large red feather.

I move forward and pick it up.

Where has this come from? I wonder. There are certainly no birds that come to this table that have feathers like it; in fact, I'm pretty sure that no birds in the British Isles have feathers this long and in this shade of vibrant red. No, this is a fake feather, the sort that might be bought for crafting or to add to a hat or fancy-dress costume.

I stand and look at the feather for a moment – twisting it to and fro in my fingers.

Have the birds left this for me, like the other items that have appeared on the bird table recently? Or has it simply blown into the garden from somewhere else?

The mystery of where these objects are coming from seems to deepen as each day passes. I'm new to feeding wild birds, but surely this can't be normal, can it?

The things that were being left for me were a very odd collection: a Trivial Pursuit wedge, pieces of a school mosaic, a fifty-pence piece, and now this red feather. It's all very strange, and I can't for the life of me work out why it's happening. Whatever the reason, I've decided I quite like it. Whether the gifts have any meaning I really don't know, but it feels like the birds might be thanking me for looking out for them, and for that I'm grateful to them.

I tuck the feather safely in the top pocket of my shirt and then I go about adding bird seed, nuts, currants and all the other different things I'd taken to feeding the birds lately. I had such a lovely variety of birds coming to the garden now, and I took so much pleasure in seeing them, that I didn't mind the expense. I was glad to have made a success of something. It had been a while.

The robin flies down on to the ground next to the bird table before I've even had a chance to finish topping everything up.

'You're keen this morning,' I tell it. 'Don't worry,' I say, tapping the feather in my pocket. 'This isn't one of yours.'

The robin cocks its head to one side and watches me.

'Go ahead,' I say, smiling at it. 'I won't hurt you. You should know better than that by now.'

The robin flaps his wings and hops up bravely on to the table. Then, still keeping a careful eye on me, it selects several mealworms in its beak, before it flies away in the swooping up-and-down motion I now recognise, across the garden and over the hedge.

'Right, that's you all set,' I say to the various birds that I know are watching me from the trees, waiting for me to leave so they can begin feeding. 'Let me just do your water, then it's all yours.'

Using the garden hose, I quickly change the water in the little metal bird bath that I'd found stored away in Evelyn's shed and put outside now the weather was getting warmer, then I head back inside to make my coffee and watch the comings and goings at the bird table that I knew would take place as soon as I'd gone.

When I get inside, I wash my hands and stick the red feather in a glass on the window sill. I make my coffee, then Merlin and I go and sit in the sitting room in our usual morning spot. With half an eye on the bird table, I pull out my phone and open Google.

'Birds bringing things,' I type in the search bar to begin with. But nothing comes up in the results to match what I'm thinking about.

'Birds leaving things on a bird table' brings up answers on how to clean bird poop from your wooden table.

Finally, I try 'Birds leaving gifts on a bird table', and I'm amazed at what I find.

There are several articles about birds, mainly crows and others from that family like jackdaws and ravens, actually leaving little presents for the people that put food out for them. It's not just random stuff, either; it becomes very clear as I read on that these birds are leaving gifts that mean something to them – buttons, beads, small toys, sweet wrappers . . . The list goes on, and they seem to do it when they feel that the person they're leaving the gifts for has been particularly kind to them.

Was that really what my birds were doing for me? Leaving me gifts to thank me for feeding them?

Even though it seems far-fetched, I feel warmed by the thought it might be true, and even keener to continue looking after them.

Merlin and I have a quiet Sunday. After a bright start, the rest of the day is a mix of clouds and April showers. In the morning we take our usual walk in the woods. Under the canopy of the trees we're slightly protected from the showers, and I can hear the church bells ringing to announce the Sunday service. I think about Callum while I listen to the bells, and try to imagine him in full swing in the pulpit preaching his sermon to the gathered congregation.

After last night I had considered going to church this morning to support him. But I felt I'd be there under false pretences. I've never really been a churchgoer, even though I used to have some belief. But any belief in a greater good had been very quickly curtailed after certain events, and I'd yet to find a reason worthy of reintroducing it into my life.

As I shelter under the trees, I allow my mind to wander back to a time I rarely wanted to return to these days, and my last experience of a man of the cloth preaching to a congregation.

What a silly pretentious man he was, standing there telling us it was all in God's plan. He had no idea of the pain people were suffering – mentally and physically. All I heard was his nonsense, which instead of making me and the others feel better, only made us feel worse.

A drop of rain falls on my face from one of the trees above, and I'm brought back to a much more pleasant reality. I'd done the right thing in staying away from the church today, I was certain of that. Staying away from Callum, however, wasn't going to be quite so easy . . .

After lunch I speak on the phone to Hannah about her upcoming visit over the Easter weekend, and I tell her how much I'm looking forward to seeing her. Matt is also due to visit before he leaves for New York on Good Friday, and I'm excited to see both of them again and show them how well things are going for me here in Bluebell Wood.

Later in the afternoon I awake from an impromptu nap in the armchair. I'm just wondering whether to have an early tea or take Merlin out again before I eat, when there's a knock at the door.

Who's that? I wonder. It's five o'clock on a Sunday. I certainly hadn't invited anyone, and no one other than delivery people or the postman ever knocked on my door, and it was unlikely they would be doing so at this time on a weekend.

Hesitantly I approach the door and look though the little peephole that I was glad Evelyn had had installed.

Outside I see a woman standing in the rain, looking extremely agitated – it's Robin's mother, Linnet.

'Hello,' I say, opening up the door to her. 'What can I do for you?'

'It's Robin,' she says, looking like she might cry. 'He's gone missing.'

Fifteen

'Oh no!' I say, staring at her. 'When?'

'About half an hour ago. He'd been banging on about seeing you and Merlin all day. I told him we couldn't just show up without warning, but he wouldn't listen. He got it into his head that he wanted to see you today and that was that. I don't suppose he's here, is he?' she asks hopefully. 'I tried to call you but you weren't answering your phone?'

'Sorry, it must be out of charge,' I lie, the truth was I'd turned it to mute just before Merlin and I took our afternoon nap. 'No, I haven't seen Robin at all.'

'Oh God, where has he gone, then? I was convinced he'd be here. He's never done this before; I have no idea where to start looking for him.'

'Come in,' I tell her, as an order rather than a request. 'You're getting soaked out there. Let's think about it together.'

Linnet looks desperately around her. 'Maybe I should just go and look for him?'

'Yes, we'll definitely do that,' I say firmly. 'But we need to think where is best to look first, and then if need be we can get some others to help us search.'

'Oh, thank you,' Linnet says, definitely on the verge of tears as she allows herself to enter the cottage. 'There's only me and Robin at home; I didn't know what to do or who to ask.'

'Come and sit down,' I tell her gently, as I help her off with her thin raincoat and lead her through to the sitting room. 'Now I know this might seem a little trivial,' I say as Linnet sits down on the edge of the sofa and runs her hand agitatedly over her damp hair, 'but it might help. Can I make you a cup of tea? Or something stronger, perhaps?' I wasn't sure I had anything stronger, but I thought Evelyn would have some cooking sherry or some such thing tucked away in her cupboards if I looked hard enough. 'You look like you need warming up.'

Linnet shakes her head. 'No, thank you, I'll be fine.'

She looked anything but fine; however, I sit down next to her anyway. 'Now, when was the last time you saw Robin?'

'He was playing with his superhero dolls in our lounge,' Linnet says quickly. 'I popped through to the kitchen to put the kettle on. While I was there I began wondering what we might have for our tea. I went to the freezer and called to Robin would he like fish fingers? He loves his fish fingers,' she says, looking distressed again.

I nod, hoping she'll continue.

'When he didn't answer, I called again, then I went back to see what he was doing and that's when I discovered he was gone. Robin likes to play hide-and-seek, so I spent a few minutes searching the house for him, then I popped out into our garden. It's only tiny and there's not many places he could hide without me seeing him. And then I started to panic. I called to him to come out if he was hiding in the house somewhere, but there was nothing. Our house is a bit like our garden,' she explains. 'It's small, so there's not many places he could hide himself, and I'd checked all his usual hideaways.'

'Is that when you came here?' I ask.

Linnet nods. 'I sort of ran here, looking all the time in case I could spy him. I thought I'd bump into someone along the way and I'd ask if they'd seen him, but I didn't see a soul.'

'It's a wet Sunday afternoon,' I explain. 'There won't be too many people out and about. Right,' I say, trying to sound authoritative and in control, when the truth was I felt neither. 'Let's assume you were correct about him trying to come here. Shall we take a look around the cottage and the garden, and then if we don't find him we'll head further afield.'

Linnet hastily nods her agreement, and we set about searching the few rooms that Bluebird Cottage has. It would have been pretty impossible for Robin to sneak in here without Merlin or me hearing him, but I felt Linnet wouldn't rest if we didn't.

But as I expect, our search of the house comes to nothing.

'Garden!' I quickly say when Linnet's lip starts to quiver again.

The rain, which has been on and off all afternoon, has taken another quick break as we head out into the garden and begin searching – in the bushes, behind trees, in the ramshackle old shed that sits at the bottom of the garden housing a few gardening tools, but again our search is in vain.

'Oh my God, where is he?' Linnet cries when I emerge from the shed alone.

'Could he have gone to the woods?' I ask gently, knowing that this was not going to go down well. 'My son loved to go exploring in places like that when he was young.'

'Robin does love the wood,' Linnet agrees, 'but he'd never go there alone – not to a creepy place like that.'

I wouldn't have described Bluebell Wood as creepy, but now was not the time to debate adjectives with Linnet.

'Why would he love the wood if he's scared of it?' I ask.

'Oh, he's not scared, I am,' Linnet admits. 'The school have taken him there a few times on nature trips. That's how I know he likes it.'

'What are we waiting for, then?' I ask. 'Let's go.'

'To the wood?' Linnet asks hesitantly.

'Do you want to find your son or not?' I demand.

Linnet nods. 'Of course I do.'

'Well, come on then.'

Linnet's raincoat is still very damp, and to be honest it doesn't look like it's kept much rain off her, so I quickly find her one of Evelyn's huge waterproof oilcloth coats that still hang in the hall cupboard. Then I pull on one of my own waterproof jackets and a baseball cap, and we head out with Merlin to look for Robin.

Linnet seems to hesitate as we reach the entrance to the wood.

I sigh. What use was she going to be if she was frightened of going in there? She'd hardly be bravely searching in the dark and out-of-the-way places Robin was likely to be hiding in, would she?

'I don't suppose you have anything on you that smells like Robin?' I ask suddenly, getting an idea.

Linnet shakes her head.

'Why don't you go back to your house and pick up a piece of his clothing that he's recently worn?' I suggest. 'Then I can let Merlin smell it and it might help him to find Robin.'

'Do you think he could do that?' Linnet asks in amazement, looking at Merlin.

'It's possible,' I reply. Merlin was a fabulous dog – intelligent and super friendly – but even I doubted whether he was up to tracking a missing child just by their scent alone. 'You go back to your house and check if Robin has turned up yet. You never know?' I say when she looks uncertain. 'He might just have wandered off and now he's come home again. If he's not there, then collect a piece of his clothing, call me and I'll come and meet you.'

Linnet nods. 'Wait, isn't your phone out of charge?' she asks.

'Er no, I'd accidentally left it on silent,' I hurriedly reply. 'And Linnet,' I say just before she goes, 'if you see anyone that you think might be able to help us look for Robin, will you ask them to come to the wood too.'

She nods again. 'Thank you, Ava. I don't know what I'd have done without you.'

'Thank me later when we've found him,' I say, trying to sound reassuring. 'Now go.'

Merlin and I head into the wood. 'Where do we start?' I ask my canine friend as he sniffs about by my feet.

I bend down next to him before I unhook his lead. 'Merlin, listen,' I say, turning his head to look at me. 'If you understand anything of what I say, then we must find Robin, the little boy you met at the school.'

Merlin looks at me with his head cocked to one side.

'I know you met a lot of children yesterday, so how about you try to find any child hidden here in the wood?' I suggest. 'There can't be more than one.' I unhook Merlin's lead and he shoots off into the long grass.

The wood looks just as pretty today as it had when I'd

stopped to photograph the bluebells. But today I don't see the flowers, or the way the light dapples delicately through the trees, my only thought is to find a missing little boy.

I felt partially to blame for his disappearance. I shouldn't, I know; he might have run off even if he hadn't met Merlin and me at the school. But Linnet said Robin had wanted to come and see us. Perhaps if he hadn't, he wouldn't be missing now.

I take Merlin's lead and follow him through the wood. I don't know if he's heading anywhere in particular, or if he's just wandering where his fancy takes him, but he knew as much as I did, so why not follow his animal instincts?

Every so often I call out Robin's name into the silence, and a few startled birds fly up from the branches of the trees.

A couple of times I think I've heard something and I stop to listen for a moment. But it must just be a woodland animal darting away from where we've disturbed it. When I come across a deep thicket of trees or a patch of dense shrubbery, I hope desperately that Robin might be hiding in them, but my hopes are quickly dashed when my search of them proves fruitless.

'Robin!' I call again as we move deeper into the wood, into an area we've only walked through a few times on our longer outings. 'Are you there? Merlin would like to see you!'

I stop and listen yet again, in case I might hear a little voice calling back to me. But instead of the silence I was getting used to, all I hear is a voice I know well.

'Ava?'

Before I see him, I hear his footsteps running towards me.

'Callum!' I call, relieved to see him appearing through some trees.

'What are you doing out here calling for birds to come and

meet Merlin?' he asks jovially as he jogs towards me. Today he's wearing long running trousers and a waterproof jacket like mine, but unlike me his head is uncovered, so perspiration has mixed with rain, leaving his hair and face damp.

'What?' I ask, not understanding.

'What you were calling just now, about a robin?' Callum says, breathing heavily as he stops in front of me. 'You're as likely to see one of those in your garden as out here in the wood.'

'No,' I say, suddenly understanding. 'I'm calling for Robin – you know, the boy I met at the school sale. He's gone missing.'

'What?' Callum asks in concern, immediately forgetting about his breathlessness. 'When?'

I look at my watch. 'About an hour ago now. If we don't find him soon, we'll have to call the police.'

'Where's his mother? Why are you looking for him?'

'It's a long story,' I tell him. 'I'll explain later. Right now we have to keep searching.' My phone rings. I grab it and answer at once.

'Linnet?' I say optimistically. 'Oh . . . oh, right. Yes, I'm quite a long way into the wood. Callum is here now too; he's going to help us search.' I glance at Callum. He nods. 'Right, yes that's a good idea . . . Okay, keep in touch and I'll let you know the minute we find him.'

I end the call.

'Linnet bumped into Lonan while she was on her way back to the wood from her house. He's going to help her round up some of the villagers to help us search.'

'Good, Lonan will be an excellent person to be involved. Right, where have you searched?'

'Everywhere we've walked so far. All our usual routes.'

'What about up by the little stream?' Callum says. 'You

know, where it broadens out into the river. Where I bumped into you that time?'

'It's possible; we haven't gone that far yet. But do you think Robin would wander that far into the wood? He's only, what, six or seven?'

'I think he might just be eight,' Callum says. 'But it's worth a try, isn't it?'

Callum, Merlin and I set off at a brisk pace, following the path towards the river. We regularly call Robin's name as we walk, stopping to listen for a moment or two when we do. Then we carry on until we get to the little clearing where Merlin and I had paused for him to drink from the cool flowing water. We split up and have a good search around, but to our dismay there's nothing, only the rhythmical pitter-patter of the rain falling on the trees above us and slowly dripping down to the ground below.

'Do you think he's sheltering somewhere?' I ask a very damp-looking Callum. Merlin's coat is also beginning to cling to him where the steady rain has slowly made it wetter and wetter. I'm the only one looking and feeling quite dry underneath my waterproof coat and hat, and I feel sorry for the other two as the weather takes its toll on them.

'Hopefully,' Callum says, running his hands over his wet hair to try to remove some of the water from it. 'Otherwise he'll be soaking wet and freezing cold by now.'

'Is there anywhere around here he could shelter, though?' I ask, looking around. 'There's only trees, aren't there?'

'Wait a minute,' Callum says, his blue eyes suddenly shining with hope. 'What about the ruins?'

'What ruins?'

'The ones up on the hill? It used to be an old manor house

back in the day, I think. That's what someone told me, anyway. I discovered it on one of my runs when I first came here. I often pass it, but I don't think anything of it any more. There's barely anything left now. But a young boy might find it extremely interesting.'

'Which way?' I ask urgently.

'This way,' Callum says, pointing, and we set off again, this time at an even faster pace and with an ever-deepening resolve.

'I think I know where we're heading for,' I tell him as we hurry along. I'm certain Callum could have moved a lot quicker than this, but he's gallant enough to keep to a pace I can cope with. 'I found Merlin sniffing around some old bricks here once.'

'These bricks?' Callum asks as the path beneath us begins to be strewn with the cream and terracotta remains of an old building.

'Yes, they were something like this.'

'This isn't what I meant,' Callum says, marching onwards as I struggle to keep up with him now. We're currently climbing up a fairly steep incline, and I'm starting to find it difficult to catch my breath. But eventually Callum reaches an opening in the trees and he pauses to let me catch up. '*This* is what I meant.'

I reach his side and I'm amazed by what I see.

We've made it to the top of the hill, and now the ground in front of us stretches out for quite a way at an even level. There are a few trees, plants and mainly tall weeds in front of us, but the planting is nowhere near as dense as where we've just come from. In the middle of all this quite clearly are the remnants of what must once have been a rather large, and likely quite grand, house.

All that remains is the skeleton of the home it once was.

There are a few exterior walls still intact, but most of them have long since fallen. I can just make out where the many windows might once have been in the front of the building, and also how many floors the house would have had from some of the fragments of them jutting across the interior walls.

'I had no idea this was here,' I tell Callum. 'We've never come as far out as this.'

Merlin is already galloping across the uneven ground in front of us towards the house.

'We'd better follow him,' Callum says. 'He might know more than we do.'

As best we can, we chase Merlin through the long grass, eventually arriving outside the ruins of the house.

'Where did he go?' I ask Callum, looking wildly around me. 'Did you see?'

'Through here, I think,' Callum says, clambering over a few large bricks covered in moss and lichen.

I follow him, entering the derelict house under a huge archway that I'm sure must once have welcomed visitors looking a lot more elegant than we did right now.

'Merlin!' I call.

'Robin!' Callum shouts. 'Are you here?'

I hear a bark. 'Merlin!' I call again, following the sound. 'Where are you?'

Merlin barks again, and I see the end of his tail wagging from behind a pile of bricks. I rush over to him and see a quite content Merlin having his chin stroked by a slightly bedraggled, but delightedly happy-looking little boy.

'Robin!' I cry, then I lower my voice. I don't want to startle him. 'Robin, are you all right?'

Robin looks up at me and nods. 'I'm dry,' he says, pointing

to a small arch of bricks above his head, and I realise he must be sheltering under the remains of a large fireplace.

'I'm glad you're dry,' I say, crouching down next to him as Callum arrives. 'But are you hurt at all?'

Robin shakes his head. 'No. I like your dog.'

'Yes, I know,' I say. 'I think he likes you too.'

'That's why he found me,' Robin says. 'Because he wanted to see me. I told Mum that he did, but she wouldn't listen. So I came and found him myself.'

'I'll ring Linnet,' Callum says.

'Here.' I unlock my phone and pass it to him.

'Thanks,' he says, moving away from us to make the call.

'Why did you come here, though?' I ask Robin. 'You could have come to my cottage?'

'I thought you lived here,' Robin says.

'In this ruined house?'

'No, in the wood. I heard you say to someone the other day you lived in the wood.'

'Did I?' I try to think what he could mean. 'Are you sure?'

'Yeah, you definitely said it. I came to the wood to look for your house, but this was the only one I found. So I waited for you to come home, and you did.'

'You must be very cold?' I ask, keen to get him out of here and back home to Linnet. 'Do you think perhaps we should go and find your mum? She'll be very worried about you.'

Robin thinks about this. 'Can't Mum come to your house and see us?'

'Yes, of course she can. But this isn't actually my house, Robin; my house is back in the village.'

Robin looks around at the ruins. 'I thought this was a bit cold and wet for you,' he says pragmatically, making me smile.

'Yes, it is. I'm sure when someone last lived here it was much drier and warmer. I think you might actually be sitting in one of their old fireplaces.'

Robin looks up in surprise.

'Do you think you should come out?' I ask, sensing this might be my chance to get him to move.

Robin nods. 'Can I come to your real house?' he asks, as he begins to remove himself from the fireplace.

'I think we should take you to see your mum first.'

'I want to stay with Merlin!' he says, sitting back down in the hearth.

'Okay, sure,' I agree hurriedly. 'If you come out, you can come back to my house with me and Merlin, and we'll meet your mum there. How about that?'

'What about him, though?' Robin asks, looking behind me.

I turn and see Callum standing back a little way, watching us.

'Is he coming to your house too?' Robin demands.

'Do you want him to?'

'Don't mind.' Robin shrugs. 'As long as Merlin is there.'

'Right, well, let's all start walking back together and then we can decide when we get there who can come in. How about that?'

Robin nods. He pulls himself to his feet, and with Merlin we walk back towards Callum.

'Hi, Robin, I'm Callum,' Callum says, smiling at him. 'I'm glad we found you.'

'It's your fault I'm here,' Robin says, pouting a little.

Callum looks at me, but I just shrug and shake my head a little. 'Is it?' he asks Robin. 'Why?'

'Because you were the one she said she lived in the wood to,' Robin says, happily following Merlin as he begins to make his way across the long grass back towards the wood.

I look at Callum with a mystified expression as we follow on.

'Oh!' I suddenly say. 'At the sale we were talking about what I'd got up to since I'd been here, and I said I virtually *lived in the wood* with Merlin because we were always in there walking! Robin must have heard us when he was browsing the stall, and thought I meant I *actually* lived here.'

Callum shakes his head and then we both grin at each other, partly with amusement, partly with relief, and partly with something else I don't quite understand just yet.

Sixteen

'I don't know how to thank you,' Linnet says, standing in my sitting room holding a mug of hot chocolate. We're both watching Robin play happily with Merlin on the rug by the window. 'If it hadn't been for you we might never have found him.'

'Oh, I'm sure you would,' I say sensibly, keen to play down Callum's and my part in all this. Linnet had been treating us both like superheroes since we'd appeared from the wood with Robin to an audience of Linnet and the few villagers that Lonan had managed to drum up to form a search party. They'd kindly stuck around to see us emerge from the wood triumphant with Robin.

As promised, I'd allowed Robin to come back to Bluebird Cottage to spend time with Merlin, but I'd insisted he let Linnet put him in some dry clothes first.

Robin had begrudgingly allowed this to take place, and then Linnet, Robin, Lonan and Callum (who has also changed into dry clothes now) had returned to the cottage to partake in mugs of hot chocolate. In fact, it didn't occur to me until I was making said hot chocolate that I had more people in my cottage than I'd ever had before.

But I'm pleased to find this doesn't bother me as much as I thought it might have done. Actually, I'm quite enjoying having this particular group of people here with me.

Lonan and Callum are currently standing by the window sipping from their mugs and discussing the history of the old ruins where we'd found Robin.

'He's really taken to both you and Merlin,' Linnet continues. 'He doesn't usually like strangers. They mess with his routine, and Robin must have routine.'

I watch Robin rubbing Merlin's tummy, and Merlin looking with delight back at him as he does so.

'Merlin really likes him,' I tell her. 'I'm just pleased we could help.'

'You're very good with Robin. Not everyone understands how to deal with him – he can be a little difficult at times. But you just seem to get him.'

'My son had a few problems when he was younger,' I say. Unusually for me, I suddenly feel the need to confide in Linnet. 'He had a lot of help when he was first at school. We were lucky, the system picked up his learning difficulties very early.'

'That must be why you get my Robin, then. How is your son now – he's not here in Bluebell Wood with you, is he?'

'Oh no, Matt is at university now.'

'Really? His problems didn't hold him back academically, then?'

'Nope, we are incredibly proud of what he has achieved. He's about to go and work abroad for a year – in New York.' I try not to think about this too much as I say the words to Linnet. Because every time I do, I feel my anxiety levels skyrocket.

I watch Linnet look with concern over at Robin and I put my hand on her arm. 'He'll be fine,' I say gently. 'I worried about Matt when he was younger, but he's grown into a handsome, confident and wonderful young man.'

Linnet puts her hand over mine. 'Thank you, Ava. That means a lot, really it does.'

'You get extra help at the school for Robin, though, don't you?' I ask, incredibly touched that my words have meant so much to her. 'That helped my Matt a lot.'

'We did, but the lady who was assigned to him has moved away from the area, and the council haven't replaced her with another teaching assistant. I heard you might be helping out at the school,' Linnet says casually, taking a sip from her mug. 'I think you'd be amazing. Especially with children like Robin. There's more of them than you might imagine that need help but don't get it.'

'I've agreed to bring Merlin into the school, that's all,' I tell her, wondering how she had heard this news already. 'Jemima thinks he might be of some help, so we're having a one-off trial to begin with when she's got all the necessary permissions.'

'Oh, I see.' Linnet looks disappointed.

To my enormous relief Lonan comes over to us. 'I'm afraid that I must go now, ladies,' he says. 'This was delicious, Ava.' He lifts his empty mug. 'You must give me the recipe sometime.'

'It's nothing special – from one of Evelyn's cookery books. That's the lady who used to live here,' I explain for Lonan's benefit.

'That's as may be, but it was still superb. It was good to meet you today, Linnet,' Lonan says, as gracious as ever. 'I'm so pleased young Robin was returned to you safe and sound.'

'Thank you so much for your help, Lonan,' Linnet says coyly. 'I'm sorry I was in such a state when you saw me earlier.'

'Completely understandable, dear lady. Any time you need any help you just call, my door is always open. Now I really must be off. I have a deadline that won't be met if I don't get on. I bid you farewell, ladies. I shall see you anon, young Robin, and you too, Callum.'

Callum amiably lifts his hand, but Robin just stares at Lonan for a moment before returning his attention to Merlin.

I see Lonan out. 'Thanks for helping today,' I say to him as I open the door.

'Not a problem at all,' Lonan says, bending his head to fit under the low cottage doorway. 'It was the least I could do. Luckily you didn't need the merry band of helpers I'd pulled together. You and Callum had the situation completely under control.'

'Well, Callum did. I didn't even know those ruins existed until he told me about them.'

'Talking of which,' Lonan says, pausing on the doorstep, 'Callum's been telling me all about the house that was originally there – as much as he knows about it, anyway. It all sounds very interesting. I'll have to do some research on it myself when I have some time.'

'I'm sure there's plenty of folk around here who will help you with any questions you might have,' I say, grinning.

'Yes, they do seem quite partial to the odd round of gossip.' Lonan winks at me. 'And we newcomers seem to be the main topic of their conversations lately.'

'Yes, indeed,' I reply, wondering what Lonan might have heard. 'Well, thanks again. See you soon, I hope.'

I head back indoors, and find Callum now sitting on the floor with Merlin and Robin, and Linnet sitting in one of the armchairs watching them.

'Callum is telling Robin all about the Romans,' Linnet says. 'They're learning about them at school this term.'

'What little I know,' Callum says. 'Actually, I think Robin is teaching me!'

Robin looks pleased by this. 'I need a hat, Callum,' he suddenly announces.

'What sort of a hat?' Callum asks.

'A Roman hat.'

'It's actually an Easter bonnet,' Linnet explains. 'The school always has an Easter bonnet parade at the end of the spring term. We haven't got around to making one yet. Robin has decided he doesn't want a bonnet; he wants one of those helmets the Roman soldiers used to wear.'

'Like a legionary?' Callum asks. 'Very smart.'

Robin nods. 'But Mum won't help me make one.'

'Robin, that's not fair,' Linnet says quietly. 'I just haven't had time yet. I work,' she explains to me, 'at the big superstore up the road. Sometimes it's getting late by the time I get home – I have to get a bus, you see. Robin stays at the after-school club a few nights a week. We'll do it, though,' she tells Robin. 'I promised you, didn't I? And I never break a promise. How I'm going to make a Roman soldier's helmet, though, I have no idea,' she adds quietly to me.

'I used to do things like that with papier mâché,' I tell her. 'When my two were small, we used to make all sorts of things using that technique. You just start with a balloon and mould bits of paper and glue on to it. It's quite easy, and Robin could help you.'

'Yes, I could try that,' Linnet says, still looking a bit worried. 'It doesn't sound too bad.'

'You'll need a big red plume on top of it,' Callum suggests to Robin. 'That's what they had, didn't they – the Roman soldiers.'

'Can I have one of them, Mum?' Robin asks.

Linnet looks even more anxious now. 'I'm not sure, Robin; it might be a bit late to get one of those now.'

'Wait right there!' I say, as an idea springs to mind. I rush to the kitchen and grab the birds' latest offering from the glass on the window sill. Then I return triumphantly to the sitting room. 'How about this?' I say, holding it up. 'Will this do?'

Robin's eyes light up at the sight of the long scarlet feather in my hand.

'It's perfect,' he whispers. 'Can I use it on my hat?'

'Of course you can,' I say, going over to him and kneeling down.

'Where did you get it from?' Robin asks as he takes the feather from my hand and holds it carefully in his own.

'Remember the magical fifty pence?' I ask.

Robin nods.

'The same place as that came from.'

Robin looks out of the French window. 'Your birds left it for you?' he asks in awe.

'Yes,' I say quietly, aware that both Linnet and Callum are listening to this as well.

'Wow, you really do have magical birds.'

'Our secret, though, remember?' I whisper.

Robin nods. 'Our secret.'

I look over at the other two and smile knowingly, hoping they understand that I don't actually believe this, it's just for Robin's benefit.

'It's very kind of you to lend Robin your feather,' Linnet says. 'Have you said thank you, Robin?'

'Thank you, Ava,' Robin says, and then, quite unexpectedly, he gives me a huge hug, which by the look on her face takes Linnet by as much surprise as it does me.

'That's quite all right,' I say, patting him gently on the back. I feel moved by his simple gesture. My own emotional door has been very firmly shut for far too long now. But this little boy could just be the one to prise it back open.

'Now, Robin,' Linnet says, smiling at us, 'I really think we must leave Ava be, and go home. We've taken up far too much of her time.'

Robin immediately pouts, but then he sees his feather, and nods. 'Can we make the helmet tonight, Mum?' he asks excitedly. 'Then you won't say you don't have time.'

Linnet smiles at me. 'Yes, we can have a go tonight. We might have a balloon somewhere at home, and if not, I'll get one first thing tomorrow, I know Jenny has some in her shop.'

Robin strokes Merlin one last time, then he leaps up. 'Okay, I'm ready now.'

'Thank you, both of you,' Linnet says as she helps Robin on with his coat.

'Any time,' Callum says.

'I'll look forward to seeing your helmet, Robin,' I tell him as we walk towards the door together.

'Can I come and show you and Merlin when it's finished?'

'Of course you can,' I tell him. 'Let me know when you want to pop round again,' I tell Linnet. 'My door is always open.'

I watch them go, pausing for a moment before I return to Callum.

'So, you have magical birds, do you?' Callum asks, turning away from the French window as I walk back into the sitting room. He grins, and I can't help smiling back.

'It would seem that way. They keep leaving me weird stuff on the table in the mornings.'

'What sort of weird stuff?' Callum asks. 'I thought you were just saying that for Robin's benefit.'

'Partly,' I say, joining him by the window, 'the magical bit, anyway. But the part about the birds leaving things is true. Along with the red feather and the fifty pence they've also left the other things I keep over there on the mantelpiece.'

Callum looks over at where I'm pointing.

'You mean those broken bits of pottery?'

'Yes, those and the yellow Trivial Pursuit piece – that was the first thing I found.'

'You've found all these things, plus a coin and a bright red feather, on your bird table?' Callum asks in astonishment, going over to investigate.

'Yep – odd, isn't it?'

'It's more than odd. How do they get there?'

I shrug. 'It says on the internet that sometimes birds bring little gifts for the people who feed them – things that we think of as junk, but they might see as little bits of treasure. But it mainly seems to be crows and those types of larger birds. I can't find anything about the sorts of garden birds I have doing something similar.'

'Some of the items are small and light enough for a little bird, I suppose; but the fifty pence, that would have to be a bigger bird, surely?'

'I get the odd jackdaw, but I've never seen anything larger. Not landing in the garden, anyway.'

'The mystery deepens,' Callum says, turning back from the fireplace.

'It's not really a mystery. Just a bit strange.'

'I meant you, Ava, you're the mystery,' Callum says, and he walks slowly over towards me.

'I am?' I ask, very aware how close to me he suddenly is.

He's a vicar, Ava! I remind myself. *A priest – a man who wholly believes in everything you don't any more.*

'Yes,' he says in that soft low voice he has, which now he's close to me is even more attractive and throwing me completely off guard. 'You're a puzzle to me.'

'Why?' I whisper, trying hard to fight my feelings, but rapidly losing the battle.

Callum reaches out his hand and gently tucks back a piece of my hair that's escaped from the ponytail I'd loosely tied it up in before we set off in search of Robin.

'You pretend to be one thing, when really I think you're something very different entirely.'

'Go on?' I whisper again. It was a *very* long time since I'd allowed any man to stand this close to me, and even when they had before I definitely hadn't ever felt anything like I was feeling right now. I was in a losing battle with myself.

'I can't explain it,' Callum says, still in his low, incredibly sexy voice, and his eyes travel over my face. 'There's just something about you. Something I want to know more about. Something I think I'm going to enjoy discovering . . . '

Callum leans in towards me, and for one terrifying but blissful moment I think he's actually going to kiss me. But the sound of a phone ringing stops him.

'Damn!' Callum says, pulling away and reaching into his pocket. 'Hold that thought.' He glances at the screen and immediately puts the phone to his ear. 'Hey, Jonah,' he says. He looks at me while he listens, and then as Jonah speaks his face changes from relaxed to fraught. 'What?' he says, hurriedly pulling back his shirt sleeve so he can see his sports watch. 'I had no idea . . . Can you start them off and I'll get there as soon as I can. Yes, I know, I know. I'm sorry.'

He ends the call and looks at me with a face full of panic and remorse. 'I've missed the start of evensong,' he says, looking around for his coat. 'We've only just started doing it on a Sunday. It's for the choir really, but it's been quite popular with some of the parishioners.'

'Oh gosh, I'm sorry,' I say, meaning it. I hurriedly fetch his coat from where I'd hung it in the hall and return it to him.

'Thanks,' Callum says, pulling it on. 'I'm sorry I have to go.' He pauses for a moment and looks at me. 'There was something I wanted to ask you.'

'Really?' I say, thinking I probably knew what it might be.

'Yes, and then we got . . . well . . . sidetracked.'

'Oh.' Maybe I didn't know, then.

'I wanted to ask what you know about the Easter Bunny.'

Seventeen

'Run that past me again,' Hannah says with a smile as we sit together on the sofa on Friday evening. 'You're going to do what?'

I give my daughter a meaningful look; she knew exactly what I'd just said. 'Early on Sunday morning I'm going to help the church hide the eggs ready for the Easter egg hunt they always have around the village.'

'No, not that bit,' Hannah says, still grinning. 'The *other* part.'

I roll my eyes; Hannah has been a mischief maker since she was small. Matt was always the quieter of my two children, and would often get cajoled into his sister's childhood pranks. I sigh. 'Everyone hiding the eggs has to dress up as rabbits.'

'Not *just* rabbits, Mum. The Easter Bunny, no less!' Hannah says with great delight.

'So? You believed in the Easter Bunny when you were small. You loved hunting for eggs on Easter morning.'

'I know, but I never thought I'd see my mother dressing up as it.'

I shrug and take a sip of the wine Hannah brought with her; we'd opened it to have with our dinner this evening – a homemade lasagne that I'd found a recipe for in one of Evelyn's cookery books. It wasn't anything fancy, but Hannah had been impressed I'd cooked it myself, and I'd been amazed that it had actually been edible.

'There's something more to this, isn't there?' she asks knowingly.

'No, I'm just helping out, that's all.'

'Hmm . . .'

'What's wrong with helping out my local church?'

'You've never been religious before, have you?'

'It's not to do with religion,' I say hurriedly, 'it's to do with helping out the village. Everyone has been so kind to me since I got here. It's the least I can do.'

'All right,' Hannah says, taking a drink from her own glass now, 'we'll leave it at that. But I'm convinced there's something more going on here.'

She was right, of course. When Callum had asked if I'd help out on Easter Sunday morning, at first I'd laughed, thinking he was joking about dressing up. Then when I realised he was being serious, I'd hesitated, but eventually agreed when he'd explained that Evelyn did it every year.

When I'd first arrived at Bluebird Cottage I wasn't bothered by the pedestal that everyone who knew her seemed to put my predecessor on, but just lately I'd begun to feel quite inferior to this wondrous person who had apparently done so much for the village and its inhabitants. So if Evelyn dressed up as a bunny every Easter Sunday then so would I.

I wanted to start making my own mark here on Bluebell Wood, and that's just what I hoped to begin doing after Easter when I would take Merlin into the school for his first trial session. I was certain he'd be absolutely fine with the children; I just hoped I'd be the same.

It was lovely having Hannah here for the weekend. Even though I'd only been in Bluebell Wood a short time, it felt like ages since I'd seen her. We'd spent the evening catching up on what had been going on in her life, and mine, and I'd been surprised at just how much I'd had to tell her about my time here so far.

The next morning, we take Merlin for a walk in the wood, and I show Hannah some of the paths we often followed on our daily trips here. It's a warm, sunny spring morning and the wood looks particularly beautiful today. The bluebells are still in bloom, and their deep purply blue is contrasted by the bright yellow of a delicate cowslip that's just beginning to push its way through.

'It's gorgeous,' Hannah exclaims after we've been walking for a while. 'So peaceful and pretty. No wonder you like it here.'

'Yes, Merlin and I have spent many a happy hour wandering these paths.'

'You look well, Mum,' Hannah says, turning towards me as we walk. 'I mean, really well. The quiet life obviously suits you. When we left you here a few weeks ago, I wondered how long you'd last, to be honest. The peace of Bluebell Wood is a little different to the hustle and bustle of London. But I have to admit solitude seems to have done you the world of good.'

'I'm not completely on my own,' I say, deliberately taking the path where I know Hannah will get the same stunning first view of the bluebells that I'd had. 'I've made a few friends here.'

'Really? That's good,' Hannah says, sounding relieved. 'Tell me about them.'

I tell her about my fellow team mates from the quiz.

'They sound great, I'm so pleased for— Oh, wow!' she says as we turn a corner and see a great swathe of blue. 'That's beautiful. I need to take a photo.'

She takes her phone from her pocket and proceeds to take a few snaps. 'The little yellow flowers are super cute amongst all these bluebells,' she says, doing the same as I had: getting down low to get a better angle.

'They're cowslips,' I tell her. 'They hadn't begun to bloom when we were here last.'

Hannah looks up at me from where she's crouching down. 'How on earth do you know that?' she asks. 'You'd have barely known these were bluebells before you came here.'

'Don't be daft.'

'Come on, Mum, you hardly knew a rose from a tulip before.'

'I wasn't that bad! Anyway, you're thinking about *garden* flowers; these are *wild* flowers.'

'See,' Hannah says, standing up. 'My point exactly.'

'I learnt from a book – several books, actually. The lady that lived in the cottage before me was a bit of a bookworm; there's a book on everything on her shelves.'

'Nice. Can I take one of you and Merlin in front of the bluebells? I want to send it to Matt. She looks at her watch. 'He'll be in New York by now.'

'Yes, I know.' I gather Merlin in my arms and smile at Hannah's phone as she holds it up.

'And you're all right with that?' Hannah asks warily.

I put Merlin down again and he scampers off. 'If you're asking if I'm happy that my son is now thousands of miles away from me – then no. Your child never stops being a child to you, and your natural instinct is always to keep them near. To keep them safe. But if you're asking if I'm happy that Matt is striking out on his own, and doing something that makes him happy, then yes, of course I'm all right with that.'

Hannah just stares at me.

'What?' I ask.

'I don't know if it's this place that has changed you, Mum, or the people that live here, but you've definitely changed since you came to Bluebell Wood, and only for the better.'

'I haven't changed that much,' I tell her as I stride off after Merlin, and she hurries to follow me. 'I don't think so, anyway.'

'You probably can't see it,' Hannah says, catching up. 'But I can, and so did Matt when he was here last week. He texted me to say I'd see a difference in you, but I didn't realise it would be to such a degree. Before, we hardly dare tell you that Matt was going to New York. In fact, we deliberately kept it a secret so it didn't stress you out. Now you're just chilled about it all. Actually, you're chilled about everything.'

'You shouldn't have kept that a secret from me,' I tell her. 'What did you think I was going to do, try to stop him from going?'

Hannah raises her eyebrows at me.

'Really? I was that bad?'

'You know you were that bad. You were always texting to check we were okay.'

'That's what parents do.'

'Dad barely ever texts.'

'Yes, well, that's your father for you,' I say, thinking of my ex-husband, never the most overtly caring of men.

'Mum, you'd be texting every day, sometimes two or three times when I was down in London.'

I stop walking and look at her.

'Can you blame me?' I ask. 'After what happened?'

'No, of course we don't blame you. I'm just pointing out how much you've changed. I don't know what's gone on here, Mum, but Bluebell Wood is working some very special magic on you.'

Eighteen

It had been quite good fun, actually – creeping around the village dressed as bunnies in the first hours of daylight on Sunday morning.

I thought I'd gone to a fair bit of trouble buying a pair of bunny ears and a fluffy tail online after Callum had asked me to help. I'd even used some old eyeliner to draw whiskers on my face and a rabbit nose – I assumed most of the other villagers helping this morning would be wearing something similar to me. And indeed, some are; but a few have gone the extra mile and are bedecked in full fluffy rabbit costumes.

We're all given baskets of shiny colourful chocolate eggs and told where our allocated houses are – then we set off, creeping stealthily around the village to hide eggs in the front gardens of those families who have agreed to take part – of which there are a fair few! Apparently, the Easter egg hunt has been taking place in Bluebell Wood since the days when the house on the hill was occupied, and the owner decided he wanted to do something special for the villagers and their children. But now, for a small donation to the church, families can have their own Easter Bunny leave eggs for their children to discover on Easter Sunday morning.

As I tiptoe about the village on my own, I realise this is the first time I've done so without Merlin. I'd left him sleeping peacefully back at the cottage along with Hannah, who had murmured something last night about coming to help me, but when my alarm had gone off this morning, I realised hers hadn't even been set! I didn't have the heart to wake her, so I decided it was best to leave her and Merlin snoozing together.

Being out and about this early feels very liberating. The early-morning dew that glistens on the grass and hedges and the slight mist that hangs in the air make it seem even more magical as I creep quietly up paths to leave eggs under bushes and upturned flower pots. Apart from the other 'bunnies' there is no one else about, and I find myself noticing more things about Bluebell Wood than I've ever done before, like the age and style of all the houses and cottages I pass: there's not one new-build amongst them, and I realise just how much this new estate is going to change the look and possibly the feel of the village when it's complete.

How have I not noticed this before? Is it because when I've been out with Merlin, I've often had my head bowed so no one tried to engage me in conversation?

I'd actually got much better at this recently. I found I was no longer quite so afraid of being caught out by a cheery 'Hello!' or a 'How are you today?' and the expectation that I should stop and have a chat for a couple of minutes.

I was almost scared to admit it, but I was becoming much more relaxed around people. It didn't feel like every stranger I met posed a threat.

Some of my egg deliveries have been to the outskirts of the

village, and so as I walk back to the meeting point where all the 'bunnies' are supposed to assemble when they've delivered their eggs, I happen to pass by the field that Merlin and I often walk by when we choose not to go to the wood, and walk around the local footpaths instead.

It's still very early, so I'm surprised to see a man using a mallet to bang a large sign into the ground next to the field. He doesn't look like a farmer; he's dressed in jeans and a casual shirt, and his shoes are heavy boots, but not the practical sort someone working the land would choose to wear, these look more like designer boots, and as I get closer I notice that both his shirt and his jeans follow the same pattern – posy rather than practical.

'Good morning!' I call cheerily in my newfound confident state, completely forgetting I'm dressed as the Easter Bunny. 'Happy Easter.'

The man jumps and drops his mallet, just missing his toes in the process. His sign slides to one side, and he turns towards me with an annoyed expression. Now I can see his face properly I think he looks familiar, but I'm not sure why?

'Yeah . . . ' he says, looking suspiciously at the top of my head. 'Happy Easter.'

'Oh,' I say, touching my rabbit ears. 'I forgot I was wearing these. I'm delivering eggs to the local children.'

The man's expression turns from annoyance to amusement now. 'I had many ideas of what the Easter Bunny might look like, but I never thought it would look like you.'

Feeling embarrassed and also a little uncomfortable under the man's steady gaze, I'm about to hurry away when a large black bird suddenly flies out of a nearby tree; it swoops, just missing the man, who ducks and sidesteps into some mud.

'What the hell?' he says, looking behind him at the bird.

'I think it was a crow,' I tell him, watching as the bird lands on a nearby television aerial. 'You probably startled it. They're not used to many people out and about this early.'

'Stupid thing,' he grumbles, looking with disdain at his mud-covered boots. 'It's a wonder the farmer hasn't had him with his gun by now.'

As I try to give him my best disapproving look, I notice that now he's moved I can see what he was doing before I disturbed him.

Cuckoo Land Homes ~ *Think above the clouds for your next home* it says in fancy black letters on the large sign behind him he'd been trying to hammer in before he was disturbed. There's a cartoon cuckoo flying away at the end of the writing, as though it's sky-written the slogan, and a bold artistic impression of several modern-looking new-build homes set against a bright blue sky, with white clouds dotted carefully overhead.

'That's who's bought this field, is it?' I ask. 'Cuckoo Land Homes.'

The man, still looking annoyed at the bird, steps back and regards the sign. 'It is! Forty deluxe houses and apartments will be built here over the next twelve months.'

'Forty?' I exclaim. 'On this bit of land?'

'Not just this bit, the three surrounding fields have been bought, too. It's going to be a marvellous new estate,' he says proudly.

'But what about the footpaths?' I ask. 'I walk my dog along there. Surely this Cuckoo Land Homes can't get rid of them?'

The man sighs like he's been asked this a few too many times already. 'As we've told your sort before, the footpaths will remain, they will simply weave in and around the houses.'

'But that will ruin the walk. The joy of walking along the footpath is you're amongst nature, not in between people's houses and gardens. And what do you mean *my sort*?' I add as an afterthought, and suddenly I remember where I've seen the man before – he was the idiot driving too fast through the village when he'd nearly mown Merlin and me down as we'd waited to cross the road.

That day he'd been in a sports car, today it would appear by the vehicle pulled up on the side of the road he's driving a sporty-looking Range Rover.

The man sighs again and puts his hand on his hips in a defiant manner. I should have been wary: I was on my own in the early hours of Easter Sunday demanding answers from a man who until a few moments ago had been wielding a large mallet. But for some reason none of this occurs to me, I don't see this weaselly guy as a threat, all I can see right now, very clearly in my mind, are all the new houses that will completely spoil the look and feel of the village.

'You're new here, aren't you?' he asks after he's stared at me for a few moments. He obviously doesn't recognise me even if I do him.

'I might be; why does that matter?'

'It would explain why you think challenging me when I've just come to put a new sign up will make an ounce of difference. We've been through all this with your parish council, and we've held meetings to try to explain what we're going to do to the local residents. We've tried to be pleasant; we've tried to listen to what everyone has to say—'

'But you're still going to build all your new houses,' I

interrupt. 'That's right, isn't it? The residents have objected. The parish council has objected. But you're still going ahead, regardless of what anyone else thinks.'

The man shrugs. 'That's progress for you.'

'That's greed for you,' I say, shaking my head. 'Don't worry, I know exactly how all this works. My ex-husband worked in the same industry. It's not personal, it's business, right?'

'Exactly,' the man says, nodding. 'People need homes.'

I watch him for a moment or two while I think. The man picks up his mallet, and attempts unsuccessfully to remove some of the mud from his boots with it.

'What do you do at this Cuckoo Land Homes?' I ask eventually.

'Why do you want to know that?' he asks, looking at me again as though he's wondering why I'm still here.

'Because I know you're not just some lackey who's been paid to come and erect this sign.'

'How could you possibly know that?'

'You're the boss, aren't you?' I suddenly say, and I glance again at his expensive Range Rover. 'Let me guess, the villagers here have given you so much trouble about this proposed site that no one else dare come and put this sign up. That's why you're doing it so early on a Sunday – no, make that *Easter* Sunday. You thought no one would see you, and you'd be long gone before anyone noticed the sign.'

The man regards me for a moment as though he's considering very carefully what he's going to say next.

'Not just a pretty face, are you?' he settles on eventually. 'Colin Cuckoo, pleased to meet you.' He smiles a cheesy smile and moves towards me, holding out his hand.

Reluctantly I shake it.

'And you're spot on. No one else would come here and put up the sign so I had to do it myself. Your fellow villagers are a scary lot when they get a bee in their country bonnets.' He grins, extremely pleased with his witty retort.

'Maybe they just care about their village and what you're going to do to it,' I reply, folding my arms across my chest.

'Look . . . ?' He waits for me to say my name.

'Ava,' I reply begrudgingly.

'Ava, very pretty.' Colin smiles again, and I recognise at once the smooth talk of a salesman. 'Just like its owner.'

My glare doesn't falter.

'Look, Ava,' Colin says, his annoyance showing again as he realises that his patter isn't working on me, 'this development is going to go ahead whether the village likes it or not. It's taken me long enough to get this far. Now it's been approved and rubber stamped, that's all there is to it. And,' he continues before I can speak again, 'if I have my way it won't stop there. This village is perfect for commuters, with the train station just up the road. It's a direct line to London from here in under an hour. Bluebell Wood is a little goldmine as far as property development is concerned, and I for one intend to mine it for everything it's worth.'

'We'll see about that,' I reply, sounding in my mind like the dashing hero of a swashbuckling drama. If I'd had a sword, I'd have drawn it. But all I had was my basket still with a few foil-covered eggs at the bottom. So, I pick that up and hold it across myself like a shield. 'I know your sort; I was married to one for long enough. You come here with your fancy cars, driving too fast through the village—'

'Whatever do you mean?' Colin asks, looking puzzled. 'You haven't even seen me drive— Oh wait, was that you on the side of the road with your little dog a while back? I thought I recognised you from somewhere.'

He moves towards me so we're almost face to face. 'You were trouble that day, and you're trouble now,' he says in a low voice. 'Can I give you a word of advice?'

Bravely, I hold my ground. Inside I'm shaking, and I want to back away – run away, even. But I'm not going to let this idiot know that.

'You clearly don't realise what I've been through to get everyone onside with this project. I'm not going to back down because a few do-gooders object to some luxury homes being built on their doorstep. The sooner you and the rest of them accept that the better. So, I politely – for now, anyway – suggest that you keep your pretty nose well out of my business.'

'Or what?' I ask fearlessly, keeping eye contact with him.

'You really don't want to know the answer to that question,' he replies, still in the same low voice, but with slightly more menace to it now.

We stare hard at each other, knowing one of us has to give any moment.

But luckily that decision is made for us.

'Hey!' I hear someone call, and I turn to see Lonan biking along the road towards us wearing cycling gear. 'What's going on?' he asks as he reaches us and dismounts from his bike. 'Are you okay, Ava?'

'Yes, I'm fine,' I say, giving Colin a meaningful look. 'Mr Cuckoo here is just leaving.'

Lonan looks between us, and to my relief seems to get it at once.

'Well?' he asks, his powerful dark figure towering over Colin's slight, rodent-like one. 'What's stopping you?'

Colin looks back at his board still leaning to one side against the fence, and decides now isn't the time to continue erecting it. 'Just because the sign isn't up doesn't mean to say it isn't happening,' he says directly to me. 'I'll be back.'

'Just because you repeat words from a movie, doesn't make you the Terminator, either,' Lonan says, and I can't help smiling.

Colin decides it's probably wise he doesn't argue any more. Sulkily he picks up his mallet and we watch him skulk back to his vehicle and drive away.

'Are you all right?' Lonan asks again once he's gone. 'I mean, really? You looked like you were just about to get into a fight with that guy.'

'Yes, I'm fine,' I tell him, but my breathing is fast and shallow as it dawns on me what just happened.

'You don't look it,' Lonan says, eyeing me with concern. 'Who is he, anyway? What is Cuckoo Land Homes? And why, Ava, are you out this early on a Sunday morning dressed as the Easter Bunny?'

Nineteen

'I cannot believe that 'orrible man was 'ere in Bluebell Wood again,' Alouette says angrily, waving her hands around her as we all meet up again. 'The nerve of 'im to come 'ere and put the sign up 'imself.'

Alouette is definitely the most attractive of all the bunnies that are standing outside the church right now discussing what has just taken place at the field. She looks like a slightly holier version of Jessica Rabbit, with her red hair cascading over her shoulders, and her white bunny ears perched on top of her head. But instead of a sexy red dress, Alouette has chosen to wear skin-tight leather trousers, heeled boots and a blue jumper with a fluffy white bunny on the front.

'He's got some nerve, that's for sure,' Jonah says, shaking his head sadly. 'And on this holy day, too.' Jonah has stuck to his usual attire of smart grey trousers, a V-neck jumper and dog collar. His grey furry ears lean towards a more natural bunny, and he has painted a cute bunny nose, whiskers and big buck teeth on his face.

'Men like Colin Cuckoo don't care for the Lord,' Jenny says, a disapproving pucker forming on her lips just under her long whiskers. 'They wouldn't dare; they look downstairs for their guidance, if you know what I mean?' She folds her arms across her ample chest and cocks her head to one side inside the hood of her fluffy pink rabbit costume.

'Sounds like it's a good job you came along, Lonan,' Gavin says, looking with approval at Lonan. 'Goodness knows what might have happened otherwise.' Gavin had until a few moments ago been wearing a Bugs Bunny face mask. It now hangs on elastic around his neck.

'I didn't do anything,' Lonan says calmly, looking strangely normal in his cycling gear among this rather odd gathering of bunnies. 'From what I witnessed, Ava had everything under control. I simply added a bit of support, right, Ava?'

'Perhaps,' I reply, still feeling a little shaky. I look at Callum; he'd been very quiet since I'd returned to the church with Lonan. He has one of the best outfits of all of us. He's wearing a full rabbit costume, a bit like Jenny's, but his is black and white and one of his long ears droops forward, making him look particularly cute. But this rabbit's eyes don't meet with mine and he looks away, so I quickly say, 'Tell me more about this housing development? Jonah told me you tried to stop it?'

'We tried everything when we knew a building company was interested in purchasing the land,' Jenny explains, 'letters, meetings, demonstrations outside the local council offices. They kept saying they were listening to us, taking all our points and objections on board. But when it came down to the final decision it meant nothing. The land was sold and permission was agreed just like that!' She snaps her fingers for emphasis, but the fur of her costume stops it making a clicking sound. 'I reckon that Colin had someone in his pocket. It all went through far too easily considering the amount of objection there were to it from all us residents.'

'What about the farmer who owned the land?'

'Died,' Jenny says pragmatically. 'Left it all to his son who lives in Southampton. He couldn't wait to get shot of it, if you ask me.'

'I'm sure Mr Covey wouldn't have left it to him if he'd known what his son was going to do with it,' Jonah says kindly. 'He was a lovely old man.'

'He knew,' Jenny says, not accepting this. 'He'd have done it himself years ago if he could be bothered with all the legal stuff and the grief he knew everyone would give him.'

Jonah opens his mouth to protest, but Callum interrupts them both. 'Whatever Mr Covey *thought* might happen, it's happened now, and it would seem we can't do anything to change it. Even though I know how much everyone has tried,' he adds when a few of the others begin to bristle again. 'And we need to remember that the development company has agreed to reserve some of the land for green areas and that they're going to build us a new village hall – which no one can deny we desperately need. So, it's not all bad, is it?'

The others don't look too convinced by this, but as usual when Callum speaks no one challenges him. 'Look, guys, let's not stand here and quarrel about this now. Do I need to remind you all you're currently dressed as Easter Bunnies? We don't want any of the children to see us dressed like this bickering with each other, now, do we?'

There are a few murmurs of agreement.

'Let's all go home and try to enjoy Easter with our families. I shall see some of you at the service later, I hope?'

Again, murmurs of 'Definitely' and 'Of course, Father'.

'Right, thank you all for your help this morning; you've done a wonderful job. Let's not allow a little unpleasantness to ruin this special time of year.'

As everyone begins to disperse, Lonan comes over to me and asks if I'm going to be all right.

'I'll be fine now,' I tell him, 'really.'

'I don't like to think of you going back to your cottage alone,' he says.

'I won't be alone; my daughter is staying with me for the weekend.' I look at my watch. 'She'll still be in bed, I expect.'

'Ah, good, it's so very agreeable to have company for special times such as this.'

'Have you anyone with you for Easter?' I ask, suddenly realising that Lonan might be on his own.

'Ah, sadly no. My children live over in the US with my ex-wife. I'll just be using the time to research and hopefully do a little writing.'

'Would you like to have lunch with us?' I suddenly ask, surprising myself as much as Lonan with this suggestion. 'Luckily for you I'm not cooking: my daughter is a great cook and is doing us a lovely roast today.'

'Oh no, I couldn't possibly impose on your time with your daughter.'

'You'll probably be doing us a favour. Hannah is likely to cook far too much for the two of us. She usually does.'

'If you're sure,' Lonan says, looking extremely touched by my offer.

'Definitely. We'll see you later, then – say around one?'

'Wonderful, I'll look forward to it. Ah, Callum. Wonderful idea this,' Lonan says as Callum walks towards us now everyone has left. 'Everyone looks marvellous dressed as bunnies – especially this lovely lady.'

Callum nods his agreement.

'I'll see you later, then,' Lonan says, still smiling as he climbs back on to his bike. 'I'll bring a bottle!'

'Someone's pleased,' Callum says, watching Lonan cycle off happily in the direction of his cottage.

'He hadn't got anyone to spend Easter with,' I explain, 'so I've invited him to have lunch with my daughter and me.'

'Very charitable,' Callum says approvingly.

'Oh,' I suddenly say, 'you're not alone, are you? I assumed you'd be spending today with Jonah after the service.'

I'd been so excited that both Matt and Hannah were coming to visit me that I hadn't given much thought to anything else. I hadn't seen much of Callum since Robin's disappearance, but I'd assumed he was busy with preparations for Easter at the church.

'Jonah has family who live close by,' Callum explains. 'But Jemima has been kind enough to invite me to her home for lunch today.'

My heart sinks.

'It's lovely of her,' Callum continues, 'but I won't be able to stay that long. I have visits this afternoon with some of the vulnerable in the community who can't get to the church today.'

'That's nice,' I try to say in a pleasant tone, even though I'm annoyed with myself for not inviting Callum to the cottage today. It would have been the perfect opportunity for us to spend time together and for him to meet Hannah. 'Nice that Jemima has invited you for lunch, *and* that you visit people today.'

'Part of my job,' Callum says, 'to try to share some kindness with those that need it.'

I wonder if he means Jemima or the other people he's visiting.

'Is your daughter staying with you long?' Callum asks. 'Hannah, isn't it?'

'Yes, Hannah. Sadly, no, she has to go back up to Lincoln tomorrow.'

'Wonderful cathedral in Lincoln,' Callum says approvingly. 'Perhaps *we* could get together tomorrow, then?' he asks hopefully. 'I'm not much of a cook, but I could probably rustle something up for us in the evening if you're free?'

'That sounds lovely,' I reply, smiling at him. 'I'm pretty awful at cooking too. Just as well Hannah is cooking for us today, or Lonan might have got beans on toast.'

'I'm sure it would still have been wonderful,' Callum says kindly.

I'm about to suggest we order in a takeaway to save either of us cooking when suddenly I hear a bark, and I look over Callum's shoulder to see Merlin bounding up the path pulling Hannah along in his wake.

'Sorry, Mum!' Hannah says as they reach us and Merlin makes a huge fuss of me. 'He wouldn't settle when he realised you weren't at the cottage. So I put him on his lead and he pulled me all the way here. Hello,' she says to Callum. 'I like your outfit.'

Callum hurriedly pulls the hood of his costume down, but he still has whiskers painted on his face, which look even stranger now he doesn't have the ears to match.

'Hannah, this is Callum,' I say, introducing them. 'Or should I say Father Crawford? He's the vicar here in Bluebell Wood.'

'Oh, hi,' Hannah says, without a hint of embarrassment. She holds out her hand to Callum. 'Great to meet you. Sorry about the costume comment. You look great.'

'Not a problem and thank you,' Callum says, shaking her hand. 'It's good to meet you too. Your mum has told me a lot about you.'

'Has she now?' Hannah says, looking with interest at me. 'Oh, you're on the quiz team, right? Mum has told me all about that, and how lovely and welcoming everyone has been to her since she came here.'

'Ava has been quite the asset both to the quiz team and to Bluebell Wood as a whole.' Callum casts a gentle smile in my direction, and I smile gratefully back at him.

'I bet she has,' Hannah says, looking between the two of us with much amusement.

'Right, we'd better let Callum go,' I say hurriedly. 'He has a service to prepare for this morning.'

'Yes, indeed I do,' Callum says, glancing at his watch. 'Hiding the Easter eggs took slightly longer than anticipated this morning.' He glances knowingly at me. 'My apologies, Ava.'

'It's fine,' I say quickly, 'these things happen.'

Again, I notice Hannah finding much delight in this exchange.

'I guess we'll see you later at the service then, Father Crawford,' she says, her eyes dancing between the two of us.

'Please call me Callum, I much prefer it,' he says, and Hannah nods. 'I didn't realise you and your mother would be coming to the Easter service, but you'll be most welcome if you do decide to attend.'

'Oh, we'll be there,' Hannah says before I have a chance to speak. 'We wouldn't miss it for the world. Would we, Mum?'

Twenty

‘When did *you* suddenly become so religious?’ I ask a little later that morning as Hannah and I walk towards the church wearing the nicest clothes we can find. We’d both struggled because Hannah hadn’t brought anything remotely smart with her, and I hadn’t worn anything the least bit fancy since I’d arrived in Bluebell Wood. Anything I own that I regard as elegant or for ‘best’ is still stored away in one of the suitcases I’ve yet to unpack.

We’d left a miserable-looking Merlin back at the cottage. He’d made it very clear that he did not appreciate me leaving him twice in one day, even though we’d taken him for an extra-long walk this morning after we’d got back from setting up the Easter egg hunt.

‘I have my moments,’ Hannah says airily. ‘When did *you* become the local siren?’

‘I’m sorry, what?’

‘You know what I mean. All these men suddenly at your beck and call!’

'What on earth are you talking about? I don't have any men at my beck and call.'

'I think you do. Let's start with this Lonan you've invited for lunch today – tell me about him.'

'Lonan is just a friend. I told you, he's new to the village too, and he didn't have anyone to spend today with. I felt sorry for him.'

'He's also the guy that rescued you from the evil property developer this morning, and the guy you went to the quiz with the first time – am I right?'

I'd told Hannah about what happened early this morning when we'd taken Merlin for his walk – mainly because I was still cross about what had happened with Colin Cuckoo and the proposed housing estate, but also so I could explain why I'd invited Lonan to lunch with us.

'Yes, but that doesn't mean anything. Not what you're inferring, anyway.'

'Hmm, I'll be the judge of that when I meet him. Okay then, what about the hunky vicar that you've avoiding telling me about, even though the sparks fly between you so clearly it might as well be Bonfire Night!'

'I think that's a slight over-exaggeration.'

'Perhaps, but you don't deny it . . . ?'

I sigh. Hannah had been pretty perceptive when she was a child, but now she was an adult I couldn't hide anything from her.

'Okay, I'll admit it: I like Callum. There, is that enough for you?'

'You like him or you *like* him?'

'It's difficult.'

'Why?'

'Isn't it obvious?' I gesture to the church we're walking towards.

'Because he's a vicar?'

'Shush,' I whisper, aware that there are others now beginning to head the same way as us. 'Yes, because of that.'

'But why? Vicars are allowed to have sex.'

'Hannah!'

'Well, they are, aren't they?'

'It's not like that. There's more to it.'

'Really? You're telling me you don't have the hots for him? I think I would if I was your age. Actually, scrub that – the guy is fit whatever age you are.'

'He is quite fit, actually,' I say, pretending I don't understand. 'I've seen him out jogging a lot.'

'*Mum*, you know what I mean.'

'Yes, of course I know what you mean. But being a vicar complicates things, doesn't it?'

'Why?'

'Because it does. You know I have my issues with ... How can I put this?'

'Your belief ... After what happened, that's totally understandable.'

'You know about that?' I ask, astonished.

We stop walking.

'Mum, I know about lots of things you think I don't. Matt and I both do. We're not blind. You went through a hell of a trauma. Sorry,' she apologises, looking at the church. 'No one would blame you for feeling the way you do.'

'I doubt Callum would see it that way.'

'You might be surprised.'

'Anyway,' I say, seeing Jemima hurrying into the churchyard

ahead of us, 'I don't think we're the only ones to notice Callum's many qualities. I wouldn't want to tread on anyone's toes.'

Hannah follows my gaze. 'Who's that?' she asks.

'That's Jemima, the head teacher of the school.'

'And you think she has the hots for Callum too?'

I shrug. 'Possibly, she seems very keen on him.'

'Right, let's find out,' Hannah says, and she sets off before I can stop her.

'Hello, Ava,' Jemima says as she sees us approaching. She glances at Hannah.

'Hi,' I say, catching up. 'This is my daughter Hannah; she's staying with me for Easter. Hannah, this is Jemima.'

'Pleased to meet you, Hannah,' Jemima says, shaking Hannah's hand.

'And you. You're obviously a keen churchgoer,' Hannah says, diving straight in and making me squirm.

'I like to support our local church,' Jemima says, smiling. 'As do most of the village.'

'I hear from Mum you have a rather fab vicar here,' Hannah continues. 'I guess that helps to attract a good crowd.'

'Yes, Callum is pretty special. He's always been very good to me.'

'Jemima is having Callum over for lunch today,' I tell Hannah.

Hannah opens her eyes wide, but Jemima speaks first: 'That's what was supposed to be happening, but my oven has decided to mess around,' she explains, looking exasperated. 'It's just packed up. I can't get someone to come out and mend it until Tuesday because it's Easter, so it's all a bit of a pickle, to be honest. What will poor Callum do?' she says and I follow her gaze to where Callum is standing welcoming worshippers into the church. He's wearing his full robes and looks incredibly attractive as he smiles at everyone he greets. 'I'm supposed to be feeding him early so he can go out and do good in the village this afternoon.'

'Why don't you both come and eat with us,' I hear Hannah say while I'm still gazing at Callum. 'We could put our dinner back so we eat later after Callum has done his thing. Couldn't we, Mum?'

'Er, yes, I suppose so,' I say, swiftly turning back to them both.

'Goodness, that's very kind of you, but I wouldn't want to put you out,' Jemima replies.

'Really, it's no bother, is it, Mum? We already have someone called Lonan coming over, so if you bring your food over after the service we can put it into Mum's huge oven and we'll all have a feast together a little later this afternoon. We can let Lonan know we're going to be eating later – I'm sure he won't mind.'

'It's really is very generous of you,' Jemima says, looking at me now. 'If you're sure, Ava?'

'The more the merrier. Hannah is a great cook.' I give Hannah a meaningful look that tells her I know exactly what she's up to, and she winks slyly back at me. 'If she thinks she can cope with everyone, then I have every confidence in her.'

It's a long time since I've been to a church on Easter Sunday.

Even though I've never been a regular churchgoer, I'd always had a belief in something – I'd never been quite sure what that thing is, only that I felt there has to be more to life than this.

That belief had been wiped out after *that day*, and until I'd come to Bluebell Wood and met Callum, I hadn't really given it much thought at all. So contrary to what I'd expected, I'm surprised to find my reservations diminishing as the service goes on. As we sing cheerful hymns together, listen to Callum's sermon, pray alongside him and wince at Mrs Bunting's slightly dodgy playing of the church organ, I join in with everybody else and enjoy myself.

I'd never really considered what Callum might be like leading a church service. I'd seen him being both the parish priest and simply being himself, and although it's still difficult for me to piece my opposing feelings for the two sides of Callum together, I understand that what he's doing today is an important part of who he is.

As Callum leads the choir down the aisle at the end of the service, he gives me a quick wink as he passes.

I can't help but smile back, but as Callum and the choir continue on by, and I sit with a silly grin on my flushed face, I inadvertently catch Jemima's eye as she watches us from the front pews.

'Thank you for coming,' I hear Callum say several times as the congregation files out of the church in front of us. 'And a Happy Easter to you.'

'Ah, Miss Swan, what a pretty dress,' he says formally, as Jemima arrives in front of him.

'Thank you, Father,' she says, swishing the skirt around a little.

Callum smiles serenely.

'I do hope you don't mind, but there's been an unavoidable change of plan,' Jemima explains quickly. 'We're now going to be eating with Ava at her cottage later this afternoon when you've finished visiting your parishioners. I'm afraid I've got issues with my cooker.'

Callum looks unruffled as ever. 'I'm sorry to hear that, but I'm sure we'll all have a wonderful time in Ava's little cottage, and I don't have evensong tonight, so there'll be no need for me to rush off anywhere. Very kind of you, Ava,' he says, looking over the heads of the elderly couple in front of me waiting to thank him.

I smile.

'Perhaps we can postpone our meal to another time, though?' Jemima says. 'It's been a while, hasn't it?'

'Of course,' Callum says, nodding. 'You know I'm always available for my parishioners. Ah, Doris and George,' he says, moving on from Jemima to greet the couple in front of me. 'Lovely to see you again. How's the hip, George?'

Jemima continues out of the church.

'Hello again,' Callum says to Hannah and me as Doris and George eventually move along. 'Did you enjoy the service?'

'Man, you rock at this church stuff!' Hannah says, making both Callum and me smile. 'Never really been churchgoers, have we, Mum? But that service was amazing. I feel fantastic.'

'Thank you, Hannah,' Callum says smiling. 'That's certainly the best feedback I've had in a long time. I understand from Jemima we're coming to yours to eat now, Ava? he asks, turning to me. 'I do hope we're not imposing?'

'Not at all,' I say. 'It will be lovely to have you there, and like I said before, Hannah is cooking, so you'll be in safe hands.'

Callum laughs and uses this as a reason to lean in towards me. 'I always feel in safe hands when I'm with you,' he whispers into my ear as he shakes my hand. 'I'll see you both later then,' he says in his normal voice, and quickly moves on to the next person waiting to speak to him.

As we walk out of the church together, Hannah is muttering something about what a great guy Callum is, but I'm still recovering from hearing his soft sensuous voice whispering in my ear to say anything at all.

Twenty-one

'Is everything all right in the kitchen?' I ask Hannah as she comes through to the sitting room wearing an apron and carrying a glass of wine.

'Absolutely fine, Mum. Stop fussing.'

'I can't help it. Cooking for this many people would worry me senseless.'

'Which is why you have me to do it for you. Now, let's go mingle with your guests. I'm eager to know more about them.'

Lonan had been the first to arrive carrying two expensive bottles of wine. He was beautifully turned out as always, in a designer shirt and tailored trousers. He'd been closely followed by Jemima, who had changed from the dress she'd worn for church into a more relaxed outfit of casual black cropped trousers and a pink silk blouse. As promised, she'd dropped round earlier with as much of her original uncooked meal as she could for Hannah to add to our own. Finally, we are joined by Callum, who I'm happy to see has also changed:

from his clerical robes into a smart pair of navy-blue trousers and a pale blue shirt.

'I didn't have anything suitable to bring,' he says apologetically as he walks through the door carrying a cardboard box. 'So I brought some Easter eggs left over from this morning's hunt.'

'Perfect,' I say, taking the box from him. 'I can't remember the last time I had an Easter egg.'

While Hannah pops back and forth from the kitchen, I keep everyone's drinks topped up. It has been so long since I've properly entertained, I feel like I've forgotten how to do it, so I'm relieved to find that all my guests are happily making their own conversation without needing me to intervene, and even happier to discover that yet again I'm able to cope with a number of people in a small space like the cottage, when a few months ago it would have freaked me out to be in this much company.

Was it the cottage that was helping me to cope? It was definitely a safe and welcoming space to be in. Or was it the village as a whole? Everyone was so friendly here that now I'd got used to it, I actually looked forward to the idle chitchat that always took place when you ventured out and about. Whatever it was, I had much to be grateful for on this Easter Sunday.

'You have a beautiful garden, Ava,' Lonan says, gazing out of the French windows. 'The birds in particular seem to love it.'

'I can't take credit for the garden; most of it was in place before I arrived. I just have to do a little weeding now and then. I do have quite a few birds visiting the table now, though, which I'm very pleased about.'

'They bring Ava gifts,' Callum announces as we all look out of the window. I frown at him. This wasn't something I wished to share with everyone – especially Jemima, seeing as I still thought the bits of pottery were from the school mosaic.

'Gifts?' Jemima asks from where she's perched on the arm of the chair. 'How so?'

I tell them quickly about the things I'd found on the bird table.

'How wonderful!' Lonan says with delight. 'They're thanking you for feeding them.'

'Perhaps.' I shrug.

'What an odd collection of things, though,' Jemima says. 'I wonder if it means anything.'

'Oh, I doubt it,' I say hurriedly, keen to move on from this. Luckily Jemima doesn't seem to notice any connection between my description of broken pottery and the school mosaic. 'It's probably just junk they've found on their travels. How is your book going, Lonan? I've inherited a lot of books, as you can see from the bookshelves, but I don't think there's one of yours on there.'

'Then I shall have to rectify that!' Lonan says. 'I shall bring you a signed copy of my latest novel.'

'Thank you.'

'I love to read but I don't think I could ever write a book,' Jemima says. 'I have no idea how you'd even go about starting one.'

Lonan and Jemima begin a long conversation about how Lonan writes his books, while Callum and I listen politely. I glance across at Callum while they're talking and he smiles at me.

Another drink? I mouth at him, noticing his empty glass.

He nods. But as I pass him on my way to the kitchen and take his glass, instead of letting me go he gets up and follows me into the hall.

'Thank you for inviting me today,' he says as we pause

between rooms. 'Jemima must have been at her wits' end when her cooker went down. I know she worries unnecessarily about these types of things. She can be a little overprotective of me at times.'

I wonder what he means.

'I'd love to take the credit, but it was Hannah who saved the day at the eleventh hour by inviting you.'

Callum grins.

'What?' I ask him.

'You may not realise it, but we both just quoted the Bible.'

'Did we?'

'Yes, both "wits' end" and "the eleventh hour" come from the Good Book, as do many well-known sayings.' He thinks. 'Like if I'd cooked for you today it might have been "the blind leading the blind".'

'Now that I can definitely relate to,' I say, smiling. 'Well, you learn something new every day, don't you? Oh, is that one too?'

'No, I'm afraid not. But I feel it should be. Perhaps I'll suggest it next time there's a rewrite.'

I glance at him for a moment, and then realise he's joking.

'Ha ha, very funny.'

'I try,' Callum says, smiling at me.

'Don't mind me,' Hannah says, suddenly appearing from the kitchen. 'Just taking a break from the magic I'm creating in there.'

'You're doing remarkably well, suddenly feeding everyone like this,' Callum says approvingly.

'I know, I'm like the loaves and fishes story, right? Feeding the five thousand on barely anything.'

Callum grins. 'Yes, exactly that. Jesus would be proud of you.'

'Too right he would.' Hannah grins back, lifting her glass.

'Miracle worker me.' And she continues on into the sitting room, but not before winking at me behind Callum's back.

I shake my head. 'Sorry.'

'About what?' Callum asks. 'I'm all about having fun with the Bible. The best way to teach people is to make them laugh and enjoy themselves.'

'You're a special man,' I suddenly hear myself saying, before I have a chance to stop myself.

'And you, Ava,' Callum whispers, looking secretly pleased, 'are a very special woman.' He moves closer to me, and for one tiny millisecond I think we're about to kiss. But then Jemima appears in the hall.

'Oh, sorry,' she says, looking startled to find us out here together. 'Just looking for the ladies' room.'

'The bathroom is upstairs,' I say, leading her to the staircase. 'First door on the left.'

'Thanks.' Jemima looks briefly at me and then at Callum. 'I hope I didn't interrupt anything . . . '

'No,' we both insist, a little too quickly. 'Not at all.'

Jemima doesn't look convinced, but says nothing before hurrying up the stairs.

I look back at Callum and pull an awkward expression. 'Perhaps we'd better get you that drink?' I whisper.

He nods. 'I'll just wait in here, shall I?' he says, gesturing back to the sitting room.

'It might be best. I'll be right back.'

I head into the kitchen and try to pour some wine into Callum's glass, but I find my hand is shaking, and I have to stop and put the bottle down for a moment to calm down.

'Oh Lord,' I say, taking a deep breath. Then I realise what I've said and I smile. This time I look up while I speak. 'Look,

I really don't know if there's someone or something up there controlling what we do down here, like some grand puppet master.' I pause for a moment to think. 'And if you really are up there, then I have some big issues I need to take up with you sometime. Although you probably know what they are already, don't you?' I pause again: although I hated myself for doing so, talking like this was actually making me feel better. 'But at this very moment, if Callum is some sort of test you're putting me through to see how I fare, then you're making it extremely hard for me to resist.'

The dinner party goes really well; better than I'd hoped.

We're just pausing before we have dessert – a combination of apple pie and ice cream from our original dinner and a chocolate mousse and whipped cream from Jemima's.

'That dinner was truly wondrous, Hannah,' Lonan says, patting his full stomach. 'And you're not a chef by trade?'

Hannah shakes her head. 'Nope, I work in the litigation department for a law firm in Lincoln. Cooking is simply a hobby of mine.'

'What a wide and varied group we are . . . ' Jemima says, waving her glass airily around the table. 'We have someone who works in law, a handsome priest, a best-selling author, and me a little ol' teacher.' She tilts her glass towards me. 'What is it you did again, Ava? Before you moved here?'

'I worked for an advertising company doing promotions and events,' I say, unsure where this is heading. Jemima has had a tad more wine than everyone else, and has been quite forthright with her questions and opinions during dinner.

'How fabulous. And that was in London, wasn't it?'

I nod.

'Your two worlds: BBW and ABW.'

We all look at her, confused by this.

'Before Bluebell Wood and After Bluebell Wood!' she cries in delight, seeing our confusion. 'Those worlds must feel very different to you, Ava?' she goes on, with a serious expression. 'However do you cope?'

'Yes, they are a bit,' I reply calmly, although I can already feel anxiety beginning to manifest itself in the pit of my stomach. 'But I really like it here. I've met some lovely people who I'd like to think of as friends.' I look across at Callum, who smiles back at me, and then Lonan, who lifts his glass. 'So I have no desire to return to London at the moment.'

'But why did you leave in the first place?' Jemima continues, unabashed. 'It's such a huge decision giving up what must have been a well-paid successful job, and moving from the capital to this tiny village in the middle of nowhere.'

'We're hardly in the middle of nowhere,' Callum interjects when he sees me beginning to look uncomfortable. 'Cambridge isn't that far down the road, and Peterborough the other way.'

'My dearest Callum, I love this village, you know I do. Everyone, including your good self, has made me most welcome since I came here. Did you know I was like you not so long ago, Ava? A newbie. But dearest Callum took me under his wing, and now I'm a true blue . . . blue . . .Bluebellian!' she cries, delighted to have found the right word. 'But you must all agree we are out in the sticks here.'

Callum, looking a tad embarrassed, gazes down into his glass, but Lonan as always has a clever retort.

'Of course we're out in the sticks,' he pipes up. 'We're living in a wood!'

We all laugh, some of us a little nervously.

I knew why I felt on edge, Jemima was pushing me into areas I didn't feel comfortable exploring in public, but why was Callum looking so uneasy?

'That's actually the origin of that phrase,' Lonan explains. 'To be in the sticks means to live where there are lots of twigs, i.e. the countryside.'

'Very good, very good,' Jemima says, tapping Lonan's arm. 'But compared to somewhere like London, there's not too much going on, is there?' She turns back to me for my response.

Hannah is looking at me with a concerned expression now; she knows why I don't want to keep talking about this, but the others, including Jemima, have no idea. I try to deflect Jemima's questions as naturally as I can.

'I thought it might be a bit like that when I first came here,' I respond calmly, 'but I wanted to come somewhere quiet, somewhere I could be alone, and that's why I chose Bluebell Wood. It seemed perfect to me: peaceful, safe, away from the hustle and bustle of the city. But I actually speak to more people here in a day than I ever did when I lived in London – people who actually seem interested in my life and how my day is going. In London, people only speak to you when they want something from you, not to make pleasant conversation or to brighten your day. And that, to me, is worth more than any over-inflated salary, fancy apartment or high-flying career.'

Lonan applauds. 'Hear, hear,' he says. 'I agree with you, Ava, give me Bluebell Wood over the big smoke any day.'

'I have to agree too,' Callum joins in. 'I spent the first couple of years of my clerical life in a tough East End parish. Don't get me wrong, it was rewarding being there, trying to make a difference, but I'd take Bluebell Wood any time over living in London. I, too, have met some wonderful people here.'

He glances at me, and I smile shyly back at him.

'Seems like the gentlemen all agree with you, Ava,' Jemima announces, in a voice just a little too loud. She tops up her glass again and smiles happily at us as she sips from it, completely unaware of any unease she might have caused me with her questions.

'I think now might be a good time for dessert,' Hannah says abruptly, standing up.

'Yes! Let me help you,' Lonan says, quickly putting down his glass.

Lonan and Hannah disappear to the kitchen together, leaving us in a strange, slightly awkward silence.

'Have I said something I shouldn't?' Jemima says, a deeply concerned expression spreading over her face. 'I sense I may have put my foot in it just now, Ava, talking about your previous life in London.'

'No, not at all,' I reply hurriedly.

'I guess I'm just a little bit jealous of you,' she says, casually leaning back in her chair, then swiftly shooting forwards again when she almost topples backwards. She reaches for the bottle of wine and distractedly refills her glass, which is only half empty, while she talks.

'You have this quaint little cottage, two successful children who obviously adore you. And you seem to have charmed everyone in Bluebell Wood since your arrival, including our lovely vicar here!' She waves her glass towards Callum.

Both Callum and my cheeks flush a shade of salmon pink.

'It took me ages to be accepted here,' she continues. 'The old head teacher was adored; no one wanted a new one when she retired and moved away – especially one as young as me. Did they, Callum?'

'I don't know about that,' Callum says diplomatically.

'Oh, come on, it was the same for you. The previous vicar had been here ages when you came along. I heard no one was too keen when you turned up with your new ideas and modern ways, but you fitted in a lot quicker than I did.'

'Perhaps,' Callum says, looking uneasy.

'Callum took me under his wing,' Jemima continues, blissfully unaware of any awkwardness around the table. Now any discomfort was much more in Callum's court than mine, but I was very keen to hear what Jemima had to say. 'Didn't you, Callum?'

Callum doesn't respond, so she continues.

'He took me under his wing when I arrived here, like the Good Samaritan he is, and helped me to become a part of the village. We were both fairly new at the time, but Callum had been here just that little bit longer, so he wasn't regarded as *a stranger to these parts*,' she attempts a southern drawl as she says this last part. 'And for that, I'll always be grateful to him.'

Jemima lifts her glass to Callum, but Callum just nods his appreciation.

'So when I noticed he was helping another newcomer to the village . . . I have to say, I was a tiny bit jealous, Ava.'

I jump a little in my chair; I hadn't seen this coming back to me at all.

'And then I realised that there was more to it than simply loving thy neighbour.' She grins. 'Have you heard what I've been doing, Callum? I've been quoting the Bible for you – how fabulous is that? The Good Samaritan and "love thy neighbour"?'

Callum nods. 'Yes, I've heard it. Very good.'

Jemima nods happily. 'Yes, I was rather pleased with both of those. Anyway, I'm getting off track, where was I . . . ?' She thinks for a moment, but neither Callum nor I feel the need to prompt her. 'Oh yes! But then I saw how the two of you look at each other, and I knew that how Callum thinks about you, Ava, is not the way he thinks about the rest of his parishioners, if you know what I mean!' And she gives us both a long salacious wink.

Callum and I don't respond, we don't even look at each other; we simply look down at the tablecloth, totally mortified.

'Ah, look at the pair of you,' she continues, smiling at us now, 'like a couple of teenagers with their first crush. I'd say get a room, but I'm not sure the Church allows that, do they, Father?'

To our enormous relief Hannah and Lonan return at that moment; Hannah carrying a plate of apple pie and a bowl of chocolate mousse, and Lonan a jug of cream and a tub of ice cream.

They pause at the door and stare at the three of us sitting awkwardly around the table, Callum and I not knowing where to look, and Jemima still appearing to be completely unaware of what she's said.

'I don't know if I need a knife to cut this pie I'm holding, or the atmosphere in this room?' Hannah asks, looking at us with a bewildered expression.

'What ever do you mean, my lovely?' Jemima says, encouraging them to bring their sweet treats to the table. 'We're simply having a lovely chat, aren't we?'

Not looking at Callum, I hurriedly help Hannah make room for the desserts on the table.

'Golly, what *have* we missed?' Lonan asks, putting his jug and tub down on the table and retaking his seat. 'It's obviously something good, by the looks on your faces?'

'I had a glance at your bookshelves earlier, Ava,' Lonan says a little later while we're all happily tucking into our desserts.

Any earlier embarrassment lingering at the table like an unwanted guest has now, much to my relief, left.

'Oh yes?'

'You've got quite the library of books there. Some of them are quite old, too. They were the previous tenant's, you say?'

'Yes, Evelyn was obviously quite the bookworm. Some of them have come in very handy since I arrived, particularly the nature books. I know all about birds and wildflowers now, and probably far too much about the different trees and plants Merlin and I find on our daily walks in the wood.'

'I've been doing some research on this area since I arrived. I always like to know the story of a place I'm staying in, and it seems Bluebell Wood has quite the history.'

'Ooh, like what?' Hannah asks keenly.

'As you all probably know, the wood here is ancient woodland, which means it's existed since at least the sixteenth century or before. But I think you can trace this area's history back even further, possibly to the reign of William the Conqueror.'

'Really?' I say, surprised. 'How do you know that?'

'It's to do with something called Forest Law – where the Norman kings of England procured areas of land for their own private hunting rights. This was mainly woodland, like here at Bluebell Wood. Which by the way was originally called Kingswood, according to the records.'

'I didn't know that,' Callum says. 'I'm surprised the church doesn't have some documentation on that.'

'You probably do if you search for it,' Lonan says with conviction. 'Churches hold a lot of useful information regarding the history of an area.'

'Jonah would probably know more,' Callum says, 'he's very good with the history of this area. He's always on at me to learn more about it.'

'I may well have to seek him out, then,' Lonan says, nodding, 'and pick his brains for further information. From what I know already, Kingswood, unusually for forest land, was allowed to have a small settlement on it – not that uncommon after 1217 and the charter of the forest was brought in, which gave some land rights back to the common man. But Kingswood was different; I believe this small area was owned by one family even before that, when in theory it should still have been owned by the King.'

'Go on,' I encourage when he pauses for effect. Lonan was obviously the consummate storyteller, both on the page and in person.

'I'm still doing my research, but I think those ruins where you found young Robin may be the house where the landowner originally lived. Like I say, he shouldn't have owned forest land, but everything is pointing that way. As a writer, I'm intrigued, I have to tell you. There's definitely a story here.'

'Sounds amazing, Lonan,' Jemima pipes up again now. She'd been very quiet since we served dessert, and I'd been hoping she might remain that way. 'But will it be a love story you uncover, I wonder?' She gives Callum and me a meaningful look.

Oh no. Not again.

But Lonan simply looks with interest at his fellow dinner guests.

'A romance is always a wonderful tale to tell,' he says thoughtfully. 'I always find some of the best love stories begin in secret.'

Twenty-two

'Thank goodness,' Callum says, as I close the door and return to the kitchen to begin clearing up.

Lonan and Hannah are currently escorting Jemima back to her house. She'd been swaying quite a bit when she'd stood up the last time, and Lonan had offered to walk her home. Hannah had volunteered to go with them for a bit of fresh air, although I suspect she had another motive, and that was to leave Callum and me on our own together.

'I didn't realise Jemima had had that much to drink,' I say, beginning to load plates into the dishwasher and dirty pans into the sink to be hand washed in the bowl of soapy water I've just filled. 'But she was certainly . . . how can I put it? *Honest* I think the word is.'

'She was that.' Callum puts the now empty wine glasses on the side to be washed too. 'Would you like me to wash or dry?'

'You don't have to do anything,' I say, putting a tab in the dishwasher and closing the door. 'You're a guest. But since you've offered so nicely,' I grin at him, 'dry?' I throw him a clean tea towel, which he deftly catches.

I pull on a pair of rubber gloves, and start with the wine glasses.

'I don't think Jemima meant to cause trouble, though,' I say, rubbing frothy bubbles around the rim of a glass with a sponge. 'It was the alcohol talking, that's all. We've all had a little too much on occasion.' I glance at Callum.

'Yes, even me.' Callum grins. 'Especially in my younger days.'

He waits for the glass to drain a little before he lifts it up to dry it. 'Did it bother you?' he asks. 'What she was saying?'

I glance at him, wondering if he means what I think he means.

'About you helping her out when she first came here?' I ask, hedging my bets.

'Er . . . yes that.'

I shrug and concentrate on washing the glass in my hand. 'Why would it? It was good of you to help her. It's obviously brought you closer.'

Callum pauses while he dries the next glass.

'Ava, Jemima is a fine teacher and a lovely young woman. I felt for her when she first came to the village. Like she said, we had a lot in common. It took a while for the villagers to accept me when I first came here too, so it seemed only fitting that I should help Jemima. She reminded me a lot of Jena, my younger sister, actually.'

'I didn't know you had a sister?' I say, looking at him.

'There's a lot you don't know about me, Ava,' Callum replies, polishing his glass extra hard. 'What I felt for Jemima was only friendship, and that's definitely as far as it goes – on both our parts. It's important to me that you understand that.'

I don't look at Callum, but I feel my insides flutter a little. 'Yes, I understand,' I say quietly.

A companionable silence falls over the kitchen again as we continue to wash up.

'I did wonder for a while if Lonan might make a good match for Jemima,' Callum says thoughtfully as he dries the last glass and rests it on the worktop. 'But if what I've heard is true . . .'

'What do you mean?' I ask, looking at him. 'What have you heard?'

Callum mischievously shakes his head. 'I probably shouldn't say anything.'

'You have now. Stop teasing me and tell!' I demand.

Callum grins. 'I'm a vicar, Ava. What I hear and say is sacrosanct.'

'And I have a bowl of hot soapy water here. If you don't want to find yourself covered in it, then share your gossip, Father Crawford – sacrosanct or not!'

'Okay, okay!' Callum says, holding up his tea towel in front of him. 'I surrender.'

'*So* . . . what have you heard?' I ask, brandishing a soap-covered wooden spoon at him.

'That Lonan has eyes for another fair lady of this village.'

'Who?' I ask, my spoon dropping.

'What's it worth?' Callum says, grinning.

'I told you: you not getting soaked!'

'How about something else?' Callum says, suddenly looping his tea towel around the back of my neck and gently pulling me closer to him.

'Like what?' I whisper, unable to look anywhere other than into Callum's pale blue eyes.

'Like this,' Callum murmurs, pulling me so close to him that our faces are barely millimetres apart.

I feel his warm breath on my lips just before he kisses me. I close my eyes and allow myself to become lost in him. His soft lips on mine, his smell, his touch. It all feels so right.

His kisses become more eager, and I feel the tea towel drop away as it's replaced by one of his hands on the back of my neck, and the other around my waist, all the time pulling my body closer to his.

My body and mind are now in total surrender, and any previous reservations I may have had about allowing a priest to make me feel like this are long gone.

Suddenly I become aware that Callum's hold on me has loosened, and he isn't quite as close as he had been a few moments ago.

I open my eyes to see him staring at me. I'd like to have described it as gazing, but it was very definitely a stare.

'What's wrong?' I ask, slightly breathless.

'I'm sorry,' Callum says, shaking his head. 'I … I shouldn't have.'

'You shouldn't have what?' I say lightly. 'I was enjoying that.' I smile at him, but he doesn't return my amusement.

'I got carried away,' he says, his head down.

'I'm not complaining.'

'Stop making a joke of this,' he snaps. 'I'm being serious.'

'Sorry,' I say, surprised by his tone.

'No, I'm sorry,' Callum says. 'Sorry about everything. I should go.'

'What do you mean?' I ask, as he suddenly makes his way towards the kitchen door. 'We haven't done anything wrong, have we?'

I follow him into the hall and watch as he grabs his jacket from the coat stand.

'No, *you* haven't done anything wrong, Ava,' he says, turning back towards me. 'But I have.'

He opens the door, and jumps as he finds Hannah and Lonan on the step about to come back in.

'I have to go,' he says to them. 'Thank you for a lovely meal, Hannah.'

'Do you have to?' Hannah says, looking surprised by his haste.

'Yes, I'm afraid I do.' He glances back at me. 'Thank you for your hospitality, Ava. It was most . . . neighbourly of you.'

Hannah and Lonan stand back to let him pass, and Callum wastes no time in speeding away along the path.

'What was all that about?' Hannah asks, closing the door behind her as she and Lonan step back into the cottage.

'I have no idea,' I reply, staring at the closed door. 'No idea whatsoever.'

Twenty-three

The wood is always so calming, I think as Merlin and I walk briskly along one of the paths a few days later. No matter what turmoil my mind might be in, the wood always has the ability to smooth it out and slow it back down to a comfortable pace.

Today, my mind is particularly chaotic due to a variety of reasons.

Hannah has left Bluebell Wood and gone back to her life in Lincoln, but not before gently breaking it to me that she'd got a promotion at work, and she's going to be transferring to their head office in central London.

'I left it until now to tell you, Mum,' she'd said the morning she was due to depart, 'because I wanted to see how you were doing. You seem so much better since you've come here to Bluebell Wood. I hoped it wouldn't worry you quite as much now as it would have done before.'

I'd immediately put on a brave face, and assured her that I did feel much better, and that of course I'd worry about her, but perhaps not to the extent I would have done previously.

Hannah had seemed happy with my reassurances, and had left content that her mother was going to be fine.

Except I wasn't fine.

I now had a son who was temporarily living in New York, and a daughter who was about to move to London permanently. I was happy for them both, of course I was, but that wasn't going to stop me worrying. Every parent worries about their offspring, especially when they leave home. But I had an added layer of fear. One that, day to day, I was gradually taking control of; but when prodded a bit too hard, that underlying torment rose far too easily to the surface once more.

That wasn't the only reason for my distress today as I stride along underneath the protection of the trees.

The way I'd left things with Callum on Easter Sunday was also causing me much anguish.

After Hannah had left on Easter Monday, I'd sat in the garden for a while just thinking. It was a lovely day, and the warmth of the sunshine on my skin, and watching the continual comings and goings of the birds to the table, had temporarily eased some of the pain that his sudden departure had caused.

Why had he left like that? Had I said or done something wrong? I'd gone over and over in my mind what had caused his change of heart. One moment he'd been all over me – which I hadn't minded in the least – and the next, his ardour had completely cooled, and it felt like what we'd been doing had been nothing but an embarrassment to him.

I sigh as we walk on, getting further into the woods.

It really was a complete mystery to me, and one Callum obviously didn't want to solve. The 'dinner date' we'd casually suggested for Monday had come and gone without a word. I hadn't seen or heard from Callum since Sunday.

I was sure everything he'd told me about Jemima had been true. Jemima had actually popped round on Easter Monday just after Hannah had left, with a bunch of flowers and a mountain of apologies.

She'd been mortified she'd got so tipsy, and could only remember some of what had gone on. But what she did tell me only backed up what Callum had said.

'Callum is very dear to me, Ava,' she'd told me over a cup of tea. 'I can be a little protective of him, I have to admit. But I only want him to be happy, and I think you two would be really good together.'

Now, as I walk through the woods with Merlin, I'm trying desperately not to stress too much about either Hannah or Callum and concentrate solely on the trees and the birdsong, and the healing power of nature, which always seemed to calm me down and soothe my soul.

'Hello, you,' I say as I feel Merlin brush past my legs. He'd dropped back, stopping to sniff something, and now he was trying to get ahead of me on the path once more. 'Not tiring yet, then?'

Merlin never seemed to tire. We could walk for hours and he would still have the same spring in his four furry feet that he'd had when we set off.

Luckily for him, I was in the mood for a long walk. The longer I spent in the woods, the more my problems seemed to ease, and currently that could only be a good thing.

When we reach the stream we both stop for a drink from the cool running water.

'Callum is right, this is amazing,' I say to Merlin, as he laps happily beside me. 'If only they could bottle this taste.'

As had happened many times over the last few days, at

just the thought of Callum, my heart, which once would have leapt at his name, now sinks deep into the pit of my stomach.

'Come on,' I encourage Merlin, 'let's see if we can get all the way up to those ruins again before we turn back.'

To my surprise, as we reach the top of the hill and approach the ruins that we'd found Robin hiding in, I notice two figures moving around.

And as we get closer, I see that it's Robin again, but this time he's accompanied by Linnet.

'Merlin!' Robin shouts with glee as he spies his furry friend galloping towards him. Linnet waves at me, and at a steadier pace we reach each other a few moments after Robin and Merlin.

'Hello. What are you two doing all the way up here?' I ask Linnet as Robin and Merlin play happily with each other a little way away from us.

'Robin loves to come up here,' Linnet says, watching her son. 'I don't know what it is, but he comes alive when he's all the way up on this hill.'

'Maybe it's the air,' I reply, half joking. 'It's so much higher up than down in the depths of the wood.'

'You could be right,' Linnet says. 'Whatever it is, it's good to see him so happy. How are you?' she asks. 'I haven't seen you since before Easter. How was your weekend?'

'Interesting . . . ' I say, and I grimace a little.

'Oh really?' Linnet asks. 'That doesn't sound too good.'

'Actually, that's not fair, most of it was great. My daughter came down from Lincoln for a few days, and I had a few guests for dinner.'

'I have to admit I have heard about your dinner party,' Linnet says, grinning. 'It sounded like quite the occasion.'

'Who have you heard that from?' I ask, surprised she'd mentioned it. 'Don't tell me the local gossip machine stretches as far as the inner workings of my cottage.'

'I heard it from Lonan, actually,' she says, suddenly looking coy. 'Robin, don't run off too far with Merlin now!'

My head turns to where Merlin and Robin are happily running around in the ruins, then back to Linnet.

'Oh really?' I ask, suddenly interested in why she's so bashful about this. 'Did you bump into him in the village?'

'He came to see us,' Linnet says, still looking self-conscious. 'Just after Robin went missing, to see how he was doing.'

'And . . . ?' I ask, smiling. Could this be what Callum was hinting at when he mentioned hearing something about Lonan?

'And we sat and chatted, and he was really nice, and then he dropped in again the day after your lunch with an Easter egg for Robin and some flowers for me.'

'Gosh, how fabulous,' I say, delighted. This is amazing, Linnet is positively glowing. She's like a different person when she speaks about Lonan. 'I'm sensing there's more to this, though?'

Linnet blushes, and checks to make sure Robin is still out of earshot.

'He's asked me out to dinner,' she gushes. 'Only to the pub, but it's still a date of sorts. It *is* a date, isn't it, Ava?'

'Sounds like one to me! This is wonderful, Linnet. I don't know Lonan all that well, but he seems a lovely man.'

'That's what I think,' Linnet says. 'I do have one problem, though.' She looks hesitantly at me.

'What?'

'I need a babysitter for Robin . . . '

'Don't look any further,' I tell her. 'I'll look after him for you. When's your date?'

'Friday night?'

'That's tomorrow, right? All these bank holidays have thrown me a bit.'

'Yes, tomorrow. I'm quite nervous. It's a long time since I've been on a date.'

'You'll be fine,' I tell her reassuringly. 'Shall I come to you, or do you want to bring Robin to me?'

'Let's ask him, shall we? Robin!' Linnet calls. 'Robin, sweetie, can you come over here please?' Robin and Merlin come scampering over to us.

'I love Merlin!' Robin says happily. 'He's my best friend.'

'That's good,' Linnet says. 'Would you like to spend some time with him tomorrow evening?'

'Ooh yes!' Robin says happily. 'At your house?' he demands, looking at me.

'If you'd like to come to mine?' I ask.

'Yes. I like your house, and I like your birds.'

'My house it is, then.'

'Do you mind if it's just you on your own with Merlin and Ava?' Linnet asks Robin cautiously.

'Where will you be?' Robin demands again, this time staring hard at his mother.

'I'm going to go out with a friend, if that's okay with you?'

Robin thinks about the question. He looks at me, and then he looks at Merlin patiently waiting for him to come and play again. Then he nods. 'Yes, I will be with my friends, Mum, so it's good if you're with yours, too. Now can we walk back with my friends to their house?'

Linnet smiles with utter relief and delight, first at Robin and then at me. 'Is that all right?' she asks.

'Sounds like a great idea to me,' I say, grinning at them both. 'Let's walk back, all friends together.'

Twenty-four

'What would you like to do first?' I ask Robin as I close the door of the cottage after Linnet has dropped him off to go on her date with Lonan.

Linnet had looked very pretty as she'd stood on the doorstep reminding Robin to be a good boy, and go to bed when I tell him to.

'Mummy has a dress on,' Robin had said, apparently not listening to anything Linnet had just told him. 'She never wears a dress.'

'Perhaps this is a special occasion,' I'd said, winking at Linnet. 'Have a lovely time, won't you? And don't worry about Robin, he'll be just fine.'

After Linnet had checked for the third time that I had her number, she'd finally left, walking carefully down the path in her strappy sandals, with the skirt of her dress swishing to and fro under her long coat.

'I want to see your birds,' Robin says now, already heading towards the French windows with Merlin in tow.

'I don't usually get too many in the evening,' I say, following them. 'But if you like we can put some food out so they might come and have a pre-bedtime snack.'

'I would like that,' Robin says, and I lead him outside towards the shed where I keep the bird food.

'How do you know what they like to eat?' Robin asks, as I let him fill the containers I use to carry the food outside. 'Do they tell you?'

'Kind of. They usually eat some of the things much more quickly than others, then I know it's their favourite. Some of the seed they always leave until last, though. I don't think they like it all that much.'

'Why do you give it to them, then?'

'This seed,' I say, pointing to a large sack of wild bird food, 'comes already mixed up. I think it must contain the type of food birds are supposed to eat. All these other things I add to make it nicer for them.'

'Mum does that with my food,' Robin says, studiously examining the different bags and containers I have full of seeds, nuts, dried fruit and fat pellets. 'She puts things on my plate I don't really like, but I'm supposed to eat. Then she lets me have treats if I'm good and eat the nasty stuff.'

'What do you think is nasty stuff?' I ask him as we make our way out into the garden with Merlin.

'I don't like vegetables,' Robin says, screwing up his face. 'They're nasty.'

'I'll let you into a little secret, I don't like them much either. But they're very good for us, and you sort of have to eat them so you can have the good stuff as well.'

'Why do the birds have a house?' Robin asks, as we approach the bird table.

'It's not really a house, it's a cover so the food doesn't get wet if it rains, and also it protects the smaller birds from predators.'

'What's a ped-a-tor?'

'Er … a predator can be a bigger bird that might want to attack the smaller ones, or even a cat.'

'Like Sylvester and Tweety Pie? I like that cartoon.'

'Yes, a bit like that, I suppose.' I'd forgotten just how many questions young children sometimes ask. Robin's quest for answers was admirable, but quite exhausting.

'What's that?' Robin asks now, standing on tiptoe so he can see on to the base of the table. 'It looks shiny.'

I follow his intense gaze, and see something round and silver among the discarded husks and seed. I reach into the table and pull it out.

'It's a tiny watch,' I say, brushing it clean. 'It looks like one that might belong to a nurse.'

'Why?' Robin asks, looking up at the silver watch hanging from my fingertips.

'A nurse often pins a watch like this on to her uniform so she can lift it up and see the time easily,' I tell him, demonstrating how it works. 'That's why it looks upside down to you and me – see?'

Robin holds out his hand, so I pass it to him to examine more closely.

'Why do your birds need to tell the time?' he asks. 'So they know when it's time to be fed?'

I smile. 'They don't need a watch to tell them that. They're clever, they just use the sun coming up and going down to tell them what time it is.'

'Why was this on the table, then?'

'That is a very good question. One I'm afraid I don't have an answer to right now.'

'You said your birds are magical. Is this one of the special gifts they leave for you?'

'I guess it must be. I wonder what it means, though.'

'Roman numerals,' Robin says matter-of-factly.

'Sorry?'

'Roman numerals on the watch. We learnt about them at school. See?' Robin points to the watch face.

'Oh yes, so there are. Clocks and watches often have them instead of numbers.'

'I know. Why?'

'I don't actually know.'

'My teacher didn't know either.' He sighs. 'I guess grown-ups don't know everything.'

'No, they certainly don't.'

'Shall we feed the birds now?' Robin asks, handing me back the watch. 'They might be hungry.'

We feed the birds together, then we return to the cottage after I've persuaded Robin that the birds are unlikely to come if we stay by the feeders.

While Robin sits on the rug by the French windows with Merlin by his side, I make us two hot chocolates – the one thing I could actually make quite successfully in my kitchen now.

'Have you seen anything yet?' I ask Robin as I return to the sitting room carrying two full mugs.

'No,' Robin says, sounding disappointed. 'I don't think they're hungry tonight.'

'They'll come,' I promise him, desperately hoping they will. 'Now come and sit up here to drink your hot chocolate. It shouldn't be too warm, but the mug is quite full.'

'Why do your birds leave you presents?' Robin asks after we've sat quietly on the armchair and the sofa for a few minutes drinking our chocolate. 'Do they love you?'

'It would be nice to think that,' I tell him as honestly as I can, 'but to tell you the truth, I don't know why they do it. It's very strange.'

'My helmet looked good at Easter. But I didn't win a prize.'

'Yes, your mum said the feather worked well. I'm sorry you didn't win.'

Robin shrugs. 'Doesn't matter. The girl's hat that won just looked like all the others. I like being different. Are you different?'

'Sometimes, I guess.'

'How?'

'I just think I am. I don't have many friends, for one thing.'

'Merlin is your friend, though, isn't he?' Robin says, looking with concern at Merlin asleep on the rug.

'Oh yes, Merlin is my friend.' *The best friend I've had in a long time.*

Robin nods happily at this answer. 'I don't have many friends either,' he says quite matter-of-factly. 'We're friends, though, aren't we?'

'Yes, of course we are,' I reassure him. 'You and your mum are my friends, definitely.'

'Is the vicar your friend, too?' Robin asks suddenly.

I hesitate now.

'He was,' I answer truthfully. 'I'm not so sure now.'

'Did you have a fight?' Robin asks innocently.

'I wouldn't really call it a fight . . . More of a misunderstanding, and he left the cottage quite quickly.'

'Sometimes I have a fight with the boys and girls in my

class. But the teacher helps us to make up by letting us colour together in the quiet corner. Maybe you should colour with the vicar? You can borrow my special pencils if you like?'

I smile. 'Thank you. Yes, maybe we could try that sometime.'

'What else makes you different?' Robin asks again.

'Er . . . ' I struggle a bit now. 'Well, I don't like crowds, that's another thing.'

'That doesn't make you different. I don't like lots of people all talking at once. I can't hear them properly.'

'No, it's not just that.' Oh, how do I explain this to Robin without going into a lot of detail? 'I'm scared of being with a lot of people at once. Actually, before I came to live in Bluebell Wood, I was pretty nervous of any people – especially strangers.'

'Mum says I shouldn't talk to strangers.'

'Your mum is right.'

'But I thought that was because I'm a kid. Why can't you talk to strangers?'

I hesitate. This was becoming very tricky. I didn't talk about this with anyone, let alone a young child. But there was something about Robin's innocence that made me want to tell him the truth.

'Something happened,' I say slowly, 'and it's made me very nervous of being around people.'

'What?' Robin asks inquisitively, looking up at me with big wide eyes.

'Something that wasn't very nice at the time; and it's made me very worried about certain situations.'

To my intense relief, Robin doesn't immediately ask me any further questions, he just stares out of the window.

'Birds . . . ' he says, pointing. 'On the table.'

I follow his gaze. 'Oh yes, so there are. Do you know what sort they are?'

Robin and I spend the next twenty minutes watching the birds feed from the table and the hanging feeders. I get one of Evelyn's bird books out for him and he happily sits, spotting the birds and referencing them to his book.

It's unusual to see this many birds feeding so late in the day, but I'm pleased they've come so Robin can see them, and so that it keeps him amused for a while.

'You see that one with the red tummy,' I say, pointing to a robin bobbing around on the grass, feeding from the food that some of the other birds had knocked to the ground. 'He has the same name as you.'

Robin looks eagerly at his namesake. 'I know. I've seen him on some of the Christmas cards my mum gets. I like him. He's funny.'

'He sings really loudly too,' I tell him. 'Quite often at night and first thing in the morning if he goes to the top of one of the trees.'

Robin gets up from the armchair and walks slowly towards the window, and to my amazement after a few seconds the robin flies across towards the little patio in front of the windows and lands on the other side of the glass in front of him.

'I think he wants to talk to me,' Robin says and he reaches for the handle of the door.

'No, don't—' I begin to say, but it's too late, the robin immediately flies up to the top of one of the large fir trees that line the back of the garden before Robin can even open the door.

'I scared him,' Robin says sadly, turning away from the

window and coming back to sit next to me on the sofa. 'He didn't like me.'

'It's not that he didn't like you. He came across specially to see you. I've never seen him do that before.'

'Really?' Robin asks, looking up at me.

'Yes, really.'

'Then why did he fly away?'

'Perhaps you scared him just a little bit. He probably wasn't expecting you to open the door.'

'Will he come back?'

'He might do. Let's just wait and see.'

'Did you scare the vicar?' Robin asks suddenly, catching me unawares. 'Is that why he left too?'

'Er … perhaps I did scare him?' I reply truthfully. 'That might explain why he left so suddenly. Maybe I opened the door a little too quickly as well.'

'Which birds do you like the best?' Robin asks, already accepting my answer while I'm still considering how right he could be.

'Gosh, I don't know, they're all interesting in their own way.'

'Tell me about them,' Robin asks, and I feel him snuggle into my side a little.

I'm touched. I haven't had a child push into me for a cuddle since Hannah and Matt were small. I put my arm around him and try to recall all the birds that come to the garden.

'Hmm … like I said, our friend the robin is pretty to look at, and he sings beautifully. But he doesn't like sharing the food, and sometimes he tries to chase the other birds away.'

'Even when they're bigger than him?' Robin asks.

'Yes, even when they're bigger – he's a brave little bird. Sometimes a thrush comes and sings at the top of the trees like the robin does. He has a really loud song, but I never see him on the bird table feeding with the others.'

'Where does he get his food from, then?' Robin asks.

'I expect he forages for berries and worms and insects. Not all birds will feed from a table. Now let's see, the blackbirds are friendly and quite brave, a bit like the robin; they will sometimes come when I'm putting the food out in the mornings and sit and watch me. The blue tits are very pretty and sometimes they hang upside down on the feeders to get food – they're like little yellow and blue gymnasts.'

'I would like to see them,' Robin says, 'they sound funny.'

'Yes, they are; maybe one will come in a minute if we're lucky. Sparrows are a bit like blue tits, only not as colourful – they have their own little characters as well. The starlings are noisy birds, and they always come in gangs all at once. The pigeons and the doves are not as clever as some of the other birds; they can be a bit silly. But they're interesting to watch. Sometimes I get a couple of jackdaws come to feed – they were wary of me to begin with. But they're very clever birds and now they're used to me feeding them, they come as soon as I put the food out. Oh, and there's a pretty little bird called a chaffinch – he's a pinkie colour, and he only seems to come when all the other birds have gone and the table is almost empty.'

'He sounds a bit like you,' Robin says in a sleepy voice. 'He doesn't like crowds.'

'Yes, I suppose he is a bit of a loner.' I hadn't really thought about it like that. 'I guess even in the bird world, they all behave differently, just like us humans. Some of them like to be in crowds, and some of them like to be alone.'

'I don't think you're alone like the chaffinch,' Robin says in a yawny voice that sounds like it's about to drift off to sleep.

'Don't you?' I ask gently.

'No, you have lots of friends here in Bluebell Wood. Merlin, me . . . my mum, and the vicar man . . . You have all your birds as friends too, and . . . you know what?'

Robin's voice has become slow now as well as drowsy.

'No, what?' I whisper.

'I think the birds of Bluebell Wood might just be the best friends of all.'

Twenty-five

I breathe a sigh of relief as I leave the school gates.

My first visit to Bluebell Wood Primary had gone amazingly well. Merlin seemed to really enjoy himself, the children looked like they were loving it, and best of all I'd had fun too.

The Year One children spent the first few minutes getting to know Merlin and asking me questions, then some of them read their reading books out loud to him – which they absolutely loved.

Merlin, like the angel he is, sat and looked attentive for a while when they were first reading, then he got a little sleepy, and I pretended the children were reading him a bedtime story, which went down very well.

The teacher, Mrs Hobby, seemed very pleased with how it had all gone, and promised to report back enthusiastically to Miss Swan.

I decide to walk the long way back to the cottage to give Merlin a well-deserved run off his lead. We take the little footpath that we'd found after our first visit to the school.

That's weird, I think, as we walk a little way along the path and I notice a couple of empty crisp packets blowing around on the ground. *It's unusual to see any litter in Bluebell Wood.*

I pick up the rubbish, and put it in my pocket to dispose of later. But it's not until we walk on a little further and begin to curve our way back towards the village around the edge of the fields, that I get a stark reminder of all the building work due to commence here.

One of the fields is now full of huge pieces of yellow machinery – fork lifts, diggers and large empty trucks waiting to be filled with the soil that would once have grown the farmer's crops, but would soon be growing many new houses instead.

There are a few men in hard hats standing around with measuring devices and clipboards, and a few others smoking cigarettes or looking at their phones, presumably waiting for instructions.

One of them, wearing earphones plugged into his mobile, finishes a chocolate bar, then he tosses the empty wrapper carelessly on the ground.

I feel my blood begin to boil as I watch them from the footpath, because only this morning I'd found another chocolate wrapper, but on my bird table this time.

'Eating chocolate now, are we?' I'd joked to the birds, as I'd removed a black Mars Bar wrapper from the table. 'Makes a change from sunflower seeds and peanuts.'

'All right, darlin',' one of the men calls, making me jump from my thoughts. The others look up from their phones to see who he's talking to.

The sensible part of my brain knows I shouldn't, but that part's rational pleading is currently being stomped on by the reckless part of my brain that is angry, and before I know it I'm pacing across the field in a pair of shoes that really aren't designed for a muddy field, with Merlin in hot pursuit.

As I approach the group of men, I suddenly feel a moment's trepidation. But it's too late to back down now, and anyway I realise I'm so annoyed I don't want to.

'No, I am not all right, as you so kindly enquired,' I say as I reach the part of the field where the men are all standing.

'What's up, love?' one of the older men asks, coming over to me. He looks at me with concern, which I hadn't expected.

'*That* is what is up,' I say, pointing to where the fallen sweet wrapper is already blowing across the field in the wind. 'That and these . . . ' I pull the crisp packets from my pocket. 'I found these blowing around up on the footpath, and this morning I found an empty Mars Bar wrapper on my bird table.'

'What sort of birds are you keeping?' the man jokes, grinning at me. His smile drops when I don't appear to share his amusement.

'It's litter,' I tell him. 'Most of which seems to be coming from this building site, by the look of what I've seen so far.'

'Now come on, love. We'll take responsibility for that rubbish,' he says, pointing at the sweet wrapper. 'Oi, Jay, pick up your rubbish, mate.' He gestures to the guy who had dropped the wrapper.

Jay shrugs and pulls out one of his earphones. 'What's up, Bert?'

'Over there,' the builder says, pointing again. 'Pick it up. Now!'

Jay nods in recognition, and mooches off to collect his litter.

'Better?' Bert asks me.

'Hardly.'

'Look, love, we can't take the blame for every bit of rubbish in the whole of the village, now, can we?'

'It's funny, I'd never seen one piece of litter in Bluebell Wood before today, and since you've all arrived, I've seen four. Three of which have been on or near this building site.'

Bert isn't looking at me with quite such a kindly expression now. 'Look, I'll try to make sure the boys are a bit more careful, will that make you any happier?'

'Nothing will make me or any of the other villagers any happier about this.' I gesture out into the field. 'No one wants this development.'

'Someone must have wanted it or I wouldn't be standing here now waiting for instructions, would I?'

'Look, I don't blame *you*,' I say, feeling myself soften a little. 'You're just doing your job, I know that. It's the money-grabbers at the top I blame.'

'I think she might be referring to me,' a whiny voice says, and I see Colin Cuckoo stepping out from behind one of the forklifts with a clipboard in his hand. Unlike Bert, who is wearing denim jeans and a checked shirt under his hi-vis jacket and yellow hard hat, Colin is wearing a grey suit with a white hard hat, and his trousers are tucked a bit too neatly into a pair of green Hunter wellingtons. 'Am I right?'

'You said it,' I reply drily.

'Look, Mrs . . . Miss?' He waits for me to say my name.

'My name is Ava, as I told you the last time we met.'

'So you did, so you did. My apologies, how could I forget?' He smiles a cheesy smile. 'Look, Ava, I'm not a monster; I know there are a few people none too pleased about this development.'

'That's an understatement, from what I've heard.'

Colin continues unabashed. 'However, as I told you on Easter Sunday, we have tried to listen to everyone's concerns and the development has been adapted to provide some additional extras to the village.'

I look at him quizzically. 'Like?'

'We are providing – at great expense, I must tell you – a brand-new built-for-purpose village hall. The original, I understand, is pretty rundown.'

'Yes, I'd heard about that. What else?'

Colin smirks at me. 'Not easily pleased, are you?'

'No.'

'We have also recently agreed that Cuckoo Land Homes will provide a new children's play park as part of the development – something you can't deny you are also short of here.'

He was right, there wasn't anywhere for children to play safely.

'That's good, I suppose . . . '

Colin shakes his head. 'It's more than we originally agreed to, I can assure you. And lastly, as part of our original deal, we have already donated a rather sizeable sum to the church fund for repairs to its exceptionally leaky roof, and we're also sponsoring a new stained-glass window – with a bird theme, of course.' He gestures to one of the Cuckoo Land Homes signs that have now sprung up all around the site.

I stare at him. Callum hadn't mentioned the church was gaining anything out of this.

'We may not have many of you villagers on our side, but it seems we do have the big man upstairs.' He looks up and crosses himself, then his beady eyes fall back on me. 'If you have any more issues with this development, may I suggest you speak to your local vicar? Because I can assure you, Ava, he's very much in favour of the benefits it will bring to the church and the village as a whole.'

'Fine,' I say, trying to remain focused, but my mind is already filled with conflicting thoughts about Callum. 'You carry on – for now. But I'll be back.'

Colin grins. 'Ah, yet again we reference my favourite movie in our delightful conversations. All right, Ava, or should I call you Arnie! You go for it,' he says, pretending to stifle a snigger. 'But I won't worry too much about your chances of terminating this project. Get it?' he says to Bert, who is still standing next to him looking rather uncomfortable. 'Terminated – *The Terminator*?'

Bert gives him a pitying look. Then he turns to me. 'Sorry,' he says, shrugging.

I'm not sure if he's apologising for Colin's poor joke, Colin himself or the development in general, but I give him a half smile and look around for Merlin so we can leave. I find him currently relieving himself – but to my horror, it's against one of Colin's pristine Hunter wellingtons.

Luckily for me Colin is still commending himself on his play with words and hasn't noticed. But Bert has. He glances at me and winks.

'Merlin!' I call, thankful when he comes at once to my side. 'Nice to meet you, Bert,' I say deliberately, smiling at him while ignoring Colin.

'And you, love,' Bert says, grinning now. 'What a great dog you have there. Very good judge of character.'

Merlin and I turn and walk as quickly as I can in my inappropriate shoes back across the field. My mind races far faster than my feet, as I try to work out what Callum's part in this might have been. Had he given his approval to this development just so he could get some money towards the church roof repairs and a new window?

No, he wouldn't, I tell myself as we march back in the direction of the cottage.

But what if he had? If what Colin is suggesting is true, how many of Callum's parishioners knew he'd sold out the village just to save his church?

Twenty-six

I spend a while back at the cottage ruminating over what had happened in the field.

Yes, it was good that there was going to be a new play park in Bluebell Wood, and yes, it was good the village hall was to be rebuilt, the church roof repaired and a new window added, but at what cost?

All these new houses would spoil the peace and calm of the village. Bluebell Wood was so quiet and remote, it just wasn't designed to house a lot of people. From what I'd been told everyone in the village seemed against this development, so why had Callum allowed himself to be swayed into giving his approval to the council? It must have been him – otherwise why would the church be doing quite so well out of Cuckoo Land Homes?

I pace around the sitting room while I'm thinking, and my gaze falls on the mantelpiece and all the gifts the birds have left me so far. The Mars Bar wrapper stands out against all the pretty, shiny, colourful things. It was someone else's rubbish, and that's just what this development was going to be – a piece of trash, blighting the beauty of Bluebell Wood.

'Merlin!' I call, suddenly making a decision. 'Get your lead. We're going to pay a quick visit.'

We stride at a brisk pace towards the church. The bell up in the clock tower strikes twelve as we walk along Church Lane towards the vicarage. The stern sound of the chimes fills me with the courage I need – my resolve has already wavered several times as we've walked towards this vital confrontation.

I open the little gate that leads into the vicarage front garden, then I march up to the door. As I raise my hand with the intention of rattling hard on the knocker, I hear a voice.

'Hello, Ava. Hello, Merlin, what brings you here today?'

I turn and see Jonah on his hands and knees doing some weeding in one of the beds behind the vicarage wall.

'Jonah ... ' I say, as the determined wind that had carried me here quickly drops. 'I didn't see you there.'

Jonah stands up, removes his gloves, and brushes his hands on his gardening apron.

'The borders needed tending to,' he says, looking back at them. 'So many weeds, I don't know where they all come from. Callum and I try our best to keep the vicarage looking smart, but it's a full-time job, I can tell you. Sadly, the budget won't run to a gardener.'

Suddenly, I don't feel quite so angry. Maybe Callum was only doing what was best for the church and his parishioners? Then out of the corner of my eye a robin lands on the wall next to us with something in his beak. He looks at me and cocks his head, then he opens his beak so the item floats down into the garden at our feet. It's a sweet wrapper.

'Well, of all the ... !' Jonah says, also seeing the robin. He picks up the wrapper. 'Littering birds, whatever next?'

'It's not their fault,' I say, my resolve returning. 'It's that building site up on the hill.'

'Oh yes, the development. They've started work now, haven't they?'

'They're about to; that's why litter is starting to blow all over the village; it's coming from there.'

'Has there been more litter about? I hadn't noticed it myself.'

'I have, it's been in my garden, and on the footpath that leads around the field, and now even the birds are dropping it.'

'That's not good. Perhaps someone needs to have a word.'

'I already have. It didn't make a lot of difference. What do you know about what's happening there?' I ask, suddenly wondering if Jonah might be in on it too. 'How did they even get permission to build all those houses if the village was so against it?'

'I don't know. We put up a good fight, but the council had the final say. Perhaps one of them wanted it and managed to swing the vote? You should ask Callum; he was more involved in the campaign than I was. He went to a couple of the closed council meetings on behalf of the village.'

'Did he now? Is he around at the moment?'

'He's at the church doing some maintenance. But perhaps today isn't the best day to bother him.'

'Why?'

Jonah looks uncomfortable. 'Just best not to. He's been away for a few days, and he has a lot to catch up on now he's back.'

'I didn't think I'd seen him around much since Easter.'

'We're allowed to take time off after busy seasons like Easter and Christmas,' Jonah explains. 'Even we vicars get paid leave!' He grins, but I don't feel like returning his smile, so he hurriedly continues. 'This year Callum took some of his. But things mount up when you're away, don't they? His to-do list is as long as your arm.'

Like my new young friend, I think my favourite of all the birds who come to visit me in my garden is the red-breasted robin. He had such a knowing, friendly way about him, and to see him dropping litter from his little beak had pushed me so far over the edge that there was no going back. Whether Jonah thought it was a good idea or not, I had to see Callum and establish what part he'd had to play in the Cuckoo Land Homes development.

'Sure,' I say, pretending to understand, 'I'll come back another day. Not a problem.'

Jonah nods. 'Are you all right for the quiz night this week?'

'Yes, of course. I'm looking forward to it.'

'Good. You're a valued member of our team now, Ava.'

'Thank you,' I say, smiling at him. None of this was his fault. It was Callum I had issues with, not Jonah. 'That's kind of you to say. Right, we'd better be going. Merlin!' Merlin appears from behind a bush, wagging his tail.

'See you Thursday, then,' I say to Jonah as he watches us go.

'Yes, Thursday.'

When we're the other side of the vicarage gate, I pretend to be clipping Merlin's lead to his collar; but what I'm really doing is waiting for Jonah to kneel back down again to attend to his weeds, so I can head in the direction of the church without him knowing. When his head has finally disappeared from view, I turn and hurry with Merlin down the road towards the church.

The churchyard is quiet as we enter, but even the calm and tranquillity I immediately feel doesn't knock my determination, and I walk with purpose along the path towards the church. I can hear birdsong coming from the trees dotted around the ancient gravestones, and this only helps to strengthen my resolve.

There's the sound of banging coming from the back of the church, so we walk around the gravel path that encircles the ancient building, until we discover the source of the noise – a hot and sweaty-looking Callum hammering a nail into the side of one of the long wooden church pews.

Merlin pulls towards him, so I let him off his lead and he gallops over to Callum's side.

'Hello, you,' Callum says, ceasing his hammering to ruffle Merlin's head. He glances up with slightly less enthusiasm in my direction.

'Hi,' he says carefully. 'Good to see you again.'

I can't help but notice the damp patterns on Callum's white T-shirt as it clings to his sweaty chest.

I swallow hard. *No, Ava, this is not the time! Concentrate.*

'Is it?' I ask airily. 'You didn't give me that impression the last time I saw you.'

Callum thinks about this. 'Right . . . yes . . . Easter Sunday. Gosh, that seems like so long ago now.'

I wonder what he means.

'It was just over a week ago, actually. Not that long.'

'No, indeed. Not that long at all.'

'Jonah said you'd been away for a while. Did you have a nice holiday?'

'It wasn't really a holiday,' Callum says, laying his hammer down on the church pew, but not expanding any further.

'What was it, then?'

'Did you want to see me about something?' he asks, his tone suddenly changing. 'Only I have to get this pew fixed and back inside the church before it rains.'

I look up at the sky but only see white fluffy clouds against a bright blue sky. Nothing that suggests rain is imminent.

Fine, if you want to be like that, I think, my resolve deepening even further. *You've just made this so much easier for me.*

'Yes, I did. What part did you play in Cuckoo Land Homes being given permission to build their houses in Bluebell Wood?'

Callum looks surprised at my question.

'What do you mean?'

'What I said. I'm asking what you did to allow this new development when the majority of the village is so against it.'

'What makes you think *I* did anything?' Callum asks, looking less surprised and slightly more annoyed now.

'Do the words a significant donation to the church roof restoration fund and a new stained-glass window mean anything to you?'

'How do you know about them?'

'Let's just say a not-so-little bird told me.'

Callum stares at me, then it dawns on him. 'Colin Cuckoo.'

I nod.

Callum sighs heavily and sits down on the pew. 'No one was supposed to know about that yet. The donations were going to be announced after the houses had been built. The play park and the village hall are the only things to be common knowledge, and not too many even know about the play park yet – that's quite a new development. Sorry, unfortunate pun,' he says, screwing up his face.

'Why?' I ask, almost feeling sorry for him. He looks genuinely distressed now.

'Why was it supposed to be kept secret,' Callum asks, 'or why did I help them to get the necessary permission to build?'

'The latter?' I ask quietly. Merlin is happily sniffing around by the church so I walk over and sit next to Callum on the pew. 'It doesn't seem like you to go against the village in this way.'

'We desperately need a new roof,' he says, waving his hand in the direction of the church. 'I know all churches seem to constantly have a restoration fund for their roofs on the go, but this one *really* needs one. I had a structural engineer in a few months ago; he said it's got eighteen months at the most before it collapses in certain places. If that happens the church won't be fit for use. No church, no services. No services, no congregation. No congregation . . .'

'No vicar?' I finish for him.

'Exactly. They'll move me somewhere else. I don't want to go somewhere else, Ava. I like it here. I like the people. I like the pace of life. I like the fact I've made a difference to the local area.'

'What about the stained-glass window?' I ask, forcing myself to continue, when what I really want to do is console him. But I have to remain calm. Callum made it quite clear on Easter Sunday that he didn't want me to be the person to console him. 'Just another sweetener?'

Callum nods. 'Before my time here, a broken window on the south side was replaced by plain glass panels because they couldn't afford at the time to replace it with much more expensive stained glass. I was still wavering when the donation was suggested to facilitate a new roof, so when they said they'd sponsor a new window as well, I'm afraid I folded. It's such a beautiful church, Ava; it deserves a spectacular window to celebrate all that is good about the village it stands in.'

'But will the village be as beautiful when all these new houses go up?' I ask. 'I think not.'

Callum looks distraught. 'I know I've let the village down.

But what was I supposed to do? It's not just the church that needed things; Bluebell Wood desperately needs a new village hall, too. Have you seen the old one? That's likely to go the same way as the church any time soon. It's not fit to house the clubs that use it on a regular basis. That's why I insisted they build a new one, and then when you became involved in all this, something struck a chord again, and I went back to them and insisted on a play park too. That idiot Cuckoo was reluctant, of course, but he eventually folded when I said I'd pull my support. It probably wouldn't have made any difference at this late stage, but I think he quite likes having the local vicar on his side, so he agreed.'

'Is that why you've been so busy since Easter?' I ask.

Callum looks at me with a puzzled expression. 'Er ... no, that was something else that caused me to be away from the village.'

He doesn't expand any further.

'Why did it make a difference when I became involved?' I ask quietly. 'I mean, I'm glad you've got the village a play park, but why did it change things?'

'It just did,' Callum says, looking like he wants to expand this time, but is choosing not to. He sighs. 'None of it makes any difference now. The fact remains I haven't been able to provide what this church or this village needs without resorting to underhand, desperate measures. I'm supposed to set an example, to uphold all that is good and pure, and instead I'm a failure yet again.' His body slumps forward and his head drops into his hands.

I wonder what he means by 'yet again'.

'You're not a failure,' I hear myself saying. 'Everyone loves you here – you know that. If I've heard one person say you're the best vicar they've ever had, I've heard twenty. You *have* made a difference, Callum. You must know that. I don't know much about being a priest, but I'm pretty sure it's not supposed to be about how much money you can raise to repair a leaky roof or build a new village hall. It's about making a difference to people's spiritual lives, to give them comfort when they need it most, and a shoulder to cry on when no one else understands.'

Callum slowly sits up again and turns his head towards me.

'Why are you so wonderful?' he asks quietly.

I don't know what to say.

'I'm really not,' I reply, totally thrown by his question.

'I think you are. That's what makes it so difficult.'

'Makes what difficult?'

'Resisting you.'

I swallow. *This conversation was not supposed to be going this way.*

'Why do you have to resist me?' I can't help whispering back.

Callum's eyes travel slowly over my face. 'I just do.'

'Is that why you ran off on Easter Sunday?'

Callum nods. 'I'm sorry about that. I shouldn't have left the way I did. But you ... you overpower me. I lose all sense of what's right.'

He wasn't the only one who felt like that!

'Have you taken some sort of oath?' I ask. 'Like a vow of chastity or something? Is that what it is?'

Callum smiles. 'That's generally the Catholic religion. No, this is nothing to do with my faith. Well,' he hesitates, 'it is a little, I suppose.'

'What do you mean?'

'A number of years ago I made a pact ... with God.'

'Isn't that what vicars do?'

Callum shakes his head. 'No, this was different. It was before I became a priest. I made a pact with him that if he did what I was asking, I would devote my whole life to serving him and nothing else would ever get in the way of that.'

'What were you asking for?'

Callum looks at me. 'I'm not sure I can say.'

'That's fine,' I reply quickly. 'You don't have to. I understand.' I stand up and look around for Merlin.

'No!' Callum yells, and I feel him grab my hand from behind so I have to turn around again. 'No, Ava. *Please* don't go.' He leaps up next to me. 'You don't understand.'

'Tell me then,' I say. Callum is so close to me that I can feel his warm breath on my cheek. I turn slowly towards him, our fingers still entwined.

Then before I know what's happening, he pulls me towards him and kisses me softly on the mouth, and just as I was at the cottage, immediately I'm powerless to resist as I melt at his touch.

'I thought you had to resist me,' I manage to whisper in between his kisses, which are becoming more ardent by the second.

'It's impossible,' Callum murmurs, as I feel his hands gently begin to caress my body.

'Father Crawford!' a stern voice calls.

Callum and I both freeze. Then very slowly we prise ourselves from each other's arms and stand side by side, looking like two naughty schoolchildren who have been caught up to no good.

'Mrs Bunting!' Callum says with an expression of amusement that rapidly changes to one of solemnity. 'Is it that time already? I wasn't expecting you until half past twelve.'

Mrs Bunting looks up as the church clock strikes the half-hour, then she looks back down at us.

'I'm perfectly punctual, Father Crawford. You, however, seem to have been a little . . . sidetracked, shall we say?'

'Yes, I'm sorry about that. I was just fixing one of the pews; you know the one that used to do all the creaking during services if anyone sat on it in the wrong place?'

'I'm aware of the fault,' Mrs Bunting says, regarding me over her half-moon spectacles. 'And Ms Martin here was assisting you, I suppose?'

'That's right,' Callum says. He turns to me and formally shakes my hand. 'Thank you for your help, Ava. I couldn't have done it without you.' His back is turned to Mrs Bunting. *Call you later?* he mouths silently.

I nod. 'Not a problem, Father. Only too pleased to be of assistance.'

Regretfully, I let go of Callum's hand and call Merlin. Then we quickly set off past Mrs Bunting, stopping to say a formal farewell to her before hurrying down the path towards the church gate. My heart is beating fast, and my head is now even more confused than it had been before we arrived.

Twenty-seven

'Will it be okay if I come to the cottage later?' Callum says over the phone. 'I think we need to talk?'

I'd been waiting for him to call since Merlin and I had left him at the church with Mrs Bunting. We'd left so much unsaid, and so many things had been discussed yet not concluded, that I was in a state of complete confusion as I paced about the cottage and the garden trying to figure it all out.

'Yes, I think you should,' I reply.

'Would around six o'clock be too early?'

'No, six is just fine.'

'Good, perhaps we could go and get something to eat after we've talked? The pub does a lovely supper.'

I end the call still no wiser, but at least now I had some hope that I might discover just what was going on with him.

As I stare out of the window at the bird table, not thinking about the birds, but with my mind still on Callum, I notice a pair of doves dancing around each other in the garden – the female showing a lot more reluctance to mate than the clearly amorous male.

'Is it that time of year already?' I wonder, as the female dove flies off with the male in hot pursuit. 'Mating season? I hope it's not as complicated for you guys as it is for us humans!'

After I've showered, I spend a little time in front of Evelyn's big wooden dressing table, tidying myself up, and wondering when I'd stopped caring quite so much what I looked like.

I didn't have to delve too deep to find the answer, I knew exactly when it was. The day that changed everything. The day when what I looked like no longer seemed so important, and whether I lived or died did.

I knew I'd made progress since I'd been here in Bluebell Wood, both Matt and Hannah had commented on how different I seemed. But that nagging feeling of anxiety, worry and self-doubt never left me completely, no matter what I did. I wonder now if it ever will.

I shake my head. *No time for wallowing now, Ava!* I quickly blow-dry my hair, pop a little lip gloss on and a wave of mascara, then I head downstairs to wait for Callum.

I feel nervous as I sit in the armchair with Merlin snoring contentedly next to me on the floor. I'm not sure why, it wasn't like this was a date I was waiting to go on with someone I didn't know. I got on with Callum, I knew him well. Or did I?

Some things that had been said earlier were nagging at me, and I wasn't sure why. Broken pieces of conversation float around in my head, like pages ripped from a novel; if I could put them together they might make sense, but torn apart they made no sense at all.

A rap on the door makes me jump, and I look at the clock. It's five to six: Callum is early.

I go to the door and throw it open, but I'm surprised to see not Callum standing on the doorstep, but Lonan.

'Good evening, Ava,' he says in his formal way. Then he

looks at his watch. 'Almost evening,' he corrects himself. 'I do hope I'm not disturbing you?'

'Er, no,' I say, casting a quick glance over his shoulder in case Callum was already making his way along the path. 'What can I do for you?'

'You remember I said I was going to do some research on those old ruins up on the hill?'

I nod.

'Well, I've found out some quite interesting information, and you said you'd like to hear about anything I discovered. I wondered if now might be a good time?'

'Yes . . . er, sure,' I say, opening the door wider to invite him in. I could hardly say I was expecting Callum for . . . Why was Callum coming here tonight? I didn't actually know if it was simply to talk or to tell me he couldn't be with me again, or something else . . . 'Come on in.'

I guide Lonan through to the sitting room, and after he's made a fuss of Merlin and accepted a glass of wine from one of the bottles left over from Easter, we settle down to talk.

'I knew this area would be filled with intrigue,' Lonan says, looking eagerly down at his notebook. 'There's just something about the place that when I originally came to visit suggested it would be of some interest to me.'

'What sort of intrigue?' I ask, taking a sip from my own glass. I'd decided when pouring one for Lonan that a bit of Dutch courage wouldn't go amiss before Callum arrived.

'It appears from the research I've done so far that the ruins on the hill were, as we suspected, once a large manor house; and the family that lived there controlled all of this area.'

'How did they control it? Wasn't there a government that did that, or a King?'

'Usually that would be correct. But it seems like I said at your delightful dinner party, much of this area was originally deemed Royal Forest, which is why it was called Kingswood before it was later renamed Bluebell Wood. However, I've discovered that Henry II actually bestowed this particular area of Royal Forest on one of his subjects as a reward for looking after and protecting one of his children.'

'Really? How exciting.'

'I believe the King, his young son and some of the King's men were out hunting one day – that's what Royal Forest was usually claimed for: good hunting ground for the King and any nobility he wished to share this privilege with. The boy got distanced from the King and his party and, new to horsemanship, he was soon thrown from his horse. A local farmer found him unconscious, with his horse still wandering nearby. He took both the boy and the horse back to his own modest dwelling, little knowing, of course, that the boy was royalty. The boy came to eventually, and after the farmer and his wife had fed and watered him, the boy told them who he was.'

'Gosh,' I say, completely enthralled in this fairy tale of a story. 'Then what happened?'

'The King's men, out searching for the lost boy, saw his horse tethered to the outside of the farmhouse. When they banged on the door demanding to speak to the farmer, they were surprised and relieved to find the King's son inside. Luckily for the farmer and his wife, the boy spoke nothing but praise for their kindness to him. When the King was told what had happened, he went back to the wood with his men and spoke to the couple himself, and as a way of showing his gratitude gave them a small area of the Royal Forest, an area that now covers both the village of Bluebell Wood as we know it today and the surrounding villages.'

'Wow, that story is like something you read in a children's book. There is definitely something magical about this place, though. How did you find all that out?' I ask.

'I began by speaking to a few of the older members of the community. It's amazing how much you can discover having a chat over a pint in the local hostelry – even in this modern day of websites and Google.'

I can just imagine Lonan chatting to the locals in the pub and getting them to spill all the gossip and tall tales about the area – even if those tales are hundreds of years old.

'And then I did my own searches on more reliable sources – the internet and local libraries. There's a wealth of information in the Cambridge University Library about the local area; luckily, I have a friend who's one of the fellows there so I could access it.'

This obviously all came very naturally to Lonan. He'd told me before how much research he did for his novels.

'I've a lot more research still to do,' Lonan concludes, 'but it would seem the ownership of the piece of land that the farmer was bequeathed stayed in his family for many generations. The ruins up on the hill are part of one of the homes his descendants built.'

'Whoever lived there really was lord or lady of the manor, then?'

'Most definitely. Like I said, I've still got some digging to do – metaphorically so – but I hope to find out more about the generations after the farmer, and also possibly before.'

'This is really interesting, Lonan; thank you for sharing it all with me.'

'Not a problem. I'm more than happy to share it with someone. It's been incredibly rewarding to find out more about where I'm residing.'

We both take a sip of our wine, but I get the feeling by the agitated look on his face that there's more Lonan wants to say.

'Why are you *really* here, Lonan?' I ask. 'There's something more than the history of Bluebell Wood you want to discuss with me, isn't there?'

'Ah, you've rumbled me,' Lonan says, nodding. 'I knew you were too bright to be fooled by my cover story.'

'Your cover story is great; I'm intrigued and definitely want to know more. But you wouldn't have come here tonight just to tell me that.'

'No, you're absolutely correct. I need your advice,' Lonan says, looking even more self-conscious. 'It's a matter of the heart.'

'You do?'

He nods. 'I know you are aware of my blossoming relationship with the lovely Linnet.'

'I am.'

'As relationships go, it's still very much in its infancy. But I think it's going rather well. I've taken quite a shine to your friend.'

I feel my heart swell, partly from Lonan talking in this way about Linnet, and partly because he had called her my friend. I hadn't had many people I could call friends in my life for some time.

'I'm pleased to hear it,' I tell Lonan, smiling. 'From what I can tell, she feels much the same way about you.'

Lonan's pale cheeks redden a little. 'That's good to know,' he says shyly. 'Very good to know.'

'So what's the problem?'

'It's not Linnet; like I said, we're getting on famously well. It's her son, Robin. I don't think he likes me very much.'

'What makes you think that?'

'I get that feeling. Obviously I haven't spent all that much time with him yet. But in the little I have, he seems a bit off with me, and I want to put that right. I know he gets on with you very well. He talks about you and Merlin a lot.'

'Does he?' I'm touched to hear that. I had a soft spot for Robin too, and a bit like Lonan, I'm glad to hear the feeling is mutual.

'Very much so, and I wondered if you could give me some pointers.'

'I'm not sure what to suggest,' I say, trying to think. 'Robin loves Merlin, but you don't have a dog, do you?'

Lonan shakes his head.

'What about a bird table?' I ask, inspiration suddenly striking. 'Does your cottage have one of those?'

'No, but I could get one, if you think it might help.'

'It might. Or what about buying one for Linnet and Robin for their garden? I'm pretty sure Robin would love his own bird table – he was fascinated with mine when he was here the other night.'

'You're amazing, Ava!' Lonan says, beaming. 'What a truly wonderful idea.'

'Perhaps you could also take Robin and Linnet birdwatching one day as well? Maybe take a picnic to the wood, or somewhere else with lots of birds?'

'Ava, I could kiss you!' Lonan cries, looking ecstatic. 'I would probably have bought Robin an expensive toy, which he doubtless wouldn't have liked, and that would have made things even worse. This is genius.'

I shrug. 'You just have to go with what a child likes. You can't force things on them you think they should enjoy. You have to let them be their own person.'

The knocker rattles on the cottage door, and I glance towards the hall.

'Oh, I'm sorry, are you expecting someone?' Lonan asks.

'Yes, actually I am.'

Lonan stands up. 'Then I must take my leave. I've imposed enough on your hospitality and your kind nature.'

'You really don't have to,' I tell him. 'At least finish your wine.'

'If you're sure?'

'Of course. I'm only expecting Callum.'

Lonan sits down again as I go through to the hall.

'Hi,' Callum says cheerily, as I open the door. 'Sorry I'm a bit late. I brought a bottle.' He holds up a bottle of wine. 'Hope that's okay?'

'It's lovely, thank you.' I stand back to let him in.

Callum is dressed casually, as he always is when he's not 'on duty'. Tonight, he wears a pale blue open-necked shirt, indigo-blue jeans and chocolate-brown suede laced boots.

'I'm sorry about what happened earlier at the church,' he says as he walks into the cottage. 'I forgot all about Mrs Bunting.'

'It's fine,' I say quickly, aware that Lonan is only a room away.

'No, it's not,' Callum says, moving closer to me. 'We had things we needed to finish—'

'Callum, Lonan is in the sitting room,' I say, throwing him a warning look. 'He popped round a little while ago to tell me about some of the interesting history he's discovered about Bluebell Wood.'

Callum looks towards the sitting room. 'Ah, I see,' he says, nodding. 'That does sound intriguing.'

Callum follows me through to where Lonan is sitting on the sofa drinking his wine. He notices at once my half-empty glass resting on the table close to the sofa.

'Seems like you stole my idea!' Callum says, holding up his bottle. 'I brought wine too.'

'Not at all,' Lonan says good-naturedly. 'I'm embarrassed to say I'm drinking our hostess's.'

'Wine left from Easter Sunday,' I stress for Callum's benefit. 'But thank you for this.' I take the wine from him. 'I'll pop it in the fridge to chill. Would you like a glass of the wine we're drinking?'

'Sure,' Callum nods. 'Why not?'

While Callum sits down in the armchair by the window, I hurry through to the kitchen. I thrust the bottle of wine into the fridge, and then I grab a glass for Callum and dash back through to them.

'Here we go!' I say cheerfully, as I re-enter the sitting room. Lonan lifts the bottle and pours wine into the glass while I hold it. I then pass it to Callum.

'Thanks,' he says. 'Lonan was just starting to tell me about the things he's found out about the wood.'

I sit back down on the sofa and listen to Lonan tell Callum what he'd told me.

'Sounds great,' Callum says at the end. 'You should do some digging into the church's history, too. I know parts of the building date back to Norman times; Jonah mentioned something once. It might help?'

'I'll do that,' Lonan says. 'Now, I must be going. I feel I might have outstayed my welcome.' He looks between the two of us.

'No, of course you haven't,' I protest. 'Stay as long as you like.'

But Lonan stands up. 'Three's a crowd, and all that. Thank you, dear Ava, for your kind hospitality and your wise words.

Both are greatly appreciated, and I shall act upon your advice forthwith.'

'You're very welcome,' I say, standing up and leading Lonan to the door.

'Enjoy your evening,' he says to Callum.

'I shall. Thank you,' Callum replies. And a knowing look passes between them.

I see Lonan out of the cottage and then I return to Callum.

'Sorry about that,' I say, sitting back down on the sofa. 'I wasn't expecting him, he just turned up.'

'Don't be silly. That happens all the time when you're the local vicar. People rarely make appointments; they think you're on call all the time!'

'And knowing you, you probably are.'

'Only when I have my dog collar on.' Callum grins.

'You haven't got it on now, does that mean we won't be interrupted tonight?'

'I do hope not . . . ' Callum says, his expression changing to a much more earnest one.

I take a hasty sip of my wine.

'What words of wisdom were you bestowing upon our friend Lonan?' Callum asks, swiftly changing the subject. 'He seemed pretty pleased with what you had to say.'

'I'm not sure I can share confessional thoughts, now, can I?' I ask, grinning at him. 'You of all people should know that.'

'Again, I have to correct you – the confessional is Catholicism,' Callum says, 'but I appreciate your discretion.'

'Let's just say matters of the heart and leave it at that.'

Callum nods. 'I understand. I think I know whose heart he might be keen to impress, though.'

'Oh really? What have you heard?'

'Could it be a certain lady who has a certain son who thinks *you're* pretty exceptional?'

'I wouldn't say that, but you might be thinking along the right lines.'

'Her son isn't the only one, because *I* think you're pretty special too.'

I glance down into my glass. Seeing it's empty, I look across at the bottle on the table, but find it's the same.

'Shall I get us some more wine?' I ask quickly, standing up. 'Your bottle might be chilled enough by now.'

'No,' Callum says, standing up to block my way. 'Not right now.'

My eyes have no choice but to look into his.

'What *do* you want, then?' I ask quietly.

'You,' Callum says without hesitation. 'I want you, Ava.'

Twenty-eight

I lie in my bed and sigh. If this felt so right, why do I get the awful feeling it might be so wrong, too?

'Are you okay?' Callum asks next to me. 'That was one big sigh.'

I look up at him from where I'm snuggled against his chest. His arm is around my shoulders, and my arm is resting on his well-toned stomach.

'I just didn't expect to be in my bed quite so early on a weekday evening, especially with a strange man lying next to me.'

'Not so much of the strange,' Callum says, winking.

'Okay then, I especially didn't expect to be lying here with a priest in my bed.'

'Is that a problem?' Callum asks.

'No,' I say a little too hurriedly. 'Of course not, why would it be? I wonder if it might be a problem for you though?'

The evening had become a whirlwind of emotions after Callum's passionate declaration.

We'd rushed to each other in a frenzy of kisses and clothes

being ripped off, and eventually ended up in the bedroom, where we'd stayed, enjoying ourselves and each other for quite some time.

Now we're lying quietly together under the duvet, in a glowing haze of happiness and, in my case, slight trepidation too.

'Why would what we just did be a problem?' Callum asks. 'From my perspective it was far from problematic!'

'Don't tease me,' I say, sitting up a little so I'm level with him. 'You know what I'm talking about.'

'Are you talking about what I told you this afternoon? Or the fact I'm a vicar?'

'Both, really. I mean, are you allowed to do what we just did?'

Callum smiles. 'Let's just say sex before marriage isn't exactly encouraged in the Church of England. In fact, it's positively *dis*couraged. But it happens – a lot more than anyone cares to admit. So, in answer to your question, I'm unlikely to be excommunicated for what we just did, unless we go around telling everyone about it – and I'm pretty sure you're not going to do that, are you?'

I shake my head.

'We're good, then?'

'Not quite. What about what you said earlier at the church ... you know, about your pact ... with him upstairs,' I say eventually.

'Yes, I've thought about that – an awful lot since I saw you earlier – and ... I'm a bit embarrassed to tell you, actually ... '

'Tell me what?'

'That I asked for a sign,' Callum says, looking uncomfortable. 'After you left. A sign that would confirm to me that what I wanted so very much right now was all right. That I wasn't going back on my word or letting him down. And you should know, Ava, I *never* ask for signs.'

'Why not?'

'I think he's got better things to be doing than sending me validation when I have a dilemma I don't know the answer to. But you mean so much to me that I felt on this occasion I had no choice.'

'And did you get one?' I ask, wondering what could possibly have happened to make Callum change his mind. 'A sign?'

Callum nods. 'I did. I was walking around the outside of the church – pacing might be a better word for it – trying to figure out what was for the best – for everyone, I might add, not just myself. Then I saw two doves billing and cooing over each other, up on the church roof.'

I like the way Callum refers to it as billing and cooing. I just thought the two doves I'd seen earlier were a bit randy; well, the male one definitely was. But Callum's way makes it seem much lovelier.

Was this his 'sign', though? I'd likely seen the same two doves this afternoon as well. I couldn't tell him that, though, if he thought this was his sign from up above.

'And that was your sign?' I ask calmly. 'The doves?'

'No, although if I hadn't seen the same two doves hanging around the church earlier, I might have thought it was – they seemed pretty loved up. No, my sign was much clearer than that, and some might say pretty unbelievable.'

What kind of miracle had taken place in Bluebell Wood this afternoon that Callum considered so amazing? After all, this was a person who believed Jesus fed five thousand people on five loaves and two fishes, and Moses parted the Red Sea.

'Go on, then?' I encourage, feeling quite apprehensive about what he was going to tell me.

'The doves eventually flew off together, but not before one of them had dropped something right in front of me.'

'They didn't poop on you, did they? I know that's supposed to be lucky but—'

'No, of course they didn't,' Callum says, looking at me with disbelief. 'Look, let me show you what they dropped instead of telling you. It's in the pocket of my shirt.'

He looks around the bedroom for his blue shirt.

'I think it got abandoned in the sitting room,' I say, feeling a little embarrassed now. 'Along with a few other items of our clothing.'

'Ah yes, so it did. Wait there.'

Callum climbs out of bed, and without pulling anything around him hurries downstairs.

I pray no one can see through any of the cottage windows. But unless someone is camping out in my garden, I think he should be pretty safe.

He returns and climbs back into bed next to me.

'This is what they dropped,' he says, holding up what looks like a pink sweet. He passes it to me.

'It's one of those Love Hearts sweets that children sometimes have,' he explains, in case I don't know. 'Look what it says on it.'

I turn the sweet over in my hand. It simply says, *Love You.*

'Can there be any clearer sign than that?' Callum asks. 'I couldn't believe it at first. I thought, *Why would a dove be carrying one of those sweets around in its beak?* And then I remembered your bird table and the gifts you've been left on there, and I knew it was the sign I needed.'

I stare at the sweet and the words *Love You*.

'It's a sign, Ava,' he says happily. 'It's a sign that God is giving us his blessing.'

'Okay . . . ' I say, still looking at the Love Heart. 'So, what you're saying is, if you hadn't been given this sweet this afternoon, you wouldn't be here now?'

Callum looks back at me and his ecstatic expression wavers slightly. 'Does it matter now? The fact is I am. I'm here with you – somewhere I've wanted to be since I first met you.' He moves closer to me in the bed, but I find myself moving away.

'What's wrong?' he asks, looking puzzled.

'I'm not sure,' I say, slipping out of the bed and grabbing a dressing gown from a hook on the back of the door. 'It's just all this . . . well, this God stuff.'

Callum looks at me like he doesn't understand.

'I get you're a vicar – that's what you do. That's your job. But *I* want you here with me because *you* want to be here, not because you think someone gave you permission to be.'

'Ava, the Church isn't my job, it's my vocation, my calling. I can't just go against its wishes whenever I feel like it. I need validation, confirmation I'm on the right path. That I'm making the right decisions in life.'

'And God always makes the right decisions, does he?' I ask, as I feel my insides begin to twist uneasily.

'Yes, of course he does.'

'You're sure about that?'

'What's this about?' Callum asks. 'I get the feeling we're not just talking about you and me now?'

'Nothing,' I snap. 'Look, perhaps you should go. I need to think.'

'Think about what?'

'About whether I can do *this*.' I wave my hands between the two of us. 'You've spent so long thinking about whether it's the right thing for you to do, you haven't given any thought to whether it's the right thing for me.'

Callum climbs out of bed now too. He pulls on his trousers, which this time are lying beside the bed. 'I just assumed this is what you wanted. You seemed pretty keen earlier.'

'I was. I mean, I am. Oh, I don't know. I hoped you being a vicar wouldn't be an issue. I mean, I wondered if it might be when I met you. But I thought I could get past that.'

'Why is it something that needs getting past?'

I stare at him standing shirtless in my bedroom with just his trousers on.

Callum couldn't look any less like a vicar right now. But he was, and he'd made it perfectly clear just how much his belief in God meant to him.

'Because I don't believe,' I tell him suddenly, knowing it has to be said before this goes any further. 'I don't believe in God, Callum.'

I look at him but he doesn't respond, so I continue.

'I used to think there might something else going on, something other than just this.' I vaguely wave my hand around the room. 'But then things changed. I changed. I simply can't accept there's some higher being up there looking down on us all. If there was, he'd protect us, wouldn't he? He wouldn't allow awful things to happen in the world. He wouldn't let bad things happen to good people.'

I stand defiantly, my hands on my hips, awaiting his response.

'So, now you've heard all that, Callum, how do you feel about me?'

Twenty-nine

Callum stares at me for a few seconds with a look of consternation on his face.

I stare defiantly back at him. But secretly I'm wishing I hadn't said something quite so dramatic.

'It makes absolutely no difference to me,' he says eventually, to my surprise. 'I still feel the same about you.'

'How can you?' I ask, shaking my head. 'How can you possibly feel the same about someone who hasn't got the same beliefs as you?'

'Ava, everybody is different in this world, that's what makes it such a wonderful place to live in.'

'Hardly,' I mutter under my breath.

'What do you mean?' Callum says, hearing me. 'Diversity is what makes us so complex and interesting as humans.'

'I didn't mean that. I meant . . . Oh, it doesn't matter what I mean. I'm going to get some water.' I try to cross the bedroom. But Callum stands between me and the door. 'Can I get past please?' I ask when he doesn't move.

'Ava,' he pleads, catching hold of my arm as I try to

pass him. 'Tell me what's wrong. Tell me what's bothering you so much?'

'What's bothering me is I'm thirsty and I'd like to go to my kitchen and pour myself a glass of water.'

Callum sighs, but stands back to let me pass.

I hurry downstairs towards the kitchen. I look in on Merlin as I pass the sitting room, but he's sound asleep on the sofa, blissfully unaware anything is awry.

I stand by the sink in the kitchen and run the tap until it's cold. Then I fill a long glass with water and stare out of the window while I sip it. Since we've been upstairs the sun has started to go down, leaving a peachy orange hue to the sky.

After a bit I feel Callum standing in the kitchen doorway behind me, but I don't turn around.

'Do you want me to go?' he asks eventually when I don't acknowledge his presence.

I turn now and look at him. He's found his shirt to go with the trousers he'd pulled on before, but his feet are still bare.

'Not really,' I reply honestly. 'But what other option is there?'

'We could talk?' Callum suggests with an earnest expression. 'It might help.'

'We could, but I don't see how that will change anything. You're a vicar, Callum, your belief is your job, your everything. I just can't understand how you can possibly be involved with someone who doesn't share that same belief?'

'Why don't you start by telling me why you don't believe?' Callum says quietly. 'That might help.'

'So you can try to convert me?'

'No, so I can try to understand you a little more.'

I was behaving like a petulant child, and Callum was being far lovelier than he need have been. But this was important to me, and I knew eventually I was going to have to explain to him why.

'Would you like some water?' I ask as a peace offering. I lift another glass from the drainer.

'Yes please,' Callum says, understanding my small gesture.

I fill the glass and walk towards him.

'Thank you,' Callum says, taking the glass from me.

'Shall we go through to the sitting room?'

Callum nods.

We move a sleepy Merlin, and sit at each end of the sofa in silence for a few minutes. Me in my dressing gown and Callum in his slightly odd state of dress – the buttons on his shirt still only half done up. I try hard to distract myself from how sexy he looks like that, by looking at Merlin, the bird table outside, and the birds' gifts up on the mantelpiece.

'Ready to talk yet?' Callum asks eventually.

'It depends what you want to talk about,' I reply, still not making this easy for him.

'You. Us. Me, if you want to? Look, why don't you go first, if that's going to make it easier. Ask me what you like?'

I think for a moment, and I'm surprised by just how many questions flash through my mind.

'Why are you so convinced there's this superior being watching over us all?' I settle on. 'What makes you so sure?'

Callum smiles. 'Start with the difficult one, why don't you?'

I shrug. 'It seems to be our biggest issue currently.'

'All right then. But if what I'm going to say is going to make any sense to you, I'll have to tell you something about my past first.'

'Okay.'

'Do you remember I told you I used to work in London when I was younger?'

I nod.

'A bit like you, I was what they call a highflier. A go-getter. A high-achiever. Any of those names that people who want to be the best at what they do are called. I worked hard in the City and I played hard in the City. I'm not proud of some of the things I got up to, I'll admit. But at the time they seemed part of the character I was playing.'

'What *did* you get up to?' I ask. Callum seemed so unsullied by the vulgarities of life; I couldn't imagine him doing anything unseemly.

'The usual: far too much drink, a few too many drugs, and too many one-night stands that were only ever going to be that. I lived a shallow and unfulfilling life. But I didn't know any other way.'

I'd always known there was something different about Callum, but I hadn't expected him to say that. It did kind of make sense, though; he really wasn't your typical vicar. I'd known that from the start.

'What happened to make you change?' I ask, genuinely interested to know. 'You clearly did.'

'I was becoming increasingly dissatisfied with my life, nothing made sense any more. I was doing things, but I didn't know why I was doing them – they weren't making me happy, but I didn't know any other way. I began to feel there might be something else to life, something much better I could be doing. But I didn't know what. And then something happened. Something that changed everything for me.'

Callum takes a quick sip of water from his glass. 'Sorry,' he says, looking nervously at me. 'I always find it difficult to talk about this.'

'It's fine, take your time,' I say, wondering what he's going to tell me.

'My sister,' he says, looking down into his glass. 'She . . . she tried to take her own life.' He looks up at me to see my reaction.

'Gosh, I'm sorry,' I reply, not really knowing what the right answer was to this. 'What happened?'

'She tried to overdose on a cocktail of painkillers, sleeping tablets and anti-anxiety meds.' Callum's face is wrought with anguish as he remembers. 'Luckily a friend found her unconscious in their flat, and she was rushed to hospital. She was lucky to survive.'

'But she did,' I try to say with positivity. 'That's good.'

Callum nods. 'It would be if she'd learnt her lesson and never wanted to do it again.'

'She tried it again?' I ask, shocked to hear this.

'A few times, sadly – luckily for us she's never been successful. She got pretty close the last time, though,' Callum says almost matter-of-factly. 'Ever since then she's been residing in a mental health hospital just north of Peterborough. She's stable for much of the time, and she has a lot of medication to keep her that way, but she's considered a danger to herself and others, so it's thought best she stays there.'

'There's nothing they can do?' I ask, again feeling totally inadequate in my replies.

'Jena has an extreme form of bipolar disorder – that's what we've been told, anyway. She lived a pretty wild life when she was a teenager and into her twenties, but there was nothing unusual about that, that was just Jena enjoying herself in the way most of us do when we're young. I was always considered the calm and dependable one back then – even when I was running amok around the bars and clubs of London. But none of us realised what else was going on until Jena tried to take her life that first time – that was the turning point for all of us.'

I wait for Callum to continue.

'It was a real wake-up call for Mum and Dad; I think they thought she was just high-spirited up until then. I knew a little more, but as her big brother I helped her hide it from them. I was always the one she called when she was in a police cell, or worse. Sometimes she'd wake up in someone's house and have no idea who they were, or where she was. I'd be the one who'd have to track her down by her vague descriptions, and go and collect her. It was about then I started to pray for the first time.'

He glances at me to see my reaction, but I consciously keep my expression neutral. 'Go on,' I encourage.

'It wasn't even proper praying to begin with – not how I understand praying now.' He smiles as he remembers. 'I just used to say a few words and look up to the sky. I didn't know who I was talking to, but it gave me comfort to feel like I was talking to someone. Someone who wouldn't judge me and what I considered were my failings towards Jena.'

I nod.

'The more Jena got in trouble and the more she tried to take her own life, the more I prayed, until one day I wandered into a church and sat in a pew. It was when Jena was at her worst. I remember properly kneeling down, hands clasped together – the full thing – and begging God to save her, to do something, anything, to help my sister to live. I have to admit I left that church questioning my own sanity. No one was going to help my sister, if my sister didn't help herself.'

Callum tries to take another sip of his water, but finds his glass is empty.

'Shall I fill that for you?' I ask.

Callum shakes his head. 'No, it's fine. I need to finish this now. Where was I . . . ? Oh yes, so the next day I was out walking when I got a phone call. Jena's name was flashing on the screen, so I answered immediately. But it wasn't Jena on the other end of the line; it was a stranger, who then proceeded to tell me that she'd been walking her dog along the Thames river path when she'd seen Jena fall from a bridge into the water. She wondered at first if it was someone larking about – kids jumping off the bridge. But when Jena didn't immediately rise to the surface, she became worried. It was then she saw a man appear from nowhere and jump into the river to try to save Jena. She ran towards them both, but by the time she got there, the man had managed to get both himself and Jena back on to the riverbank. Jena was in a bad way, and the man had begun to give her CPR. The woman immediately phoned for an ambulance, but it was shortly after this that she discovered Jena's shoes, phone and a note placed carefully on the side of the riverbank.'

'Was it a suicide note?' I ask quietly when Callum pauses again.

Callum nods. 'This time she'd tried drugs *and* drowning.' He takes a deep breath and continues. 'Even though Jena appeared to be living on a different planet most of the time, she managed to remain quite organised when it came to attempts to end her life. She'd left her phone unlocked and my number on her note, so the lady rang me immediately to tell me what had happened. By the time I got to the hospital Jena was in a pretty bad way, and this time she had around-the-clock suicide watch on her.'

'I'm really sorry, Callum,' I tell him again. 'That must have been awful for you.'

'I'm not telling you for pity,' Callum says, 'I'm telling you to try to help you understand.'

'Sure, go on.'

'After I'd seen Jena, I asked the nurses if they knew what had happened to the man who saved her – the one who dived into the river. They didn't. Jena had been brought in on her own in the ambulance. So I contacted the woman who had rung me, to see if she knew. But she said, and this is where it gets interesting, that as soon as the ambulance arrived the man had disappeared – even though he'd been on the ground trying to save her, soaking wet and exhausted. Once the paramedics had taken over, he'd vanished.'

Callum looks at me with expectation, and I'm not sure how I'm supposed to respond.

'Don't you see, Ava? The man had gone, vanished into thin air, the woman said. Jena had a guardian angel that looked out for her that day – just like I asked for. Okay, I'll admit before you say it, it was likely just a passer-by who didn't want to get involved and left as soon as he knew she was all right. Some people don't want to be heroes, I get that. But my point is, it didn't matter how she was saved or who saved her, her life was spared that day, just like I'd prayed for in the church. I didn't realise it at the time, but it was like a light bulb lit up in my mind. I suddenly began to notice all the people who were doing selfless things, day in and day out. Whether they were have-a-go heroes, nurses by Jena's bedside or the volunteers that gave their time to the hospital for free, and I knew it was my time to start giving something back to society, instead of taking all the time.'

'So you decided to become a vicar?' I ask doubtfully.

'No, not to begin with. I volunteered for charities; I went overseas to distribute relief with Christian Aid. It was then I began to think more about how I could make a difference in my own country.'

'When you were overseas, I bet you saw some terrible things,' I say as carefully as I can. 'Instead of making your belief stronger, didn't it make you wonder why those things had been allowed to happen in the first place?'

Callum nods his head slowly. 'Yes, if I'm totally honest, I did begin to question things. Some of the poverty and conditions people were living in were appalling. But I believe for every bad thing that happens in the world, something good always comes from it. I'm not suggesting for a moment that the bad thing isn't terrible for those that are living through it, but even in the darkest of times you can find light, Ava. There's always light.'

'But there's evil, too,' I challenge. 'You can't deny there's evil in this world, can you?'

Callum looks calmly back at me. I can tell he's trying to work me out, but his expression remains tranquil and composed.

'I think it's my turn now,' he says steadily. 'My turn to hear your story, Ava. What happened to change your path in life and bring you here to Bluebell Wood?'

Thirty

'How do you know something happened?' I ask innocently. 'I might have decided like you to take a different path in life.'

'But you didn't, did you? I get the feeling something pretty big happened that didn't just change your path, it knocked you completely off course.'

'I need some more water,' I say, grabbing both our glasses.

I hurry through to the kitchen and stand for a moment filling our glasses at the sink. While I do, I gaze at the same spot outside as when I'd last been standing here.

I'd thought before it was a coincidence, but it's still there, exactly where the dove had dropped it in front of me.

I head outside and quickly pick up the discarded item from the kitchen window ledge, then I return to Callum with the glasses of water.

'When we were in the kitchen before arguing, a dove flew into the garden,' I tell him carefully as I sit down. 'It dropped this on the kitchen window sill.' I pull a cutting with grey-green leaves from my dressing-gown pocket. 'It was still there when I went back just now.'

Callum takes the cutting from me. 'Is it from an olive tree?'

'I think so.'

Callum glances at me to see if I might be thinking the same as he is.

'It's an olive branch,' I say, confirming it for him. 'The dove offered us an olive branch, didn't it?'

'The sign of peace,' Callum says, still gazing at the leaves in his hand.

'You're thinking about Noah and the dove that flew back to the ark carrying an olive branch, aren't you?'

'Not necessarily; olive branches were offered by the Romans, too. In battle the defeated would offer them as a sign of surrender.'

'But it's the Bible story that's the most well-known, isn't it?' I sigh. 'Even the birds seem to be on your side.'

'This isn't about sides, Ava. If you want to see this as a sign, then perhaps the dove was simply suggesting that there be peace between us. You said you saw it earlier when we'd just been arguing – your word, by the way, not mine. I like to think of what we were doing more as a healthy discussion.'

'Oh, stop being so nice!' I plead. 'How can I argue with someone who is so calm and understanding all the time?'

Callum grins. 'Like I said, why argue at all? This isn't a competition. I just want to understand you more and what happened to cause you to have such an extreme distrust of the Church.'

'I don't distrust the Church as such,' I admit. 'I just can't believe there's this all-knowing, all-seeing, all-powerful being watching over us.'

'Why can't there be?' Callum asks softly. 'Tell me.'

'Because ... bad things happen, and they shouldn't. Not to good people, anyway.'

'What bad things, Ava?'

I sigh. He's brought me back to this again.

'You see it all the time on the news, don't you? Wars, famines, incurable diseases, natural disasters, terrorist attacks . . . '

'Yes, sadly you do. But I'm interested in which one happened to you,' Callum says perceptively. 'I doubt it was famine or war, and possibly not a natural disaster either . . . '

He waits to gauge my reaction.

'That leaves an incurable disease or a terrorist attack. Does someone you know have an incurable disease?'

I shake my head a tiny bit.

'That only leaves a terrorist attack, then,' he says quietly. 'Is that what it is, Ava? Were you involved in a terrorist attack when you lived in London?'

I nod this time. Still silent.

'Oh, Ava,' Callum says softly. 'Do you want to tell me about it?'

'Not really,' I reply quietly. 'I've only ever talked with my therapist before.'

'What about your family?'

I shake my head again. 'I couldn't. They tried to talk to me about it – lots of times. But I just clammed up. I wanted to protect them.'

'That's totally understandable.' Callum reaches out his hand, but I pull mine away before he can touch it.

'Sorry,' I say, jumping up and walking over to the French window. 'It's difficult, even now.'

Callum sits quietly on the sofa, while I watch a couple of blackbirds and a pigeon picking the last of the day's food off the ground around the bird table. A robin joins them in the garden, but instead of pecking at the ground with his fellow feathered friends, he sits on the edge of the bird bath. He looks at me, his head cocked to one side as if he's listening intently to what I'm about to say.

'I was working in London on the day of the attack,' I say suddenly, not looking at Callum but still watching the birds, who have now been joined by a couple of sparrows that hang off one of the feeders. 'Usually I'd be in my office, but we had an event on at a large hotel just off the South Bank. I'd been planning this one for ages; it was for an international finance company, so we had people attending from all over the world. This was the last day of a three-day conference, and I have to admit I was secretly congratulating myself that everything had gone so smoothly.'

I glance at Callum; he nods his encouragement, so I turn my attention back to the robin, who's still watching and listening. It felt easier to tell him than talk directly to Callum.

'While one of the seminars was going on in the main conference hall, I stepped out for a moment to take an important call. I couldn't get a good signal so I had to go a little way along the corridor to pick one up. It was then I heard the first scream. I thought it was someone outside in the street messing about, but then there were more screams, and a noise that gradually built until it felt like there was a tidal wave of sound about to crash towards me along the corridor. Suddenly, accompanying the sound was a mass of bodies, they streamed down the corridor in a huge panicking mess of pushing, shoving, shouting and screaming.'

I pause to take a deep breath. Just the memory of that day was making my heart race faster, and beads of sweat begin to break out on my forehead. I was forcing myself to return to a place I never wanted to visit again, and it was painful both physically and mentally.

The birds outside suddenly start chattering. Something has spooked them and they all fly off in different directions. A jackdaw has swooped down and landed in one of the trees. All the birds have left except the plucky robin; he simply waits patiently for me to continue from his perch on the bird bath.

'I had no choice but to join them in their panic,' I continue again. 'I was carried down the corridor in a sea of people. I didn't know why they were panicking, no one was stopping to chat, everyone just wanted to get out of there as quickly as they could. There were no alarms going off, so I knew it wasn't a fire. I thought perhaps there had been a bomb scare, but I'd been in a large building before when that had happened, and although there had been a sense of fear, the majority of people had been much calmer and in control. The feeling here was just total terror. Eventually we reached the foyer at the front of the hotel – at last we can get to the exit, I thought. It was hot and stifling in the crowd, everyone was breathing heavily, and it was beginning to feel like there was no oxygen in the air – even I was struggling to breathe normally.'

I pull at the collar on my dressing gown, trying to loosen it a little, but I still feel like I'm beginning to suffocate, so I ease open the French window to get some more air. I expect the robin will fly away like he had when Robin had done the same, but he doesn't, he just sits and waits patiently, while I draw in welcome breaths of fresh air.

'Are you all right?' I hear Callum ask. 'If it's too much for you—'

'No,' I interrupt him. 'I want to tell you. Just let me take a minute.'

I'd only ever relayed this story to one person before, and that was my therapist. But even then, I'd cut corners and missed out bits so I didn't have to relive the full horror all over again. Now it felt important that I share everything with both Callum and my feathered friend outside. So when I feel a little calmer, I continue my story.

'I can see the exit now,' I say, dropping right back into that awful day. 'On the other side of the elegant art deco foyer. It's a huge ornate revolving door that's seen thousands of people come and go in its time. But everyone wants to get through it at once right now, and they can't. There's pushing and shoving, and people are shouting for others to calm down, but they don't, they just keep pushing forwards.'

As I talk, I can feel those hands and bodies pushing into me, the heat and panic in that hotel foyer as hundreds of people tried to escape at once.

'Someone shouts that the emergency exits are open on the other side of the hotel, and so half the people decide to head for them. This creates even more chaos because now some are trying to push against the crowd still surging forward towards the revolving door; not everyone has heard the new message, and many of the people are foreign and simply don't understand. And still I don't know why everyone is panicking, why everyone is so desperate to escape, and I'm sure I'm not the only one.

'I see an old lady sobbing near me, and then her husband, who has been knocked to the floor and can't get up. Some people are trying to help by creating a human barricade around them, but others are still pushing into them, selfish, not caring that someone has fallen.

'I don't know what to do. Do I stop and help? Do I continue trying to get to the revolving door, or do I heed the advice still being shouted above our heads to head to the emergency exits?'

I open the French window a little further; at least I could control this exit if I needed it.

'Then I start to feel even hotter, and my head starts to spin. I think for one awful moment I might pass out in this sea of bodies, that I too might get trampled underfoot. But then something happens: there's a burst of fresh air, and we all move again, but this time towards the front of the hotel, and suddenly before I have time to think about it, I'm outside on the pavement. There are still people everywhere, now they're trying to find friends, colleagues and loved ones as everyone spills out of the hotel to safety.'

I can feel my own breathing begin to calm as I take in the cool evening air from the garden, just as I'd done on the pavement that day.

'Once we're outside, police officers are trying to calm everyone down. I can see barricades in the distance stopping people coming near us. We're being filed one way down the street, for some reason we're not allowed to go in the direction of the bridge.

'I'm walking next to a man in a black suit who I recognise as one of the hotel concierges. "What's going on?" I ask him. "What happened?"

'The man turns to me with an ashen face. "Attack," he says slowly, as if he can't quite understand it himself. "In the hotel ... just rushed in and—" He shakes his head and begins to sob.

'I stop walking. In the middle of the sea of people all heading in the same direction. People knock into my shoulders as they pass, but still I don't move. My feet feel like lead, but my head feels light, too light, and I begin to sway.

'"Hey," a man says, putting his hand supportively on

my shoulders this time instead of knocking into me. "Are you okay?"

'He helps me along in the crowd, until we get somewhere we can stop and rest, then we sit down on a low stone wall by the Thames.

'"What . . . what happened?" I ask him. He too looks pale and drawn, like the concierge had.

'"From what I can gather a man rushed into the hotel with a knife and began stabbing people at random."

'"Oh God," I say, as my hand shoots up to my open mouth. "Where?"

'"Some conference that was being held," he says. "I don't really know. I was just checking out of the hotel when it happened. Next thing I know there's screaming and suddenly the whole foyer is rammed with people trying to get out. But apparently the main exit was blocked by the police because the guy was still on the loose outside. I believe they've taken him out now."

'"Taken him out as in . . . ?"

'He nods. "On the bridge."

'My head drops into my hands again.

'"Do you want me to phone someone for you?" the man asks. "I'm lucky I had my bags with me when it happened. My suitcase got lost somewhere in the melee, but I still have my phone."

'I stare at his phone for a moment, and for the first time I realise that my own phone must have been knocked from my hands in the panic. But I shake my head.

'"No, I have to go back there. I was in charge of that conference. I have to find out what went on, who's been hurt."

'I go to stand up, but the man puts his hand on my arm to stop me.

'"They aren't going to let you anywhere near there right now," he says. "Let me phone someone for you, at least to tell them you're safe. This will be all over social media and the news in minutes. There's nothing you can do now."'

It's dusk now and the jackdaw has left the garden. But the robin still remains – watching and waiting. As I stop talking, he bows his tiny head, gives me one last knowing look, and then takes off on his strange bobbing flight path, over the garden boundary and out towards the wood.

It's over.

I turn to look at Callum. I'm not sure exactly what I've told him over the last few minutes, and what I was simply remembering in my head.

'It could have been me, Callum. I could have been one of those people that got stabbed if my phone hadn't rung and I'd still been in the meeting room.'

'Thank God you weren't,' Callum says quietly. 'It was your conference, then? There weren't others being held at the hotel that day?'

I shake my head. 'No, it was mine. Four people lost their lives. Two were delegates and two were hotel staff that tried to stop the attacker. Several others were badly wounded.'

'Do you know why this guy did what he did?'

'The police said it was just a random attack. But we found out afterwards, during the inquiry, that the company that was holding the conference had had some shady financial dealings with the country the attacker came from. He was taking what he saw as justified revenge on them.'

Callum sighs. 'That seems to happen all too frequently now.'

'Doesn't it just? The finance company organised a memorial

service some weeks later, which I attended with some of my colleagues.'

'Did that help you at all?'

I look at Callum. I don't want to tell him, but he has to know.

'It did until the priest taking the service started going on about God's Plan and how the victims were in a better place, etc., etc. It was totally inappropriate and I was mortified when I heard him saying it. Those people are not in a better place, they're dead, and their families will never be the same again, they'll never heal from this trauma, like so many of us that were there that day. The repercussions from one evil person's actions go on for ever.'

Callum, still keeping his distance, watches me carefully.

'We don't always get it right, Ava,' he says. 'I'm sure he only meant his words to help and to heal.'

I turn back to the window, but the birds have all gone now. The garden is still, ready to bed down for the night. The only movement comes from one of the bird feeders that swings rhythmically to and fro in the breeze.

'Possibly,' I say diplomatically. 'But his words didn't do either of those things. That memorial service was the first time I'd left my flat in weeks. I was already on sick leave by then, and the last thing I, and probably so many others, wanted was to walk into a church full of people that reminded us of what had happened. But instead of offering words of comfort that would help us find a way through our pain and suffering, all we found was someone telling us it was all part of some long-term plan! The attack changed me, Callum; it may not have taken my life, but it might as well have done. I was a mess then, and I still am now.'

'Don't say that,' Callum pleads. I turn and face him again. 'You might have been a mess then, Ava, and rightly so; what you experienced was a terrible thing for anyone to go through. But you're certainly not a mess now.'

'On the outside perhaps, I put on a damn good show. But inside, Callum, that's a different story.'

'Tell me.'

I sigh. I'd come this far. 'As you know, I have a big issue with crowds – mainly indoors, but often outside, too, for some strange reason. I can't deal with strangers and I've developed an extreme distrust of people I don't know. I don't sleep well, and when I do I have nightmares and flashbacks. When I was in London I didn't go out; I spent weeks cooped up in my flat on my own. The only time I left was for appointments with my therapist, a well-meaning woman called Genevieve, who would listen and try to help, but never really did. I worry constantly about my children, mainly being in big cities in case the same thing happens again, but to them this time. Oh, and apparently the name given to all this is PTSD – Post-Traumatic Stress Disorder. When really what it should be called is hell. There, is that enough for now? I could go on if you like?'

Callum looks at me with his usual understanding and compassion.

'That is plenty,' he says calmly. 'More than enough for anyone to have to deal with in a lifetime.'

I just nod.

'Feeling like that is completely understandable,' Callum says in the same steady tone. 'You experienced something dreadful, Ava, something that no one should ever have to go through. It would be more worrying if you weren't affected by it, don't you think?'

'It doesn't make it any easier to live with, though – just because I'm reacting in the right way.'

'No, I know it doesn't.' Callum stands up slowly, like I'm a wild animal he doesn't want to scare. 'But do you think you might have got a little better since you came here to Bluebell Wood? I didn't know you before, but even I've seen a change in you since we first met.'

He begins to move towards me, still moving slowly and carefully.

'You were like a deer caught in the headlights when I stumbled upon you and Merlin in the wood that day. You looked petrified and barely spoke. You were probably relieved when I ran off and left you.'

'Yes, I was.'

He looks a tad crestfallen, but tries not to show it.

'I'm glad you're here now.' I reach my hand out towards him and Callum moves a little closer. 'You're the only person I've confided in about that day, you know? The only person I've wanted to tell, that I've trusted with it. I want it to go away, Callum. I want to be able to close my eyes and not think about it. But it's always there, it won't leave, and just when I think the memory might have faded a little, something happens to bring it all back.'

'Like when we were at the quiz – all those people crowded together?' Callum asks, standing in front of me now. 'That must have brought back painful memories for you.' He's only inches away, but we remain apart and he doesn't attempt to come closer, which I appreciate.

I nod. 'It's like a wave of nausea and fear that engulfs me, and I feel like I can't escape again. After the attack my flat became my protection from the outside world, and just recently it's been this cottage. I came here to cut myself off, to escape, to protect myself from people, crowds and situations that make everything worse, and it was working at first, but then this village, its lovely people and its odd wildlife . . . ' I gesture to the bird table. 'Instead of being a threat, something I want to push away, it's become something I want to pull closer to me, to embrace. I can't explain it, Callum, but Bluebell Wood has begun to heal me, in ways expensive therapy sessions and endless talking about my problems could never do. The last thing I wanted or thought I needed was to meet someone – a kind, lovely someone, who I'd fall for in ways I didn't think I'd ever do again. But I have, and here he is standing in front of me, listening to me babble on about something awful that happened to me, and instead of running away because I try to goad and push him into doing so, like so many others I've done since that awful day, he remains, looking like he doesn't give a damn about my weird ways or my many problems. Instead, he looks at me like . . . ' I pause now. I can't say it.

So Callum does for me.

'Like he loves you?' Callum asks quietly. 'Because if you don't see that, Ava, then I need to start working harder on my expression.'

Callum doesn't move, but I do. I step forward and wrap my arms around his neck. Then I kiss him with as much meaning as I can. I want him to know I feel exactly the same way about him as he does about me.

Callum's arms wrap tightly around me, and immediately I feel safe, protected and more comforted than I have in forever.

Thirty-one

Over the next few days Callum spends as much time as he can with me and Merlin. In between the duties he performs in the parish, and my now regular trips with Merlin to the school, we manage to spend a fair amount of time together both at the cottage and walking in the woods.

We talk a lot. About normal things like the weather and what's happening in the village, including Lonan and Linnet's blossoming romance. We talk about Callum's sister, and I realise that's why he has periods where he seems to disappear from the village: he's visiting Jena. Also, it's why he is so desperate to remain in Bluebell Wood – so he can be close to her. Apparently, she'd had quite a bad turn after Easter, and Callum had spent most of his leave at the hospital with her. Jonah's words of warning about not bothering Callum suddenly make sense, and I feel bad for troubling him about the housing development when he had so much more on his mind that day. And we also talk more about the day of the attack. Callum doesn't push me to confide in him, but since the evening at the cottage, I've been finding it much easier to talk about, and I had to admit it was definitely helping me to do so.

We don't talk about our fight – if it ever was that. And I don't bring up 'The God thing', as I've taken to calling it in my head. If Callum was happy to be with someone who didn't have quite the same beliefs as him about everything in life, then who was I to make an issue of it?

We also attend the quiz together – at a pub in a nearby village this time. Callum and I do our very best to remain apart for most of the night, but there are a number of coy, flirty looks across the table at each other, which I'm sure some of the others must notice, and they only add to the enjoyment we have at the end of the night, when we are finally allowed to be together back at the cottage.

But unlike the first quiz night, when I'd had to escape outside in a state of anxiety and panic, I'd remained quite calm when the pub had got busy. I couldn't honestly say I hadn't felt a little rattled on the inside, but I'd manged to remain calm and in control; and for me it was a huge step forward.

Today Callum and I take a different route with Merlin than the quiet ones we've so far stuck to through the wood. We're walking along the footpath that leads from the school, around the fields and back into the village.

'Aren't you worried someone might see us?' I ask as we walk past the school. So far we'd managed to keep ourselves away from the well-intentioned but prying eyes of the rest of the village.

'Nope,' Callum says, smiling at me. 'We're not doing anything wrong, are we, taking a walk together?'

'Just as well no one saw us at the cottage last night, then. Otherwise they might have something to say!'

Callum waits until we enter the footpath and then he pulls me to one side and kisses me quickly but eagerly.

'I don't care what people say. You make me happy, Ava, and a happy man is a happy vicar! That's all anyone here needs to worry about.'

I take his hand and we walk blissfully along with Merlin, who, delighted as always to be out on a walk, runs about on the path, sniffing and leaving his scent.

So caught up am I in my little bubble of adoration and love, that I've completely forgotten where this footpath emerges, and it's not until we reach the top of the hill and look down, that I see the field with all the building work going on.

Callum clearly sees it at the same time as me, because I feel his body stiffen.

'It's fine; we don't have to go past there,' I say hurriedly, seeing his stricken face. 'We can turn back and go the other way.'

'No, I let this happen. The least I can do is face up to what I've done. We're carrying on this way.'

He sets off with Merlin, and after a moment or two I follow him.

'You know,' I say, catching up with him and slipping my hand into his again, 'this development might still have gone ahead even if you hadn't given your blessing.'

'Don't try to make it seem better by using words like blessing. I sold my village out for the price of a roof and a stained-glass window.'

'You gave them the gift of a fully functioning church, a play park and a new village hall that so many people will benefit from when it's built.'

Callum stops marching down the hill and turns to look at me. 'For a person so caught up in the darkness of life, you do a good job of attempting to make everyone else see the light.'

'What's that supposed to mean?' I ask, my hand slipping away from his.

'Nothing.' He goes to walk off, but I don't follow him.

'Are you coming?' he says, stopping when he realises I'm not beside him.

'What do you mean I'm so caught up in the darkness of life?' I ask again. 'I thought you understood what I've been through.'

'I do. Of course I do,' Callum says, walking back to me. 'But every time I try to lighten your burden, try to help you understand that what happened wasn't your fault, you ignore everything I say. Brush it aside as if it's meaningless.'

'Just because I refuse to believe that what happened was part of some "bigger plan",' I say, wiggling my fingers to make air quotes, 'it doesn't mean I dismiss everything you say.'

'I don't mean that. I've simply been trying to give you some meaning to what happened – a reason. Something that will make it easier for you to live with the event itself and its repercussions.'

'I'm not one of your disciples,' I say firmly. 'Hanging off your every word while I wait for you to fix me. Hoping you'll perform a miracle and magically cure me of my plague.'

'You've just confused several moments in both the Bible and history there,' Callum says, smiling a little. 'But I get your gist.'

'Don't laugh at me!' I say, feeling like he's mocking me. 'Just because I don't know the Bible inside out like you do, it doesn't make you better than me!'

'It's not only the Bible, it's . . . Oh, it doesn't matter,' Callum says, shaking his head. 'Honestly, Ava, I really and truly don't see you as one of my parishioners in need of help. Goodness,

I would be in trouble if I felt the way I feel about you about everyone in my congregation. I'd definitely get some very odd looks distributing Holy Communion!'

I can't help but smile. Callum has this wonderful way of defusing my anger, and making whatever was riling me seem not quite as inflammatory as it had been moments before.

'That's better,' Callum says. 'One of your smiles is worth a million of your frowns. However sexy you are when you're angry.'

'Stop trying to flatter me,' I tell him. 'I'm not dark all the time, am I?'

'No, of course you're not, and when you are you have every reason to be. I know I can be one of those annoying sunny people who try to see the good in everything.'

'Ah, he praises himself as well!' I say, grinning. 'Is there no end to your talents?'

'I'll show you later if you like,' Callum says, grabbing me and pulling me to him.

'I might take you up on that!'

'Oi, oi!' a voice says as we're just about to kiss. We both turn towards the voice and see a man coming out of the trees behind us doing up his belt. 'Don't mind me, call of nature!'

It's one of the builders from the site.

'Is it absolutely necessary for you to do that?' I say. 'Don't you have a Portaloo or something?'

'We did, but it's out of order today – blocked up. A man has to relieve himself somewhere!'

I turn and look at Callum, who looks as appalled as I feel.

'Aren't you the one that was here the other day?' the man asks, looking at me. The one giving Cuckoo Boy grief?'

'Yes, I was.'

'Nice one,' he says, to my surprise. 'Royal pain in the arse, he is. None of us like doing jobs for his lot. But we have to go where the money is, don't we? Sorry your village doesn't want these houses. Just between the three of us, I think you're right: it'll ruin the look of the place. A lovely little old-fashioned village like this needs houses sympathetic to the current ones, not the sort we're building. But that's Cuckoo all over isn't it – cheap and not very cheerful.'

I'm not sure what to say. I hadn't expected this response at all.

'Thanks,' I say eventually. 'Just a shame we can't do anything about it now.'

The builder shrugs. 'That's life, I guess; money always wins in the end.'

Callum remains strangely quiet throughout this exchange.

'Right, I'd best be getting back to the site, enjoy your . . . ' He waves his hand between us and grins. 'Your *walk*.'

We watch him go.

'Are you all right?' I ask Callum, who still hasn't spoken.

'You heard him: "Money always wins in the end." He's right, isn't he? Everything always comes down to that – even I was swayed by the promise of it.'

Callum looks so pale that I'm actually quite concerned.

'There has to be another way,' I say with determination. 'There must be a way of stopping this development, and yet allowing Bluebell Wood to get all the things it desperately needs.'

'Unless you've got a stash of gold coins sitting around in an unused bank vault somewhere, then I really don't think there is.' He gestures towards the building site. 'I allowed this to happen, and now I have to live with both the consequences and the guilt.'

Not if I have anything to do with it, you won't, I think, even more determined than ever to help him.

Thirty-two

'Are you sure you don't mind?' Linnet says on Saturday morning as she drops Robin off at the cottage. 'I feel like I'm imposing on you.'

'Not at all,' I reassure her. 'I love having him round. We have fun, don't we, Robin?'

Robin nods enthusiastically. 'Lonan is getting us a bird table,' he announces. 'I've asked him for one like yours where the birds bring gifts.'

'I don't know if he'll be able to manage that,' I reply, looking uneasily at Linnet. 'But I'm sure he'll get you the best one he can.'

Robin nods, seeming to accept this. 'Are you going now, Mum?' he asks. 'I want to show Ava my project.' He lifts the carrier bag he's holding up in front of him.

'Sounds like I'm not wanted any more,' Linnet says, but she smiles at me. 'We hope to be back around six-ish, depending on trains. Possibly a little later. Is that all right with you?'

'Of course, take all the time you need. Now go and enjoy yourself.'

Linnet kisses Robin on the head and then she walks back up the path, where I can see Lonan in his car waiting for her at the top. I wave to him, and he waves back.

'Right, what shall we do first?' I ask Robin as I close the door.

'Have you fed your birds yet?' Robin asks eagerly.

'Nope, I waited until you got here,' I tell him. 'I thought you might like to help me do it.'

'Great!' Robin says, putting down his bag and hurrying towards the kitchen. 'Let's do it now.'

We collect our bird food and head outside to the table. We fill the hanging feeders first, so I don't see anything unusual until we come to the table. As always, the flat of the table is covered in the husks from the previous day's food, but once we start to clean it away to make room for the new seed, something appears in the corner.

'What's that?' Robin asks, peeking over the top of the table. 'It's something metal.'

I reach into the corner of the table and retrieve a flat circular piece of metal. It's a bit battered, but when I blow the remaining seed away it's immediately clear what it is.

'It's a coin!' Robin and I say at the same time.

'It's not like the fifty pence you found before, though, is it?' Robin asks, looking eagerly at the coin in my hand.

'No, this looks much older.' I pick the coin up in my fingertips and examine it in the sunlight. 'We'll have to look it up when we get inside and see if we can date it.'

We finish feeding the birds and head inside.

When we've washed our hands and run the coin under the tap to try to clean it up a little, we place it on a piece of kitchen towel and I find my phone so we can try to date the coin together.

'It's not a modern coin,' I tell Robin as I open Google and search for 'old coins'. 'Because it doesn't have a recent monarch's head on it.'

'What's a monarch?' Robin asks, wandering over to the window to watch the few birds that have already come down to feed on the new food.

'A king or a queen,' I tell him, as listings of websites promising to date my coin load on to the home page. 'Our modern money has the Queen's head on it. Before our current Queen it was her father, and when she's not here any more all our money will have her son's face.'

'There's a blue tit on the peanuts,' Robin says, already seeming to lose interest in the coin in favour of the birds. 'He's upside down!' he cries excitedly.

I do my best to try to read about dating old coins on the website I've chosen, in between talking to Robin about the various birds that are arriving in the garden.

'I think it might be Roman!' I say excitedly, as a photo of a coin that looks very similar to our coin appears on my screen.

'Which one?' Robin says, still transfixed by the bird table.

'No, I mean the coin. I think it's Roman. It's pretty worn away, but the head looks just like the one in this photo. It says on the website it's the Emperor Claudius. Wow, how amazing is that? I wonder why it was on the bird table.'

'Why are the pigeons trying to piggy back with each other?' Robin asks innocently. 'I don't think the one underneath likes it much, it keeps flying away.'

'They're just playing,' I say quickly.

Robin doesn't seem all that interested in the coin, so I leave it on the table, and decide I'll do some more research later.

'What have you seen so far?' I ask him as I come across to the window. 'Has your friend the robin been yet?'

We spend a lovely day together. We watch the birds, play a couple of board games that I'd discovered in one of Evelyn's cupboards, and then after lunch we take Merlin for a walk.

'I've had the best day,' Robin says later, sleepily from the sofa.

'I'm glad you have,' I call from the kitchen.

It's five thirty and I know it won't be long before Linnet and Lonan return. Lonan has taken Linnet down to London on the train to have lunch and see a matinee of a West End show. She'd texted a little while ago to say they were on a train that gets in just after six o'clock and depending on traffic they'd be back about twenty minutes after that, so I'm just getting us both a glass of juice and a biscuit before it's time for Robin to go.

I carry the glasses and biscuits on a tray back into the sitting room, half expecting I might find Robin has nodded off, but to my surprise he's up and standing in front of the mantelpiece.

'What are all these?' he asks, staring at the strange line-up of things I have displayed there.

'They're all the things the birds have left for me on the table,' I say, putting the tray down on the table.

'Why is my fifty pence up there?' Robin demands. 'I paid for my bear with that. It should have gone to the school.'

'Don't worry, I put a different fifty pence in the takings that day,' I tell him. 'After I met you, I wanted to keep your coin because it was special to me.'

Robin lifts his coin down from the mantelpiece. 'Britan-nana,' he says, looking at it.

'What?'

'Britan-nana,' he says adamantly. 'On this side of the coin.'

'Oh yes, all the old fifty-pence pieces used to have Britannia on one side of them. They seem to put all sorts on the new ones now to make them more collectable. I'm surprised we have one with her on.'

Robin puts the fifty pence back and considers all the other things.

'Roman,' he says matter-of-factly.

'Are you talking about the coin we found earlier?' I ask, taking a sip of my juice.

Robin shakes his head. 'No, all your gifts from the birds. They're all Roman. We've been learning all about the Romans at school.'

I put down my glass and join him in front of the fireplace.

'What do you mean they're all Roman?'

'Britan-nana – she was a Roman Goddess,' he begins, pointing at the coin. 'Then there's these bits of pottery and glass – we made a Roman mosaic at school using things like this. Some of the bits went missing, though.' He looks accusingly at me.

'I just found them on my bird table,' I reply. 'I don't know where they came from.'

'The nurse's watch has Roman numerals on it – remember I told you that when we found it together?'

'Oh yes, so you did.'

'Mars is the Roman God of War,' he says, looking with interest at the chocolate wrapper. 'And I'm not sure what this piece of plastic is?' he says, looking at the Trivial Pursuit triangle. 'But the feather you gave me for my Easter bonnet – that was just like the Romans had on their helmets, wasn't it? That's why I used it.'

I stare at the odd arrangements of objects on the mantelpiece.

'You know, you're right, Robin,' I say, astonished that I hadn't noticed this link before. 'And that matches perfectly with the coin we found today. I think that might be Roman, too.'

'What does it mean?' Robin asks, collecting his juice from the table. 'Are the birds doing a history project too?'

'History – of course!' I exclaim. 'That's why it's a yellow Trivial Pursuit piece. Trivial Pursuit is a quiz game that adults sometimes play,' I explain for Robin's benefit. 'The yellow triangle means you get questions on history.'

'See,' Robin says assuredly, wandering over to the table. 'I told you it all matched.'

'You did, and I think you might be on to something . . . If only I knew what, though?' I look at the objects again and wonder why the birds had left them all. It couldn't just be a coincidence, could it? Maybe I was getting carried away with this Roman theory for Robin's sake. But it made so much sense . . .

'Your coin isn't as pretty as mine are,' Robin says.

I turn around and see him holding the coin we'd found earlier.

'Do you mean in comparison to your pocket money?' I ask. 'Your money is much newer than this – it will be a lot cleaner, for one thing.'

'No, I mean my other coins – the ones I found in the ground.'

I walk over to the table. 'What coins did you find?' I ask slowly.

'Some that look a bit like this, only they're much shinier.'

'Where did you find them?' I ask, as a shiver runs through me. Could Robin's coins be the same as this one? Were there more of them?

'Me and Mum went for a walk one day to see the big machines.'

My mind runs through what he could mean.

'The big yellow ones on the field.'

'Oh, you mean the machinery that's digging up the fields on the hill?'

'That's right. I like them. So Mum said we could go and have a look when no one was there.'

'And you found the coins there in the field?'

Robin shakes his head. 'No, I found them just by the field on the other side of the footpath. Mum got a phone call, and while she was speaking I saw a lot of birds on the ground. When I went over to them they flew away, but there was something shiny on the ground where they'd been. It was sort of buried, so I pulled the leaves and earth away, and there were some shiny coins.'

'How many?' I ask excitedly.

'Two that looked a bit like yours, and two that were shinier, like gold.'

I stare at Robin for a moment.

'Did I do something wrong?' he asks anxiously.

'No, no, not at all. What did you do with them? Did you tell your mum?'

'No, she was too busy talking, then we had to rush back because Mum had to go into work, so I put them in my pocket and when I got home I put them in my special box, where I keep my special things.'

'So they're still there now?'

Robin nods.

'And you think they look like this one?' I ask, pointing to the coin.

Robin nods again. 'Yes, they have a head on them that looks like this one, but mine are much shinier. That's why I wasn't as excited as you to find a coin; because I already have some of my own.'

'And you're sure you didn't find yours on the field with the machines?' I ask again, realising what this could mean if he had.

'No, just next to it. When is my mum coming back?'

'Very soon. In fact,' I hear a knock at the door, 'this might be her now.'

As I walk through to answer the door, my mind is racing.

Could Robin's coins actually be Roman too, like mine? If there were Roman coins near to the housing development – what else might there be? And if there was anything else buried in the ground nearby, might it be enough to stop the building work from going ahead?

Thirty-three

'This could be an amazing find,' Lonan says as we wait for Linnet and Robin to come back with his coins. 'If these coins are Roman and they're gold – goodness knows what other things might be buried close by.'

When Linnet and Lonan had returned to collect Robin, I'd asked them to come in for a moment while I had a quiet word with Robin. Robin had clearly kept his find a secret from his mother, and I didn't want him to think I'd betrayed his confidence by telling Linnet about them without his permission.

After I'd assured him he wasn't in any trouble, he'd seemed quite happy for me to tell the others, and Linnet and Robin had immediately headed back to their house to retrieve the coins.

'I know, that's what I thought,' I tell Lonan as we wait in the sitting room. 'If there's other things buried there it might be enough to stop the building work going ahead.'

Lonan considers this. 'Yes, you could be right. The builders would likely have to cease their work while it was excavated by experts. Hmm . . . ' He pauses.

'What's up?' I ask.

'It's odd because all new developments like this usually have to have the land looked at by experts before any work can proceed. The land next to where Robin says he found his coins should have been examined already. If it was, I'm surprised they didn't discover anything then.'

'Knowing Colin Cuckoo, he probably didn't bother.'

'He'll be in a lot of trouble if he didn't. There are huge fines for that sort of thing. I've actually been researching the possibility that there might have been a Roman settlement around here.'

'Really?'

'Yes, this whole area was heavily populated by Romans both BC and AD. The largest settlements came AD when the Romans started to build all their infamous roads. We are, of course, very near the original Ermine Street here, some of which is now the A10 and A1.'

'I don't know the name Ermine Street, should I?'

'Ermine Street was the name of a major Roman road that ran from London to Lincoln and then York. If they are indeed Roman, our coins wouldn't be the first Roman remains to be found in this area. I really do think we might be on to something here.'

'I hope so, Lonan,' I say, thinking again of Callum's face when he'd seen the building site. 'I really do.'

Linnet and Robin return with Robin's coins, and after we've examined them Lonan proclaims he is very confident they not only might be Roman, they might be gold, too.

'We have to report this find at once,' he says gravely. 'I had a quick look on my phone while you were making our tea, Ava, and we have fourteen days to report it to the local coroner, otherwise we might face criminal charges.'

'What!' Robin cries. 'Mummy, I won't go to jail, will I?'

'No of course not, Robin.' Linnet gives Lonan a stern look.

'Sorry, Robin,' Lonan says softly. 'No, you won't go to jail if we tell them about your coins now. Also, you might get a reward if we tell the right people quickly.'

'A reward?' Linnet asks. 'Like what?'

'As the finder, Robin would be entitled to half the value of the coins should they be sold. The other half would go to the land owner. If we don't tell anyone and it's later discovered we had these coins, the whole value could go to the Crown.'

'Then we must tell someone at once,' Linnet says keenly. 'We don't want to get into trouble, and my Robin might get a little reward.'

'It won't be a little reward if these coins are found to be Roman gold. It will be an almighty big one. These things sell for thousands – tens of thousands sometimes.'

Linnet goes quite pale.

'But surely we can't do anything until Monday, can we?' I ask.

'No,' Lonan replies. 'The office will be closed over the weekend and it's only a few days since Robin found the coins, so we have plenty of time.'

'So, if we wanted to, there's nothing stopping us heading up to the field and having another look around?' I suggest carefully. 'Seeing if we can find anything else before we declare it?'

I was worried that the coins had been found just off the field where the houses were being built, so it might not be enough to stop the work.

'No, I guess not. Where did you find your coin again, Ava?'

'On her bird table,' Robin says before I have a chance to

reply. 'Her birds brought it to her like all her other Roman things.'

Lonan looks confused. 'You've found other artefacts?'

'Not exactly . . . '

'I'll tell, shall I?' Robin says excitedly, and he begins to explain about the little collection on the mantelpiece.

'How wonderful,' Linnet says when he's finished. 'It seems your little birds knew all about this long before we did. They were trying to give you messages, while you were feeding them food.'

Lonan looks a little less convinced.

'Maybe they don't want the nasty men to build the houses either,' Robin says, pouting.

'They're not nasty men, Robin,' I tell him. 'They're just doing their job. It's the greedy developers I blame,' I say to Linnet and Lonan. 'Like that Colin Cuckoo.'

Robin giggles. 'His name is Cuckoo!' He thinks hard. 'Cuckoos steal other birds' homes and lay their eggs in their nests,' he says. 'We learnt that at school.'

'Yes, I think you're right,' I tell him.

'Maybe the birds think he's stealing their homes by chopping down trees to build his houses?'

We all smile at Robin – sometimes only a child can see life as it really is.

'Perhaps they do, Robin,' I say reassuringly. 'But do you know what? We're going to do our very best to help the birds by stopping him. Just you wait and see.'

'Remind me again why we're up this early on a Sunday?' Callum asks, yawning. 'I'm usually up early on a Sunday for obvious reasons, but not before it's even light.'

'You know perfectly well why we're up,' I reply, passing him a coffee. 'So we can meet the others at the field just as it's getting light, then hopefully no one will see us searching.'

'Trespassing, you mean,' Callum says, sipping on his coffee.

'Can *you* think of any other way?' I ask, drinking from my own hot mug. 'And it's not really trespassing, we're just checking to see if there's anything else there.'

Callum had arrived at the cottage last night, just as we were discussing the possibility of there being more Roman artefacts up on the hill and in the field where the development was happening.

I'd almost forgotten he was coming; I'd been so caught up in our discovery.

'Hello, Callum,' Linnet had said, smiling knowingly at him as he'd entered the sitting room. 'Fancy seeing you here.'

Linnet, and subsequently Lonan, were the only people I'd confided in about Callum and me. I felt I had to tell Linnet, because I knew so much about her and Lonan, and actually it had felt good to confide in someone new.

Linnet had been overjoyed for me, and not at all shocked.

'We could all see you liked each other,' she'd said, beaming at me. 'It was only a matter of time.'

So even though no one is surprised to see Callum arrive at my cottage on a Saturday evening carrying an overnight bag and a bottle of wine, to their credit neither Linnet nor Lonan made a big deal about it. Even Robin didn't seem in the least bit bothered. Neither did Merlin, who after he'd fussed around Callum, returned to his bed to doze again.

Callum had then been told everything that had happened, including Robin's theories about the birds' gifts.

He'd looked knowingly at me and simply said, 'Remember the doves?'

I'd forgotten all about the doves that had left Callum a Love Hearts sweet outside the church, and me an olive branch on my kitchen window sill.

'What about the doves?' Linnet had asked.

'More bird gifts,' I'd explained. 'One of them was an olive branch left outside my window – apparently the Romans used them as peace offerings.'

We'd then gone on to talk about what we should do next, and I'd come up with a plan for a few of us to go to the footpath and the field early the next morning to see if we could find anything else buried there – it was a long shot, but we had to try.

'We've got plenty here already, you know?' Lonan tried to reason with me. 'More than one gold coin is definitely considered treasure. We don't need anything else; these coins alone should be enough to stop building work for a while.'

'But they weren't found on the site, were they? Robin said he found them near the footpath.' I'd glanced over at Robin all cuddled up on the sofa sound asleep next to Linnet. 'And my coin was found on my bird table. It could have come from anywhere around here. They might only look at the area where the gold coins were found if Colin has had the site looked into before.'

'And what if you *do* find something on the building land?' Callum asked. 'You won't be able to say we found it there, because then we'll be found to be trespassing and likely get sued. Also Cuckoo Land Homes will get a cut of any reward because it's their land.'

It had been a dilemma we'd tossed back and forth between

us. Eventually we'd settled on a few of us going up to the footpath and the field early this morning to see if we could find anything, either outside the field or just within its boundaries.

So, as the sun is rising over the trees, Callum and I meet up with our small group of bleary-eyed, yawning helpers. There's Linnet and Robin, of course, then Lonan, Jemima and Jonah, and Alouette and Jack from the pub. It was a slightly bigger group than I'd envisaged, but apparently Alouette and Jack had been an integral part of the group that had been opposed to the development in the first place – which I was surprised to hear, considering they ran the local pub. But Alouette had come from a small village in France that had been ruined by a new development on its outskirts, so she was very keen to preserve the integrity of the village. Callum had remembered that the school had a metal detector donated to them a couple of years back for the children to experiment with, so we had asked Jemima if we could borrow it for an hour or two this morning, and she'd agreed as long as she could come along too.

'Right,' Jonah asks as we assemble by the school at the beginning of the footpath. 'Where should we begin?'

Jonah had taken the 'no one must see us' instruction a little too literally, and had arrived this morning looking like the Milk Tray Man, dressed from head to toe in black. Everyone else was simply wearing clothes appropriate for digging or scraping around in the earth. A few had brought shovels and trowels, and Jack had helpfully brought a large garden sieve for sifting through the earth.

'We'll walk along the footpath to where Robin found his coins to begin with, and then we'll decide from there where we're going to dig.'

We all set off along the narrow path, looking not unlike the

Seven Dwarfs off to mine for diamonds, except there's nine of us and we're off to dig for our own type of treasure.

'Where exactly did you find your coins?' I ask Robin, as we near the field. I felt bad he'd had to get up this early, but we needed him there to show us exactly where he'd found his treasure, and Linnet had been so desperate to be involved that I don't think she'd have stayed at home without him.

'This way,' Robin says, proudly leading the way towards a wooded area by the footpath. 'It was here. I was kicking around in the leaves when I saw something shiny.'

'This is council land, isn't it?' I ask Callum, who's joined us. 'It's nothing to do with the field with the building work?'

'I don't think so,' Callum says, looking hesitantly around him.

'Stop worrying, Callum,' I say. 'We're not trespassing here, are we?'

'I don't think we're going to be trespassing anywhere today,' Jack says, walking back up towards us from the direction of the field.

'What do you mean?'

'They 'ave put the barbied-wire up,' Alouette says, looking appalled.

'What my wife is trying to say is it seems someone has recently erected barbed-wire fences around the perimeter of the building work,' Jack explains, looking annoyed. 'Doesn't look like we'll be given the chance to trespass.'

'Damn,' I say. 'We'll just have to look as best we can and as close as we can around the edge.'

We split up into small teams, with Jemima covering as big an area as she can with the metal detector. There's much excitement when the detector occasionally beeps, and someone rushes over with a spade to dig where she's standing.

But all we find for our troubles are a couple of tin cans and a rusty old key.

We dig thoroughly around the area where Robin says he found his coins, even though the metal detector doesn't beep, but we find nothing. And everywhere we dig we have to cover back over and mark, just in case someone comes by and notices what we've been up to.

'We're going to have to stop soon,' Callum says, as I dig furiously in a small patch of land in some trees where Jemima has told us the detector had alerted her to something.

I'm down on my hands and knees with a trowel, carefully throwing the soil I've dug into the sieve that Robin is vigilantly shaking from side to side to see if he can spot anything.

I turn and look up at Callum, sweat pouring from my brow.

'We've already had an early-morning jogger come past,' Callum continues, looking around him. 'It won't be long until more people start arriving for Sunday-morning walks and jogs. Plus, you look exhausted, Ava. Everyone else has stopped at least once for a rest and a drink.'

'But we haven't found anything,' I groan in anguish. 'If we don't find anything else, how can we be sure they'll stop the building work?'

'According to Lonan, what we have already is more than enough,' Callum says. 'He's done his research.'

'No!' I insist, raising my voice. 'We must make absolutely sure we stop it. We have to. We can't let them win, Callum. Evil can't win against good, it just can't! Not this time.' I beat my fist down on the ground for emphasis.

'Why don't you go and get a drink from your mum?' Callum tells a shocked-looking Robin. 'You must be very thirsty?'

Robin nods. He carefully puts down his sieve, and then as

he passes me he gently pats me on the back. 'Don't worry, Ava,' he says, 'I won't let the bad people win. I'll look after you.'

Then he disappears through the trees towards Linnet, while I stare after him, tears springing into my eyes and slowly rolling down my dirty face.

'Come on,' Callum says, gently lifting my arm. 'Stand up.'

I allow Callum to lift me up. He takes a clean white handkerchief (he would have one!) from his pocket and attempts to wipe my face.

'What was all that about?' he asks. 'Evil can't win against good? Are you talking about the builders, or is this more to do with another issue?' He looks with meaning at me.

I shake my head and try to look down at the ground, but Callum catches my chin and gently tilts it up.

'You scared young Robin just now.'

'I know; I shouldn't have said that in front of him.'

'You can't win every time, Ava. We all try to do good, but sometimes it's just not meant to be. We have the gold coins Robin found, hopefully that will be enough.'

'It's not enough, though, is it? Why would the birds have gone to all that trouble to leave me those clues if they didn't want me to find something special buried here, something that would save their habitat?'

'Maybe their gifts weren't to do with this?' Callum suggests. 'Maybe they meant something else, and you just fitted it to your Roman narrative.'

I shake my head. 'No, what else could they mean? Look, you lot,' I call out to the trees around us, 'I know you want me to find something here. So why not help me to do it? *Please!*'

Suddenly there's the sound of flapping wings, and at least

twenty birds – mostly wood pigeons – rapidly take flight. Then I hear Merlin barking.

'Where's Merlin?' I ask, looking around.

'I'm not sure,' Callum says, doing the same.

'Merlin!' I call. 'Merlin, where are you?'

He barks again, and we attempt to walk in the direction of his bark, but it's difficult, we're in a particularly dense patch of trees here, denser than the wood we're used to walking in near the cottage.

'Look,' Callum says, pointing upwards. I follow his hand and above the trees I can see a huge flock of birds circling in the sky.

'He's there!' I cry. 'He must be.'

We follow the birds until we're almost underneath them, and it's then we see Merlin in the middle of a clearing. He's pawing at the ground.

'Merlin!' I cry, running to him. 'What is it?'

Merlin looks up at me for a moment then continues with his digging.

'Is something there?' Callum asks.

'I can't see anything,' I say, kneeling down next to Merlin. 'Can you get the metal detector?'

Callum quickly returns with Jemima, the metal detector and the others, who've heard the commotion.

I hold Merlin back from his digging, and Jemima hovers the machine over the ground. To our immense delight it beeps.

'There's definitely something down there,' she says.

Jack digs the area with a shovel while everyone else keeps a close eye on the earth that he's removing.

'Yes!' Jonah calls after Jack has been digging for a few minutes. 'Here's something!'

We all stop what we're doing and rush over to him.

'What is it?' I ask excitedly.

'I don't know,' Jonah says, holding up a small piece of silvery metal. He rubs it over a little with his sleeve. 'But there's some engraving on it.'

The metal is passed between all of us but no one knows what it could be.

'It looks familiar,' Callum says, holding it in the palm of his hand, 'but I have no idea what it is.'

'It does look familiar, doesn't it?' Jonah agrees. 'But I don't know why?'

'It could be anything,' Lonan says, examining it. 'Sadly it doesn't look as though it's of any value – it doesn't look like silver, just an engraved metal. This pattern could be anything too – it's just swirls.'

'Why would the birds have gone to all the trouble of pointing this out,' I say, taking the metal from Lonan, 'if it isn't anything special?'

'The machine isn't registering anything else,' Jemima says, shaking her head. 'That must have been it.'

'I think it might be time to go now,' Jonah suggests. 'Callum and I have Sunday service in a few hours.'

'Yes, and we have a pub to open later, too,' Jack says, putting his arm around Alouette's shoulders. 'I'm sorry we didn't find anything better, Ava. But hopefully what we do have will be enough to build a decent case for the building work to stop for a while.'

Quietly, one by one, everyone begins to gather up their belongings and head back down the hill, and I have no choice but to follow. I couldn't expect them to stay here all morning; Callum's right: other people will be using this footpath soon, they'd see us and wonder what was going on. Questions would be asked, and then we'd have all sorts of problems.

I sigh as I trail behind the group making its way, with slightly less exuberance than it had on the way up, back down the hill towards the school.

None of this made any sense. Nothing that was happening added up. Was I just imagining all this stuff with the birds? Was it like Callum suggested: because of what Robin had said? Was I making it fit my own agenda about stopping the development?

I pull the piece of tarnished metal from my pocket and look at it while I walk.

For all my doubts, I'm still certain this means something. I'm convinced the birds wanted me to find this today.

But why? How does this small piece of engraved metal fit with everything else that's going on?

The others might have given up, content that we've done enough, but I'm determined to discover exactly what the birds of Bluebell Wood want us to know . . .

Thirty-four

'How did you get on?' I ask Jemima on Tuesday afternoon when Merlin and I have finished our first reading session of the week at the school. 'Did you find anything?'

'As a matter of fact, we did.' Jemima looks cautiously around the playground in case anyone might be listening. 'The children discovered quite a few interesting bits and pieces.'

I'd been wrong about everybody else being content after our excursion on Sunday morning. Later that day, when I was feeling pretty down about our lack of success on the dig, I'd had a phone call from Jemima, who had come up with an ingenious idea.

'Why don't I see if I can get permission to take the children on to the field with the metal detector as part of their history lessons?' she'd suggested. 'It will be educational for them, and hopefully helpful to us. I'm pretty sure Cuckoo Land Homes won't say no. They seemed pretty keen to keep the village onside when we had dealings with them before. I'm sure I can persuade them that this will be a great idea.'

I had of course agreed, and I'd waited most of Monday for

Jemima to get the go-ahead from Colin Cuckoo, and then all of Tuesday morning, when I knew she was heading up there with a class of children, to hear if they'd found anything.

I still wasn't sure if my passion for stopping this development came from a need to give something back to the village and the people that had helped me heal so much in the last few months or from a desire to help Callum feel better about what he'd done, or if my drive actually came from something much deeper inside me – as Callum had suggested – a need for good to prevail over what I considered to be the evil party this time.

Whatever was pushing me on, I was determined to stop the development and keep Bluebell Wood as the picture-perfect village it had always been.

'Really?' I ask Jemima eagerly, keen to hear her news. 'What did you find?'

'Some of the things we found were quite modern – you know, decimal coins, more keys, nails, screws – that kind of thing. The children were excited every time the detector went off. But we also found some interesting bits that look like they might be from broken utensils – one looks like a spoon, and the other could be a handle, and several of the children found pieces of broken pottery on their own, which might not be that old, but I think could be.'

'Wow!' I reply, astonished to hear this. After Sunday, I'd begun to wonder whether the coins Robin had found might be a one-off. 'What did you do with them?'

'I just collected everything up together in a box. When one of the builders stopped us on our way out to enquire if we'd found anything, I just showed him the modern stuff that was on top.'

'Great! Well done.'

'I felt bad, though, because he seemed really interested in what we were doing.'

'I bet he did; Colin Cuckoo probably told him to keep an eye on you.'

'That was the weird thing,' Jemima says, with a puzzled expression. 'When I rang up on Monday to ask permission to take the children on the field, I didn't speak to Colin Cuckoo, he wasn't in the office, I spoke to someone else in his company. It was them that agreed to us going on the site, as long as we stayed at the top of the field where the construction work hadn't started yet, for safety reasons. That was fine with me because I didn't want the children anywhere near the big machinery, so we were confined to the end close to where Robin said he found his coins, which is, of course, where we wanted to be.'

'What was weird about that?'

'It might be nothing, but when we arrived the builders were very welcoming; they'd obviously been told we were coming by someone. But they also seemed quite surprised we'd been allowed on there.'

'How do you mean?'

Jemima shrugs. 'I don't know, it just seemed like they were really keen for us to find something, and when we left, they seemed slightly disappointed that all we'd found were the modern things I chose to show them.'

'I've met a couple of them, they seem like nice guys. They don't like Colin Cuckoo, that's for sure. I expect they were disappointed for the children.'

'Perhaps.'

'Anyway, this is great news. If you've found items that might be Roman actually on the field, they will be counted as treasure, and will mean the building work will have to be stopped.'

'I guess so,' Jemima says, sounding a bit hesitant again.

'Why do you say it like that?'

'I really don't want to put a downer on your plans, Ava, honestly I don't. If what we've found *is* of historic interest, the building work will definitely have to stop for a while to allow the area to be excavated, and what they find then will depend on how long the work is paused for. But it won't be for ever, will it?'

'Why not?'

'I think the work only stops while the area is looked at by the experts; once they're happy they've found all they can, then the work continues. It would have to be an area of *extreme* historic interest to prevent the houses *ever* being built. So while we've probably done a great job in pausing the development, I don't think we can assume we've stopped it completely.'

I stare at Jemima. I hadn't thought about it like that. I'd been so pleased we might have found a way of stopping the development, I hadn't paused to consider that it might go ahead again at a future date.

'I could be wrong,' Jemima says hopefully, seeing my forlorn expression. 'You never know what they'll find once they start digging; we might all be living on a complete Roman settlement?'

'But we might not,' I reply desolately. 'It might just be a few odd things that have survived in a field, and if they find anything valuable like Robin did, Colin will get half the profits as the owner of the land, according to Lonan. So, we've probably done him a favour in the long run: not only will he get to build all his houses, but he might make an extra few quid out of it as well.'

*

The afternoon is wet, so Merlin and I spend it cuddled up on the sofa together. Merlin is tired from his trip to the school, and I'm just miserable about life in general. Even Callum calling to ask about the school's trip to the field and to enquire whether he can come round tonight doesn't cheer my mood as much as it should do, and I feel annoyed with myself that I can't even see the positive in that.

The rain ceases for a while and one of the young birds that have recently begun to frequent the garden bobs about on the grass a little way from the bird table looking for food. This youngster's feathers haven't come through properly yet, but it has a small flash of yellow on its wings that makes me think it might be a greenfinch, and I make a mental note to check one of Evelyn's books later.

I watch the little bird for a while, wondering at what stage a mother bird decides it's safe for her young to venture out on their own, and if she still worries about them constantly, like I do with my two grown-up children. I'm half watching the bird, half thinking about Hannah and Matt, when out of the corner of my eye a large shadow is cast over the garden as something drops quickly down from the sky. Before I have time to react, I realise the shape has swooped down on top of the little bird.

'No!' I cry, as the huge bird I now recognise as a sparrow hawk beats its long wings and takes off again with the little greenfinch in its talons. 'Stop!' I shout at the window, banging on the glass. But it's too late; the cunning predator has caught its innocent prey, and is probably retreating back to its own nest, where the young bird that had been happily searching for food a few moments ago is now likely a meal for the sparrow hawk and its own chicks.

I stand silently at the window, completely shocked that

something so violent has taken place in my garden, right under my nose.

I feel guilty that the little bird had been under my bird table when it was taken, as if it should have been better protected here than out in the wild somewhere. It had put its trust in me and my garden to forage for food, somewhere it should have been safe, and yet it had been savagely attacked by a predator it didn't stand any chance against.

I feel cold and numb as I stand at the window, and I realise after a while I've started to shake. Merlin, sensing something is wrong, rolls off the sofa to come and stand supportively next to me. He nuzzles his nose up against my leg, so I slide down on to the floor and pick him up, holding him close as I sit cross-legged on the carpet.

'Why do the innocent fall prey to those that wish them harm?' I ask Merlin, finding his closeness immediately calming in a way I hadn't expected to. 'Those innocent people had trusted they'd be safe coming into the hotel that day. They thought no harm would come to them, but it did. Those that meant them harm got to them, just like the sparrow hawk got to the young bird – an innocent life taken in an instant.'

Merlin wriggles in my grip, and I realise I'm holding him a little too tightly.

'Sorry,' I tell him, snuggling against his soft fur. 'I just don't understand anything any more, Merlin. It seems you can't win whatever you do, however you try to help; it all just goes wrong.'

Just then the friendly little robin that so often visits the garden lands on the grass not far from where the bird had been taken a few moments ago. I'm about to warn him to leave in case the sparrow hawk returns, when I notice he has some pink paper in his beak, which he drops purposefully on the ground in front of him. Then he looks at me in that knowing way he always has, with his little head cocked to one side.

Merlin spies the robin and pricks up his ears.

'No, Merlin, leave him,' I say, trying to calm him by stroking his back firmly. Merlin growls, in what I know to be a playful way, but it's too much for the robin and he decides to leave.

'Merlin!' I complain good-naturedly. 'Now you've scared him away.'

The piece of pink paper blows towards us across the grass. So I put Merlin down and open up the French window, then I chase the paper a little way across the lawn as it blows gently along in the breeze.

When I finally catch up with it, I pick it up and open up the folds to reveal what the robin has dropped – it looks like a torn corner from a bingo card, with the numbers 12 and 21 remaining.

'Well, you've stumped me now,' I call out to the garden, in case the robin is still about. 'Did the Romans play bingo? Is that what you want me to know this time?'

There is, of course, no answer. However, I do feel a little better as I stand outside in the fresh air and realise what Merlin and I probably need is a good walk to clear away the drama of this afternoon, and put it in perspective.

So that's exactly what we do. And as always, the peace and tranquillity of the wood doesn't totally heal my woes or take my worries away, but it makes them seem just that little bit easier to deal with. So when Callum arrives that evening, I'm already in a much better state of mind.

I tell him about what had happened earlier in the garden, and how I'd reacted. When I get to the part about the robin and the pink paper, he smiles.

'What's funny?' I ask, annoyed that he's finding this amusing.

'Nothing is funny at all. I'm smiling because of what the robin left for you – the piece of paper.'

'What about it – do you understand what it means?'

'Possibly. You won't like it, though.'

'Why?'

'Because I think it's a quote from the Bible.'

I stare at Callum, so he continues: 'Twelve: twenty-one is a line from the book of Romans, would you believe? And it says, "Do not be overcome by evil, but overcome evil with good."'

I still stare at him, and then I glance out at the bird table through the window.

'Are you sure?' I ask.

'Has Evelyn got a Bible on her bookshelves?' Callum says, getting up and walking over to them. 'Yes, here.' He pulls the Bible from the shelf and begins to flick through the pages. 'It's sometimes translated slightly differently, but the meaning is the same. Here you go,' he says, passing me the book and pointing to the page.

I read what it says aloud: '"Do not be overcome by evil, but overcome evil with good." They knew what I was thinking,' I say to Callum in amazement as he stands next to me. 'They were trying to give me some comfort.'

'And some guidance, too,' Callum says, sitting down next to me. 'I think that all the gifts the birds have left for you are trying to guide you in some way.' He looks up at the mantelpiece, where the birds' gifts still remain, except for the Roman coin, which Lonan has taken to present to the local coroner as part of our treasure finds.

'Just because you might have had a setback with stopping the development completely, it doesn't mean you should give up. Good will always win out eventually, Ava. And that's not me quoting from the Bible this time, that's me telling you what I believe. And if you won't take my word for it, listen to your bird friends. They seem to know exactly what's going on, even if we don't.'

Thirty-five

Lonan returns from his visit to the local coroner a few days later with good news.

Although they couldn't say for certain without further official examination, off the record they were pretty sure that the things we had discovered were indeed Roman and treasure. If their suspicions prove to be correct, then the building site and the area around it will have to be thoroughly examined by archaeologists before any further disturbance of the ground can take place.

According to Lonan, the building site will likely be closed down within the next few days.

'They didn't even seem that surprised when I walked in with our things,' Lonan says as he sits with me in the cottage drinking coffee one morning and telling me everything that had happened. 'Apparently, there have been quite a few finds in this area. It was only a matter of time before someone came up with something of real value like Robin's coins. They were particularly excited about those.'

'But unless the archaeologists find something of significant interest when they start looking in the area, then the building work will eventually begin again?'

Lonan nods. 'I'm afraid so.'

I sigh.

'There was one other bit of news, though,' he says, pulling something from his pocket. 'The strange bit of metal that Merlin helped you find. They don't think that's old enough to be of interest. Apparently, the Portable Antiquities Scheme only record things dated before 1700. They photographed it, though, in case they should want to record it and look at it further, and I said that was fine. So it's all yours again.'

He hands me back the small piece of engraved metal.

'Thanks,' I say, sounding less than grateful.

'What's wrong, Ava?' Lonan asks. 'What you've done in discovering all this lost history is amazing. I know we've probably only stopped the building work for a short while, but it's better than nothing.'

'I know, but I just wanted to do something more,' I tell him. 'We're new to Bluebell Wood, aren't we, you and I? I don't know about you, Lonan, but this village has done more for me than I could ever possibly try to explain. I just wanted to give them something in return for everything they've done for me.'

Lonan nods in agreement. 'I know what you mean. I only came here to get some intense writing time. Usually when I rent properties, all I see is the inside of them, and on occasion the inside of the local hostelry. But Bluebell Wood has been so much more than just a base for me this time. I've been lucky enough to meet some wonderful people – you included – who've made me feel welcome and a part of the community. But most importantly, I've met and fallen in love with a delightful and amazing woman, and she and her remarkable son have taken me in and made me feel wanted again, and I haven't felt wanted for anything but my stories for a very long time.'

I'm surprised to hear Lonan say this. He always came across as such a strong, confident character, so to hear him sound vulnerable, even lonely, comes as quite a shock.

'It seems like we're both in debt to Bluebell Wood, doesn't it?' I tell him. 'If only we could find a way of repaying the village for what it's given to us.'

I look at Lonan, but he's staring out of the window.

'Lonan? What's wrong?' I ask, seeing his troubled face.

'If I said what I'm going to say now to anyone else, Ava, they'd think me mad. But I think I just witnessed a jackdaw leave a gift for you on your bird table ... '

Lonan and I rush outside to the table and discover that a jackdaw has indeed left something, and this time it's immediately clear what it is: a gold locket on a chain.

I carefully lift the locket from the table and blow the few pieces of bird seed that have already attached themselves to it down on to the grass.

'I wouldn't have believed it if I hadn't seen it with my own eyes,' Lonan says, staring at the locket. 'But the bird flew down with it in its mouth and then purposefully dropped it on the table.'

'I'm not surprised in the least,' I say, examining the locket. 'I've become quite used to it now. But they've never left anything like this before. I wonder where it's from and what it means.'

'Does it open?' Lonan asks. 'Maybe there's something inside?'

Carefully I prise open the locket, and just as Lonan had

suggested, in one half there is a worn sepia photo of a man with a beard.

'He looks Victorian, maybe even Edwardian,' I say, squinting at the photo. 'I wonder who it is.'

'The plot thickens ... ' Lonan says, shaking his head, and then he laughs. 'You know, I might have to change my writing genre after witnessing all the things I have recently. I think my historical novels might have to be given the push, in favour of a mystery. I've certainly got enough material to use!'

'I thought the bingo numbers were strange enough, but this? This is on a different scale.'

'What bingo numbers?' Lonan asks. 'Have you had more gifts that I don't know about?'

As we go back inside, I quickly explain about the pink paper left by the robin and how Callum had interpreted it for me.

Lonan looks even more astonished than he had when the locket had been presented.

'Goodness, you have been left some treasures by these birds, haven't you? Some tiny treasures that might have seemed insignificant at first, but now are painting a much more fascinating story than I could ever hope to tell.'

'I like that,' I say, smiling, 'they are tiny treasures, aren't they, each and every one. Until a few days ago I thought they might just be junk, and it was all a weird coincidence the birds leaving these things. Then we found the Roman connection and I thought they were to do with that, but now ... now I think they have a much more significant meaning, one that I hope to discover very soon.'

That afternoon, I can't help but allow my walk with Merlin to pass by the building site.

It's just gone three o'clock so I'm surprised to see the men packing up for the afternoon. Bert, the builder that I'd spoken to on my first visit here, recognises me and comes over to the edge of the field.

'Looks like you got your way,' he says, smiling at me. 'We've been told to pack up for a while. Apparently, they've decided this is an area of historical interest after all. They're going to excavate it properly and have a look around.'

'Really?' I say, trying to sound surprised. 'What happened, did you find something?'

'Someone else did nearby, then we had some kids on here from the local school with a metal detector and they found some bits and pieces – enough to stop us working, anyway.'

'I'm sorry,' I say, genuinely meaning it. I hadn't considered the builders, who now wouldn't have work; I'd only thought about stopping Colin Cuckoo. 'Will you be paid while the work stops?'

'Yeah, we'll be put on another site. We won't be out of pocket. Cuckoo Land Homes has new builds going up everywhere.' He looks around to see if anyone else is within earshot, then he leans in closer to me. 'Just between you and me, I'm glad someone else found more artefacts. From what I've seen, this land seems riddled with old stuff people might find interesting. It seemed a shame for it to be forgotten and just built over.'

I look at Bert and it takes me a moment to process what he's trying to tell me.

'Are you saying that you've been finding things while the building work has been going on?' I ask. 'Things that might be classed as of historical interest?'

Bert nods. 'Not only us, but I heard that the original excavation found things too, but it was all hushed up.'

My heart is beating fast now.

'Do you think someone bribed those in charge of the original excavation to say there was nothing here?'

Bert nods again. 'I don't think so, I know so. You didn't hear it from me, though, right?'

I hurriedly nod my agreement. 'Just one more question: were you told not to say anything about them by someone with the name of a bird, by any chance?'

Bert looks at me, then he makes the sound of a cuckoo.

It's all I need to hear.

Thirty-six

'I can't believe they're not going to do anything,' I say to Callum for about the fifth time since he got to the cottage. 'How can they not?'

'You don't know that for sure,' Callum says patiently as he watches me pace about the sitting room. 'Lonan said they'd look into it.'

'If they look into it they won't find anything, will they? Colin will have hushed everything up. He may be rude, annoying and a pain in the arse, but he's not stupid.'

'Maybe one of the builders will come clean?' Callum suggests.

I shake my head. 'No, they'll be too afraid of losing their jobs, and the person that got paid off will keep quiet or the same will happen to them. It's no good, Callum, Colin Cuckoo wins again!'

'Ava,' Callum says, standing up and coming over to me, 'you need to calm down. This isn't helping anyone – especially not you.' He tries to comfort me by placing his hands on my arms.

'I know,' I wail, 'but I'm just so frustrated. Whatever I do it doesn't work; I can't stop them. I want to help Bluebell Wood.

I want to help you, Callum, and if I'm honest I want to help myself, too. This has become about more for me than just stopping some houses going up. It's about doing what's right and, more importantly, preventing what's wrong.'

'I know it is,' Callum says supportively. 'I know you need to do this, and I understand why. If they do find Colin Cuckoo has been concealing things he believes to be treasure, then he'll be in a lot of trouble. Lonan said a fine, possibly imprisonment.'

'I bet he'll wriggle his way out of it,' I grumble. 'He's that type.'

'But you'll have sullied his reputation in the process,' Callum says. 'And that counts for a lot in the business world.'

I know he's trying to help me, but I can't help but think there must be something else we can do. I can't and I won't give up now.

We sit back down on the sofa and I snuggle into Callum while he wraps his arm around my shoulders.

'How's your sister?' I ask, hoping a change of subject might help my mood.

'Yeah, she's doing okay. Things have calmed down a bit now her meds are kicking in again.'

'They wanted to put me on anti-anxiety medication after the attack,' I tell him, 'but I refused.'

'Do you think it might have helped you?'

I shrug. 'Maybe. At the time I didn't want to have everything I was feeling dampened down, though. I think I needed to feel those emotions, to allow them to process properly.'

'Do you think you've processed it all now?'

'Probably not. You've seen how I've been reacting to everything that's going on.'

'That might not just be because of what happened. Perhaps

it's in your nature to root for the underdog – to try to protect those around you from what you perceive as harm.'

'What do you mean what I *perceive as harm*? Are you saying the houses are a good thing now?'

'No, of course I'm not. But sometimes bad things have to happen to us to make us stronger humans. The process we go through while we're dealing with what we consider bad things sometimes makes us a better person as a result.'

'I know you're a vicar,' I say, looking up at him and smiling, 'but do you have to always find the good in everything? It's very annoying!'

Callum smiles too. 'That's not my profession, that's just me. And you're the one who sees everything as black and white. Good and bad. Life has many grey areas, in my experience.'

'You're probably right,' I say, sighing a little.

'But that shouldn't stop you from fighting for what you think is right. That's one of the things I love about you – your clear sense of right and wrong.'

I gaze up at Callum.

'I love you, Ava Martin,' he repeats, as my heart feels like it's going to burst with love for him.

'And I love you, too, Callum Crawford. More than you know.'

We kiss, and as our passion grows and I rearrange myself on the sofa to get closer to him, I feel something in my pocket prodding into my side.

'Hang on,' I say breathlessly as I sit back for a moment to remove whatever it is. I reach into my pocket and retrieve the object: it's the locket.

'What's that?' Callum asks, beginning to kiss my neck now.

'Something the birds left earlier,' I whisper. 'Don't worry about it now.'

But Callum pulls away to look. 'Is that a locket?'

'Yep, they left it on the bird table while Lonan was here. He actually saw a jackdaw land and drop it there.'

'That's a step up from the other stuff they've left, isn't it?'

'Just a bit.' I try to put the locket on the side table, but in my haste I drop it and it slides on to the floor, falling open as it does.

'Don't worry, I've got it,' Callum says, leaning towards the locket. He lifts it up and his gaze falls on the photo.

'What is it?' I ask as he stares intently at the picture. 'What are you looking at?'

'This man,' Callum says, still looking at the photo. 'I think I recognise him.'

'How can you?' I ask doubtfully. 'That photo must be a hundred years old at least.'

'I'm not sure ... but I'm certain I've seen him somewhere before.' It's clear as Callum sits up that any amorous intentions he might have been harbouring have been put on hold. He stares hard at the photo. 'And you say the birds left this for you?'

'Yes, Lonan saw a jackdaw drop something on the bird table. When we went outside this was on there.'

'I've got it!' Callum suddenly says. 'This guy was once a vicar to this parish.'

'How do you know?'

'When I moved into the vicarage, I did a lot of clearing out. The previous vicar died without any family, so the place was quite a mess – full of junk and other stuff that Jonah and I didn't need to keep. One of the things we found, though, was a box of old photos – lots of them were of the previous incumbents to the parish. I'm sure this guy was one of them.'

'Where are the photos now?'

'At the vicarage, in the attic.'

Callum stares at me, and I hope he's going to suggest what I want him to.

'Do you want to go and look now?' he asks a little sheepishly. 'I mean, I know what we were about to do . . . '

I lean over to him and kiss him firmly on the lips.

'Let's go,' I say without hesitation. 'That can wait. I've a feeling this can't.'

We hurtle over to the vicarage with Merlin in tow, and I realise as Callum unlocks the front door that this is the first time I've come further than the garden.

The inside of the vicarage is much like I imagined it would be – slightly old-fashioned and traditional. But clean, and immaculately tidy.

'Jonah!' Callum calls as we enter into the hall. 'Are you home?'

'What's wrong?' Jonah asks, appearing in the hallway. 'I thought you were— Oh hello, Ava.'

'Do you remember that box of old photos we found when we moved in – the one with all the previous vicars?'

'Er . . . yes, I think so.'

'Is it still in the attic?'

'I expect so, why—'

But Callum is already thundering up the stairs.

I smile politely at Jonah. 'Do you remember this man from the photos?' I ask, showing him the locket.

'Possibly,' Jonah says, 'but there were a lot of photos. The locket looks familiar, though . . . Where did you get it?'

But luckily I don't have to explain because Callum's muffled voice shouts from upstairs. 'I have it! Back down in a moment.'

Callum reappears carrying a cardboard box which he carries through to the kitchen and puts down on the table. Then he rips open the top and begins to thumb through the contents.

'Can I get you a cup of tea, Ava?' Jonah asks politely as we follow him into the kitchen. 'My friend here seems to have mislaid his manners.'

'Thank you, Jonah, but I'm fine.' I watch Callum pulling photos from the box, then discarding them on the table.

'Gosh, you have got some really old photos here,' I say, looking at a few of them as they come flying our way.

'Here it is!' Callum says triumphantly. 'I knew it was here. Look, this is the same guy, isn't it?'

I compare the sepia photo in the locket with the slightly crumpled one Callum has thrust at me.

'Yes, I'd say it is. What do you think, Jonah?'

But Jonah is looking through the discarded photos on the table.

'Here!' he says, looking as elated as Callum had been. 'I knew I'd seen it before. Is this your locket?'

I look at the photo that Jonah is holding out to me. It's a photo of an Edwardian lady. She has her long hair piled up on top of her head, and she's wearing a long dark skirt tightly nipped in at the waist, and a high-necked white blouse, and I'm astonished to see that she's wearing a locket around her neck that looks exactly like the one I'm holding in my hand.

But what's more amazing is she's standing next to a man with a beard, who not only looks exactly like the man in the photo that Callum has just found, but is the spitting image of the man in my locket too.

Thirty-seven

'Where did you say you got this locket?' Jonah asks, while we all sit at the kitchen table examining the photos in front of us.

'Ava found it in her garden,' Callum says quickly, before I can answer. 'Didn't you?'

'Yes,' I reply, 'earlier today.'

'When Ava showed me the photo in the locket,' Callum explains to Jonah, 'I knew I'd seen the man with the beard somewhere before, that's why we came rushing over. I had no idea that there would be a photo of the locket inside this box too.'

'The locket must have belonged to the bearded man's wife, by the look of the photo Jonah found,' I say. 'I can only assume it's his wife if he was the parish priest. They look like a couple, don't they?'

Jonah turns the photo of the couple over. 'It says Father Corbin Hawkins and his wife Mavis. So yes, they were married. It doesn't surprise me that the locket turned up in your garden, though, Ava.'

'Why?' Callum asks.

'Oh, Callum, I've told you before you should read up on the history of the parish you're rector of.' He shakes his head. 'There're books all about the history of our church in your study. Which, luckily for you, I spent some time reading when I first came here.'

Jonah gives Callum a reproving look, which Callum chooses to ignore.

'If I remember correctly,' Jonah continues, 'Mavis was the daughter of the main landowner around Bluebell Wood at the time when she married Corbin. Back then, something called a glebe was in place to help maintain churches. They supported themselves by taking taxes or a living from the land near to where the church was housed; often that land would extend far further than the church grounds. So when Mavis married Corbin, her father granted them part of the benefice that his ancestors had been given by the Crown, sometime back in the twelfth century, I think, if my memory serves me correctly.'

'Lonan told me about that!' I say excitedly. 'Something to do with a horse and the king's son?'

'Yes, that's the one,' Jonah says, nodding keenly. 'I believe the story goes a farmer was given part of the Royal Forest by the King, in gratitude for looking after his son following a riding accident. As a result, the farmer eventually became a wealthy landowner, living off the benefits that land gave you back then with tithes and so on.'

'Lonan seemed to think the farmer's descendants built the manor house that's now just ruins up on the hill at the top of the woods,' I say excitedly, while Callum watches us, looking slightly bewildered that we both appear to know so much about the history of Bluebell Wood.

'Yes, I believe his family did build that house eventually.

But the original land the farmer lived on was where your cottage is now.'

'Really? How very exciting. I had no idea. I thought his house was where the ruins are.'

'No, that building came much later. The farmer had a very meagre home, probably a small cottage not unlike yours, on the outskirts of the wood.'

'How do you know all this?' Callum asks Jonah dubiously.

'I told you, most of it is written in books in your office. The past rectors were very good at keeping records of everything, and the church dates back to Norman times, doesn't it? You'd know there are records of everything if you'd just spend some time reading them.' Jonah folds his arms across his chest and gives Callum another disapproving look.

'All right! Stop making me feel bad that I've not had time to read some dusty old books. I prefer to concentrate on looking after the parishioners I have who are living and breathing, not those that passed on centuries ago.'

Jonah purses his lips, and I want to laugh at the two of them bickering. I feel like I'm in the middle of some seventies sitcom taking place in the village vicarage.

'Please continue, Jonah,' I ask sweetly. 'I'd like to know more.'

'Thank you, Ava,' Jonah says, rolling his eyes at Callum. 'At least someone is interested.'

'I'll be interested when you get to the point!' Callum joshes good-naturedly.

'*Anyway*,' Jonah continues, 'so that Corbin could not only support the running costs of his church, but his new wife and their future family too, he was bequeathed some land by Mavis's father. Mavis's family were by then living up in the manor house on the hill, like you correctly said. The land the couple was bequeathed is the land your cottage is on now, Ava, the family's original home. This became, upon their marriage, the vicarage – or rectory, as it's correctly known in this parish. The house we're in now was bought by them at a later date, because it was a little closer to the church and it had more space to house their ever-growing family. Seven children they had!' he says, looking shocked. 'Seven! Can you imagine?'

'So what you're saying,' Callum says, trying to clarify this in his own head, 'is that the land Ava's cottage is on was part of the original bequest to the farmer from the king?'

Jonah nods.

'And it originally belonged to Mavis's family – well, her ancestors?'

'Yes.'

'And because Mavis married the vicar of the parish, some of that land was then bequeathed to them?'

'You're following it so far,' Jonah says.

'And even though they moved to this house we're in now, they didn't sell the land the original vicarage was on?'

'No, surprisingly, it must have held sentimental value for them, so they just continued to rent it out.'

'What happened to it after they passed away, then? It just passed down through their families?'

'Not exactly.' Jonah shakes his head. 'It's a bit of a sad tale at this point. Mavis and Corbin may have had seven children, but only one survived. Four died in infancy of various childhood diseases, and two were killed in battle in the First World War. Their only surviving child, a son, also became a priest, so when both Corbin and Mavis passed away, their son took over the parish and the land continued to be his. But it was when *he* passed away, without leaving any direct heirs, that he left the land his parents had been given to the Church in his will, and it's remained that way ever since.'

'So technically the Church owns my cottage?' I ask, my mind still racing. 'I thought Evelyn did?'

'No, Evelyn rents it from us,' Jonah explains. 'Officially we shouldn't actually see any revenue from it. Since 1976 all profits from glebe land – i.e. land that brings in any money for the Church – should go directly to the Diocesan Board of Finance. But because this particular section of land has such an unusual history, an exception was made and the land is still owned directly by us at St Francis, and we keep any revenue from it – which in our case is rent from the cottage.'

'I knew Evelyn rented it from us,' Callum says, looking astonished, 'but I had no idea of the cottage's history.'

'Again,' Jonah says, 'if you'd read the books—'

'In my office, yes I know, I know.'

'But if that's the case,' I say, still trying to piece this all together, 'the Church might not only own the land where my cottage is, it could still own much of the land that was originally bequeathed to the farmer.'

'It's highly unlikely,' Jonah says. 'I'm sure much of it would have been sold on over the years. Our records only show that Mavis and Corbin were given the land your cottage is on when they married because it related to the vicarage at the time. I'm not sure what happened to the rest of the land her father might have still owned. I guess there must be records of it somewhere.'

'Let's stop and think for a second,' I say, as my mind continues to race. 'What if the land around Bluebell Wood wasn't sold by either Mavis's ancestors or her son? That would mean the Church could still own it now if her son left everything to them? And if that land happened to include the fields that were sold for building . . . '

'We might be able to stop the development!' Jonah cries, catching on immediately. 'Oh my goodness, you're right, Ava.'

We both turn and look at Callum, our eyes wide with excitement.

'You two are getting completely carried away,' he says, shaking his head. 'What are the chances that the land wasn't sold on officially over the years, decades, centuries even? People are always looking for ways to make money. There's no way that the Church could possibly still own land around here and no one knows about it. Na-ah. No way in the world.'

Both Jonah and I sit silently, neither of us willing to be discouraged.

'All right, all right,' Callum says, yielding a little. 'Suppose I go along with your theory for a moment, and the Church might really own a large section of Bluebell Wood. You're suggesting that old Mr Covey, and then subsequently his son, didn't officially own the land that was sold to Colin Cuckoo for the development. They simply lived and worked on it using some sort of gentlemen's agreement?'

I shrug. 'It's possible?'

'Surely a solicitor would have copies of the original title deeds, though? All land belongs to someone; those sorts of documents don't just go missing in the mists of time, do they?'

'But what if they did?' I ask. 'What if over the years the land became occupied by different people who laid false claim to it, and then it just became known as their land? That would be impossible these days, but we're talking a long time ago here, Callum. Stranger things have happened than a bit of misplaced land.'

'It would be a miracle if the owner of the land your cottage stands on still owned vast swathes of land around here because a king supposedly gave it to a farmer hundreds of years ago. It's not going to happen.'

'But miracles do sometimes happen,' I tell him quietly. 'And *you* of all people should believe in them, Callum.'

Thirty-eight

Merlin and I walk along the footpath and down the hill, and as always when we come this way we pause for a few minutes to watch the work going on in the field.

There is still excavating taking place, but unlike a few months ago when the site had been full of bright yellow diggers and large industrial machinery, today it's full of people digging up the earth in a much more careful and precise way.

As we had hoped it might be, both the fields and the surrounding area where the development had originally been planned had now been declared a site of historical interest. Several other ancient finds had been discovered on an initial scout of the area, and so the development had been paused, the diggers, trucks and machinery had moved out, and a bunch of friendly archaeologists had moved in to take their place.

And to both their and our delight, every day more interesting items were being unearthed – pieces of broken crockery and utensils that suggested this area may have indeed once been a Roman settlement. The fresh spring water that ran through the wood apparently backed up this idea, as the Romans would usually settle near a source of fresh water.

Since they've been here they've found rudimentary tools that had been used for building, small pieces of jewellery and various coins, including more gold to add to Robin's original find, which had caused great excitement among both the archaeologists and the villagers, who often come to the field to watch what's going on.

All in all, everyone was extremely pleased with the progress being made on the Bluebell Wood dig. Even Colin Cuckoo, who once he'd got over the fact his development had been put on hold had realised that he could benefit from everything that was being found on the dig, had been spotted once or twice watching what was being found on his land.

As I'd suspected, no one could be found to back up my theory that Colin had known this land was of historical interest, either before the work had begun to take place or during. And it was a constant source of annoyance to me that not only was he going to get away with it, but that he actually might benefit from this delay to his building plans.

Colin Cuckoo wasn't my only source of frustration. Progress in other areas was currently at a standstill too.

After the excitement of finding the photos and hearing about the history of the land in and around Bluebell Wood, we'd been unable to find anything else that would back up my theory about the Church still owning some of the land.

Jonah had searched through the records at St Francis's, Lonan had searched land registries and any other sources he could think of, and Callum and I had spoken to as many of the locals as we could, to try to find out if anyone knew anything, or could remember any of their own family talking about the ownership of land.

We'd even got Alouette and Jack helping us again. They'd been engaging the regulars in their pub with as much chat as they could about the subject. But they too had drawn a blank.

Only Bran said he remembered seeing an argument between a farmer who had owned the field previously and one of the former vicars. But he said he didn't know what it was about; he just remembered it because it was unusual to see anyone arguing with a man of the cloth.

So our initial enthusiasm that we might have found a way of stopping the build before it began again when the dig finished had so far amounted to nothing.

I felt some of the others had lost a little of their eagerness now we weren't getting anywhere, but Jonah and I were still determined to discover the truth.

'Morning, Ava!' Tori, the site administrator, calls as she sees Merlin and me gazing over the fence. 'How are you?'

We'd got to know Tori well. When the dig team first arrived, she'd had a lot of questions for us about where exactly we'd found our items and when, and if anything had been found anywhere else in Bluebell Wood. We'd showed her the engraved piece of metal, but she hadn't seemed that interested in it, saying it was from a much later date than they were concerned with. I'd then had to tell her, a little red-faced, that the Roman coin that I had discovered had been found on my bird table. But Tori hadn't been as surprised as I thought she might be.

'You'd be amazed how often that happens,' she'd told me. 'Birds often seem to be drawn to the sites we later excavate. Do you get a lot of magpies on your table?'

'Occasionally.'

'One of them probably dropped it when it was getting food.

It's likely it came from the main site, though. Do you have anything else the birds have left?'

I didn't think it necessary to go through every single one of the birds' gifts, but I decided it best to mention the locket.

'Oh, that's lovely,' she'd said, examining it. 'But again, much later than we would be looking for. You say you think you know who the man is in the photo?'

We'd told her about Corbin once being the rector of the village and how the cottage where I lived had once been the vicarage, and she seemed happy with our explanation.

'Very nice. All history is interesting. It's someone's story, isn't it? But I have to concentrate on a fairly narrow window. Although your locket and that funny piece of metal you showed me are lovely. You can keep them; they won't be treated as treasure.'

Today, Tori makes her way across the field towards Merlin and me.

'We're good, thank you,' I reply. 'How's it going in there?'

'Great, we've had a bit of luck today, actually.'

'Oh yes?'

'It's a bit odd, really, but I thought of you when it happened because of what you discovered on your bird table.'

My ears immediately prick up.

'We all arrived this morning at eight, like we usually do, and almost at once we noticed a huge flock of birds circling over a part of the field we haven't started excavating yet.'

'Go on,' I say, keen to hear more. It was beginning to sound very similar to what had happened on the morning of our secret dig.

'We didn't think anything of it at first, but the birds seemed to be persistently diving close to the ground, a bit like seabirds do when they're trying to catch fish. This struck me as unusual behaviour for country birds, so a couple of us went over to investigate what they were doing, and we found they were actually digging at the ground with their beaks, disturbing the earth. We were about to turn away and leave them to it, when my colleague noticed that there was something sticking up from the area they were attacking. We didn't know if we could get any closer to it because the birds were constantly taking turns to dive on the ground, but when we tried, they immediately stopped to allow us near, and then they simply circled over our heads like they were watching us.'

Even though I sensed Tori was struggling to believe this had actually happened, I had absolutely no problem in imagining the scene. I'd seen the birds of Bluebell Wood in action before.

'And what did you find?' I ask eagerly, knowing without a doubt that there was going to be something.

'To begin with it looked like the stone tip of a bird's wing, of all things. So immediately we got some tools and began to carefully pull back the earth. As we got deeper we discovered what we thought must be a stone statue. Usually when we find things like this, it turns out to be something like a Victorian garden statue or a gargoyle from a derelict building, but very quickly we realised not only were we unearthing a bird, but it looked very much like an eagle.'

'An eagle,' I repeat, amazed to hear this. The birds had presented me with many small items over the last few months, but this was on another level. 'Really?'

Tori nods. 'We tried not to get too excited at this point. Just because it was an eagle, it didn't mean it wasn't still from a modern era, even though eagles are, of course, synonymous with the Roman Empire.'

I hadn't realised the significance, but I nod anyway.

'It took a while, but finally we were able to ease it from the ground. We could see then it was very definitely an eagle; it's missing a part of its wing and a little of its beak, but it's in incredible condition for its age. I can't tell you how exciting this is for us, Ava – this eagle is possibly over two thousand years old, according to our initial tests on the stone.'

'Wow! That's incredible. What was the eagle used for – decoration?'

'More than likely in this case it would have been to decorate a mausoleum for burying their dead. People think of Roman legions proudly carrying eagles on their standards as they marched across the country, but they were also a funerary emblem and often stood at the entrances to cemeteries.'

'There could have been a cemetery here too?' I say, looking out into the field.

'Perhaps not right here. Roman cemeteries were usually a little removed from the settlement, so the decaying bodies didn't infect the water supply. But there would definitely have been some sort of cemetery in the area. The Romans thought a lot about death; what happened to your body after you died was very important to them, and remember we're not that far from Cambridge here, and the Roman road at Ermine Street, so nothing turning up here would surprise me. Roman artefacts, and coins in particular, turn up all over this area in great abundance, not from Roman soldiers' barracks necessarily, but more likely from small settlements of people living off the land.'

'Gosh,' I say, looking out over the fields, the houses and the trees, trying to imagine Bluebell Wood as it might have been back then.

'Would you like to see the eagle?'

'Yes please.'

'Pop Merlin on his lead, then, and I'll show you.'

We walk across the field towards a large white tent. Tori opens up the flaps and we go inside.

In the tent a few trestle tables are filled with some of the items the dig has found so far, all lined up and individually tagged. Around that are a few chairs and bags belonging to the dig staff, some tools, and a small stove and kettle next to a table with some mugs, plates and cutlery.

'I've just brought Ava in to see the eagle,' Tori explains to a woman sitting at one of the tables with a laptop and several large books in front of her. 'Ava is one of the reasons we're here in Bluebell Wood.'

The woman nods, and smiles at me.

'Over here,' Tori says, walking over to a tarpaulin laid out on the ground. There's a large mound on the tarpaulin covered in a sheet. She lifts the sheet carefully to reveal what looks to me very much like an old stone garden ornament. 'Here he is,' she says proudly.

I stare at the eagle; it's hard to imagine it could be two thousand years old. It looks just like something someone might have purchased from a garden centre, and had sat discarded in their backyard for a bit too long. Considering its age, I'm surprised I can clearly make out the eagle's face, beak, and the details of its feathers.

'I can't believe you found something that size here in this field,' I say, strangely captivated by the bird.

'Neither can I. I still can't quite believe how we discovered it this morning. Those birds obviously wanted us to find it for some reason.'

Yes, I think, *I bet they did.*

'I'm not one for believing in things I can't see or prove, Ava. That's why I became interested in this particular area of historical research. We see and find some strange things on these digs, but we find them through careful and meticulous investigation of the ground, there's a pattern and a logic to what we do. But even I can't deny what those birds were doing this morning. You obviously have some very clever birds here in Bluebell Wood. If you think they might be trying to tell you something when they leave things for you on your bird table, then I for one think you should definitely listen to them.'

Thirty-nine

'I'm sorry,' Lonan says, as several of us sit around a table at The Daft Duck later that evening. 'I just can't find anything to link the cottage to any more land in Bluebell Wood.'

'Don't worry,' I tell him, even though I'm disappointed. 'I didn't think you would. I know you've tried really hard to help us.'

'Yes, Lonan, you've been amazing,' Linnet says, putting her hand on his shoulder.

Lonan gazes lovingly at Linnet, and I can't help smiling.

'What do we do now?' Jonah asks. 'We're starting to run out of ideas.'

'But luckily not time,' I say. 'By the look of what's happening on the dig, they're going to be there for some time yet. Did you all hear about the eagle they found today?'

Everyone nods. Gossip – or should I call it *information* – spreads with great ease around this village. It hadn't, of course, taken too long for the news to spread that the much-adored parish priest had a new girlfriend, and I'd been surprised at how easily the news had been accepted by all Callum's parishioners, including the older ones. We were still attempting to keep Callum's overnight stays at my cottage secret, though; we didn't want to push our luck too far!

The villagers of Bluebell Wood weren't the only ones that had taken the news of our relationship well. I'd recently gone with Callum to meet Jena at the hospital. I'd been extremely nervous, not because of the place of our visit, but because I wasn't sure how Jena would take to me. But I needn't have been concerned. Jena, who Callum had assured me was very settled now on her new meds, was lovely, friendly and very welcoming.

I was pleased to find she had a wicked sense of humour, and would mercilessly take the mickey out of her older brother. It was also lovely to see Callum interacting with her, and I left the hospital not only promising to come back and visit again, but loving Callum just that little bit more after seeing how wonderful he was with his sister.

Hannah had, of course, been ecstatic when I told her that Callum and I were now an item, and Matt, even though he'd yet to meet him, had been extremely pleased I'd found someone that was making me happy, and that his sister wholly approved of.

So apart from our still unsolved mystery regarding the land around Bluebell Wood, life was going very well for a change, and I was happier than I'd been in years.

'*Bonsoir, mes amis*,' Alouette says, coming over to our table and sitting down with us. 'I am so sorry I 'ave not been able to get over 'ere earlier; we 'ave been so busy tonight.'

Some of the workers from the dig would stay and have a drink after they finished at night, and often they'd eat at the pub too, so Alouette and Jack were also doing quite well out of the excavations on the field.

'They are all celebrating the eagle!' she says, her hands gesticulating in the air like wings. 'They are very excited by it.'

'It's quite a find,' I say, waving to Tori, who is in the pub tonight, too. 'Tori says she's never found anything quite as big and as complete as this on all the digs she's been a part of.'

'Do I hear right that Jack is thinking of changing the pub's name?' Callum asks. 'I believe he's considering changing it to The Eagle to commemorate the find.'

'Ah!' Alouette says, waving her hand dismissively in the air now. ''e 'as wanted to change the pub's name since we came 'ere. I like The Daft Duck; it is funny, no?'

'That's a bit sudden, isn't it?' I say, surprised to hear this.

'He thinks the pub sign falling down today is a symbol,' Alouette says, wrinkling up her nose. 'A symbol we 'ad a windy day today, that is all.'

'Well, I like The Daft Duck,' I tell her. 'It's different.'

'Yes! That is what I think too, Ava.'

'Eagles seem to be the in thing right now,' Lonan says, looking slightly embarrassed. 'I heard from my agent today that one of my past novels, *The Eagle Soars*, is going to be adapted into a television series.'

'Wow, that's amazing,' I say, truly pleased for him. 'Well done!'

We all raise our glasses in a toast.

'While we're sharing good news,' Callum says, putting down his glass, 'I have some news that I hope will be good too.'

I turn to Callum. He hadn't said anything to me. Linnet had obviously known about Lonan's exciting news; I wondered why Callum hadn't shared his with me.

'I had a phone call from Evelyn just before I came out tonight.'

Immediately there are calls of 'How is she?', 'Isn't that lovely', 'How wonderful', and I feel even more put out.

I'm sure Evelyn is lovely, everyone certainly seemed to adore her, but I still felt I'd never quite lived up to my predecessor's reputation.

'She's very well,' Callum says, trying to answer everyone's questions at once. 'And her daughter is much better now.'

'That's good to hear,' Linnet says. 'She was very worried about her before she left.'

'Is that the good news?' I ask, hoping that was the end of us talking about Evelyn tonight.

'Yes, in part. The good news, as far as you're concerned, Ava, is she's decided to stay on in Australia indefinitely. She's going to retire there permanently to be with her daughter and her grandchildren.'

'Oh gosh, really?' Jonah groans. Then he catches my eye. 'I mean, that's great news for you, Ava, and of course we *love* having you here in Bluebell Wood, but Evelyn was such an important part of the church, she'll be sorely missed.'

'Yes,' Callum says, looking a tad uncomfortable, 'she will indeed. But,' he says, turning to me, 'as Jonah has already pointed out, that means that you are more than welcome to stay on here in Bluebell Wood if you'd like to. I'm sure I'm not alone in saying that we all love having you here, and you've become an important and valuable member of our village. I know you only took out a lease on the cottage for six months, but I really hope you'll think about extending that now?'

I feel a mix of emotions as I look at Callum's hopeful face. I'd become so used to being here in Bluebell Wood that I'd almost forgotten I was only renting the cottage temporarily. My plan had always been to come here for a few months' peace and quiet, to get my head together, and decide where I saw my future going. But what I hadn't banked on, as I'd chosen my little cottage with its pretty-sounding name, in its even prettier sounding village, was that by moving here my life would change quite as profoundly as it had.

I'd come here a lonely, fearful shell of a women who went out of her way to avoid human interaction at every opportunity. But I'd emerged some five months later a different person. I was in a new relationship with a rather fabulous man, I had some amazing and wonderful friends, and I could never ever have believed what a difference to my life having a wise and loyal little dog like Merlin would make. In a few short months I'd found hope and happiness here in Bluebell Wood, and I couldn't wait to see what might happen next.

I lift up my glass. 'A toast,' I say. 'To Evelyn!'

'Evelyn!' everyone repeats, lifting their own glasses.

'I hope she finds as much happiness in Australia as I've found in Bluebell Wood with all of you.'

Forty

'Ava!' I hear a voice call as I'm just on my way back from the shop with Merlin early one morning. 'Ava, wait up!'

I turn to the voice and see Jemima walking quickly towards me along the street.

'Hi, how are you?' I say. 'How are the long summer holidays treating you?'

'Why I went into teaching!' Jemima says, grinning. 'I'm kidding, of course; but I can't lie, it is one of the perks. Which leads me neatly into what I want to ask you.'

'Oh yes?'

'I hear you're going to be staying on in Bluebell Wood now Evelyn is not returning?'

I only decided a couple of days ago. That got around quickly, even for here.

'Yes, that's right,' I tell her.

'Great! I wanted to ask how you found last term with the children?'

'Merlin and I really enjoyed it, thank you. We'll be happy to come back next term if you'd like us to. I can't guarantee how often, though; I'm going to have to look for a job now I'm staying permanently. Bluebell Wood was only ever supposed to be a stopgap.'

After the initial euphoria that I was going to be staying here had worn off, I'd realised that the generous lump sum my previous employers had provided in exchange for me taking voluntary redundancy due to my health was not going to last for ever.

I needed to earn a living from somewhere, but where? I really didn't want to go back into the publicity industry. After the gentle, peaceful life I'd grown used to here in the village, I couldn't imagine going back into the cut and thrust of events and promotions in a big city, and I definitely didn't want to commute back and forth to London again.

'That's just what I want to talk to you about,' Jemima says keenly. 'I need a classroom assistant to start next term and I think you'd be perfect for the position.'

I stare at Jemima for a moment.

'Me? Really?'

'Yes, you're wonderful with the children, and most of them know you already because of Merlin. You'd be great. I know it's likely nowhere near as much money as you were getting before in London, but—'

'Yes!' I say before she can change her mind. 'Yes, I'd love to come and work at the school.'

'Gosh, I didn't think you'd agree so quickly. I mean, it's hardly a high-flying career like you're used to, but it can be very rewarding.'

'I don't want that sort of job any more,' I tell her, 'something that's all about the money and climbing a never-ending career ladder. I've done that. I want to do something that I enjoy, and I know I'll enjoy working at the school.'

Jemima grins, and then to my surprise she reaches out and hugs me.

'I'm so pleased for you,' she says, standing back again. 'I mean it. You've found a place in life you're happy and content in. Happiness and contentment are very underrated, in my opinion.'

'You're right,' I tell her. 'I am lucky, very lucky indeed.'

After talking to Jemima for a little longer about the job and what I would need to do before I started at the school in September, Merlin and I head back to the cottage. We had some packing up of Evelyn's things to do before Robin came over later for the afternoon.

Evelyn had been in contact again with Callum, via email this time, and had sent a list of things she'd like packing up and sending off to her in Australia, if we didn't mind doing so. In return, she said she'd be more than happy for me to keep anything that was left. If I didn't want her things, then we should sell them and give the profits to St Francis's church. She was just pleased that her cottage was going to be lived in by someone that Callum thought was deserving of it.

I had to admit she sounded rather lovely in her email, which Callum had forwarded to me. Evelyn had obviously loved this cottage, and cared deeply about what happened to it.

'Are you sure this is all she wants me to pack up for her?' I'd asked Callum when I'd seen the list. 'It doesn't seem like much?'

'I don't think she needs much,' Callum replies, sounding very vicar-like, as he did on occasion when he wasn't thinking too much about it. 'She has everything she needs in her family.'

'I'm sure she does,' I agree.

'I know she's sad to leave Bluebell Wood, though; she was telling me she'd lived in your cottage since she was a child. Apparently, her family have lived there for over a century – they were the first to rent it after it stopped being the vicarage.'

'I don't suppose . . . ?' I ask hopefully.

Callum shakes his head. 'No, she knew nothing about what we're looking for. As far as she is aware, her family has always rented it from the Church. She said there were always stories told about King Henry and how he'd bequeathed land to the original owner of the land the cottage is built on. But as far as she knows, there was never any actual proof – only rumours. She did say one thing that was interesting, though . . . '

'Oh yes?' I ask, as always clinging on to anything that might help us solve this mystery and stop the housing development once and for all.

'She has a vague memory of her grandfather talking about some maps that had apparently gone missing.'

'Maps?'

'Evelyn wasn't sure, but she thought it might have something to do with the rumours. She said she was just a little girl then and might have got it mixed up.'

What Evelyn told Callum had sounded promising, but as usual it didn't take us any further forward. So I'd sourced some old boxes from Jenny's store and Gavin's farm shop and decided that there was no time like the present to begin packing up the old and bringing in the new. Evelyn's old house had given me a wonderful place to stay over the last few months, but I already had a few ideas of what I'd like to do with the place to really make it mine.

'Right, books!' I say to Merlin as I stand in front of the large bookcase and he curls up on the sofa to watch me packing. 'Now, where's my list?'

I begin to sort through the books on the shelf, making three piles: books Evelyn wanted me to send to her, books I wanted to keep and books we could sell.

The only thing was, I kept getting distracted and opening up the books to look at them. I'd only ever made a small dent in reading the vast quantity of books that Evelyn had collected over the years, even though when I first came here I'd thought it was one of the things that might keep me busy, and fill in the many hours I'd expected to spend alone in the cottage.

Funny how things turn out, I think, as I put the book I'm holding down on the pile to keep. *It feels like I haven't had enough hours to do all the things I've wanted to, let alone needed things to fill them up!*

I pick up a group of old annuals that must once have belonged to Evelyn's children. There's a mix of *The Beano*, *The Dandy* and *The Eagle*, and I wonder if Robin might like to look at them later. I stare at the small pile of *Eagle* annuals. 'There you are again,' I say to the books. 'It seems you're everywhere right now.'

When I'd fed the birds this morning, I'd found a new gift had been left for me. This time it was a tiny silver brooch in the shape of an eagle, its wings spread in flight.

'This seems more appropriate!' I'd said to the birds, as they'd waited in the trees for their food. I was no longer surprised by what I found on the table. 'It's one of your own this time.'

The brooch was an extremely pretty little thing, and, like the locket, quite a step up from some of the other things the birds had left. The insignia seemed familiar to me, so before I'd taken Merlin out for his walk, I'd looked it up, and the internet had revealed it to be a vintage RAF sweetheart brooch, for servicemen to present to loved ones before they left for battle. 'Where are you getting these things from?' I'd murmured as I'd studied the brooch in my hand. 'This would have been very special to someone once upon a time.' So I'd placed it on the mantelpiece with my other gifts.

Now I put all the annuals in a pile on the table for Robin to take a look at later, and then I carry on. I'm almost at the end of the last shelf when I find a thick old book with a plain brown cover; there's nothing on the spine so I open it to see what's inside.

As the pages fall open in the middle, I'm surprised to find not lines of typewritten font, but pages of handwritten notes instead. The notes appear to be about many different subjects, but they're all written in ink, in the ornate scroll of someone who has been taught beautiful penmanship.

I carefully turn the page to the front, to find written in the same pretty handwriting:

Miss Mavis Fowler
Teaching Lessons for St Francis Junior School.
1895

Could this be the same Mavis that later married the local vicar? I wonder. Fowler could have been her maiden name, and she might have been a teacher?

The lessons on the pages are basic, but I can just imagine an Edwardian lady – no, she'd have been Victorian then, wouldn't she? – teaching them in the part of the Bluebell Wood school that dated back that far.

'Wow,' I say, suddenly feeling a strong connection to Mavis

as I read through her words and touch her handwriting. 'I can imagine you now. You're a real person to me, not just a rather stern-looking woman in a photo.'

I glance at the clock and realise that I've spent longer than I thought sorting the books, and I'd better get ready for Robin coming soon. I reach over to put Mavis's book on the table next to the annuals, with the intention of finishing it later. But I don't quite get it far enough on to the table, so it immediately topples off. I just manage to catch it as it falls, but in the process the pages fan open again, and this time something falls out.

It's a faded brown envelope.

'What's this?' I ask, carefully opening the thinning paper.

Inside are two black-and-white photos. One I recognise as Mavis: she's standing by a blackboard, a white piece of chalk in her hand.

'You were clearly proud of your job,' I say, smiling at the photo.

The second is a photo of Mavis and Corbin together on what looks like their wedding day. Mavis is in a long white lace gown, and Corbin is wearing his formal priest's robes, and they both have their hand on a large tome of a book – a Bible, I assume. I imagine this photo would have been of particular significance for a man of the Church on his wedding day.

But it's when I look at the photo a little more closely that I notice the detail on the Bible. It has a very elaborate cover, almost like it's made entirely of metal, and there are . . . I squint as I look at the photo . . . it looks like tiny jewels encrusting the cover.

But the most interesting thing of all is the very edge of the Bible, because it looks like it has a clasp on it. A clasp that might have held or even locked the covers together. Nothing odd about that, except this book's clasp looks exactly like the strange piece of engraved metal we'd found outside the wood. The one Merlin was digging for, and the one the birds had alerted us to . . .

Forty-one

Robin looks around the room as he comes through the door.

'What are you doing?' he asks, seeing all the books lying everywhere.

'I'm sorting out the bookshelves. I have to send the lady who lived here before me all her old books.'

Robin thinks about this.

'Isn't she coming back, then?' he asks.

I shake my head.

'Does that mean you're staying?' he asks, looking apprehensive.

'I am,' I say, smiling at him. 'Are you happy about that?'

Robin doesn't say anything; instead, he dumps his bag down on the table next to the annuals, runs over to me and hugs me around my waist.

'Yes,' he says simply, so I lean down and hug him tightly.

'I've brought my project to show you today,' Robin says, already moving on to the next thing on his mind.

'Have you, which one?'

'The Roman one we did at school. I thought you'd like to see it.'

'I would indeed. Shall I get us both a drink and then we can look at it together?'

We settle down at the table with two glasses of orange juice and look through Robin's school project. I ask him questions as we go along, and I'm impressed that he remembers so much about what he's learnt.

'Mum says they're finding lots of real Roman things on the field,' Robin says, proudly turning the page of his exercise books. 'Is that because of us?'

'Yes, if we hadn't declared what we'd found then no one would have known about it. It's very exciting, isn't it? Have you seen any of the things they've found?'

'Miss Swan says we're going to have an exhibition at school next year to show us everything.'

'That's great.' I look at the page Robin is showing me. 'Look, that solider is wearing a hat like you wore at Easter.'

'It's a helmet,' Robin corrects me.

'Of course it is.'

'Do you like my eagle,' he asks, pointing to a picture he's drawn of a Roman soldier carrying a standard. At the top of the standard is a huge eagle.

'Yes, it's very good,' I reply, still staring at the eagle.

'It's called an Aquila,' Robin says. 'That's Latin for eagle. All the Roman legions had them. They stood for power and courage.'

'Another one . . . ' I murmur almost to myself.

'What?' Robin asks. 'I mean, pardon. Mum says I should say pardon.'

I smile. 'I've seen quite a lot of eagles recently, that's all.'

'Where, on your bird table?'

'No, eagles are rare in this part of the world. You usually only see them in the north of the country, in places like Scotland.'

'Where have you seen them, then?'

'They dug a huge stone one up in the field a few days ago.'

'Yes, I know; Mum said.'

'And Jack at the pub said he might change the name of the pub to The Eagle because of it.'

'I know that, too. Mum said she didn't like it, and she preferred the duck one.'

'And the birds left me a little badge today with one on.' I go to the mantelpiece and collect the brooch, which Robin examines with much interest.

'And then I found these annuals today on the bookshelf. I thought you might like to read them. Some of those have the name *The Eagle*, too.'

Robin puts down the brooch at once, and picks up one of the annuals.

'There just seem to be eagles everywhere at the moment. I wonder if I'll see any more.'

'You could go to the church,' Robin says, his nose already deep into one of *The Beano* annuals.

'The church – why?'

'There's a huge one inside, isn't there?'

'Really?' I ask, wondering where he could mean.

'Yes, when that vicar man Callum stands up to talk to everyone, he stands in front of it.'

I think back to when I was last in the church.

'Do you mean the lectern?' I ask. 'The big wooden thing Callum sometimes stands at?'

Robin lifts his head for a moment. 'Yeah, that's the thing. There's a big eagle carved at the top of it. I always look at it when I'm bored of people talking and reading from that big shiny book.'

'You know, I think you might be right,' I say, trying to remember. 'I think there is an eagle carved there. Wait, why did you describe the book as shiny?'

'Cos it is,' Robin says, still turning the pages of the annual. 'It's all silvery and the light coming in through the pretty windows sometimes makes coloured patterns on it.'

I grab Mavis's book of teaching notes from the table and retrieve the wedding photo.

'Robin,' I say carefully, not wanting to lead him, 'you see the book in this photo?'

'Uh-huh,' Robin says indifferently.

'Is this like the book you've seen on the eagle in the church?'

Robin looks a little more carefully at the photo.

'Yeah, that looks like it. Those people are *old*!'

'How do you fancy a walk with Merlin in a bit?' I ask him, my heart pounding. 'I think we might take a quick trip past the church ... '

'How on earth did you recognise it?' Callum asks as we hurry towards the church with Robin and Merlin. 'Did you remember it from Easter Sunday?'

'I only had eyes for you on Easter Sunday,' I tell him.

'My male ego is flattered by that, but my alter ego thinks you should have been listening to what I was saying.'

'It matters not now. It was Robin that recognised it, actually, wasn't it, Robin?'

Robin nods. 'I like to look at the big eagle and the pretty patterns on the book.'

Callum glances at me.

I shake my head. 'Don't worry about it. Do *you* think it's the same one as in the photo?'

'It looks very much like it. That Bible cover is pretty old; I'm told it would have been what's called "treasure binding". It's lost a lot of its gems over the years, and the clasp on one side of the cover, but the engraving is still visible.'

'You did say you recognised that engraved piece of metal we found in the wood . . . '

Callum stops hurrying and turns to look at me. 'You think that's what that is, the missing clasp from the cover?'

'I can't tell for sure until we get there. But it looks a lot like it.'

We all rush into the church, Robin going along with our excitement, even though I don't think he entirely understands what's going on.

'There's the big eagle,' he says, pointing down the aisle of the church.

We all walk towards the lectern at a much calmer pace now we're inside. Callum lifts the open heavy Bible down from where it rests on top of the eagle lectern and closes its covers.

'It is the same one,' I whisper. Not sure if my whispering stems from the fact I'm in total awe at what we've discovered, or because I'm inside a church. 'Here.' I hold out the engraved clasp.

Callum takes it from me and holds it to the cover. The size, width and pattern of the metal match perfectly to the area the clasp is missing from.

'The birds wanted you to find this Bible, Ava, that's for sure. But how do we discover just why they did?'

'Can I take a look?' I ask, sitting down on one of the pews.

Callum passes me the heavy Bible and I rest it on my lap. Then carefully I flick through the pages. 'I'm not really sure what we're looking for,' I say, looking up at him. 'Maybe I got a bit over-excited with the eagle link and the photo turning up today.'

'Once I got a book from the library and when I took the outside cover off I found a five-pound note inside,' Robin says, watching us. 'Mum told me I had to give it back to the library, though,' he says regretfully.

'Can we remove the Bible from the cover?' I ask, looking at the inside of the book.

'I don't know if anyone has ever taken the cover off,' Callum says. 'If they have it's not been for a very long time.'

'Do you want to try?' I ask him.

'You do it,' Callum says. 'I trust you.'

As carefully as I can, I try to remove the heavy cover, but it won't budge. The outside is a heavily engraved metal, but the inner part is a taut leather that has thinned and worn over the years so it's like a tight skin covering the Bible inside. Instead, I try reaching my fingers in between the cover and the front of the book. But there's nothing, my fingers reappear with only dust on them. The back, however, is a different story. 'I can feel something!' I say, trying to force my fingers that little bit further into the tight space. 'No! I can't get to it,' I cry in frustration.

'My fingers are smaller than yours,' Robin says, looking at his hand. 'Shall I try?'

I look at Callum, who nods.

'Be very gentle,' I say to Robin as he sits next to me and pushes his small fingers in between the leather and the book.

'I can feel something,' Robin says, wrinkling his face up as he wriggles his fingers. 'It feels like thick paper.'

Very slowly, and very carefully, Robin begins to pull something from underneath the book jacket until it's visible for us all to see.

'Shall I do it now?' I ask, desperate for him not to tear whatever it is.

'Yes, I think it might rip,' Robin says, turning the book back towards me.

As gently and as carefully as I can, I ease the paper slowly from the book until it's all the way out.

Then I look at the other two watching me.

'Shall I open it?' I tease, knowing exactly the response I'm going to get.

'Yes! Yes!' Robin shouts.

'Of course!' Callum encourages.

I open up the first page of thick yellowing paper and try to read what it says.

'The writing is tiny,' I say, squinting to decipher the ornate script. I pass it to Callum. 'Can you do any better?'

Callum takes the paper from me. 'It's like parchment,' he says, feeling the paper. 'If it is parchment, then this writing might be in old English. Try opening up the other paper.'

Again, as gently as I can, I slowly open the folds of the second piece of paper.

'What is it?' Callum cries in torment as I silently stare at what's inside.

I turn it towards him.

'It's a map,' I say quietly. 'A map of Bluebell Wood. Only it says at the top it's a map of King's Wood and it's dated 1165.

Epilogue

Twelve months later . . .

Callum, Merlin and I snuggle together on the sofa in the cottage while we watch the birds through the window, as they feed on the table outside.

'You know something?' Callum says, adjusting his arm slightly where it's wrapped around my shoulders. 'There's been a number of times my faith has been questioned over the years by things that have happened, and a number of times it's been strengthened. But since you came to Bluebell Wood, Ava, and the birds started bringing gifts to your table, my belief has only gone from strength to strength.'

'Do you think my birds were acting as messengers from some higher being, then?' I ask, surprised to hear him say this. Usually Callum steers clear of talking about his faith with me, even now.

'Do you?' he asks.

'Nice try,' I reply. 'But you're not pulling me in with that old trick. You know I believe in the birds of Bluebell Wood. But why they did what they did remains a mystery I don't want to solve.'

After we'd found the documents in the church Bible, we'd wasted no time in getting them looked at and transcribed by an expert. After a few nervous weeks – which then turned into months, when even more interested parties became involved – we'd had to submit all the evidence we had, including the photos of Mavis and Corbin. Eventually we'd heard the news we'd hoped to hear for so long.

According to our evidence, not only did the Church own the land that the cottage was on, but much of the land in and around Bluebell Wood, including the fields sold for development. The ancient documents had been proven not only to be evidence of the land that King Henry II gave to the farmer, but both they and the cover that protected them were thought to be the originals that the King had presented to Mavis's ancestor, and they were now on display at the Fitzwilliam Museum in Cambridge, on loan from the British Museum in London.

Callum had been shocked at first to find that everything he knew in Bluebell Wood had suddenly changed, and he'd been put under a lot of pressure by the local landowners to sort things out in a way that would keep everyone happy. Which, of course, Callum and his diocese had done their best to do, along with help from a top London solicitor, who Hannah had been happy to recommend.

The housing development was still on pause while the dig continued to find interesting artefacts buried beneath the soil, and Colin Cuckoo had been lucky to get away with only a hefty fine and a suspended prison sentence, after his part in concealing what was buried in the soil all around the village was finally uncovered.

Callum was currently trying to come to an agreement with a new development company to build some homes that would be sympathetic to the style of the current houses and cottages in Bluebell Wood, so that no one missed out, including the Church, who would still get the money for the roof repairs and a new window.

The new church hall and the play park were already being built with the proceeds of some of the treasure found in and around the field, as well as the money that Callum had made in appearance and interview fees from media companies wanting to hear the story of King Henry II and the missing documents.

Lonan and Linnet were still going strong, and Lonan regularly took Robin on birdwatching weekends to various places all over the UK. Lonan had also pitched a new idea to his publishers, and was currently writing the first draft of his next novel about Henry II, a farmer and a small village by a wood in Cambridgeshire.

So all in all, the strange events that had befallen Bluebell Wood had turned out extremely well for everyone involved.

Callum looks up at the glass box frame where I now display all my gifts from the birds.

Sometimes I'd explain to people if they asked what they were, and sometimes I'd just say they were things I'd found in the garden, if I didn't think they'd understand.

Everything was there: the yellow Trivial Pursuit piece, the pieces of broken mosaic, the fifty-pence piece, the red feather (that Robin had returned to me as a gift), the nurse's watch, the Mars Bar wrapper, the Love Hearts sweet, a now well-wilted olive branch, the corner from the torn bingo card, the Roman coin (which had also been returned as it wasn't of any particular value) and the gold locket. The RAF brooch with their eagle insignia had turned out to be Evelyn's father's, which he'd given to her mother, and she'd been overjoyed when I told her I'd found it 'in the back garden'.

I'd spent a lot of time thinking about the gifts the birds had given me and why, and for some reason it didn't feel right to have this one item in my collection. I knew it must mean something to someone, and that someone would more than likely want it back. So I too had been thrilled to find it meant something to my predecessor in this cottage, and I could give her back something for what she'd given me by allowing me to stay here.

'Do you still think the only meaning in the gifts the birds left you was the Roman theme?' Callum asks, looking at the frame. 'Was it really only so we could unearth all those treasures in the field and discover who really owned the land?'

'I think those birds had a dual purpose in every single thing they gave me,' I tell him. 'I may not have known it at the time, but each of those gifts represented something that was going on in my life back then. Each gift told me to be braver, stronger, and to believe in things that I never thought possible.'

I look at all the special gifts lined up together in the frame. Only this morning I'd had a new gift, which I hadn't shared with anyone yet, not even Callum.

When Merlin and I had gone outside as we always did first thing to fill up the bird feeders and spread my special mix of seed, nuts and fruit on the table, I'd discovered something waiting for me. It had been over a year since the birds last left anything, so I'd been surprised to find it there. This was very different to anything they'd left for me before: it was a tiny stuffed toy owl wearing a mortar board and a gown, and printed on its little white sash were the words: *Best Teacher Ever*.

I'd held the owl in my hands for a few moments and stared at it.

I'd spent the last ten months working as a teaching assistant at the school and I'd loved every minute of it. Jemima had been incredibly supportive and had told me on more than one occasion what a wonderful teacher I would make.

I'd thought about it a few times, but I'd always talked myself out of it. Was I too old to retrain? Would I be any good at it? Was it too late to start a new career at my age?

I was still undecided what to do for the best.

Until now.

'Best Teacher Ever?' I'd read out loud to the birds and my friend the robin, who'd flown down into the garden to watch me like he always used to, with his head cocked to one side.

'If you guys think so, then who am I to argue with the birds of Bluebell Wood?'

Extras

Did you know every character's name in the story has a bird meaning?

Ava (Little Bird) **Martin** (A breed of bird)
Merlin (Type of falcon)
Callum (Dove) **Crawford** (From the old English word Crawa – Crow and Ford)
Evelyn (Irish: Beautiful Bird)
Bran (Crow)
Jenny (Jenny Wren: nursery rhyme) **Bird**
Gavin (White Hawk) **Peacock**
Mrs Bunting (A Bunting is a breed of bird)
Eileen (Bird)
Arnold (Eagle Power)
Jonah (Hebrew for Dove) **Finch**
Alouette (Lark) **Daw**
Jack Daw (Jackdaw!)
Jemima (Dove) **Swan**
Lonan (Blackbird) **Adler** (Eagle)

Linnet (A small finch that eats flaxseed)
Robin (I don't think I need to explain that one!)
Colin Cuckoo (Again, self-explanatory!)
Jena (Little Bird)
Mrs Hobby (A Hobby is a bird of prey)
Bert (Bertrand – magnificent crow)
Jay (Jaybird)
Mr Covey (Covey means 'brood of birds')
Tori (In Hebrew means my turtledove)
Mavis (Song Thrush) **Fowler** (Catcher of wild birds)
The Reverend Corbin (Raven) **Hawkins** (diminutive of Hawk)

Bluebird Cottage – Many cultures across the globe have folklore and beliefs about the bluebird. It is a symbol of cheerfulness, happiness, prosperity, heart and home, good health, new birth, and the renewal of springtime.

The Church of St Francis – St Francis of Assisi is the patron saint of animals, birds and the environment.

The bird's gifts didn't just have Roman meanings. They were also messages to try to help Ava:

The yellow Trivial Pursuit triangle – Encourages Ava to go to the history-themed quiz at the pub.

The pieces of mosaic – Gives Ava the connection to the school and Jemima.

The fifty-pence piece – Helps Robin to trust Ava for the first time.

The red feather – Helps Ava bond with both Robin and Linnet.

The nurse's watch – To try to help Ava understand about Callum and Jena, and where Callum disappears to so regularly.

The Mars Bars wrapper (Mars the God of War) – To give Ava courage in her battle with Colin Cuckoo.

The Roman coin – To help Ava find her first way of delaying the housing development. This gives her hope and purpose.

The Love Hearts sweet – To help Callum allow himself to love Ava.

The olive branch – To suggest there should be peace between Ava and Callum.

The torn bingo card – To help Ava understand the best way to overcome her issues with what she perceives as evil in the world. 'Do not be overcome by evil, but overcome evil with good.'

The gold locket – To lead them further along the path to finding the real owners of the land in Bluebell Wood, and connect Ava with Mavis, the teacher.

The Eagle RAF brooch – To help Ava find the connection to the eagle on the lectern, to find a bond with Evelyn, and to confirm the 'sweethearts' that Ava and Callum now are.

The toy owl – To encourage Ava to retrain and become a teacher in the future.

Acknowledgements

Super quick thank yous this time!

Not because I'm any less grateful for all the help I get when putting my novels together, but because I hope you know how much I appreciate you all by now.

So massive thanks go to:

Hannah Ferguson – my amazing agent

Darcy Nicholson – my excellent editor

Tamsyn Berryman and the terrific team at Sphere.

Jim, Rosie, Tom and our darling dogs, Oscar, Sherlock and Teddy – my fabulous family, without whom none of this would ever be possible.

And to the little robin who landed by my feet on Christmas Day 2019 and gave me the idea for this story – thank you!

'A perfect, sparkling, summer read' Cathy Bramley
Ali McNamara
Kate and Clara's Curious Cornish Craft Shop
Craft Shop

Discover the glorious little Cornish town of St Felix – where romance and magic glitter in the summer air